W9-AVL-644

"From cutting-edge science to a magician's trade secrets, *Placebo* by Steven James is a fascinating journey into American politics, business, and the military. The characters are utterly alive, the story memorable. Gripping and intense, it will keep you on the edge of your seat until the last page."

—**Gayle Lynds**, *New York Times* bestselling author
of *The Book of Spies*

"With every new book, Steven James elevates his game and lifts his readers with him. *Placebo* is a winner! Highly recommended."

—**Davis Bunn**, bestselling author of *Lion of Babylon*

"A good novel is interesting. A great novel is entertaining. An unforgettable novel is both. Steven James's *Placebo* is all that and more."

—**Alton Gansky**, bestselling author of *Angel*
and *Director's Cut*

"There's no exaggeration in calling Steven James a master storyteller. *Placebo* delivers a thrill ride but also emotional depth and intriguing characters you'll lock into immediately. I devoured the story."

—**James L. Rubart**, bestselling author of *The Chair*

"Fascinating, gripping, and thrilling—I loved this book. The master storyteller has woven another spell in *Placebo*, where the lines of science, reality, and fiction blur in one compelling tale. Intelligent and absolutely un-put-down-able. You will lose sleep over this one."

—**Tosca Lee**, *New York Times* bestselling author
of *Demon: A Memoir* and the Books of Mortals series
with Ted Dekker

PLACEBO

Books by Steven James

THE JEVIN BANKS EXPERIENCE · BOOK 1

PLACEBO

A JEVIN BANKS NOVEL

STEVEN JAMES

Revell

a division of Baker Publishing Group
Grand Rapids, Michigan

ST. JOHN THE BAPTIST PARISH LIBRARY
2920 NEW HIGHWAY 51
LAPLACE, LOUISIANA 70068

© 2012 by Steven James

Published by Revell
a division of Baker Publishing Group
P.O. Box 6287, Grand Rapids, MI 49516-6287
www.revellbooks.com

Printed in the United States of America

All rights reserved. No part of this publication may be reproduced, stored in a retrieval system, or transmitted in any form or by any means—for example, electronic, photocopy, recording—without the prior written permission of the publisher. The only exception is brief quotations in printed reviews.

Library of Congress Cataloging-in-Publication Data
James, Steven, 1969–
    Placebo : a Jevin Banks novel / Steven James.
        p.   cm. — (The Jevin Banks experience ; bk. 1)
    ISBN 978-0-8007-1934-0 (cloth) — 978-0-8007-3425-1 (pbk.)
    1. Title.
    PS3610.A4545P53 2012
    813'.6—dc23   2012018412

This book is a work of fiction. Names, characters, places, and incidents are the product of the author's imagination or are used fictitiously. Any resemblance to actual events, locales, or persons, living or dead, is coincidental.

The internet addresses, email addresses, and phone numbers in this book are accurate at the time of publication. They are provided as a resource. Baker Publishing Group does not endorse them or vouch for their content or permanence.

12   13   14   15   16   17   18   7   6   5   4   3   2   1

To Pam Johnson,
For all of your help, all of your smiles,
all of your insights

Have you ever had a dream, Neo, that you were so sure was real? What if you were unable to wake from that dream? How would you know the difference between the dream world and the real world?

—Morpheus to Neo
in *The Matrix* (1999)

Is all that we see or seem
But a dream within a dream?

—Edgar Allan Poe
(1809–1849)

Who knows but that we all live out our lives in the maze of a dream?

—Weng Wei,
eighth-century Chinese poet

Part I

ENTANGLED

The Shore

September 24
Heron Bay, New Jersey
1:12 p.m.

You are there when they recover the bodies.

The day is gray with thick, somber clouds hanging heavily in the sky. Mist lurks above the bay, circling in a breeze that comes in damp and cold off the water.

You stand onshore watching the divers position their boat at the place where the witnesses say they saw the minivan go in. As you wait for them to reappear, your heart squirms like a thick, wet animal trapped inside your chest.

It was your wife's minivan.

And she had your two sons with her.

The silence is stark and chilled, disturbed only by the wet slap of waves against the shore.

For some reason, even though the van disappeared into the bay more than two hours ago, you still hold out hope that somehow Rachel and the twins have survived, that some inscrutable miracle has drifted down from heaven and stopped the water from pouring into the van.

You try to convince yourself that the vehicle has become a safe haven filled with air, a metal bubble of life—proof that a loving God exists and cares enough to step into time and save lives; you tell yourself that someday you'll all look back at this and stand in awe of the unimaginable possibilities of divine intervention.

You tell yourself that.

But then a pair of divers surface, tugging something with them.

And you see that it is one of your sons.

The body doesn't look real, more like a mannequin or a CPR dummy—frighteningly motionless, its skin pasty gray, its eyes open and staring unblinkingly at the blank, indifferent clouds.

It's only because of his clothes that you recognize which of your two boys it is—Andrew, the oldest by three minutes. You recall seeing him in that outfit earlier in the day, before you headed to the rehearsal for the show. Yes, it's Andrew.

Five years old and now he's dead.

As they lift him into the rowboat, his head lolls your way and water dribbles from his loose, gaping mouth. His eyes still refuse to blink.

For a moment you think it's some kind of mistake, a cruel joke the universe is playing on you.

No, no, that's not really him, that thing in the boat. Andrew is alive, of course he is. Any second now he's going to come running up the shore and yell, missing his r's like always, "Daddy! I'm okay! Don't wuwy, Daddy! I'm wight hewe!"

You catch yourself gazing along the shoreline. A few emergency medical personnel and police officers stand near the pier staring quietly at the divers, but that's all. No media. The cops have kept them professionally cordoned off on the road beyond the boat landing's parking lot. Besides the paramedics and police, the shoreline is empty: just a long line of lonely sand and jagged rocks curling toward the far shore now lost in the fog that wanders restlessly across the water.

Of course Andrew doesn't appear running up the shoreline. The body is real. Your oldest son lies dead on the rowboat, and now the divers are going back down to retrieve the rest of your family.

The pulsing beast in your chest writhes again and you find it getting harder to breathe. You want to leave, to turn away, to run and run and run forever until your heart is finally in a safe, emotionally dead and distant place and you get a phone call outside of time from the police explaining everything in objective, detached detail, but you know you have to see for yourself what happened to Anthony and Rachel.

You have to.

And so you stay.

And stare at the water rippling beside the boat, afraid to even blink. You wonder if this comes from what you do, the knowledge that so many things can be faked, that there are so many ways to make people's minds play tricks on them in that fraction of a second of misdirection, either through the gentle deception of sleight of hand or the almighty power of stage lights or camera angles. If you blink you miss everything. The old line, the clichéd standby: *Now you see it, now you don't!*

But nothing is faked here today.

It isn't long before the divers bring up Anthony. It takes longer with Rachel.

You hear some whispered words through a radio that one of the officers has and realize that it was her hair. It got tangled in some branches as they were removing her from the van. Then he turns down the volume, and the rest of the words squibble away and drop out into an uneven static.

For some reason as you watch the men bring the three corpses to shore in the boat, you don't cry. You know enough about how people react to tragedy to realize that this is shock, you're in shock. But naming the condition doesn't help; in fact, it almost seems disrespectful to label the numbness, like a subtle move toward objectivity, which is the last thing you want right now.

"Mr. Banks?" A voice, scratchy and soft beside you. You turn and see that it's one of the police officers, a sturdy woman, maybe forty, with dark eyes and a tight bun of sandy brown hair. "Is there anything I can do for you?"

"No."

"We'll have someone drive you to—"

"No. I want to see the bodies up close."

She takes a small breath as if she's about to dispute that and you brace yourself for an argument, but she replies simply, "I'll go with you."

You realize that letting you spend time with the bodies now, rather than at the morgue, might not be protocol, and you respect that this officer seems to care more about you than about policies and procedures. You hold back from telling her that you want to be alone with your family, and silently accept her offer.

The boat arrives at the pier and the two of you walk toward it.

None of the officers are joking around or using gallows humor like cops do on TV: "Looks like today's special is three for the price of one!" Maybe screenwriters stick those lines in the shows because treating death honestly would be too hard on viewers and ratings. Better to lighten the mood, tidy up reality, let us escape—at least for a few hours during prime time—into a more sterile kind of pain.

You arrive and look into the boat, then climb aboard and kneel beside the three corpses that used to be your family—the boys you ate breakfast with this morning, the woman you kissed goodbye just before you walked out the door.

You reach for her cheek and hesitantly touch its wet, claylike surface. You slide the snarled, wet hair from her eyes, and though you try to hold back your tears, you fail, and the rising squall of wind brushes wisps of fog across your face as if its ghostly, curling fingers are trying to wipe the tears away. Or maybe the mist is just trying to taste the pain and carry it farther ashore.

———

She did it on purpose. Rachel did.

Four people saw her veer off the road, drive through the parking lot beside the bay, and then accelerate as she hit the pier. Later, the investigators found nothing wrong with the van. Neither the steering wheel nor the gas pedal had jammed; the brakes were working fine. The trip off the pier was no accident.

Rachel had survived impact. There was water in her lungs, which meant she'd been breathing when the minivan filled with water. The air bag had inflated and there were no cracks spiderwebbing across the windshield, no contusions on her head that would've indicated that she was knocked unconscious.

Still, I hope that somehow she was. I can hardly imagine her just sitting there conscious and aware, waiting for our two sons to drown, but by all indications that's exactly what she did.

The boys were strapped into their car seats and had never been good at getting them unbuckled on their own, so even if they'd known how to swim, they wouldn't have been able to get out of the van.

Though it chills me to think about it, I can't help but wonder what it was like for Drew and Tony in those final moments—feeling the minivan speed up, experiencing the momentary weightlessness as the vehicle left the pier, then the jarring impact as it hit the surface of the water.

And then.

Sinking. Slowly at first, but then more rapidly as water began to fill the van. And the questions a five-year-old might ask: *What's happening? When is Mommy gonna help me?* Or perhaps even a thrill of curiosity as the water passed the windows: *Is this what it's like for a fish?!*

But then, of course, the troubling realization that this was scary and bad. And, as the instinct for survival took over, struggling uselessly to get free, crying, then screaming as the water rose.

The boys' lungs were filled with water too.

They were breathing as the water rose to their lips, passed their mouths, swallowed their cries for help. I've done hundreds of underwater escapes over the years, and I know all too well how terrifying it can be when your breath is running out and you can't find a way to free yourself from your bonds. You try to remain calm, but there comes a moment when sheer terror eclipses everything. Six times I've passed out and had to be revived.

At least my sons only had to drown once.

And now.

Over and over I've searched through my conversation with Rachel earlier that day for any hint of what she was planning to do, any warning, however slight, of her dark intentions.

Everything had been so suburbally normal for a Saturday morning— I was slipping off to work for a few hours, then I'd be back to mow the lawn; Rachel was heading out with the boys to grab a few things at the grocery store for our dinner that night with the Andersons. Before I'd left, she'd seemed a little tired, but that was all.

I'd offered to ask her parents if they could watch the kids next weekend so we could sneak away—just the two of us—find a bed-and-breakfast in the country, somewhere outside of Atlantic City where we lived, take a little time to reconnect. To relax. Before the new season began.

"It'd be a good break for both of us before the new show opens," I told her.

"That would be nice," she said softly.

"That would be nice," not, *"Sorry, I'll be dead by then. And so will the boys. I'm going to drown them as soon as you leave the house."*

My friends, my family, the media, law enforcement—everyone who was touched by the case—searched for a reason why she did what she did: *Did she show any signs of depression? Was she noticeably upset that morning when you left? Were you having marital problems? Can you think of anything at all that would have caused her to do this?*

No, no, no.

No, I could not.

It was as if all of us were desperate to compartmentalize her actions under a specific heading—anger, loneliness, depression, despair—as if naming the motive, channeling all the terrible confusion and pain into one word, would have softened the blow, brought some sort of closure.

But we found no motive, no cause, no explanation.

A mother had inexplicably murdered her sons and committed suicide for reasons only she knew. Reasons that had drowned with her in Heron Bay.

I've tried to hate her for what she did, tried my hardest to despise her, to slice all the positive feelings I ever had for her out of my heart, but I can't make the love go away. Even after she killed my sons, even after that, I haven't been able to find a way to hate her. Part of me feels wretchedly guilty for still loving her, as if it's a failure on my part, as if it cheapens my love for the boys.

No reasons.

We found no reasons.

But something motivated Rachel to accelerate off that pier, and to make any sense of it I felt compelled to find a person to blame for not stopping her.

In the end I did. I found him. A man who'd missed a warning sign, some subtle indicator, some tiny clue as to her intentions—or possibly he'd said something, did something, without even knowing it, that'd pushed her over the edge.

He needed to be punished for his failure, and so I've reminded him of it every day for the last thirteen months.

And he has suffered acutely, just as he should, for letting his wife and his two sons die.

Sleight of Hand

Thirteen months after the drownings
Monday, October 26
1:53 p.m.

The highway snakes along the Oregon coastline like a great eel, twisting around the foothills that skirt the wild sea.

Surprisingly, the sky above us shines clear and bright and starkly blue. In the Pacific Northwest, this is a rare and welcome sight, and the Monday afternoon traffic is heavier than I would've expected. By the number of backpacks inside the cars and surfboards on top of them, I can tell that many of the drivers are outdoor enthusiasts heading home after a long weekend of enjoying the clear weather here on the coast or hiking in the nearby mountains.

I'm at the wheel of the van, and my friend Xavier Wray sits beside me. At fifty-two, he's nineteen years older than I am, but he still has a closetful of tie-dyed clothes and still uses the word "groovy."

He shaved his head last year because he didn't think the ponytail went well with his receding hairline, and, as he said, he only had control over one of the two factors in the equation: "Start losing your hair and you look old; get rid of it all and you look timeless."

I can tell he's been watching me but trying not to be too obvious about it. Figuring he would say something soon enough, I wait him out, and just as I start thinking about the television exposé we're working on, he breaks the silence: "It reminds you of that day, doesn't it? The ocean? The shore over there?"

"Yes."

Silence.

"You want some advice, Jev?"

"Xavier, we've been through this before."

"Sure, but do you want some advice now?"

"No."

"You sure?"

"Yes."

"Okay, here it is." He brushes some lint from his faded season-one *X-Files* T-shirt imprinted with a picture of David Duchovny (looking quintessentially cool) and Gillian Anderson (looking urgently concerned), and the words "The truth is out there."

"Stop trying to move on."

I look at him quizzically. "That's your advice?"

"Yup."

"Stop trying to move on."

"You got it."

"That's what's going to help?"

"Yup."

"Well"—I give my attention back to the road—"thanks, Xav. I'll keep that in mind."

"Thinking about what's done, man, dwelling on it, trying to deal with it, I'm just saying, that creates a lot of emotional drag. Be where you are; let where you've been alone. Do that and the universe will lean in your direction."

"That's very Zen of you."

"There're always going to be holes in your heart in the shape of your wife, in the shape of your kids."

19

"And you're telling me, what? That I need to fill the holes with something else?"

"No. I'm telling you to stop staring into 'em and let 'em be there, a part of your story, a part that affects your future, sure, but not what defines it. Stop feeding your pain and it'll dissipate. Okay, that's it. That's what I wanted to say. I'm done."

"How long have you been waiting to tell me all that?"

"It just came to me. I'm in the zone."

"Uh-huh." I take a small breath. "Listen, I appreciate it, really, but let's talk about something else."

A long pause. "What do you want to talk about?"

"Nothing really comes to mind."

"Okay." He sounds a little defeated. "Right."

Xavier and I have been close friends ever since we met three years ago in Las Vegas, when my new show "Escape: The Jevin Banks Experience" opened. That was before moving to Atlantic City. Before everything happened and I gave up performing.

He'd worked backstage on the strip for nearly thirty years before coming to work pyrotechnics for me. He lives in an RV, loves to blow stuff up, doesn't believe we landed on the moon, thinks Bush was responsible for 9/11, and still insists that Obama's birth certificate was a fake: "Why do you think it took him so long to produce it? And who surrounded him *every day*? *The Secret Service*, Jevin. And they're in charge of investigating counterfeit money. Right? *Counterfeit documents?* See? Just google it. It'll make you a believer."

Now I drive in silence and he quietly fiddles with the button camera I'll be wearing. Moving from stage pyrotechnics to cinematography has been an easier transition for him than I thought it would be. He has an eye for it. So much of it is about angles and staging and lighting, just like in a stage production. And since I'll be working incognito, he gets to use some of his favorite gadgets, like the button camera.

A Suburban passes us. A boy who looks about ten years old peers through the window at me as they go by. Even though my sons wouldn't be nearly that old by now, I wonder what they would have looked like if they'd have reached that age. It seems to happen all the time these days when I see kids.

They'd be taller, stockier, possibly into football or soccer or playing piano, but that would've been Drew, I'm guessing, rather than Tony. Probably video games for both of them. I would've taught them to ride their bikes, they'd have navigated through most of their years of elementary school and—

Stop it, Jevin. This isn't helping anything.

No, no it's not.

Emotional drag.

If nothing else, Xavier was right about that much.

I try to follow his advice and leave where I've been alone in order to get the universe to lean in my direction, but it's not as simple as he makes it sound. I've never been able to just tell myself to be happy—or sad, or angry, or anything. Something significant has to happen for my emotions to pendulum that far in another direction. It would be so much easier if I could just tell myself what to feel and then feel it, but that's not how things work for me. I only seem to learn the important stuff in life the hard way; I have to suffer before I change.

Setting the camera aside, Xavier finger-scrolls across the screen of my iPad to check my messages. "Looks like Charlene's gonna be a little late, but I think you two should still make it to the center by five thirty."

"It's what, about two hours from Salem?"

"Maybe a little less, but about that, yeah."

"Fionna send the files yet?"

He checks. "Not yet. Just another shot at a simile."

Fionna McClury, who works logistics and "information gathering" for us, is a single, stay-at-home mom who homeschools her four kids and works as a cybersecurity consultant to pay the bills. Fortune 500 companies hire her to try hacking into their companies in order to test their firewalls. Nine out of ten times she's successful.

Her kids help her sometimes for homework.

And sometimes she freelances.

For me.

She's a real pro at teaching her kids everything except English. Her Achilles' heel. Lately she's been trying to teach metaphors and similes and keeps sending us some of her own to critique before using them with her kids.

A little apprehensively, I glance at Xavier. "What is it this time?"

"The plane was as fast as a metal tube flying through the air at six hundred miles an hour."

"Um . . . it's accurate."

"I'll tell her that." He types. Hunt and peck. It takes awhile. "Hey, I forgot to mention, I need this weekend off. There's a convention I'm going to."

"Bigfoot or UFOs?"

"Very funny. It's about tectonic weapons."

"Tectonic weapons."

"They're for real, I'm telling you. There's credible evidence that the Air Force has the U2, the HAARP antennae, microwave technology. Just blast another country's fault lines with electromagnetic waves, take out their infrastructure without firing a shot. No boots on the ground. It's the weapon of the future. Intense stuff."

"Let me guess—Peru a few years ago? Haiti, Japan—test runs?"

"See, even *you* made the connection. Go to YouTube, search term *tectonic weapons*. It'll blow your mind."

"I'm sure it would, but why on earth would the US attack Haiti, Japan, or Peru?"

He taps his finger against the air as if to accentuate that my question was a way of agreeing with him. "Precisely, Jev. That is *exactly* the question we need to be asking."

Aha. "Okay."

"Okay?"

"You can have the weekend off. And you should text her, tell her we need those files tonight."

"Fionna."

"Right."

I guide the van along the highway and think about the TV series we're filming—another step in my transition from the stage to the screen.

For the last year, I've used my background as an illusionist to replicate the tricks and effects of dozens of fake psychics, televangelist con men, and fortune-telling scam artists.

I know all too well what it's like to search desperately for answers, and I can't imagine deceiving someone who's in that situation just to make a buck.

My stage shows did well; money's not the issue. I'm really not sure anymore what I want out of life, but I figure if I debunk hucksters who are taking advantage of vulnerable and hurting people, well, at least that's something positive. Something small but worthwhile.

The exposés have become a staple for cable's Entertainment Film Network, and while not paying nearly as much as my stage shows did, they've helped me keep my skills sharp.

Three episodes left under contract. Then I'm not sure what I'll do. It feels a bit like I'm in a sea with nothing on the horizon to sail toward. And nowhere I really want to sail.

Two shows ago, Entertainment Film Network's executive producer told me I needed to branch out in a new direction, merge my work with more of a bent toward investigative journalism—sort of an undercover illusionist. I'd studied journalism for a few years in college, so (at least to the producer) it seemed like a natural fit.

I don't have the name or face recognition of a Copperfield, Blaine, or Angel, and in this case anonymity would be to my advantage.

So, here I am.

But this trip is nothing like debunking a roadside psychic. The Lawson Research Center, or LRC, headed by theoretical physicist and Nobel laureate Dr. William Tanbyrn, has big dollars, big names, and a lot of credibility behind it.

It's true that since Dr. Tanbyrn started getting deeper into the study of the roots of consciousness, he'd fallen out of favor with some of the mainstream scientific community, but most of those scientists were discounting his findings without analyzing or carefully investigating them. It seems that for a lot of people, just the fact that he's now at the Lawson Research Center—a facility known for investigating the paranormal while also serving as a New Age conference center—is enough to undermine his credibility.

Needless to say, his most recent test results on mind-to-mind, non-local communication were controversial; the findings were widely disputed or simply disregarded, as were Dr. Dean Radin's in the books *The Conscious Universe* and *Entangled Minds*. However, Dr. Tanbyrn's research had made it into three peer-reviewed journals and, supposedly, had been replicated by two researchers in Sweden, although as far as Fionna and Charlene had been able to tell, that study hadn't appeared yet in any of the literature.

In essence, Dr. Tanbyrn and his team were claiming proof of unconscious psychic activity, or psi, saying they actually had hard data to back up the existence of some forms of telepathy. They claimed to have facts—scientific evidence, not just anecdotes of folks saying they could read other people's thoughts.

I find that all pretty hard to swallow.

Whenever someone claims psychic activity—whether it's a TV psychic, the gypsy at the fair doing cold readings, or a multimillion-dollar research center, my con-man radar goes up. As Xavier likes to say, "Wherever there's someone out to make a buck, there's someone about to lose his shirt."

I have some ideas on how Dr. Tanbyrn and his team are faking the findings, but I need to be sure. Get it all on film. That's what my three friends are going to help me do.

Charlene isn't at the rest stop when we arrive.

While Xavier heads to the vending machines for some Gatorade and Cheetos, I look over my notes about the center where Charlene and I will covertly spend the next three days.

But after a few moments I hear a girl in the vehicle next to me crying and see the family with the ten-year-old boy that passed us earlier. The stressed-out-looking mom is urging her two kids out of the SUV.

"I don't care if it's a ten-hour drive." She's clearly exasperated. "Please, you have to get along with your sister." Her kids look as weary as she does. The girl, who's about seven or eight, wipes a tear from her eye.

Go on. It might help.

I slip out of the van, lean against the door, and pull out the 1895 Morgan Dollar I always carry with me. Rachel and I didn't wear wedding rings, but since I was a numismatist, she insisted we exchange coins. This is the one she'd given me at our wedding seven years ago. It was by no means my most valuable coin, but being worth $125,000, it wasn't one that I was about to use to buy a lottery ticket.

I accidentally-on-purpose let it drop. It rolls toward the boy.

After a glance at his mother for permission, he picks it up and hands it to me.

"Thanks." But as I accept it, I vanish it from my hand. "Hey, where did that go?" I act shocked that it's gone.

Both he and the girl search my hands, then the ground. I turn my pockets inside out to show them that they're empty, and that's when I palm the rest of the coins I'll need. Then I pretend to notice something beside the boy's arm. "Hang on. There it is."

I reach over and pull half a dozen, more commonplace silver dollars one at a time from his left armpit, letting them drop to the parking lot.

"Did you see that, Mommy!" the girl exclaims. She's definitely not crying now. Her brother searches both of his armpits for more coins. I gather up the ones that fell.

"Yes. I did." Their mother is eyeing me a little suspiciously, as if I'm the psychopathic magician she's heard about who lures kids away from their parents by doing coin tricks for them in rest stop parking lots.

Xavier is returning now, snacks in hand. He sees me entertaining the family and tries to hide a half-smile.

I do a couple more tricks—I'm in my element and it feels good—then I see Charlene pull into a parking spot a few cars away, and I tell the kids, "I didn't realize it before, but I can tell you two are good at magic too."

They look confused.

"Go on, reach into your jacket pockets." With the sight angle of the mother and the attention of the kids focused on my right hand, the two left-handed drops I did a few moments ago while I was finishing the second-to-last trick hadn't been easy, but after twenty-five years of doing this, I'd managed to pull it off.

The kids reach into their pockets and are each astonished to find a silver dollar.

"I told you. It's magic."

"That was really good," the woman tells me, finally sounding a little more at ease, then nudges her kids toward me. "Go on, give the nice man back his money. And thank him for the magic show."

Though visibly disappointed that they can't keep the coins, the children obediently offer them to me.

"Oh, those were in your pockets, not mine. I couldn't take those." I wink at their mother. "I hope you have a great trip."

At last, with a word of thanks, she allows the kids to accept the silver dollars, then corrals them toward the restrooms.

Charlene is getting out of the car, and Xavier, who has a mouthful of Cheetos, waves to her but speaks to me in between crunches. "You just can't stand it, can you?"

"Stand what?"

"Seeing kids cry when you know you can make 'em laugh."

"What can I say. It's my only redeeming quality."

"You're pretty good at blackjack."

"True."

Charlene rounds the van. "Hello, gentlemen."

We greet her and she watches me pocket my remaining coins. Xavier, who's deep into his bag of Cheetos now, licks some cheese powder from his fingers.

Charlene sighs good-naturedly. "I see you're both up to your usual tricks."

"Old habits." I put the last coin away.

"How many silver dollars have you given away to kids over the years?"

"A couple, I suppose."

"Uh-huh."

She smiles and it looks nice. Brown-haired and congenial, Charlene Antioch has a girl-next-door innocence about her, but also a slyly sexy side that she keeps hidden except when onstage in my show—that is, when I still did stage work. I don't know how many times in the last six years I've made her vanish, sliced her into pieces, or let her chain me up and seal me in a water tank. But I haven't done an escape in over a year. The thought of Rachel and the boys in the van, trapped, drowning, has just been too much for me. I can't even stand being in small, cramped places anymore.

An escape artist who's claustrophobic.

So now he makes films exposing fake psychics.

Pathetic.

Today Charlene, who's thirty-two but looks twenty-five and is a chameleon when it comes to outfits, has her hair in a ruffled, earthy hairdo that might've actually looked more natural on Xavier than on her. Birkenstocks, a button-up shirt, and tan Gramicci climbing pants round out her neo-progressive nature-lover outfit. Undoubtably, she chose it because of the center we're heading to. I, on the other hand, wasn't so particular—black jeans, a faded T-shirt from one of the half-marathons I ran last year, a three-season leather jacket. Also black.

"How was your drive?" I ask her.

"Good."

Xavier crumples up the empty Cheetos bag, aims for a trash can ten feet away. Tosses. Misses. Goes to retrieve it, but rather than drop it in, he backs up for another ten-foot shot.

I glance at my watch. "We should probably get going. They're expecting us by five thirty and it's still almost an hour to the Three Sisters." The famous mountain range wasn't far at all from the Lawson Research Center and, coincidentally, was near the town where I grew up.

On his fourth try, Xavier finally hits his shot, and the three of us remove the cameras, the heart rate monitor, and the radio frequency (RF) jammer from the van. Even though Charlene and I have used them all before, Xavier insists on re-re-re-explaining how they work, how to keep them concealed, how Charlene would use the jammer and heart rate monitor tomorrow when she was in the chamber.

"Right." She takes the nearly invisible monitor that'll record her heart rate and, in a gesture of modesty, turns to the side before unbuttoning her shirt to press it against her chest, just above her heart. Xavier confirms that it's recording her heart rate, prints out the results on the small portable printer we're going to take with us. Then, monitor removed and shirt rebuttoned, Charlene climbs into the rental car.

I turn to Xavier. "So you're going to get B-roll of the mountains?"

He pats his video camera. "I'll get footage of everything around here. By the time you're done with your little study, we'll be ready to edit this puppy. Get it to the network. Actually meet a production deadline for once."

"Great." I grab the gear we'll need and join Charlene in the car while Xavier closes up the van.

He takes off, and a moment after I start the engine, Charlene turns to me. "I saw you with that family in the parking lot. You really are good with kids, Jevin."

"Thank you."

"With everyone."

"Thanks."

A pause. "It's been a long time since you were onstage. Do you ever think you might—"

"No."

Another slight pause. "Okay." As I'm backing out of the parking spot, she reaches over and gently places her hand on my knee. Despite myself, I feel a tingle of intimacy at her touch.

I stop the car. Let it idle.

"We need to get used to this," she says softly.

"Yes."

On the video we sent to the LRC, we'd portrayed ourselves as being deeply in love, and from what I could tell, it was one of the main reasons we'd been chosen for the study. Consequently, I know that if we're going to pull this off, I can't let on that her touch makes me uncomfortable in any way.

But yet it does, because in the last few weeks my feelings for her have strayed beyond the kind a co-worker can comfortably have for someone if they're going to remain simply co-workers. Part of me knows that, yes, it's been long enough since Rachel's death that I should be able to move on and start dating again, but another part of me isn't so sure that I'm over the loss in the ways I should be before delving into another serious relationship.

Charlene removes her hand. "What are you thinking?"

"I'm thinking it's not going to be easy being a couple."

"I'm not trying to make you uncomfortable. If you're not up to—"

"I'll be fine."

A moment passes. The car is still idling. "We were good on stage together." Her voice is gentle, like a brushstroke on canvas. It's an enigmatic statement and I do my best not to read too much into it.

She's just trying to tell you that you're a good actor, that together the two of you can pull this off.

"Yes."

"So then," she takes a small breath, "I'm not sure how to put this, but . . . you're going to be alright being my lover for the next three days?"

Pretending to be your lover. Pretending.

"Ready as I'll ever be." I have a sense that there's another layer of meaning beneath my words, a layer that I may not have intended, and a wash of slightly uncomfortable silence fills the car. Rachel's ghost seems to drift between us. Linger beside my shoulder.

Finally, I pull out of the parking lot and Charlene nods. "Good." But by then I've nearly forgotten what words of mine she's responding to.

I merge onto the highway and head toward the Lawson Research Center. Despite the meta-analysis Fionna ran on the test results, I'm still convinced that Dr. William Tanbyrn and his team are faking it somehow, because if they're not, if their findings are true, I don't have any idea how to wrap my mind around the implications.

Hollow Bones

From an early age Riah Colette knew that she was different.

She would go through the motion of hugs and good-night kisses with her mom and dad and little sister, Katie, but rather than enjoying the gestures, she would only notice how firm the hug was or how wet the kiss.

Her parents and sister spoke about love, said that they loved each other, that they loved her—but she couldn't understand what they meant, not in the sense of feeling something nice or meaningful toward someone else, which seemed to be the case with them.

Riah wasn't blind to the cues of affection that her dad gave her—the smiles and winks and the way he would position himself just so as he brushed against her when he passed her in the hallway.

He preferred her over Katie. That became especially clear by the way he began to treat her when she turned thirteen and started to look more like a young woman than a little girl.

And then there were the nighttime visits.

Katie wasn't old enough yet to earn that kind of special attention from their father, and at first Riah thought she should probably feel bad about it—that there was some sort of shame or injustice in her dad's favoritism toward her, but since he was her father, she had the sense that it was a good thing to please him. And so, the times in her bedroom late at night when he would knock on her door and she would tell him to come in, well, after a while they stopped feeling so awkward and became a way of making him happy.

Besides, he almost always gave her a present the next morning—a hairbrush, a pair of earrings, new underwear—as long as she promised not to tell her mother or Katie about the visits and as long as she kept the gifts a secret. And she had agreed.

One time when Riah was fourteen and she and Katie were in the woods near the stream on the edge of their property, Katie found a bird with a broken wing and brought it to her. Katie, who was nine at the time, was clearly troubled by the prospect of abandoning the bird in the forest. "We have to help it. If we leave it out here, it might die."

Of course it'll die, Riah thought. *All things die. So will you. Someday.*

But she didn't say any of that.

"Here," she said instead, "let me see it."

Riah had always been good at pretending that she cared about animals, and she could tell that her sister had no idea what was about to happen.

Katie handed Riah the bird, and she was struck by how light it was, as if its bones were made of air or the rest of its body was made entirely of feathers.

The lightness of the bird made it seem like what was about to happen would not be all that significant—after all, since the bird was so small, so tiny and young and helpless, not much would be different in the world after it was dead. Not really.

Riah didn't know what kind of bird it was, but it had blue feathers with streaks of gray and an orangish-yellowish beak. She could see the concern in Katie's face but felt only curiosity herself: *What will it be like to watch this bird die?*

It didn't struggle, didn't try to move its broken wing or attempt to squirm from her hand.

"What are you going to do?" Katie asked.

"I'm going to help it."

A few seconds passed, then Katie said quietly, "How?"

Cradling the bird in one hand, Riah placed her other hand gently on top of its head.

"Let's take it back to the house," Katie offered. "Then we can see if Mommy can help."

"It's okay." Riah closed her fingers around the bird's fragile head.

"What are you doing?" Now a sense of urgency. A nervousness—Riah twisted her hand.

One quick and abrupt movement. The bird let out a tiny chirp that was cut off in the middle, but that was all. It didn't quiver, just became still.

"No!" Katie screamed.

That easy. That quick. Limp and still.

Riah lifted her hand to see what the bird looked like and saw that it didn't look very different at all. Just lay so, so amazingly still.

She knew that sometimes nerves cause animals to twitch after they're dead, that chickens will run around even after their heads had been chopped off. In fact, she'd seen something like that firsthand herself when she was about Katie's age. But that wasn't with a chicken. "I killed a snake," her dad had told her. "But it's not dead yet. Come on. I'll show you."

Riah couldn't understand how the snake could be killed but not yet dead, but her dad led her past the line of tomatoes in the garden behind their house, where she saw a shovel with a dirty red stain lying beside the body of a three-foot-long black snake. The head lay a couple feet away and was motionless, but the snake's body was curling and writhing furiously on the grass.

Killed, but not yet dead.

After a moment Riah had gone over and picked it up, then held it while it continued to squirm and spasm, held it while its severed neck leaked warm, sticky blood onto her hands, held it until it stopped moving for good.

And now, as she cradled the dead bird in her hand, she thought of that writhing, dead snake.

But the bird didn't squirm at all.

So still.

Katie, who was crying loudly, had almost made it back to the house. Riah wasn't surprised by her sister's reaction. Honestly, she wasn't surprised by her own, either. It'd been so easy to stop that bird's life, to quiet it into death, and now she realized that it didn't either bother her or please her, gave her no sense of accomplishment or of loss, no satisfaction or disappointment.

She knew that she should probably feel something, that normal girls would feel bad or guilty or sad in some way, or get upset and start crying like Katie had, who was now calling for their mother.

Katie, a normal girl.

Riah, the freak.

She laid the bird gently on the ground in a patch of dandelions near the stream, hoping that the gesture would somehow make her feel more reverent or more considerate of the bird's death, but all she really felt was a sense of curiosity at the angle of the bird's head and how it looked so odd twisted that way.

She tilted her own head and studied her reflection in the water, tried to see what it would've looked like if her head was bent in the same way as the dead bird's, but she couldn't quite get the angle right.

Back at the house, her mother had yelled at her, but her father had laughed it off. "Same as a racehorse," he said in his wet, thick-tongued way. "Those things break a leg, the owners put 'em down right there on the track. Doesn't matter who's in the stands—women, kids, makes no difference at all, they make everyone watch."

Riah's mother gave him a scolding look. "Hank, that's enough."

He gazed at his youngest daughter, who was still sniffling, and his tone became firm: "Day comes when you gotta learn that everything dies. Just a matter of time. Better to learn that now than later."

He went back to his corn bread and ham with a renewed passion.

"You don't need to upset Katie and you don't need to encourage the older one," Riah's mom said.

It'd been right around the time when Riah turned thirteen and her dad began visiting her bedroom that her mother had stopped referring to her by name and just started calling her "the older one."

Her dad grunted at the comment from his wife. "I'm just saying, killing a crippled bird isn't cruel. Put it out of its misery. It's the caring thing to do."

"Caring? Really?" There was unusual defiance in her mother's tone.

"Yeah." His eyes narrowed. "Really."

Riah watched Katie stifle back a tear. The girls had learned long ago not to argue with their father. He didn't take it very well—especially after he'd been drinking, as he had already this afternoon.

Her mother's leg got a little jittery beneath the table. "And is that what you'd want us to do to you? Snap your neck if you broke your leg? Would that be the caring thing to do?"

"Don't challenge me, woman." Each word had become a hammer blow. "Don't make me put you in your place."

Riah noticed a tiny tremor in her mother's hands and saw her throat tighten. She knew that on those nights when her father visited her bedroom, he often stopped by his own room first. She didn't know exactly what he did to her mother on those nights, but she knew enough. There was usually yelling and crashing and sometimes sobbing. Her mother typically wore more makeup than usual the next day. But even then, the bruises were still visible.

I wonder how long it takes her to put all that makeup on.

Now her mother seemed to compose herself and looked at her husband harshly, but she did not challenge him. Instead she rose stiffly, picked up her plate, and headed to the kitchen. "Come on, Katie," she said. "Help me with the dishes."

Katie quickly left the table and hurried to the kitchen, and then, when Riah and her father were alone, he gave her a wink and put his hand on hers.

Your mother yelled at you and he defended you. You should thank him. That's what you're supposed to do when someone helps you.

She smiled back at him, playing the role of a girl who cared about her father.

"Alright," she said, her voice soft, meant only for him. "After they're all asleep."

She knew he would understand.

"That's my girl." He stabbed his fork into his ham. "That's my good little girl."

Now, twenty years later, Riah headed across the Benjamin Franklin Bridge toward RixoTray Pharmaceuticals' corporate headquarters in central Philadelphia.

She knew that the CEO, Dr. Cyrus Arlington, was working late. It wasn't quite 8:30, and Riah hadn't told him she would be swinging by. He'd been in London, and she hadn't seen him since he'd left two days ago. Tonight she wanted to see how he would respond to the surprise.

That's what she did sometimes. Tested people to see how they would react to the unexpected.

To observe what normal people do.

To learn what it would be like to be normal.

It might have been her curiosity into human nature that was one of the reasons she'd become a doctor in neurophysiology: to understand how people think, communicate, feel—and maybe to begin to understand more of what it means to be human.

That was before joining Cyrus's neurophysiology research team to work on the neural decoding studies, before seducing him to try and discover more about the meaning of love.

Over the years she'd realized that if there was one thing she wanted, it was to find out what it would feel like to care about somebody or something the way other people did—where family members or friends mattered, where your heart might get warmed or anxious or broken. What would that be like, to feel more than just curiosity about someone else's joy or pain?

Riah paid the toll and guided her car toward the sixty-story mirrored-glass skyscraper that was rivaled only by the Comcast building for prominence in the Philadelphia skyline. Tonight she had a question to ask Cyrus, a proposal, as it were.

A way she had thought up over the last few weeks to find out more about the limits and depths of true love.

Serenity

5:28 p.m. Pacific Daylight Time

I'm anxious to get to the center, and it's not far, only ten minutes or so.

As we pass through Pine Lake, I realize it's exactly like I remember it: the Cascade Mountains rising majestically from the horizon with Mt. Hood dominating the range, creating a picturesque backdrop to the town that the demise of logging in the region had turned into a virtual ghost town.

I haven't been here in over fifteen years, but when I was a boy, I used to gaze at Mt. Hood every day on my way to school to see if it had snow on it. Usually there were a few days a year when the snow on the very top would disappear. One year, though, when I was in sixth grade, the snow stayed up there all summer.

Tapping the brakes, I slow down and guide the car off the highway and onto the winding mountain road that leads toward the Lawson Research Center's entrance.

I can still hear my dad talking about how the year-round snow cover was going to help the tourists stay longer. Good for the economy, the town. Good for the ski shop he ran.

That was two months before my mom left us and moved to Seattle, where I only saw her twice before she remarried and left for France with her new husband.

As a kid I thought that no matter how much the snow might've helped the local economy, it didn't help us, and in my childhood naïveté, I blamed the snow for what happened to my family, as if it were some sort of convoluted cause and effect. It's funny what you associate together when you're young, things that aren't related at all but that seem to be somehow interconnected.

I'd dabbled in magic before that, but that was the year I started taking it seriously. In the hope of somehow making my mother reappear.

"Jevin?" Charlene's voice draws me back to the moment. "Are you okay?"

"Sorry, I was . . . Yeah, I'm fine."

"I was saying, we're almost there. The turnoff is in a quarter mile."

"Right." A stillness passes between us. For some reason I feel the need to explain myself. "I was just remembering the last time I was here. As a kid."

"Good memories or bad ones?"

"A little of both."

I make the turn.

The newly paved access road winds through the towering pines of the old-growth forest. A large sign sits at the entrance, painted with both the name of the center and a symbol of a rather rotund woman in the lotus position with lines that make me think of electric sparks emanating from her head. I can't decide if it looks more like she's morphing into a porcupine or getting electrocuted while meditating.

We park and grab our bags from the back of the car.

Charlene closes the trunk. "I've been thinking a lot about this study, Jevin, wondering if it might be legit. I mean, this isn't the first research in mind-to-mind communication."

We haven't been on the same page with this project since I first proposed that we debunk the research. "True. But that's over the last seventy years, and with every year that passes, you have a more discernible decline effect: with more stringent testing procedures, the results are less and less conclus—"

"Conclusive, yes, I know, but this one was replicated nearly four dozen times with hundreds of subjects. I just don't see how they might have faked it."

"Nonrandom timing on the video-image generation, selective reporting, coached participants, confirmation bias, or something to do with the movement or focusing of the camera. It could be something as simple as switching the equipment or using a computer to mimic the sender's responses and create the atypical results before the external review of the findings. We'll find out."

Silence.

We head toward the main building. She looks at me. "Your dad still in the area?"

"My dad?"

"Yes . . . Is he still in the area?"

"He is."

"I was wondering . . . ?"

"He's still here."

"Okay."

"Yes."

"I was wondering if you might want to see him."

"You were wondering . . ."

"Go over to his place and—"

"Probably not a good idea. And I have to say, this conversation is starting to sound like a David Mamet script." As a fellow filmophile, I figured she would know what I was talking about.

"A script? You think? By Mamet?"

"Would you stop already."

She smiles.

Two elegant Japanese rock gardens with Native American symbols engraved in sandstone sculptures lie to our left. They look like they might've been more at home in New Mexico than here in Oregon.

I've never explained to Charlene why I ended up living with my grandmother the last four years I was in Pine Lake, and this doesn't feel like the right time to get into all of that.

"There should be time after the study," she offers.

A pause. "We'll see."

I imagine she must know this is a way of saying no without actually saying it.

"Right. Okay."

The path leads to a surprisingly modern building with solar panels, a garden to the south, and a fountain that's gurgling from the top of a three-dimensional sculpted peace sign. Beside the office door is another sign of the overweight, spiky-haired porcupine lady.

I open the door.

Gentle sitar music, along with the fragrant scent of a flowery incense, welcomes us as we enter the building.

The young woman at the counter has blonde dreadlocks dangling across her shoulders, a loose-fitting Indian shirt, an indiscernible number of bead necklaces, and a disarming smile. "Welcome to the Lawson Research Center. I'm Serenity."

I can't imagine that it's her real name, and despite myself, I end up trying to think of a cool New Age nickname for myself to help me fit in.

In lieu of a handshake, Serenity presses her palms together in front of her chest in a posture of prayer and gives me and Charlene a small, reverent bow from behind the check-in counter. I see that she has intricate tattoos on the back of her hands. Symbols from nearly every religion I'm aware of, and some that I am obviously not.

Charlene and I return the gesture.

"Is this your first visit to the LRC?" Serenity's voice is tiny and melodic. Birdlike.

I nod. "Yes. We're here for the study with Dr. Tanbyrn."

"Of course."

She glances at a sheet of paper taped to her desk, reminding me of a flight attendant referring to note cards on her first attempt at solo-announcing the preflight instructions. An open journal with a half-finished entry lies beside the cheat sheet. Scribbles fill the margin of the journal. "And you are?"

Charlene takes my hand and leans close to me as she tells Serenity the aliases we used when we sent in the video to apply for the study: "Brent Berlin and Jennie Reynolds."

"We prefer Wolverine and Petunia," I tell Serenity.

Charlene looks at me questioningly.

I shrug.

Our New Age nicknames.

"I'm Wolverine," Charlene explains.

"Actually, I—"

"He's Petunia."

"That's nice." Serenity nods understandingly. "Yes, of course."

Charlene winks at me. "Right, dear?" There's no way I'm going to be Petunia for the rest of our stay, but arguing in front of Serenity doesn't seem like the loving thing to do, so I let it drop. I'll reaffirm my identity as Wolverine later.

"Sure," I mutter. "Dear."

Serenity consults her notes again. For walk-around and street magic, you need to be able to read other people's handwriting upside down and backward so that when you use mirrors you can decipher what they've written on cards you're not supposed to see. In time I got pretty good at it, and right now that skill was coming in handy.

"I think you'll find our campus inviting and restful. A place to quiet your thoughts, still your spirits, and bring a more harmonic centeredness to your inner being and to your relationship with each other." The words are obviously scripted, but she makes them sound authentic, like she genuinely means them, and I like that about her.

"Thank you, that sounds nice," I tell her honestly.

Charlene thanks her as well, then mentions something about how we'd been so looking forward to this, but I'm giving my attention to the lobby, taking in the simple, rustic setting that also carries an air of high-end architectural design. Outside the window lies a porch with elegant stonework and round porch tables with umbrellas spreading above them like protective canvas wings. I imagine the metal is recycled, that the canvas is organic and somehow both waterproof and biodegradable.

Charlene is still holding my hand, which is okay by me.

"They're serving in the dining hall until six, if you haven't eaten yet," Serenity tells us. I want to get settled, so I'm thankful Charlene and I grabbed a bite on the way here. "Breakfast is in the morning, six to eight. Dr. Tanbyrn will meet you at nine at the Prana building."

Charlene looks at her curiously. "I'm sorry—the piranha building?"

"Prana." Serenity seems surprised that Charlene doesn't know the word. "The life force. The life-sustaining force. Hindu."

"Right."

Charlene lets go of my hand.

Serenity holds out a map uncertainly. "I'm sorry, did you say you've been here before?"

"No." It's a dual-purpose answer—I hadn't said that, and we haven't been here. I accept the map from her.

Serenity settles back into her script: "There's a 7:00 yoga class tonight that you're welcome to attend, all at your discretion, of course. Here at the Lawson Research Center, we care more about your experience than your attendance at any of our quality scheduled events."

She hands Charlene a schedule. "We want this to be a place apart from the normal distractions of daily life. Too many people are tethered to technology, and it gives them a false sense of connection with other sojourners but splinters their attention from the most vital relationships, those with the people around them, and all too often it keeps them from being present in the moment."

Serenity makes it through all of that in one breath, which I find pretty impressive.

"So"—now she looks nervous—"Wolverine, Petunia, I will need to ask you not to use your mobile phones or other electronic computerized devices here on our campus. It's our policy." She sounds like she's apologizing.

Fionna and her kids had researched this place extensively, and Serenity's request comes as no surprise. We don't have any intention of forsaking our electronic devices during our stay, but Charlene fishes through her purse, produces her phone. Shuts it off. "Of course."

I turn off my cell as well. I wonder what the reception up here in the mountains will be like anyway.

Serenity directs us to our cabin, wishes us well, and prayer-gesture bows to us again. We reply in kind.

As we're walking down the path toward the cabin, Charlene shakes her head. "Wolverine and Petunia?"

"I was trying to fit in. And I'm supposed to be Wolverine."

"I kind of like you being Petunia."

"I'll bet you do."

We walk in silence until I make my suggestion for the evening's plans. "Tonight, instead of going to yoga, I think we should have a little look around the research center."

"Jevin Banks, you read my thoughts."

"Well, if I can actually do that, tomorrow's test is going to be a piece of cake."

I'm toting the bags, so when we reach the porch Charlene opens the cabin door and we step inside.

The Doll

The cabin is nothing special. No TV. No telephone. A kitchenette, a small living area, a bathroom. A bedroom with a king-sized bed lies at the end of a short hall.

Ah, that was something I hadn't thought through very well. One bed.

I consider going back to ask Serenity for a cabin with two beds, but I doubt that would help Charlene and me look like a couple who's deeply in love. I catch myself eyeing the couch to see if it'll be big enough for me.

The autumnal smell of wood smoke permeates the air, although it must be from somewhere else since there's no woodstove or fireplace in the cabin.

A sweep of the room with Xavier's latest gadget—a pen-sized radio frequency detector—tells us there aren't any bugs and that Charlene and I will be able to talk freely while we're in the room. It's probably an unnecessary precaution, but in Xavier's mind you can never be too careful about these things.

It doesn't take us long to put our things away, and as Charlene is closing the dresser drawer, she turns to me. "So you're thinking wait till it gets dark? Go check out the Faraday cage?"

"Yes."

"And how do you propose we get into the building?"

I hold up a second hotel-style key card in addition to the one to our cabin.

"How did you get that?"

"At the front desk while you were talking with Serenity."

"You . . . how?"

"The key card coder. Serenity had a journal open and stopped writing in midsentence when we arrived. The slant, baseline, and connecting strokes of the passcode she'd written in the margins matched those on the sheet of paper containing her orientation notes."

"And you swiped the key without either of us noticing?"

"Yes."

She shakes her head. "You really are good, Petunia."

"Wolverine."

"Well, let's hope you're right about the code."

"We'll find out soon enough."

"As soon as it gets dark?"

"Exactly."

I pull out the two thick volumes that Dr. William Tanbyrn wrote—one before and one after his interest shifted from theoretical quantum physics to consciousness and its relationship to quantum entanglement. The words on the back of the second book touted:

Dr. William Tanbyrn, who received a Nobel Prize in physics for his contribution in the development of mechanisms for studying the existence of loop quantum gravity, has embarked on a daring new field of study—the human mind and its interaction with the universe around us.

As I sit on the couch, Charlene leans close. "Didn't quite finish them yet, huh?" I can smell her perfume. I hadn't noticed it so much earlier in the car, but it's nice. A gentle touch of lavender.

"Barely got started." I'd been hoping to get through the books before our meeting this week with Dr. Tanbyrn, but he wasn't the most concise author I'd ever read, and I'd found the two five-hundred-page tomes a bit hard to decipher. "They're pretty dense."

"Well, tell me one thing you've learned so far."

"Not even quantum physicists understand quantum physics."

"Ah."

"Oh, and something else I found interesting: when electrons jump from one level in orbit around the nucleus to another, they don't travel through the space between the rings, they just appear at the next ring."

"What do you mean? Like teleporting? 'Beam me up, Scotty'? That sort of thing?"

"That's one way to put it."

"Where do they go?"

"No one knows."

"Sounds like science fiction to me."

"Me too. Except it's reality."

"Huh." She sounds more interested now. Peers over my shoulder as if she's going to stay for a while.

Her perfume really is nice.

I try to redirect my attention from her to the books.

"Let me read you a quote." I flip through the pages, but it takes me awhile to find the one I'm looking for. "Okay. Here: 'Nothing exists except atoms and empty space; everything else is opinion.'"

She considers that for a moment. "Sure. Even solid objects are mostly space, the electron orbiting the nucleus. Who wrote that? Dr. Tanbyrn?"

"Not quite. A little bit before his time."

"Einstein?"

"Democritus. He died in 370 BC."

"That's amazing."

I hand her one of the books. "Here. You can read this one if you want. I highlighted all the good stuff. Up to chapter 9."

But she straightens up. "Actually, I was thinking I'd take a quick shower, freshen up. It was a long day in the car."

"Ah, yes. Well, maybe later."

She pats my shoulder. "I'll let you do all the heavy lifting. You can fill me in when you're done."

Then she leaves me alone to my reading, and I settle in with my pen, highlighter, and the shorter, more recent of the two textbooks, and flip to the chapter on quantum entanglement and theories about the results of a meta-analysis of studies on identical twins. As I do, I can't help but think of Drew and Tony, who, just like so many identical twins, seemed to communicate with each other in unexplainable ways—finishing each other's sentences, making up words that the other boy seemed to instinctively know the meaning of, even, at times, giving the impression that they knew what each other was thinking.

As I begin to read, the memory of my two sons pinches my heart, and I can't help but wonder if this research will help me to understand them better or just make me miss them all the more.

Riah Colette showed her ID to the security guard in the RixoTray Pharmaceuticals corporate headquarters' lobby, took the elevator to the top floor, and entered the suite where her paramour worked in his corner office.

Whenever Cyrus was in his office—no matter what time of day—his secretary, Caitlyn Vaughn, would be stationed at the reception desk out front. Riah nodded to her, and the young woman gave her a half-frown but waved her through.

Since Cyrus was a married man, he'd wanted to avoid his place from the beginning of their relationship, and Riah never let him come to her apartment, so that limited their choices. Sometimes they would slip off to a hotel room, but more often than not they stayed here in his office.

Riah had the sense that the twenty-something redhead was jealous of her liaisons with her boss, and she wondered how many times Caitlyn had leaned close to the door to listen to the sounds coming from inside the office during her visits. It was something to think about. Perhaps she would ask her about it one of these days.

Quietly, Riah gave the door a light one-knuckle knock, just enough to let Cyrus know someone was there, but then entered before he had a chance to call her in.

He was on the phone, and she could tell he was taken aback by her arrival, but he quickly put on a smile and signaled to her that he would be with her in a moment, then gestured toward a chair: *Have a seat.*

She chose not to, but instead angled toward the window.

Impeccably dressed in a suit that cost more than most people's entire wardrobes, Cyrus looked sharp, powerful, confident. But also stern. Any gentleness he might've tried to portray was betrayed by his eyes, which were like two steel balls, blank and emotionless. Two miniature shot puts embedded in his head. Riah had seen him enjoy himself, oh yes, but had never seen him happy, not really. And that intrigued her. Because she couldn't remember a time when she'd been happy either.

He let his gaze drift from her face and slide down her body, along the curves of her dress, and she didn't discourage it. She felt no shame in using her looks and figure in her research into human nature, into attraction, into love. She kept in shape for this, and at thirty-four she'd been told that she was still striking, and she was used to eyes following her wherever she went.

Long ago, Riah had learned that sex was the way to please men. And when they're pleased they trust you, and when they trust you they share their secrets with you. As she'd overheard a female co-worker say one time, "If you can't tell someone your secrets, you make intimacy off-limits."

So, it seems, sharing secrets leads to intimacy.

Riah wasn't sure yet if intimacy would lead to the one thing she wanted to feel most—love—but she held out hope that in time it would.

She knew Cyrus's office well: the wide windows overlooking central Philly, his framed degrees and awards hanging prominently on the walls, bookshelves that were neatly lined with medical textbooks and packed with paraphernalia from his travels around the world. In the center of the room sat his imposing mahogany desk that she and Cyrus would clear off sometimes when they decided not to use the leather couch in the corner.

And of course, at the far side of the room, the two aquariums: one filled with buzzing emerald jewel wasps, the other with inch-and-a-half-long cockroaches. It was a curious thing. Riah had asked him about that, but he'd never explained why he kept them.

She went to the shelf and picked up the voodoo—or, more accurately, *vodou*—doll that he'd brought back from his medical humanitarian visit to Haiti after the earthquake. In one sense, it was oddly appropriate that he'd brought it here to Philly. After all, there was a large Haitian population in the city, and some people said there were between five hundred and one thousand houses where people practiced voodoo in their basements. With estimates of twenty to fifty people participating in the services, that meant there might be as many as 50,000 serious voodoo worshipers in Philadelphia, putting it on par with Miami and even New Orleans.

The cloth doll had a painted-on face with pin marks through the eyes and in the groin area. Most of Cyrus's visitors found the doll disturbing, and he seemed to enjoy using it as a conversation piece and a chance to offhandedly mention his volunteer work in developing countries. Personally, Riah wasn't bothered by the doll, just wondered who, if anyone, the pins had been intended to harm.

Holding the doll, she stood beside the window and looked at central Philadelphia's streets spreading out before her like spokes from a wheel. She'd always thought that there were too many one-way streets in downtown Philly, probably caused by the disrupted traffic patterns around the monolithic city hall.

A proud city.

The city of the nation's birth.

And, historically, a good place to base a medical center or a pharmaceutical firm.

While studying medicine at Drexel, she'd learned that Philadelphia was the home of the first public hospital in 1751, the first school of pharmacy in 1812, the first private biomedical research institute in 1892.

In addition, the greater Philadelphia area was the home of eleven other pharmaceutical firms' corporate headquarters. Rixo Tray, though the smallest of the twelve, actually had the second-highest profit margin. Due, in large part, to having Dr. Cyrus Arlington at the helm.

Riah stared out the window at Philadelphia's nighttime skyline while she waited for Cyrus to finish his call. Tonight she would ask him for the first time to come over to her place after work, and when they got there she would see how he responded to the surprises she had waiting for him.

Perhaps it would lead to love, she wasn't sure, but if nothing else, seeing his reaction would give her more information on how men respond to shared secrets.

Twilight

I hear the shower running in the bathroom.

Charlene had asked me to fill her in, so now I look over a two-sentence summary of quantum physics: "The observer's intentions and expectations about reality actually affect the outcome of reality. Without the observer the quantum wave function never collapses." Admittedly, the collapsing quantum wave was a concept I needed a little more time to really grasp.

As far as I could understand it, quantum physicists claimed that since possibilities do not become reality without conscious observation, matter could not exist without consciousness. So, according to Dr. Tanbyrn, philosophers ask, "If a tree falls in the forest and there's no one to hear it, does it make any sound?" but physicists are forced to ask, "If there's no one there to observe the tree fall, does it even exist?"

As he writes:

> Our universe is both a puzzle and an answer, both a mystery and an adventure. From the earliest explorations of the human mind to probing the mysteries of existence, we as a species have always been question-askers. And now, with the advancement of quantum physics, the answers we find only produce more profound questions about what is happening on the subatomic level of the universe.

Remarkably, none of the explanations used to explain the activity of subatomic particles has been proven. Not M-theory, superstring theory, the multiverse. Basically, in understanding quantum physics, you need to remember that scientists still don't understand the nature of life, that although they can test how energy reacts under different circumstances, they still don't really understand what it is.

In some quarters it's even debated whether quantum physics should be considered science or a field of metaphysics.

My mind is spinning, not only because of the mystical-sounding quantum theories I'm reading, but also, admittedly, at the thought of Charlene showering in the next room over. I try to concentrate on the intricate concepts of the book, but the sound of the running water and the knowledge of who it's washing over is a little too distracting.

Hoping to divert my thoughts, I step outside.

Clouds have rolled in. The evening is cool. Jacket weather.

A light mist touches the air.

Almost dark.

I read for a few more minutes but can still hear the water running inside the cabin, so I take out my cell and go on a walk to check if I can get a signal and to see if the files Fionna was going to send me have arrived.

～

Two miles away

Glenn Banner did not think of himself as an assassin.

Yes, he had killed people, eleven so far, and always in the name of money, but still, when he thought of assassins, he pictured slick, highly paid professionals who hide on rooftops, snap ten-thousand-dollar rifles together, take out opposition-party political figures, and then, fake passport in hand, melt into the crowd on their way to another country to lie low for a couple weeks before their next hit.

When Glenn thought of an assassin, he didn't think of a guy who worked most days as a mechanic, a guy who was just trying to make ends meet, a divorced dad who was doing the best he knew to put food on the table and have enough cash left over to spend some time with his daughter on weekends. Mary Beth was six and lived with her mother and her stepfather two miles from Glenn's mobile home that lay on the outskirts of Seattle.

No, he didn't think of himself as an assassin.

But none of that changed what he was.

Lots of people had unsavory jobs they needed done, and that's where Glenn came in. Sometimes it meant getting compromising photos of someone, or scaring off an ex-spouse, or beating some sense into a young punk who wouldn't leave a guy's daughter alone. Small jobs really, but they were the sort of thing Glenn was good at, and they helped pay the bills.

But two years ago he'd moved up the food chain.

Toward more permanent solutions.

Yes, he looked more like the guy who lives down the block than he did a professional problem solver, but his low visibility was part of what made him so good at what he did. He was truly gifted at playing the role of a neighbor who enjoyed a few smokes with his friends, drank a few Buds on the weekends, and always bought his little six-year-old princess a toy from a truck stop on the way back from his assignments.

But truthfully, to him she wasn't a little princess. The kid was just a set piece in the life he was acting out. In the bigger game he was playing. But she served his purpose of creating sympathy among the people he knew, and that was reason enough to put up with spending time with her.

He parked the car at the edge of the county road that made a circuit around the center's sprawling campus.

He didn't want to drive onto the property, so he'd decided earlier to access it by hiking through the surrounding old-growth forest.

Tonight—collect the information that he could use against his employers. Tomorrow—solve the problem, pick up his paycheck, then blackmail the people who'd hired him.

No, he didn't think of himself as an assassin. He was just a guy heading off to work in a job that happened to be somewhat messy.

He made sure he had his knife—a 170 mm blade, Nieto Olivo series—with him just in case. After all, as the saying goes, "Chance favors the prepared mind." Then Glenn began picking his way through the dying daylight that was filtering through the forest around him.

Sleepover

Though he was trying to keep his voice low, Riah heard Cyrus wrapping up his phone call: "Yes, we have a man in the area . . . He's good, he'll take care of everything . . . No, of course . . . Alright. I'll be there within the hour . . . Yes. By tomorrow afternoon it won't be a problem . . . And the video is on its way. You'll be impressed with the results."

An intriguing end to the conversation.

He said goodbye, hung up, and turned toward Riah. His eyes landed on the cloth doll she was still holding. "We've come a long way since then." He gestured toward it. "Shamanism, witchcraft, sorcery. Voodoo."

She turned it over in her hands. Studied the punctured eyes. "Some people still believe in those things. How was London?"

"Wet. Dreary. Tedious. And yes, I know."

"You know?"

"That some people still believe in those things. I saw a voodoo ceremony myself while I was in Haiti. A bit troubling, if you ask me. The whole goal is for the participants to get possessed."

"By a Loa."

He seemed surprised that she knew. "Yes."

"They call it being 'ridden,' as if the spirit was the rider and the person was the horse."

"You've done your homework."

Riah considered what type of response to give him, what a normal woman might say, then asked, "Why do you keep this thing around anyway? It's kind of creepy."

"To remember the trip, of course, but also to remind myself that superstition is erased by science. The more we advance in medicine, the less we need to believe in the supernatural. I didn't expect you tonight."

She strolled toward the bookshelf. "Is it a problem that I'm here?"

"No, I . . . No." But his body language told her that perhaps it was.

She placed the voodoo doll back on the shelf and considered how he thought, how she could play off that to get what she wanted. "I can leave. If that's what you'd like."

He seemed to consider that, then said, "No. Stay."

He came toward her, kissed her. She kept her eyes open while he did, studying his face as he pressed his lips against hers. Though she'd learned over the years to kiss in a way that turned men on, and did so now, she felt nothing—no attraction, no repulsion, no excitement. It was as if he were an object to her, a lab specimen. She knew that thinking about him in this way would not have been considered by most people to be healthy, but although she desperately wanted to, she didn't know how to think about her lovers in any other way.

At last, as he pulled away, she decided to try something that might convince him that he would want to spend the night with her. She lifted his right hand, kissed his index finger, then trailed it across her cheek down her neck, around the fringed neckline of her dress, and brought it back, touched it lightly to her tongue. She let her lips pucker to greet the moist tip of his finger. A light kiss, yes, but she had the feeling it would be terribly seductive and exciting to him.

She let go of his hand, and Cyrus let it linger beside her lips for a moment, then lowered it slowly to his side.

He took a deep breath to collect himself, then looked at his watch. "I do have a meeting in forty-five minutes."

"Forty-five minutes? That's plenty of time."

"Well, actually, I need to leave now to get there. It's at the R&D facility."

When she'd first applied for her job, she hadn't understood why RixoTray had built its research and development complex thirty minutes away, just outside of Bridgeport, but the more she'd thought about it, the more it made sense: keep the facility isolated, at least a little ways, from any terrorist threats to the country's fifth largest city, the one that held more symbols of freedom and independence than any other, the city that was known as the birthplace of modern democracy.

After all, if you were an Islamic terrorist group trying to strike at the heart of the Great Satan, you might choose New York City, the financial capital of the West, or Washington DC, the political capital of America, or LA, the home of the entertainment industry that spreads all those corrupt Western ideas around the world. Or you might choose Philly, the historical symbol of democracy. And since your people had already dramatically attacked NY and DC and targeted LAX, that left Philadelphia as a primary target. It was just a matter of time.

She looked at Cyrus, responded to his comment about the meeting by asking the natural question: "At this time of night?"

"It's with Daniel and Darren."

Well, that made sense. The twins didn't exactly keep normal office hours. "I thought they were in Oregon?"

"We flew them in earlier today."

Earlier today. She hadn't heard. "I'll come."

"No, that won't be necessary."

"I'm the principal investigator on the project. I'm the one who implanted the electrodes. I should have been told the two of them were back."

He was quiet.

She put a hand lovingly on the side of his neck. "I'll join you, then you can join me at my place. Actually, that's why I came here, to invite you to a sleepover."

He considered that. "A sleepover."

"Mm-hmm. It'll be fun." She sat on his desk and crossed her legs, making the most of the slit in her dress. "I have some new outfits to wear. A few sleepover games I thought we could play." She could tell he was definitely interested now.

Riah handed him the phone receiver from his desk. "Call your wife. Tell her you just got sent out of town on an urgent business trip. Something pressing that can't wait." In his position as CEO, it wasn't an unusual occurrence, and they'd used this excuse to their advantage before.

She waited for him to finish lying to his wife, then led him out of the building to the parking garage. She knew where his Jaguar would be and figured she could pick up her car tomorrow morning when they returned to his office.

They slipped into the Jag.

And took off to see the twins.

Undetermined States

No phone reception, not even one bar, not even enough of a signal to send a text.

Since the sun has dipped below the tree line, I click on the porch light and take a seat on the swing that overlooks the sweeping valley of tall, long-shadowed Douglas firs to wait for Charlene. The main research building lies somewhere across campus on the border of these trees.

After taking a little time to study the map Serenity had given us of the grounds, I scan the chapter on quantum entanglement that I read yesterday, jotting a few notes so I can summarize it for Charlene.

When I look up, I see that all the light has drained from the forest, and I can feel a growing twitch of excitement about our little foray into the research center. However, despite my anticipation, I can also feel myself getting uneasy about the thought of entering, even for a few moments, the Faraday cage.

When Charlene joins me on the porch, she has changed clothes but is still toweling off her hair.

She gestures toward the book I'm holding. "Learn anything new?"

"A couple things, yeah. I'll tell you on the way."

"I've been wondering . . . You don't think there'll be security?"

"It's possible. We'll use the back entrance on the lower level, the one by the woods. According to the info Fionna pulled up last week, it should be clear, but if we see any guards or security cameras, we'll bail."

I take the key card that I'd lifted from the front desk, a flashlight, and my friendly neighborhood lock-pick set just in case I'll need it, secretly hoping that I will. After all these years of practice, I can get through most locks in less than fifteen seconds. Most handcuffs in less than nine. It's a private game I play—always going for the record.

Charlene grabs the RF jammer and heart rate monitor and we leave for the research facility.

～

Glenn came to the edge of the property. He'd been prudent with the use of his flashlight and was confident no one had seen him moving through the forest.

There was no fence to scale, so after getting his bearings, he turned his flashlight off, quietly walked through a dark channel in the woods, and emerged on one of the walking trails that led down the mountain toward the main campus.

～

The night is cool and damp, a mountain night.

With the cloud cover, there's no moonlight, no stars to guide us. However, pools of hazy light escape from the windows of some of the buildings, and there are enough outdoor lamps mounted on the posts that parallel the walking paths for us to easily follow the meandering trail.

Charlene is close beside me, and I summarize the information I'd read at the cabin about the basics of quantum theory. "According to the Copenhagen interpretation, without measurement—that is, observation—a quantum system remains in an undetermined state of existence."

"An undetermined state of existence . . ." She mulls that over. "So, you're saying that reality isn't determined yet, so—what? Objective reality doesn't exist?"

"Quantum physicists would say that's right, at least not in the way we normally think of it. Unobserved reality exists, just in a fuzzy state of flux that they call a state of quantum uncertainty."

"A fuzzy state of flux?"

"Well, yes, but they say 'quantum uncertainty.' Sounds more scientific. Anyway, it doesn't stop there. The Copenhagen interpretation also states that upon observation, the quantum system collapses. In other words, it's forced into becoming one of its possible states—which basically refers to how it manifests itself. It's a little confusing."

"But how does it know which state to manifest into?"

"The intentions and expectations of the observer determine it."

While she chews on that, I mentally review the map of the grounds. There are more than two dozen buildings, including cabins, a retreat building, conference and dining facilities, a prayer garden, and a meditation chalet. It seems that whoever designed this place did his best to include everything a New Age devotee could want. One-stop shopping for spiritual seekers.

And of course, there was the research facility on the west side of the campus, the one founded by Thomas Lawson and now run by Dr. Tanbyrn.

The one we were heading to.

We pass the prayer garden and Charlene rubs her chin. "We're talking about subatomic particles, though, right? So how can a photon know the thoughts or intentions of the scientist observing it?"

"That's a good question. Physicists don't really have an answer to that."

"So, according to quantum physics, reality as we know it doesn't exist, and somehow subatomic particles can figure out when you're looking at them and form into what you anticipate you're going to see."

"Pretty much."

"And no one knows why or how any of this works."

"Exactly."

"Science sure has come a long way since Democritus."

Her hint of sarcasm isn't lost on me. Actually, I'm on the same page. "And here's something else: if you don't know where a particle is, you need to understand that it could be in any of its possible states or locations and treat it that way."

"Okay."

We come to a looming stand of trees, dark pillars on the fringe of light from one of the ornate streetlights sporadically positioned along the path.

"But," I go on, "you have to treat the particle as if it's in every one of those—at the same time."

"But it's not."

"It might be. Actually, it is."

"You're confusing me."

"Welcome to the club. And then you've got time and gravity and they basically muck everything up. With quantum states, there really is no past, present, or future. Physicists can't understand why we're not able to remember the future."

"Are you serious?"

"Yeah, and if you use quantum mechanics to do the calculations, gravity shouldn't exist in the weak state that it does."

"How's gravity weak?"

I pick up a stick. "See? Gravity should hold this down. I'm able to overcome the gravitational force of the entire planet."

"Huh. I never thought of it like that."

"Gravity is the least understood force in nature and seems to be incompatible with quantum measurement, which has really bugged scientists for the last eighty years. And that brings us to superstring theory and the search for the grand unified theory—"

"Okay, okay." She's beginning to sound exasperated. "But what does any of this have to do with the research they're doing here?"

"Well, from what I can tell, it's related to how particles act when you separate them. They're somehow connected, or entangled, in a way physicists can't really explain."

"Surprise, surprise."

"Right, well, if you split a particle and do something to one of the halves—say, change the orientation of an electron—the other half will instantaneously respond the same way."

A pause. "Go on."

"And they do this even if they're in different parts of the laboratory, or the planet, or the universe."

"That doesn't even make sense."

"Not when you think in terms of three or four dimensions, but the math of quantum mechanics leads physicists to postulate that there have to be at least nine or ten dimensions, probably eleven. As well as an infinite number of parallel universes."

"Of course. Parallel universes. Why not. And why stop at a few? An infinite number is so much more reasonable."

"My thoughts exactly."

We pass the dining hall. The research facility isn't far.

Rather than have the sterile, institutional appearance of a hospital or university research center, the building is constructed of beautiful pine logs and, in the trail's lights, has the look and feel of an Alaskan lodge.

Charlene looks at me. "So if I'm hearing you right, the particles might be separated by space—could be light-years apart—but somehow they're still interconnected?"

"Physicists typically call it nonlocality, or quantum entanglement."

"And that's what the study tomorrow is about. Only this time involving people."

"It looks like it. Yes."

"To see if people who are in love are somehow entangled?"

As we continue down the path, one confound I'd only briefly considered earlier comes to mind: in these studies, the results depend on the subjects being in love, or at least having a deep emotional connection with each other, but Charlene and I were only pretending to be lovers. If there really was anything to the test, that relational dynamic would inevitably affect the results.

I contemplate how the relationship of the participants to each other could possibly alter the outcome, and decide I'll try my best tomorrow to follow the test procedures in order to find out.

We leave the trail, skirt along the edge of the woods, and meet up with the path to the lower level of the research facility's exit door.

There are no visible video surveillance cameras, but to be prudent, as we approach the door we keep our heads down, faces hidden.

The key card reader has a number pad beside it. Serenity hadn't written down a password, and I'm not sure what I'll do if there is one.

I slip the card into the reader, and thankfully, the indicator light immediately switches from red to green. I hear a soft buzz and the door clicks open.

Nice.

"Here we go," I tell Charlene.

Then, snapping on my flashlight, I lead her into the building.

Third Floor

We find ourselves in a long, windowless hallway. Apart from the soft light emitted by the exit signs at each end, the only light comes from my flashlight.

In her research, Fionna had discovered that while some of the financial contributions to the LRC came from private donors, Dr. Tanbyrn's research had received a twenty-million-dollar grant from RixoTray Pharmaceuticals for a "cooperative research initiative."

Which seemed like an awful lot of money to me for research that might end up being bogus.

When we were first exploring this project, to make her poking around legal, Fionna had managed to land a consulting job with Rixo-Tray to test their cybersecurity.

While she was doing her research, she'd stumbled onto some connections to research into the DNA segments called telomeres (which shorten as cells split, causing aging), and the enzyme telomerase, which seems to stop that process. In fact, in one 2010 Harvard study that appeared in the scientific journal *Nature*, telomerase was shown to actually reverse the aging process in rats.

Imagine being the pharmaceutical firm that developed a drug that stopped—or even reversed—the effects of aging in humans.

The financial rewards would be astronomical.

Fionna is still working on getting through the firewalls without being detected, and that was about all she'd come up with so far—no clear connection between the telomeres research and the Lawson Center. Last I heard, she had her seventeen-year-old son, Lonnie, working on an algebraic equation to hack the IPSec VPNs (whatever those are) for an extra-credit assignment.

I sweep the beam of light ahead of us, targeting the end of the hall.

"So, the Faraday cage?" Charlene whispers.

"Yeah, let's see if it really does block out all electromagnetic signals."

"You going to be okay with that?"

I'd made a decision earlier regarding the chamber. "I don't need to go inside. You can take care of that."

"Of course."

I see that she's eyeing the line of doors to our right. "So, do you know where it is?"

"Third floor. North wing, east side, end of the hall."

She stares at me. "How do you know that?"

With my flashlight I motion for her to follow me, and we head toward the stairwell. "In the LRC brochure, there was a photo of a researcher monitoring someone who appears to be resting on a reclining chair. Right?"

"Sure. That was the sender."

"Exactly. The person who's supposed to be transmitting loving thoughts—good energy, that sort of thing."

"Be nice, dear. That's going to be your job tomorrow. I don't want any negative vibes coming from you." She thinks for a moment. "But I don't understand the significance of that picture. The guy in the photo isn't in the chamber. So how can you tell where it is?"

We reach the stairs. Start to climb to the third floor. "Beyond him is a window. You can see trees outside the glass, but neither the tree trunks nor the canopy are visible. The forest is on this building's east side. Also, based on the relatively uniform height of the forest canopy behind us, I'm guessing that the floor the chamber is on—"

"Ah, I get it. The third story."

"Yes. And from the journal articles, we know that the distance between the sender and receiver is 120 feet. I'm anticipating that the easiest way to measure the distance would be if the chamber were on the same floor as the sender's room. Also, as we approached the building, I saw windows uniformly placed on the west side of the wing, but the room with the Faraday cage wouldn't have any. So, based on all those factors, including the length of the hall, the chamber will be located on the third floor, north wing, east side, at the far end of the hallway."

At the top of the stairs Charlene pauses. "There were blueprints in the material Fionna sent you, weren't there, Sherlock?"

I clear my throat slightly. "Come on. It's down here to the left."

~

Glenn arrived at the building, picked the lock of the first floor's exit door, and stepped inside.

Now to find the computer with the files.

Knife in one hand, flashlight in the other, he started down the hallway.

~

As Cyrus and Riah swung into a gas station on the way to Bridgeport, Riah couldn't help but wonder about this meeting with the twins. As the lead researcher on the team, she should have been notified that they were back in town.

After all, she was the one looking at ways of recording and electrically stimulating neural activity in the brain's language recognition center—in the Wernicke's area of the temporal lobe. Before a person speaks, neural signals command the body to produce those vocal sounds. She was the one searching for ways to decipher the signals and correlate them to specific linguistic patterns.

So. Questions.

Why hadn't she been told?

Why was Cyrus meeting with them after hours at the R&D complex?

And what was that phone conversation of his about: "We have a man in the area . . . He's good, he'll take care of everything . . . By tomorrow afternoon it won't be a problem"?

She had the sense that something dealing with the research had gone unexpectedly wrong.

Or maybe something has gone unexpectedly right.

Cyrus guided the Jag back onto the highway, and she took note of her boss's demeanor. Over the last four months she'd grown good at reading him, and though he always looked focused, intense, now she thought he looked a bit ill at ease. Nervous? Possibly. But something else too.

Afraid?

Hard to say.

She would watch him closely, note his reaction when they met up with the twins at the R&D facility, and see what that might tell her about what was going on.

The Faraday Cage

The door to the room containing the Faraday cage, or anechoic chamber, is not locked, and the hinge gives a faint squeak as we enter.

The soundproof chamber sits in the middle of the room and looks like a giant walk-in freezer, but of course it wasn't designed to insulate food or regulate temperature. Rather, the metal walls were constructed to stop all electromagnetic signals from entering. There's no way of communicating with a person once he or she is sealed inside.

After all, if you were able to send radio signals into the chamber, faking a test like this would be easy. It was one of the oldest tricks in the book for televangelists or psychic healers who claimed to hear voices from "on high" or "the great beyond."

Simply have the "evangelist" wear a tiny earpiece radio receiver. A cohort reviews people's application forms and transmits to the guy the names and ailments of people in the audience. Then he "miraculously" calls folks out by name and announces that God has told him their disease or disability, and while everyone in attendance is in awe of his abilities, he "heals" the person.

True, those with enough faith might actually be helped simply because of the placebo effect, but most people wouldn't be healed at all. And then of course, the blame gets shifted back onto them: "God wanted to heal you, but you didn't have enough faith. I'm sorry. You just need to believe more."

Then comes the offering time for "gifts to the ministry."

A very slick racket.

Charlene opens the chamber door, and my thoughts cycle back to where I am now, here inside the research building.

I peer into the chamber. Someone has made an effort to try and make it look homey. Crammed inside are a reclining chair, a small end table with a stack of spirituality books, and a countertop with instruments to monitor the participant's heart rate, respiration, and galvanic skin response. A floor lamp sits nearby. But the feeble attempt at interior design doesn't do much to soften the impersonal atmosphere of the chamber's stark, copper interior.

During the test, only air will be fed into the chamber.

That's it.

A video camera hangs surreptitiously in the corner of the chamber.

Hmm . . . *That carries digital signals to the room with the sender. Is that how they do it? Somehow use the video cable?*

I notice a release mechanism on the inside of the door and realize that even if the door were latched shut, even if I were trapped inside, I would easily be able to escape—even without having to get out of cuffs or a straitjacket first.

Still, the idea of being in a closed space like this brings to mind my wife and sons drowning in our minivan, and I immediately feel my breathing tighten, my heart tense. I turn from the chamber and set up the equipment Xavier gave me at the rest stop.

I don't let Charlene see me trying to calm my breathing.

She closes herself inside the chamber, and we test the RF jammer to make sure that if Dr. Tanbyrn's team does try to send any signal other than the video feed into or out of the chamber, it'll be blocked.

Nothing gets through.

I take some time to check different frequencies and settings to make sure that Charlene will truly be isolated from all means of communication tomorrow during the test. There's no Wi-Fi in the building, perhaps for some sort of security reasons, and none of our mobile devices get through the walls of the chamber.

There are still lots of ways they might be faking the studies, but I feel confident that at least we won't be dealing with radio interference or frequency tampering.

In addition, the heart rate monitor Xavier gave us—the one Charlene will secretly wear to make sure that the center's findings actually match ours—is working and undetectable outside the chamber.

As we're finishing up the tests, she proposes that we place the RF jammer beneath the chair cushion so it'll be in place for tomorrow's test, but I don't want to take any chance it'll be discovered or removed before the test begins. "Palm it," I tell her, "and then place it when the research assistant turns her back." Over the years I've spent hundreds of hours rehearsing magic routines with Charlene, and although she isn't quite as good at sleight of hand as I am, she can certainly hold her own.

"Okay."

Thinking about the chair, I look for any ways of running low-voltage current through metallic threads to trigger the test subject's physiological responses, but find nothing. Charlene agrees to check it tomorrow again before the test.

We're gathering our things when I hear footsteps in the hall.

Charlene and I freeze.

I click off my light.

A flashlight beam dances across the crack at the bottom of the doorway.

Okay, maybe they do have security guards here after all.

"Into the chamber," Charlene whispers, but I shake my head.

The intensity of the light skimming beneath the door is getting stronger. The person is definitely coming our way.

"We have to." Her voice is urgent. "Now."

She's right and I know it. There's nowhere else to hide. I take a deep breath and step into the Faraday cage with her. I try to tell myself that I'm really still simply in the room, not in an enclosed metal cube, but it doesn't work.

She swings the door nearly all the way closed so that no one would be able to see us—as long as they don't decide to open the door and have a peek inside.

Probably for my sake she leaves it open just a couple inches.

But already I can feel the walls pressing in on me. I shut my eyes and try to relax, yet immediately I feel like I'm no longer in the chamber but in the minivan with my family. It's filling with water and there's no way out. The doors won't open—I try them, the water is rising, the boys are begging me to—

The hallway door creaks open.

I open my eyes.

Through the crack in the chamber door, I see the flashlight beam cut through the thick blackness of the room. A person enters, and the abrupt heaviness of the footsteps leads me to think it's a man. Possibly quite large. He sweeps the beam through the room, and it slices momentarily into the crack of the chamber's slightly open door.

Charlene and I edge backward. Thankfully, the footsteps don't approach us but rather head toward the computer desk positioned against the south wall.

As the man passes by, it's hard to see what he's wearing, but it appears to be all black. No insignia, no uniform. So, not a security guard, not a custodian. I half-expect a ski mask, and though I catch only the briefest glimpse of his face, I can see that it's not covered. He's Caucasian. That's all I can tell.

My heart is racing; it feels like a meaty fist opening and closing inside my chest, but I realize that the nervousness is just as much from being in the chamber as it is from the presence of the intruder.

The office chair at the workstation by the wall turns, and a moment later the bluish light of the computer screen glows on, faintly illuminating the room.

Though I want to focus on this man and what he might be doing, my curiosity is overshadowed by my strangled breathing from being inside the chamber.

I lean closer, edge the door open slightly, then draw in a breath of air from the thin opening leading to the room. It seems to help.

From this angle I can't see what might be on the screen, but I do see that the man has placed a combat knife with a long, wicked blade beside the keyboard, and I find myself thinking of how I might defend Charlene if things turn ugly, if the man opens the chamber door. She's a tough and independent woman, in great shape from lap swimming and yoga, but she's slim and small-boned and she's not a fighter.

I've been taking TaeKwonDo for three years, but I'm only a brown belt. Besides, I'm weaponless; he has a knife and a big size advantage. Still, I've spent a lot of time sparring and I can take care of myself pretty well in a fight.

However, I've never fought an armed assailant.

And I've never sparred in a space this small.

Though mostly shadowed, the look on Charlene's face tells me that she has noticed the knife as well. She is fingering the cross she wears around her neck.

I rest my hand on her shoulder to try to reassure her, to tell her without words that things are going to be okay.

A tiny nod, then her hand goes on top of mine.

The intruder types for a few moments. The color of the monitor's glow changes, becomes brighter and white, and I guess that he has moved past the desktop to some specific program or file.

As the moments pass I'm caught up again thinking about the tight quarters, and I don't know how long I can stand being in here.

Based on what I've seen, people who've never experienced claustrophobia have no idea how desperate and frantic it makes you feel, when—

It's all about your breathing.

Calm. Stay calm.

I breathe, yes, I do, but it's not calm breathing at all.

Trying to distract myself, I think of the escapes I've done, all the closed-in spaces I've been in and how I've survived them—sealed tanks filled with icy water, the coffin I was buried alive in for two days, the controversial million-dollar bet I accepted from a TV psychic I'd debunked. He challenged me to an escape even I couldn't have come up with on my own: I was put in a straitjacket, locked in a trunk with a parachute beside me, then dropped from a plane at 22,000 feet.

To give the chute enough time to open, I only had ninety-one seconds to get out of the straitjacket, strapped into the chute, and out of the trunk. It hadn't seemed like such a bad idea at the time, but free-falling made it a lot harder to get out of the jacket than I expected, and then when I popped open the trunk, I didn't quite have the chute buckled and almost lost hold of it.

But I made it down safely and took home the million dollars.

And I had to admit that the adrenaline rush was something else.

You did that, you can at least stand being in here for a few more minutes.

But then the chair squeaks, alerting me again to where I am, and I see the saber of light from the flashlight swing around the room.

Toward the chamber.

The man's footsteps follow it.

My heart is beating.

Beating.

I grip my flashlight, which really is too small to serve as much of a weapon. "Get back," I tell Charlene softly. She steps backward.

The man aims his light at the crack.

And then the door to the Faraday cage flies open.

Blood

It happens all at once, in a swirl of light and shadow and movement, blurred and swift.

I flick on my flashlight and shine it into the eyes of whoever opened the door, hoping to momentarily blind him, perhaps give us a chance to push past him and escape, but he's quick and knocks it away. The flashlight goes spinning around the chamber, clattering to the floor.

Whipping, twisting shafts of light.

Dizzying in the darkness.

Directing his own flashlight into my eyes, he slashes the knife toward me, and as I avoid the blade he swipes it at Charlene.

She jerks backward but is too slow, and the knife slices through the sleeve of her shirt.

She gasps.

I see blood. The cut is deep. It's in her left forearm.

I go at the man, who's now in the chamber with us, and instinct and three years of TaeKwonDo sparring take over. I use an inner forearm block to knock his knife hand to the side. Then, despite the close quarters, I'm able to land a fierce front kick to his thigh. I aim a punch at his throat, but he's able to partially block it.

He feints at me, then swishes the blade in a figure-eight pattern in the air.

76

But he's holding the knife in his right hand, which is good for me because I'm on his right side. I avoid the blade, almost manage to trap his wrist. He expertly flips the knife around and raises it to bring it down toward my chest.

An ice-pick grip.

Bad idea.

I step forward, wrists crossed, and snap them up against his forearm to keep him from bringing the knife down, then I move toward him as I twist my right hand, grasp his wrist, and swing the knife he's still holding down, fast and hard, toward his leg.

The blade must be sharp, because it goes in smooth and quick and deep, not to the hilt, but far enough to do some serious damage.

Amazingly, he doesn't back off, only lets out a small grunt of pain. He holds his ground, levels his flashlight at me, and with the other hand grabs the hilt of the knife and pries the blade, dripping wet with his blood, out of his thigh. "Do not move." A coarse, low whisper.

This guy is either unbelievably tough or on drugs, or somehow the adrenaline was blocking the pain, because his voice remains slow and measured.

Still I cannot see his face.

My arm is hidden in shadows, and I pocket the item I took from him when I brushed my hand across his arm. Sleight of hand. I did it without even thinking. My heart is churning, my breathing fast. He didn't see. He didn't notice.

My TaeKwonDo instructor's words flash through my mind: "A tense muscle is a weak muscle."

I know that from my escapes as well.

Relax. Relax.

But I can't seem to. Charlene is here and this guy just cut her and I wasn't about to let him get close to her again. My fists are tight, my stance ready, my muscles tense and flexed. It's not ideal, but it's not an easy time for a tai chi state of mind.

I could make a move, but if something happened to me, I couldn't imagine what he would do to Charlene.

I edge in front of her.

Relax.

Relax and respond.

A wire-tight silence stretches through the air.

He backs up a little, but Charlene and I are still trapped in the chamber. She's pressing her right hand against the wound to stop the bleeding.

I'm about to ask if she's okay, but before I can the man speaks, keeping his voice in the gravelly whisper. "Who are you?" I say nothing. He swings his light toward my face. "Tell me who you are and who sent you."

I blink against the brightness. Don't reply.

"You tell me"—now his voice is ice—"or I will kill you both. Right where you stand. Do you understand me? Who sent you?"

He might have more weapons, a gun.

Based on the size and type of the knife he brought with him, I take the guy seriously. I search for what to say.

Think, Jevin, think—

"Who sent you?" He tightens his grip on the knife and tilts the blade first toward me, then toward Charlene.

I have an idea, go with my gut.

"RixoTray," I tell him. "To verify everything."

He keeps his flashlight directed at us. "RixoTray," he repeats softly, but it doesn't sound like a question and he doesn't ask me to elaborate.

Okay, don't let him ask a following question. Please don't let him ask a follow-up question.

All I can think of is helping Charlene. I don't want to fight this man, but in a rush of emotion I find myself wondering how far I would go to defend her if he came at us again. Would I die for her? Would I be able to kill for her?

Yes to the first. I wasn't sure about the second.

And thankfully, I don't have to answer it, because finally, without another word, our attacker backs slowly through the room and disappears out the door to the hallway.

I hurry to Charlene's side. "Are you alright?"

She's still holding her hand against her wounded arm. Her sleeve is soaked in blood.

"I'm fine."

"Let me see."

"No, Jevin. It's okay."

I lay my hand softly on her shoulder. "Charlene. Let me see."

Gingerly, she lifts her hand, revealing a dark, bleeding gash over four inches long, visible through the slit fabric.

Not good.

She quickly puts her hand back on her arm.

"Here." I take off my belt, wrap it around her arm, and carefully cinch it off, not as a tourniquet, but snug enough to serve as a pressure bandage, to slow the bleeding. "We need to get you to a hospital; you're going to need stitches."

"We have that test tomorrow."

"That doesn't matter."

"Jev, a man just tried to kill us. This is no longer just about some kind of ESP test. We need to find out what else is going on here, and we're not going to be able to do that from a hospital room. I'll be okay, we'll just bandage it up. I saw a first-aid kit in the bathroom at the cabin."

She knew first aid, had to, working as my assistant. CPR too. She was the one who'd brought me back after the water escapes I didn't quite succeed at. I figure she should be able to evaluate how serious the cut is.

But still—

Argue with her later. Just get her out of here.

"Okay, come on." I help her to her feet.

"You stepped in front of me, Jevin. I saw that. Thank you."

"Sure."

"Where did all that come from, by the way?"

"All what?"

"Those moves. How you swung the knife down into his leg? I've never seen you do anything like that before."

I've never had to.

"I guess those Bruce Lee movies are paying off."

"I guess they are."

Gently, I lead her out of the chamber and into the room. I'm not certain if she needs me to or not, but I support her with one hand under her armpit. She doesn't pull away.

Before we head to the hallway, she insists that we check the computer to see what the guy might've been accessing. "Go on. I'll be okay."

Though I want to keep moving, I tap the keyboard and wake up the screen, only to find that the computer is password protected. As Fionna had pointed out to me more than once, you *hack* a site, you *hash* a password. I had no doubt she could hash this one in seconds, but it might take me hours.

Obviously there was no time for that.

Did the guy hash it, or did he already know the password?

It was impossible to know.

"Let's get out of here, Charlene. Get back to the cabin and take care of that arm."

"Yeah. Okay."

A voice in my head: *That guy might not have been alone. Watch out in the hall.* Edging open the door, I tip the light quickly in both directions. After making sure the coast is clear, we head in the opposite direction from the spotty blood trail our assailant left behind.

Unfortunately, even though Charlene has her wound covered, we leave our own sporadic trail of blood as we go, and I wonder what kind of suspicions it might raise in the minds of whoever would be cleaning this floor tomorrow, but—

She whispers to me, "What made you think to say RixoTray when he asked you who sent us?"

"Follow the money." We reach the stairwell, cautiously start down the steps. "Where there's a twenty-million-dollar investment, there's a lot at stake. Behind every dollar sign there's an agenda. RixoTray has a dog in the hunt, and I took a stab that our guy would know that."

"A stab."

"Bad choice of words."

Obviously, Charlene knew that our shows in Las Vegas and Atlantic City were by no means financial failures and money wasn't a big concern for me. Over the years I've made some sizable investments, and I always keep an eye on them. After all, unless your income is in the stratosphere, you don't throw millions of dollars, or in this case, tens of millions, into a project and then fail to monitor its performance—even if that means doing so in unorthodox ways.

We reach the lower level, the other end of the hall from where we first entered.

"But Jev"—she's been thinking about what I said—"it's just as likely that he was sent by a competitor to find out what the research was about. In fact, that might even be more likely."

Hmm. "True. Come to think of it, all he did was repeat 'RixoTray' when I told him they'd sent us. He could've just been muttering that because it gave him information he didn't already have."

"Exactly."

Near the exit I see a small waiting area with six chairs and an end table just outside a door with Dr. Tanbyrn's name on it. We quietly leave the building and pick our way through the woods until we reconnect with the trail that leads toward our cabin.

I'm worried about her arm, about nerve damage, but I'm also thinking about our assailant, wondering who he might've been, what he was looking for.

And why he'd brought a knife like that along with him into the building.

Wound for Wound

Riah and Cyrus finished passing through the last of the three security checkpoints to RixoTray's R&D facility.

An ultramodern fortress of steel and glass, the building was surrounded by razor-wire fence, a myriad of electric sensors, even a fifteen-foot-deep moat that was made to look like an innocuous, landscaped stream.

This was where RixoTray researched the effects of its experimental drugs and developed new strategies for pushing out pharmaceutical products faster than their competitors. It was here where their biggest secrets were kept, here where they coordinated placebo tests for their drug trials, and here where they were close to a breakthrough in developing a commercially available telomerase enzyme to reverse the effects of aging.

In this building, tens of billions of dollars could be generated by a single discovery or lost by a single miscalculation.

Cyrus strode beside Riah through the main corridor on the east wing. The hallway was high-ceilinged and bright, with pictures of scientists and plaques of patents decorating the walls. The conference area they were heading toward was at the end of the hall, next to the renovated research rooms that served as a two-bedroom office apartment for the twins when they were in town.

It was just down the hall from Riah's lab. She was involved with electrical brain stimulation, specifically deep-brain stimulation (DBS), which had most often been used for treating people with Parkinson's disease, although it had also been used to help people manage obsessive-compulsive disorder, depression, and even the symptoms of epilepsy and Alzheimer's.

Primarily she used an EEG to scan specific areas of the brain involved in speech production, then, by identifying the sounds or syllables those brain waves represented, she was working toward translating those signals into actual audible messages.

A pair of guards stood sentry at the terminus of the hallway.

"We're here to see Daniel and Darren," Cyrus told them.

The broad-shouldered, shorter man nodded. He tapped his fingers subconsciously together, which Riah took to be a sign of nervousness. She wasn't surprised. When people close to the project found out what the twins had done, uneasiness was the natural reaction. Especially if you were going to be alone in a room with them. "Okay, sir. Yes. I'll get them."

He left, and as she and Cyrus waited for the twins to arrive, she found herself reviewing what she knew about them.

The best way to describe the two brothers was that they were practitioners of death—apparently two of the most effective ones the Army's Delta Force had ever trained.

As identical twins, Daniel and Darren shared something fundamental that so many twins share—the ability to communicate on a seemingly subconscious level in ways that defy typical categorizations. Of course, since she was the principal investigator on the team, part of Riah's job was to find out what those ways were.

According to the information she was privy to, the twins had been born to a teenage girl who'd been raped and decided to give her sons up for adoption rather than abort them.

Because of a clerical error, Daniel and Darren were separated at birth, adopted by different families, and raised separately in New Jersey and South Carolina, respectively. They never met until they were in their twenties, yet the similarities between their lives were striking.

They both lettered in soccer and wrestling in high school, both had girlfriends named Julie with whom they had their first sexual encounter, both tinkered with cars in their spare time, both worked in fast-food restaurants—not unusual for teenage guys, but both were fired for spitting on the hamburger bun of a female patron. Who was wearing a blue dress.

Yes, a blue dress.

The stories were astonishing, and when Riah first heard them, she'd thought they were manufactured to create a sense of awe or amazement at the two men. Or even that they were simply an honest mistake, an inadvertent misrepresentation of the facts, but after reading more identical twin studies—some dating back to the nineteenth century—she'd found herself believing the seeming inscrutable coincidences between Darren's and Daniel's lives. In truth, the similarities weren't nearly as incomprehensible as many of those found in the rest of the literature.

Both Daniel and Darren joined the Army.

Which is where they met.

A colonel visiting Fort Bragg saw Darren at the shooting range and mistook him for a soldier he'd seen the previous day at Fort Benning. After some inquiries and a bit of deciphering, Colonel Derek Byrne made the serendipitous connection. Some people might call it chance. Or fate. Or coincidence. Cyrus once told Riah it had to do with quantum entanglement, but whatever the reason, the colonel was able to reunite the two brothers.

They both made it onto the Delta Force and eventually moved into the United States Army Intelligence and Security Command.

Some people think that the CIA is responsible for the majority of the United States' political assassinations carried out abroad, but over the last few months, Riah had found out that those people are wrong.

After a little research of her own and some frank and astonishingly forthcoming conversations with the twins, she'd learned that the military's covert operatives were happy to work in the shadow of the CIA and let the spooks take the brunt of the media's scrutiny and Hollywood's ever-watchful eye.

Daniel once mentioned to Riah that he and his brother had "found their niche" in their new line of work. She could see that they were patriots through and through, and could only guess that they did as they were told by their supervisors without question, without reservation, without hesitation.

A month ago, out of curiosity, she'd asked Darren straight-out how many people he and his brother had killed. "None," he'd told her evenly. "But we have eliminated certain targets when necessary."

Riah knew this differentiation between "targets" and "people" was a psychological ploy used by the military to make it easier for soldiers to kill—depersonalize the enemy by calling them *combatants* or *targets* rather than allowing the soldiers to think of them as fellow human beings, as fathers and brothers and sons, as mothers and sisters and wives.

When Darren used the word *target*, however, it'd struck her that the difference in terminology wouldn't have affected her if she had their job.

Actually, as troubling as it might be, she realized that given the right circumstances, she would have found it relatively easy to kill, no matter what anyone called the victim.

Just like the bird when you were a kid. Grab the head. Twist.

And it goes still.

Limp and still.

She remembered that Darren had studied her face carefully as he waited for her to respond.

She didn't want the brothers to realize that she was like them in certain fundamental ways, so she hadn't pursued the matter any further. However, she'd gotten the sense that Darren saw something in her eyes that'd given away more than it should have.

Now in the conference area, Cyrus looked at his watch. "They're late."

"I'm sure there's a good reason," she told him softly. "They're very reliable men."

Back at the cabin, Charlene still refuses to let me take her to a hospital, so in the end I'm left to simply do what I can to cleanse and disinfect the wound with the rather ill-equipped first-aid kit in the bathroom.

Throughout the process, she gives me instructions, wincing at times but not crying, and I'm impressed by how well she's handling it. We're both rattled from the attack, of course, but surprisingly, still focused.

Finally, I butterfly the wound closed with alternating strips of tape and wrap her arm with the first-aid kit's Ace bandage.

She digs out some Advil, and after she's taken a couple capsules, she positions herself on the couch, then states the obvious: "Alright. Just so we're on the same page, we're no longer here just to debunk some research on mind-to-mind communication."

"Agreed."

"Should we go to the police?"

It was a good question, one we shouldn't take lightly. "Did you see his face?"

"No."

"Me either." I join her on the other end of the couch.

Honestly, I want to stay here at the center, keep looking into things, especially now that there seems to be another layer to everything that's going on. "So we wouldn't be able to identify him by anything other than his voice. Would you be able to do that?"

"Not the way he spoke, whispering like that."

"The same for me."

"So we could report it to the police, but they would, of course, ask what we were doing in the building."

I evaluate everything. "I think we should hold off contacting them until we know more."

"So you don't think we should back away from this?"

I have the feeling she already knows the answer to that.

I've never been one to back away from a challenge, and I can't see myself doing so now—even if it ends up being a little dangerous. It isn't about money or fame or anything like that. It's about the challenge. And about uncovering the truth. "No. I'm in."

"And you know me, Jevin."

"Petunia never backs down."

"Wolverine."

"Whatever."

To cover all my bases, I offer one last time to help her: "I still think we should take you to a clinic or something."

"Jev, think about the timing here: a thug with a combat knife shows up, sneaking around looking for some sort of computer files the night before this round of Tanbyrn's study begins. That has to be more than a coincidence."

"But it was a coincidence that we ended up in the same room as him in a locked building, wouldn't you say?"

"Maybe it was more than that."

"What do you mean?"

She sighs. "I don't know. I'm just saying we need to find out as much as we can about Tanbyrn's research and what that guy might've been looking for. Being part of the study tomorrow is our best shot at doing that."

Of course, I feel the same way. Fighting that guy had awakened something in me that imitating the tricks of psychics never had—a taste of danger that I used to know when I was doing my escapes. A surge of adrenaline, the paradoxical tightening of focus and widening of awareness that danger brings with it. There was a time when I wouldn't do an escape unless there was a chance I could die from it—something that I know was always hard on Rachel.

I contemplate what to say.

"Alright. So we keep an eye on your arm, but after the test tomorrow, I want to have someone who knows what he's doing take a look at that cut. Within the next twenty-four hours. Deal?"

She's a little reluctant but finally agrees. "Deal." Then she leans forward. "So, who do you think he was?"

"Honestly, I have no idea, but based on what I saw, I'd say he's not specifically trained in knife fighting, more of a street fighter."

"The grip he used?"

Nicely done.

I nod. "Yes, too easy for me to deflect. It wasn't one a pro would choose. So I'm guessing his background isn't in law enforcement or military. He learned to fight the hard way."

"By actually fighting."

Or killing.

"Probably. Yes." I stand. Pace. Take the 1895 Morgan Dollar from my pocket and flip it quickly through my fingers. Habit. Helps me think. "We really need to find a way to reach Fionna or Xavier. I want to know what files that guy might've wanted from that computer."

"Go outside. See if you can get a signal."

"It's no use. I tried earlier."

"Try down by the road, where we parked the car. It's more in the clear down there." I don't want to leave her alone, and I think she can sense my hesitation because she adds, "Go on. I'll be okay. Just lock the door behind you."

I glance at her forearm one last time, and when she folds her arms, apparently to show me that she's fine, I finally agree. "Okay. I'll be back in a few minutes. The light switch for the exterior porch lights is just inside the front doorway. I'll keep an eye on the cabin. If anything comes up, anything at all, flick the porch light on and off a couple times. I'll be watching; I'll get back here right away."

Taking both my phone and hers so I can try each of them, I leave the cabin, lock the door behind me, and head to the parking lot.

∾

Glenn limped up to his car.

He was not happy.

If what the guy in the chamber had said was true—that RixoTray had sent him and the woman—then there was an awful lot his contact was not telling him, and Glenn did not take well to having his employers keep things from him.

He opened the car door and tried to slide in without wrenching his leg but found it impossible. A flare of pain shot through him.

He cursed. Thought of what happened in that chamber.

In prison he'd learned to trust his instincts, and as it turned out, tonight they were right, because just before the fight he'd had a feeling, nothing more, that someone was watching him. That was what had caused him to turn from the computer and open the door to the chamber.

But then the guy inside had flashed his light in his eyes and Glenn was forced to defend himself.

Why would RixoTray have sent those two?

Unless they hadn't.

Unless the guy was lying.

With a great deal of pain, Glenn was able to position himself in the driver's seat. He started the engine.

Thankfully, the blade hadn't pierced an artery.

He knew enough about anatomy to know that if it had, he would already be dead.

Quietly, slowly, he guided the car onto the road.

He used his right hand to press down on the knee of his injured leg to keep from flexing the thigh muscles as he accelerated.

The trek back to the car had been brutal, pain rocketing up his leg with every step, no matter how hard he tried to keep pressure off it. But he'd dealt with it just like he'd dealt with things when he was locked up and took a shiv to the stomach and still managed to dig it out and slice out the eyes and cut off the ears of the block-mate who'd tried to kill him.

Glenn headed down the mountain road.

Whoever had been in that chamber had been quick. Strong. Had known how to fight.

But who was he? Who was the woman?

What were they doing there?

RixoTray Pharmaceuticals?

It could have been a lie, but it was a place to start.

Glenn prided himself on being self-controlled, on viewing things objectively, but as he drove back to the motel to take care of the leg, he felt fire rise inside of him.

He was a person who kept his word, so, yes, he would take care of the old man tomorrow afternoon at three like he'd been hired to do. But he wasn't going to stop there. He would find that guy from the chamber and return the favor, wound for wound, as the Bible put it in Exodus 21:25.

An eye for an eye.

Or in this case, a stab for a stab.

God's kind of justice.

Or at least Glenn's kind.

He found himself planning how things would go down: incapacitate the guy, cuff him, and then make him watch as he played with the woman for a while. At last, when he was done with her, stab him in the thigh—and if the blade just so happened to slice through his femoral artery, well, justice in real life didn't always have to stick to the letter of the law.

So, the plan for tonight: take enough OxyContin to kill the pain in his leg—God knows he had plenty of it on hand—then in the morning call his contact to identify the two people who'd been in that room. Tomorrow, after he'd completed his paying gig, he would deal with them.

He glanced at his wrist to check the time.

But noticed that his watch was missing.

He let out a round of curses. It must have fallen off during the fight in the chamber.

The Twins

I have the assailant's watch in my pocket.

I'd happened to lift it when I slid my hand across his wrist just before I shoved the blade of his knife into his thigh.

Truthfully, removing the watch was pure instinct from all my years of sleight of hand and street magic, not something I'd consciously planned. During the fight, the last thing I was thinking was how I might remove the guy's wristwatch, but in any case I have it now, and it might serve as some small clue that could lead us to identifying who our assailant was.

After trying unsuccessfully to reach Fionna or Xavier, I pause beneath one of the path's lights. Holding the watch in my shirt to keep from getting any more of my fingerprints on it, I carefully study it.

It's a Reactor Poseidon Limited Edition. Very nice. In my line of work you get to know watches, and even though Reactor is a small company, their watches are amazing. This one won't even get scratched if you shoot it with a bullet. I couldn't help but think that a regular street thug would have sold a watch like this for cash if he knew how much it was worth. So the guy we were dealing with might very well be better trained, more of a pro, than I'd earlier assumed.

The watch is relatively new. No engravings. No unique identifying marks, which isn't exactly surprising considering the craftsmanship and the durability of the materials.

Who knows, Xavier is into CSI kinds of things and would probably jump at the chance to dust the watch for prints. I could get it to him as soon as we meet up again, tomorrow sometime.

Inside the cabin I find Charlene at the table, flipping through the notes we'd used to prepare for this project. "Any luck?"

"No." I show her the watch, and we discuss it but can't come up with any other clues, and in the end I stow it in the bedroom and return to her.

I point to the RixoTray research documents that she'd spread out around her when I was outside. "What about you? Did you find anything?"

"Nothing related to quantum entanglement or mind-to-mind communication research. But they are doing research on the temporal lobe—the language-recognition capabilities of the Wernicke's area—by using an EEG to record brain images and identify thought patterns that relate to linguistic communication. It's similar in a way to helping paralyzed people communicate by identifying their neural responses to questions."

"Interesting."

"Once you know which parts of the brain control which parts of your physiology, you can send electrical currents to those areas to elicit a physical response. Scientists have been experimenting on helping paralyzed people move their limbs, blind people see variations in light, insomniacs sleep, obese people curb their hunger, and even doing work on reducing aggression in criminals. They can even cause hallucinations that patients can't tell from reality and reduce or eliminate intractable pain."

She goes on, "Researchers at a number of universities have implanted electrodes into monkeys' brains and then trained the primates to move robotic arms. At least four computer gaming companies are developing EEG-controlled games in which the games respond—"

"Let me guess—to the player's thoughts."

"Yes."

"Wow."

"Anyway, one division at RixoTray is focusing on direct brain-computer interfaces and communication. It's mentioned on a number of grant applications. A neuroscientist named Riah Colette, she's in charge of the study."

"Might be helpful to talk with her. See what the specific connection might be to what Tanbyrn's doing."

"Couldn't hurt."

We agree to follow up on that tomorrow. Then, after a little more discussion about who the attacker might've been, I can tell that Charlene's energy is fading and I realize I'm drained as well—both physically and emotionally. She goes into the bedroom to change and I grab a blanket from the bathroom closet.

When she emerges in the hallway, she's wearing a pair of sweatpants and a gray T-shirt. Nothing Victoria's Secret seductive, but it's easy enough to tell she's in good shape and I'm careful not to stare.

I hold up the blanket. "I'll take the couch."

"Really, you don't need to sleep on the couch, Jevin." Before I can respond, she catches herself and goes on quickly as if to avert any misunderstanding: "I mean, that is, there's plenty of room on the bed. I'm just saying it's okay if you want to sleep with me—next to me. Right? On the other side of the bed."

"Right."

"I'm not suggesting at all that we do anything other than sleep." She doesn't blush often, but she does now, and it's a little endearing.

"Of course."

This conversation could get awfully awkward awfully fast.

As if it hasn't already.

I have no doubt that if I climb into bed with her, even if she ends up sleeping like a baby, I'll be too distracted to sleep at all. And I know I'm definitely not ready for her to inadvertently snuggle up to me or accidentally drape her arm across my chest sometime during the night.

"The couch would be best," I tell her.

"Sure. Okay."

"Alright . . ." I search unsuccessfully to say the right thing. "So then. Good night. And . . . just be careful with that arm."

"I will."

"Don't roll on it or anything."

"I'll be careful. I promise."

I pass the blanket to my other hand. I really have no idea how to wrap up this conversation. "We'll see what it looks like in the morning. I still want to take you to the hospital."

"Noted." She smiles. "Good night, Petunia." Her tone is light, the blush is gone, the moment feels natural and familiar. She glances at the couch. "Seriously, if you can't sleep, you're welcome to the other side of the bed."

I nod. "Gotcha."

With that, she leaves for the bedroom and I drop onto the couch. It's a little short, but I usually sleep kind of scrunched up anyway and I figure I'll be alright.

As I lie down, I can't help but think of the attacker in the chamber, and I realize that what bothers me most is the fact that I wasn't able to stop him from hurting Charlene.

I promise myself that if we run into each other again, I won't make the same mistake, then I close my eyes, hoping to sleep, to clear my head, hoping that the dreams I've had so often over the course of the last year won't return.

But I'm anticipating, of course, that they will. After all, the nightmares of my children drowning while my wife sits just a few feet away and waits for them to die have been plaguing me for months.

It wouldn't be so bad if it was just a dream. But it's not. It's history.

For a while I'm caught in the time-between-times world of waking and sleeping where you wander into and out of awareness, then I'm vaguely aware of the fact that scientists don't really understand sleep, why we do it, what biological purpose it actually serves. We're never more vulnerable than when we're asleep, and if the most vulnerable members of a species die out, then natural selection should have weeded us out. From an evolutionary point of view, it makes no sense.

Never more vulnerable . . .

And then I drop away from where I am and tip into the world of my dreams.

~~

The twins stepped into the conference room.

Gentle-looking, both of them, with an easy, measured confidence. No swagger. No posturing. Medium build. Wiry. Clean-cut. Soft-spoken.

If it wasn't for the scar snaking across Darren's left cheek, Riah wouldn't have been able to tell them apart.

She noticed that Cyrus was keeping his distance from them, and though it didn't entirely surprise her, she did find it informative.

She greeted each twin with a half-hug. Their friendship allowed for this, made it seem like the natural greeting. After all, when you've inserted nanowire electrodes up someone's artery and into his brain, it tends to engender a certain degree of trust.

Deep-brain stimulation used to be highly invasive and involved dozens or even hundreds of electrodes implanted in the brain through small burr holes drilled in the skull.

Not anymore.

Now, tiny polymer nanowire electrodes less than six hundred nanometers wide are used. Since their width is far less than that of a red blood cell, they can be inserted through an artery in the arm and guided through the vasculature up and into the brain, where they're used to deliver electric signals to stimulate the neurons in the hardest-to-reach parts of the brain.

The process had been around since 2006, but Riah had made advances that allowed for electric stimulation of the Wernicke's area, the temporal lobe's language-recognition center. She'd implanted the electrodes in the brains of the twins three weeks ago.

After a brief "How are you doing?" conversation back and forth, Cyrus cleared his throat slightly and offered Riah a smile that wasn't really a smile. "Riah, really. I think it would be best if you waited outside the room, gave us just a few minutes alone."

The words were condescending, but her feelings weren't hurt, though she had the sense that given the social context, they should have been.

Daniel and Darren watched Cyrus quietly. Before Riah could reply to him, Darren spoke up: "We trust Riah. She can stay. It's time we brought her in on the broader nature of the project."

"No." Cyrus shook his head. "I'm afraid that's—"

"Nonnegotiable," Daniel said firmly. He gestured toward his brother, who was still staring steadily at Cyrus. "We've been talking about it, my brother and I, and we were going to tell you tonight. That's one of the reasons we requested you come. She needs to know about Kabul or we don't move forward. It's time to integrate the findings from Oregon. It's the only way to make things work. As my brother said, we trust her."

Riah watched Cyrus. Having the twins contravene what you'd said like that would cause most people to squirm or backpedal or acquiesce immediately, but she could see a storm of resistance on Cyrus's face, a narrowing of his dark eyes. If he had been afraid before, he didn't appear to be so now.

It struck her that for all of his talk of trusting her, he hadn't been all that forthcoming but had been keeping things from her—that the twins were back in Pennsylvania, the nature of this visit tonight, why he wanted her to step into the hallway even though she was the head researcher on the electrical brain stimulation program.

Had he lied to her? Perhaps not lies, technically, but not the truth either.

As she thought about that, she realized that all the men she'd been with over the years, even her father when she was a little girl, had deceived her at some point, and eventually—some sooner than others—betrayed her in the most intimate ways possible.

A thought came to her, an epiphany about human nature that was both disquieting but also quite possibly the truth: *Betrayal is a facet of love.*

Could it be?

She waited for Cyrus to respond.

Could betrayal be as natural to our species as attraction is?

And another thought, almost poetic in its simplicity: *If familiarity breeds contempt, then what kind of dark children does intimacy breed?*

She was considering this when Cyrus replied to Daniel, "I'll have to clear it with Williamson."

"Yes."

"She'll be in bed by now. I'd be waking her up."

"Yes." Daniel reached into his pocket, produced his Droid. "Would you like to use my phone or yours?"

Testing Love

Tuesday, October 27

I wake up, tense, my heart clenched tight in my chest.

The residue of my dreams still circles through me. Dark and restless and unnerving.

I check my watch.

5:02 a.m.

An hour earlier than I'd planned on getting up, but I know I won't be able to fall asleep again.

I stare at the ceiling, rub my eyes, try to forget the places my sleep took me, but the harder I try to put the images out of my mind, the clearer they become.

So I tell myself again that it was just a dream.

Only a dream.

I'm the one driving the minivan, Rachel sits beside me, and we're talking about something like the bills or getting the boys to their T-ball practice or something—it's not really clear, and of course that's the way dreams work—and then suddenly I'm not on the highway but veering off the road. Rachel gasps, "Where are you—"

I drive through the parking lot.

"Jev—"

Toward the pier.

"—Stop! You're going to—"

We fly off the pier, hit the water. The impact is jarring, and almost immediately Rachel is shouting and the boys are crying loudly, scared, terrified.

I'm the one at the wheel.

I'm the one killing my family.

We begin to sink rapidly, more rapidly than I would've thought.

It's a dream.

No it's not.

It's—

The twins are screaming and Rachel is climbing back to free them from their car seats, but I'm sitting motionless, watching the water rise inside the van. I realize that for some reason we're tilting backward and so the boys will drown first. I notice this in my dream—notice it, but do nothing.

The murky water outside the window swallows sunlight as we sink, but not enough to enshroud us completely in darkness. I can still see, I can still—

"Help me, Daddy!" It's Andrew, but I don't move, I just tell him it's going to be alright, that everything is going to be alright. Then Rachel is beside me again in the front—I don't know how, but she is; time and space have shifted and brought her here to my side because we are still in the dream.

The boys are strapped in the car seats, helpless and about to die.

Rachel doesn't threaten me or question me or accuse me but holds me close and tells me that she loves me. I say nothing, just turn around and watch the water rise over the terrified faces of our two sons.

Only then do I respond.

Only after it is too late do I scramble back, grab a breath, duck beneath the water that's pouring into the vehicle, and try to save them.

Only then.

When it is too late.

And that's when I awaken, at the same point I so often awaken when I have the dream—staring into the open, lifeless eyes of my sons with Rachel by my side. Sometimes, like tonight, she's holding my hand. Other times she's already dead, drifting motionless and bloated beside me.

Some days I wish I wouldn't wake up at all but would join my family in whatever realm of eternity they ended up in, good or bad, heaven or hell, as long as we could be together again.

But so far I haven't been that lucky.

I take a deep breath, sit up on the couch.

Exhale slowly.

The dream is fading away, but it leaves a dark thought-trail behind as it does, one that roots around inside of me and doesn't want to let me go.

Charlene, who'd studied religion in college, once told me that in Acts 14 Paul mentioned four things that serve as evidence of God's existence—rain, crops, food, and joy.

Joy as evidence of God. In a world as hurting and pain-filled as ours, where death always wins in the end . . . what else besides a divine gift of joy divvied out to the hurting could explain how people can laugh at all?

Unfortunately, God wasn't seeming all too real to me over the past thirteen months. Not if the evidence of his love was joy.

I hear something in the bedroom, the soft, comfortable sound of Charlene turning over in her sleep. I don't want to wake her, so as quietly as I can I find my shoes and jacket and slip out the door to the porch.

It's still dark, but in the porch light I can tell that the emerging day is drenched in early morning mist and a sad, drizzling rain.

From growing up in the area, I know it's a typical Pacific Northwest morning, the kind of weather people in the rest of the country might use as an excuse to stay indoors, settle down with a cup of tea and a good book. But in Oregon and Washington, rain is a way of life and mist is welcome, and being damp means feeling at home. The sayings I grew up with:

"Oregonians don't tan, they rust."

"Enjoy Oregon's favorite water sport. Running."

"I saw an unidentified flying object today—the sun."

In order to stretch my legs and clear my head, I start on a brisk walk along the three-mile trail that loops around the main part of the campus. The decorative streetlights beside the path glow languidly through the haze. It's as if I've stepped into a nineteenth-century London novel.

What happened last night in the Faraday cage seems to have occurred in its own distant dreamworld somewhere. Time does that to memories—unfurls them at different speeds and in ways you wouldn't expect, putting more distance between events than the hours should allow.

Or sometimes it swallows the space between experiences and time becomes compacted, seems not to have passed at all.

But now it's as if last night's altercation happened so far in the past that the Lawson Research Center should've changed dramatically since then.

However, after a few minutes I see its exterior lights through the trees and it looks like it should: rustic and rugged, sedately awaiting our visit for the test later this morning.

I think of the attacker, of the blade swiping through the air toward Charlene, meeting her arm, slicing into her. I hope she'll let me take her to the hospital later today, or at least to a clinic in Pine Lake, but based on her response when I tried to do that last night, I'm not optimistic. In the meantime, we seemed to be on the same page as far as going on with the test.

The reason we came to the center in the first place.

A test so simple it might actually be hard to debunk.

First, find a couple who are in love with each other. That's a prerequisite, at least for this specific line of research. Isolate one of the

ST. JOHN THE BAPTIST PARISH LIBRARY
2920 NEW HIGHWAY 51
LAPLACE, LOUISIANA 70068

lovers in the Faraday cage, position the other in a room somewhere else on campus. Or, in this case, 120 feet down the hall.

The person in the chamber is the receiver, the other is the sender.

Next, set up equipment to record physiological changes in the receiver, and at random intervals show the sender the video of the person in the chamber, instructing him to think loving thoughts, give focused positive attention to her. If the receiver experiences physiological changes while he does that—and only while he does—it would be evidence of some type of nonlocal, unconscious psychic connection.

And that's exactly what Dr. Tanbyrn and his team claimed their tests showed.

According to them, in almost every instance, within seconds of the sender thinking focused, loving, positive thoughts, the receiver's heart rate, respiration rate, and galvanic skin response change—almost imperceptibly, yes, but enough to be measured. And when the sender stops focusing his thoughts and emotions on his partner, her physiological condition returns to a baseline state.

That was the claim.

But how was that even possible? How could that happen?

Entanglement on a quantum level? That seemed to be Tanbyrn's take on it. But even if that were the case, why would the person in the chamber be affected by only that one person's thoughts?

In other words, what about all the other people who care about her and might be thinking about her at the same time as the test's sender? After all, if the connection is truly nonlocal, it wouldn't matter where the other people were, how far away they might be.

So why would their positive (or maybe negative) thoughts fail to affect the person in the Faraday cage while just her lover's thoughts did? Couldn't other people love her just as much? What about a mother or a sister or a child? Couldn't their love be just as impactful? Just as resonant?

And how could you ever hope to design a test that would account for those other people's thoughts? Tell everyone who cares about the woman not to think about her at all during the test? But even if that were possible, how could you rule out the possibility that they hadn't done so anyway?

After all, one of the best ways to get someone to think about something is to tell him not to.

And of course, how much of a connection, how much love, was needed for any of this to work? What measurements could you ever come up with to test the depths of true love?

Really, as inexplicable as the results were, there were so many variables and confounds that at best it would only be possible to identify a relationship that was highly correlational, not one that was causal.

But still, even that much would be hard to explain naturally.

And so, as I walk the trail toward the river on the east side of the campus, that's what I try to think of a way to do.

Pathology

Philadelphia, Pennsylvania
8:16 a.m. Eastern Daylight Time

Riah lay awake, alone, in bed.

She had a lot to think about after her visit to the R&D facility last night.

When she and Cyrus left, he'd refused to come over to her apartment and had gone home instead to the arms of his wife.

Riah wondered what explanation he'd given Helen for his unexpected arrival—especially since there weren't any other flights that left for Atlanta last night after the one he'd told her he was going to take out of town—but Cyrus was an experienced liar and Riah was confident he'd found a way to be convincing.

Now as she repositioned her head on her pillow and stared at the wall, it occurred to her that she was disappointed—not that he hadn't come over to sleep with her, but because his absence hampered her study about secrets and intimacy and love.

Actually, it might tell you something about love after all.

She rose from bed, gathered the toys she'd purchased for her "sleepover" with him. Perhaps she would need them later, it was hard to tell. After all, their relationship had reached a crossroads; she was aware of that, but she was still open to seeing what the future might bring, might teach her.

Carefully, she put everything away—the chocolate sauce in the cupboard, the handcuffs and other slightly more exotic, harder-to-obtain items in the closet.

She guessed that Cyrus had gone home rather than come to her place because the twins had pressed him to tell her about the research, and sleeping with his wife would've been his way of punishing his mistress for tagging along and putting him in that uncomfortable situation.

But fortunately—or unfortunately, depending on how you look at it—Riah didn't feel punished. As much as she wanted to, she didn't know how to feel heartbroken or thankful or excited or sad or any of those other emotions normal people have.

No.

No shame. No guilt. No anxiety about the consequences of her choices.

And of course all of this troubled her because she knew what it meant; what her lack of a conscience and lack of empathy and lack of concern for other people, in addition to her remorselessness for her actions—she knew what all of this was indicative of.

A condition that the Diagnostic and Statistical Manual of Mental Disorders described under the category "personality disorders."

Admittedly, by themselves those traits might not have been enough to convince Riah of her condition, but when you took into account high intelligence and charismatic charm, the diagnosis was pretty clear.

Riah Colette was a psychopath.

Not a murderer, no.

But a psychopath nonetheless.

True, many people with her disorder were violent, but not all of them were. Some were lawyers, others were used car salesmen, businessmen, politicians, athletes. Usually psychopaths took up professions in which narcissism, self-promotion, and deception served as assets. Often, of course, that meant careers with high levels of competition.

All competition requires putting aside a certain degree of empathy and understanding toward those you're trying to beat, so it made sense that people who lack a sense of moral accountability and compassion would be attracted to it. To compete is, essentially, to participate in an act of self-promotion. After all, how can you love, serve, and honor someone above yourself while you're wholeheartedly trying to defeat him?

Attempting to assure someone else's failure requires setting aside concern for his well-being, and to treat anyone that way requires a certain degree of psychopathology.

Once, Riah had been invited to a volleyball game between two Christian colleges. The fans on each side cheered when their team did well, but they also cheered when the girls on the other team made a mistake that put their own team ahead. Curious about this, Riah had asked the man who'd invited her, "Don't Christians believe in supporting each other?"

"Of course."

"So that doesn't apply when a girl is wearing a different color jersey?"

She'd meant no offense by the question, but he'd studied her in a subtly judgmental way. "It's just a game."

"Aren't you all part of God's family?"

"God is our Father, so all believers are brothers and sisters in Christ. Yes."

"Then why would you cheer when your sister misses the ball or fails to make a successful hit? Doesn't she feel bad enough already after making a mistake in front of hundreds of people? Why would you celebrate her failure or add to her embarrassment or shame under *any* circumstance at all?"

He glared at Riah and, perhaps as a way of showing he didn't buy into her reasoning, almost immediately joined the other fans around them in applauding when a girl from the other college missed a serve and put his team within one point of winning the game.

Riah had taken something away from that experience, something that might be an important insight into the way normal people think. Psychopathology is at least culturally pervasive enough to cause re ligious people to set aside some of their prophets' and leaders' most cherished values of selflessness, service, humility, and encouragement when they're watching or participating in a sporting event.

Even though it didn't make Riah sad exactly, it did confuse her. She could only imagine that if she were able to feel something as precious as compassion, she wouldn't be willing to give it up so readily over something as inconsequential as watching a group of girls hit a ball back and forth over a net.

Honestly, when Riah saw things like that, she wondered if she wanted to be "normal" at all.

But of course, for her, all of this was not just an academic question or a cultural milieu. It went much deeper, because she knew that she was a true psychopath in every sense of the term.

Over the years she'd tried telling herself that she wasn't like the psychopaths who kill, that she was different, that she could control her condition, master it even, and eventually learn to experience the emotional and experiential ups and downs that healthy, mentally well-adjusted people do.

She'd tried to convince herself that the difference between her and normal people was one merely of degree, not of kind, one that she could overcome with effort and understanding. But in the times when she was most honest with herself, she had to admit that the instinct to kill had burrowed inside her long ago.

The bird that she killed in front of her sister.

The other animals over the years when no one was looking.

The inexplicable curiosity she felt while watching things die.

And those nagging questions about what it would be like to take the life of another human being.

And so far all of her research into neurophysiology had failed to show her how she might change, how she might learn to control the urges she had.

Notwithstanding all she knew about the brain, its pleasure centers, the way it processed reality, and even taking into account direct brain-computer interfaces and ways to elicit muscle responses by exciting certain parts of the brain, she had not managed to find the answers she was looking for.

Riah walked into the kitchen and looked at the clock on the microwave.

Almost 8:30.

She was mostly in charge of her own schedule at RixoTray, as long as she checked in. Today she was supposed to be at work by ten and wasn't sure now if she would be going in at all.

She had a lot to think about after the meeting with the twins last night.

Finally, Riah decided she needed to process that discussion in light of her thoughts about who she was, what she was capable of, and what the two men whom she assumed shared her condition were working with Cyrus Arlington to do.

After a few minutes of reflection, she texted her supervisor and told him she was taking the day off for personal leave.

~⌒~

Dawn.

Returning to the cabin, I find Charlene awake and finishing a cup of coffee. The air smells of dark-roasted java.

She looks up, gives me a slightly concerned smile. "Hey, I was looking for you. Where were you?"

"Went for a walk." I decide not to tell her how long I've been up already.

I see that she has set out a mug for me by the coffeemaker in the kitchenette, and I angle across the room toward it. "How's your arm?"

She holds it up and stares at it as if she hadn't noticed before that it was injured. "Hurts some, but not as bad as I thought it would. I think it's going to be alright. How was the couch?"

"Not too bad."

She already knows that over the last year I've had trouble sleeping, and it probably goes without saying that my dreams had taken their toll on me last night as well. She doesn't ask and I don't elaborate.

"So then, dear"—she drains her coffee and goes for her purse, confirms that she has the RF jammer and the tiny, concealable heart rate monitor—"I believe we have breakfast and then a meeting with Dr. Tanbyrn."

I take a long draught of my coffee, finish most of it. Set down the mug. I can feel my stomach rumble. Truthfully, breakfast sounds like just what I need. "Yes, dear. I think we do."

On my walk I hadn't come up with any specific plan on how to debunk this research—or how I might replicate it through illusions or the tricks of mentalism. But getting video footage of this morning's test would be a good place to start.

I put on the small button camera that Xavier provided for me, and since I'll be needing the lap function on my stopwatch when Charlene is in the chamber, I make sure that it's working too.

It is.

Good.

To keep up the illusion that Charlene and I are in love, we walk to the dining hall hand in hand.

～

Riah stepped out of the shower.

Dressed.

And thought back to the events of last night.

In the end it was probably best that Cyrus hadn't come over because this way it gave her some time to sort through what the twins had told her.

109

Daniel had explained that the research being done in Oregon was meant to complement her own work here in Pennsylvania. "Dr. Tanbyrn and his team are mostly interested in studying the physiological changes in one person while another person who is emotionally or genetically close—"

"Or in our case, both," Darren cut in.

"Is attentively focused on him—"

"—in a positive, loving way."

"Mind-to-mind communication," she said dubiously.

"Yes," Darren answered.

Riah considered that. Even though she knew RixoTray was financially supporting the research, Cyrus had kept most of it under wraps and she knew surprisingly little about the nature of the research in Oregon.

She used diffusion tensor imaging, magnetoencephalography, fMRI, and EEG to measure the excitement patterns in the Wernicke's area of the temporal lobe. By better understanding how the two men processed communication, her team had been hoping to—

Aha.

"So, are you saying that if we could learn to excite the section of the brain related to mind-to-mind communication, you could heighten the—what? The connection? Intensify it somehow?" She was thinking aloud, and by the looks on the twins' faces, she was right on track. "Enhance the ability to . . . connect with each other?"

The twins exchanged glances and then nodded almost simultaneously. Cyrus's gaze crawled toward the clock on the wall as if he were perhaps expecting someone, or maybe he was just biding his time until he could maneuver the twins out of this uncomfortable meeting.

Riah knew that the Department of Defense was funding her research in the hopes of eventually developing a brain-computer interface to help troops communicate in the field by creating a device that could detect, decode, and then transmit neural linguistic information to other troops.

110

It could be used to help soldiers communicate in field conditions that wouldn't allow for normal speech, such as in the middle of a firefight when words couldn't be heard, or when any sound would alert the enemy, such as sneaking into a terrorist compound.

Communication of neural linguistic information.

Now she wasn't so sure that was all the study concerned.

Riah draped her necklace around her neck.

Began to brush her hair.

She might've felt used by Cyrus and the twins, might've felt that her research was part of a big picture that she'd never been told about, and that was essentially true, but to a certain degree that was true about all the research at the R&D facility.

After all, the financial implications of an information leak were so devastating that just like in any sensitive government or private-sector medical research project, nearly all the researchers at RixoTray did their work strictly on a need-to-know basis. Progress was more often than not about one person piggybacking on the work of another to answer a question neither of them fully understood.

After the discussion about the center in Oregon, the conversation had shifted away from the Lawson Center's research, and Darren turned to Cyrus. "I was told you have the video."

"Not yet. But I will. Tomorrow. A courier will be delivering it."

Daniel addressed Riah: "When you see the video, you'll know what we mean. What the research concerns."

"Kabul?" she asked, referring back to what he'd mentioned earlier in the evening, when she and Cyrus first met up with them.

"Yes." Darren sounded pleased that she'd made the connection.

After that they discussed her findings at length, and it was almost as if she was the one who'd been brought in to do the briefing, even though she was the only person there who hadn't prepared for it at all.

Honestly, Riah didn't understand why the twins' conversation with Cyrus couldn't have all happened over the phone, but apparently they

were the ones who'd called for the meeting, and their motives were
not always easy to decipher.

At last when Cyrus stood to go, Darren had asked him, "So tomorrow, the video. What time will it arrive?"

"In the afternoon. Sometime between five and six."

"We'll see you at six then. In your office. And we would like Riah
to be present as well."

A pause. "Alright."

"Williamson will be there?"

"She won't land in Philadelphia until six thirty. She's coming in
at seven."

"Well, let's come at seven then too, so we can watch it together,
make sure we're all on the same page. Everything happens when the
president—"

"I know when it all happens." Cyrus was looking at Riah, and she
understood that he was cutting off Darren to keep something from her.

"Alright," Daniel said. "So, seven?"

"Yes," Cyrus said coolly. "Seven."

So now, Riah decided to start an online search of journal articles
concerning the findings of the center in Oregon. Even though she had
until this evening to look into things, if the research was anywhere
near as complex and detailed as hers, it might take at least that long
to sift through it all.

She put on a pot of coffee, positioned herself in front of her computer. And began to type.

Dancing Pain

I'm anxious to get started with the study, anxious to get moving. But still, my early morning walk had left me famished, and I was glad there was a substantial breakfast laid out for us.

Now we're almost done. Charlene is finishing her plate of fruit, and I slide my empty bowl of oatmeal aside, then polish off the last of my cheese-smothered hash browns. "Too bad Xavier isn't here. I have to say, this food is amazing."

"By the way, what's the deal with him and cheese anyway?" She's looking at the smear of melted cheddar cheese left on my plate.

I shake my head. "I have no idea. About a month ago he just started eating it in some form every couple hours."

"That's so random."

"That's so Xavier."

"Good point."

The dining hall has nearly a hundred people in it, but since there'll only be ten or eleven couples in the study, the rest of the retreatants must be here for the yoga and centering conference that's going on at the same time on the other side of campus.

I gaze around, curious if the man who attacked us last night might be here. I hadn't seen his face well enough to identify him, so the only way I could hope to find him is by his limp, especially if he was limping *and* missing a watch.

From what I can see, there's no one here who fits the bill.

After dropping off our trays at the cafeteria's conveyor belt to the kitchen, Charlene and I cross the campus toward the Prana building.

The quiet fog hovers around us, and it reminds me again of my dreams, my family, of that day at the shore when I watched the divers bring up the bodies.

Fog.

And a chill.

And a cloud-covered sky.

And the terrible questions that have never gone away.

Why, Rachel? Why did you do it? Why did you kill my boys? Why did you kill yourself?

Perhaps the timing is coincidental, but Charlene reaches for my hand, and it seems like she's reading my mind and trying to reassure me, but in this case I don't hold on. It's almost like I want to dwell in my pain for a while alone.

Yesterday Xavier told me that there're always going to be holes in my heart in the shape of my wife, in the shape of my sons. Now his words come back to me: "Stop feeding your pain and it'll dissipate."

But maybe I don't want it to dissipate. Maybe I want it to cling to me, to remind me that if only I'd been more astute and attentive—if only I'd noticed what was going on in Rachel's heart or what was troubling her so much that death seemed like the only option, if only I'd been able to see her desperation—maybe I could've intervened and stopped things before they went as far as they did.

But I had not.

And it had happened.

And now she is dead and so are my sons.

Charlene doesn't say anything, and even though she isn't moving any farther away from me, I sense the distance between us grow slightly wider.

We enter the small retreat center that Serenity had told us was named after the Hindu word meaning "life-sustaining force." The reception desk is empty, but I tap a set of chimes hanging beside it and hear a male voice call from the back room that he'll be with us in just a moment.

As I think of a life-sustaining force, I have to admit that it sounds like something I could really use, but I also can't help but think of the *Star Wars* movies: "May the Force be with you." I'm not sure what I believe about unseen forces altering the universe, but gravity and magnetism seem to do alright, and even when you're in the debunking business, you have to keep an open mind.

However, disappointingly, George Lucas killed the whole Force idea in *Episode 1* when Qui-Gon Jinn referenced a connection with the Force depending on your midi-chlorian count. In the end even Lucas shied away from allowing the unexplainable to remain unexplained and came up with a scientific reason for why some people rather than others could live more in tune with the Force.

It was more scientific-sounding this way, of course, but from a storytelling perspective, a lot less satisfying.

Prana.

A life-sustaining force.

"Hope" would be a better name for it, for the force that really sustains us.

My thoughts cycle through my dreams and then land back in this moment.

The reception room is adorned with well-coordinated earth-tone furniture, a small conference table, and windows that offer a broad view of the fir and pine forest that stretches out of sight in the ethereal, otherworldly fog that has engulfed the campus.

When we were preparing for this assignment, I'd anticipated that Dr. Tanbyrn would do a general briefing this morning with all the couples who'd be taking the test today, but no one else is here. As I consider that, a man with thick 1970s sideburns emerges from the back and introduces himself as Philip, a grad student from Berkeley who was "honored to be one of the great Dr. Tanbyrn's research assistants."

"Brent Berlin," I tell him, using the name I'd registered under here at the center. "And this is Jennie Reynolds."

We shake hands, then he gestures toward three of the chairs.

"Have a seat. Let's get started."

Glenn Banner was high.

It helped with the pain, but it made his thoughts curl around each other in odd ways, as if they were made of elegant colors all dancing across the needles of discomfort that bristled up his leg.

That's what he thought of as he sat in his motel room and sharpened his knife: dancing pain.

Did he feel the stab wound in his quadriceps?

In the sense of pressure, of a tingling sensation, yes—but did he feel it as acutely as he should have for a deep-muscle puncture wound like that? Absolutely not.

Drugs can be wonderful things.

Still, he couldn't help but think that he should've gone after that man and woman last night. Should have killed them both and then gotten photos of their bodies to remember the night. Act on his impulses.

But what's done is done. You can't change the past.

But you didn't find what you were looking for either. You didn't find the files.

No, he hadn't.

Leaving right after he'd been stabbed had meant not having the opportunity to find the information he'd gone in there looking for, the data he'd planned to use against his employer to pick up a little extra cash.

The information he was interested in concerned the military's involvement in the study. The connections were still fuzzy, but while researching his employer before taking this job, he'd come across evidence of meetings between him and Undersecretary of Defense Oriana Williamson, as well as mentions of Project Alpha, which included amorphous references to two men, "L" and "N," whose existence—let alone identity—Glenn hadn't been able to confirm.

Since early this morning, he'd been trying to reach the man who'd hired him, but so far had been unsuccessful.

The guy just wouldn't answer his phone.

Glenn tried the number again.

Nothing.

It was supposed to've been an easy gig: take out an old man who didn't have long to live anyway, pick up the payment, buy some little gift for his daughter, Mary Beth, in order to keep up the appearance that he loved her, then get back to Seattle and blackmail the guy who'd hired him.

But now everything had gotten more complicated.

Glenn had been wounded, had failed to dig up the dirt he wanted to find on his employer, and had ended up with two special people he wanted to pay a visit to.

He tried to shift his focus to the task he needed to accomplish today.

Killing the doctor.

Honestly, he had no idea why the old man needed to die, but he doubted it was revenge, which left the most common reason you would hire someone like Glenn—the guy knew something he was not supposed to know.

Perhaps something to do with Akinsanya, the man who seemed to be behind everything? The one who'd connected his employer with him in the first place?

Glenn wasn't sure.

It was too much to think about.

He closed his eyes and disappeared into the swirl of euphoria and irritation and adrenaline that the wound and the OxyContin gave him.

Dancing pain.

After a long moment he drew in a breath that seemed to be made of liquid air, opened his eyes, collected himself, and pulled out the manila folder his employer had given him, then flipped through the sheaf of papers until he came to the doctor's schedule.

Personally, he would've preferred taking care of the old geezer this morning while he was asleep in his cabin, get the photo of the body, and get out, but for whatever reason the man who'd hired him wanted it done this afternoon at three, during the doctor's office hours.

Just another odd demand in a series of odd demands. This guy was obviously used to micromanaging his people, and Glenn did not like being micromanaged.

He was tempted to leave a message that he was going to take care of this assignment on his own time frame, in his own way. But admittedly that might not be the most prudent way to get paid, so although it was tempting, Glenn decided to stick to the original plan.

Three o'clock this afternoon.

Tanbyrn's schedule: the doc would begin the day at his cabin, get breakfast at the dining hall, head to the Prana building for a meeting with the people in his research study, then spend the rest of the morning and the early afternoon working with them before heading to his office from two to six.

Where he would die.

At three.

Yes, there might be other people in the building, but the place had a state-of-the-art design, and considering the method Glenn was leaning toward in regards to taking out the doctor, he was sure that collateral damage wouldn't be a problem.

Well, okay, not *sure*, but at least *reasonably* sure.

Glenn tried the guy's number again.

Still nothing.

Alright. Enough.

He'd gotten a pretty good look at the couple in the chamber, and he didn't figure it would be that hard to hack into the LRC's computer files, see if they showed up on any surveillance footage, see if—

So then why'd you even go there last night, Einstein? If you could've just hacked in? Why did—?

The anger he was feeling at himself was eclipsed by the subtle shift in the way he was experiencing his limbs, his legs, his hands, the stab wound in his thigh.

It felt like the drugs were beginning to wear off. He was tempted to take more OxyContin but was hesitant to do so. He needed to be on top of his game today.

Focus.

See if you can find the files, then find out who those two people are.

Start with the staff and current retreatants—that shouldn't take too long—then move out from there.

Focus.

He went to find his laptop to see if he could hack into the Lawson Research Center's video surveillance archives. To find this couple he'd decided to kill for free.

A little pro bono work.

Two photos to add to his collection.

The Cane

The interview and pretest procedures take longer than I expect and end up chewing up most of the morning.

As time passes, three more couples come and meet with other research assistants, but Philip stays with us.

I'm getting frustrated that things aren't moving along more quickly, and by 11:30 I'm seriously annoyed and wondering why all of this couldn't have been taken care of before we came to the center.

A few minutes later, Serenity enters the room, pushing a cart containing our lunch—coffee, a platter of fresh fruit and veggies that I imagine were probably grown here at the center, and vegetarian subs on gluten-free bread.

I eat quickly.

Just as I'm finishing, Dr. Tanbyrn arrives.

He looks like he's in his early eighties and walks with an elaborately carved cane. He's bald with a grizzled beard, wears thick, out-of-style trifocals and thrift-store clothes, and has a dusty, professorial look about him.

At first I catch myself thinking that he doesn't dress anything like a Nobel laureate should dress, but then I'm struck with the thought that he's wearing exactly what I would expect an eighty-year-old physics genius to wear.

After a cordial greeting and some genteel small talk with all four couples, Tanbyrn spends some time reviewing the study's procedures, most of which Charlene and I are already familiar with. And, frustratingly, some of which Philip had already gone through earlier.

I want to ask Dr. Tanbyrn about the center's connection to Rixo-Tray, who the assailant from last night might have been, or what he might've been looking for, but I know that if I bring up these issues with him at all, it'll need to wait until we're alone sometime after the test. After all, I'd have to admit that Charlene and I were sneaking around the Lawson building after hours, and after hearing something like that, it would be reasonable for him to demand that we leave the center.

When my wandering attention shifts back to him, he's in the middle of a sentence. ". . . so quantum waves are not elementally trapped in space and time as we are—or at least as we appear to be. Because of this, because of their entanglement with each other, even though they might be separated by time or distance . . ."

"They really aren't separated at all," one of the men interjects.

A nod. "Quite right. One thing is certain in quantum physics: the more we learn, the more we realize how little we know; and subsequently, the less sure we are of 'knowledge,' the blurrier the lines become between our understanding of animate and inanimate objects, our definition of life, our understanding of what it means to be alive. And the more mysterious the universe seems."

The woman next to me looks reverently at Dr. Tanbyrn. "It's so mystical, so spiritual."

"Beneath the veneer of the visible is an entirely different sphere, a fabric of dimensions and reality that holds this physical, observable one together. I am not by any means the first to explore this inexplicable quantum entanglement—this nonlocal connection between subatomic particles—but my research does lean in a slightly unique direction.

Here at the Lawson Research Center, we are looking at the matter that those particles make up. In this case, organic matter."

"People." It's the woman beside me again. "To see if they're entangled." She giggles lightly, then corrects herself: "If *we* are."

"Yes," Tanbyrn replies. "Although I perhaps misstated myself. I'm not just looking at how people might be entangled or connected, but how their awareness of reality might be. In other words, how one person's individual consciousness might nonlocally affect another person's awareness, thoughts, or physiology."

There it is. The crux of the whole matter.

He announces that Charlene and I will be the first couple to do the test, then takes us to a side room and meets with us privately. "Have you decided who'll be the first sender and who'll be the first receiver?" His voice is aged and faltering but also kind, and he reminds me of my grandfather, who died when I was still in my teens.

"I'll be the sender," I tell him. "Jennie's better at deciphering my thoughts than I am at deciphering hers."

Charlene gives me a playful jab. "What? You can't read my mind?"

I shrug. "What can I say? I'm a guy."

"I knew you were going to say that."

"See what I mean?" But then, suddenly, the doctor's words sink in. He'd said *first* sender. *First* receiver.

"But," I explain, "Jennie will be the only receiver. I'm not going to be in the chamber."

Dr. Tanbyrn taps a finger against his chin. "We like to repeat the procedure, reversing the roles so that we can test the receptivity of both participants."

"I think we'll just keep it to Jennie. The truth is . . . I don't do so well in small places."

"Aha, well. Yes, of course." There's no judgment in his voice, and I get the impression that he's dealt with claustrophobic participants before.

He rises unsteadily, leaning on his cane for support. "Well, come along then. It's not far. Just two buildings over."

But as he takes his first step, the cane slips on the pinewood floor. He flails his hands out to regain his balance and ends up grabbing Charlene's wounded arm. Despite herself, she cries out and pulls back, causing him to plummet toward the floor, and I'm barely able to drop down fast enough to catch him.

For a moment the air in the room seems to hold its breath.

Then eases.

Gently, I help him to his feet. "Are you alright, Doctor?"

"Yes, yes, quite." I'm still holding his shoulders, steadying him. "Oh my." He's shaken, breathing hard, gazing at Charlene. "But are *you* alright, my dear?"

She's grimacing, and I can't imagine how much it must've hurt to have him squeeze her arm like that. "Yes, I'm okay."

"I am so sorry." He sounds deeply distressed. "I just lost my balance. I—that's never happened to me before."

Once he's standing on his own, I hand him back his cane.

He gestures toward Charlene's arm. "Are you sure you're alright?"

Only then do I notice the blood that's seeping through her sleeve.

He has a curious, perceptive look in his eyes, and I wonder if perhaps earlier this morning he might've seen the blood on the third floor of the Lawson building and is now somehow piecing things together.

Charlene presses her hand tenderly over the wound to quell the bleeding, and when she replies to Tanbyrn, she avoids explaining how the blood got there. "I better go get this cleaned up."

I offer to go with her but she declines.

"No. I'll meet you two there." Then she excuses herself to return to the cabin, leaving Dr. Tanbyrn and me alone.

He waits for me to speak, as if it's my responsibility to absolve him of the guilt of harming her. "Don't worry, it wasn't you. She hurt her arm last night. The scab must've just broken open. It's not serious." The only thing I'm not really sure about is that last part. Because the cut might be serious. "Are you sure you're okay?"

"Yes, Brent. I am. Thank you for arresting my fall."

"Glad I was close enough to help." I gesture toward his cane. "Do you need a hand?"

"I believe I'll be fine. Thank you."

After a slight pause, he leads me to the lobby. I slow my pace to remain next to him just in case he loses his balance again. His cane taps heavily on the floor beside me as we walk past the reception desk, out the door, and into the gray morning mist.

Kindling

Glenn Banner was able to connect the dots.

On his hacking attempts, even though he hadn't uncovered the incriminating information he'd been searching for last night, he had found his way into the Lawson Research Center's video surveillance archives and had been able to pull up the footage of the two people he'd seen in the chamber as they registered at the front desk late yesterday afternoon.

He paused the video.

Zoomed in on the screen of the computer on the registration desk.

Saw the names: Brent Berlin and Jennie Reynolds.

And the name of the cabin they'd reserved.

Hmm.

So, whether it was RixoTray who'd sent them or another firm altogether, by staying on campus the pair would be close enough to poke around in the evenings. Perhaps trying to dig up information on the military's involvement—that is, if they were aware of it.

Of course, it was always possible they were looking for something else.

Additionally, if they were participating in the study rather than attending the yoga retreat, they would have the chance to speak with the doctor, perhaps squeeze information from him.

Glenn googled their names, but they were both so common it was like looking for a needle in a haystack. He couldn't help but think they were quite possibly aliases anyway.

It was possible that the couple would've left the center last night after the altercation, but the cut on the woman's arm hadn't been life-threatening, and if the secrets buried in the computer files at the center were as important as Glenn thought they might be, he wasn't convinced that the two intruders would've left the center yet.

He really needed to talk to the man who'd hired him.

Glenn tried the phone number once again.

And this time, at last, the guy picked up. "What is it?" The voice was as blunt and impatient as always.

Glenn filled him in on what'd happened last night at the research facility, leaving out the part about being too slow to stop the guy from swinging the knife down and plunging it into his thigh. And of course, leaving out the fact that he himself had been there trying to find information that he could use in his blackmail attempts.

"What were you looking for?"

"I was doing research on Tanbyrn."

"I provided you with all the information you need. I even gave you the passcode for—"

"Listen to me, there are things you're not telling me, and I don't like being kept in the dark."

Rather than respond directly to that, his employer returned to the topic of what had happened in the chamber. "You say there were two of them there? A man and a woman?"

"Yes." Glenn gave him a description of the couple. "Who are they?"

"I don't know."

"The guy said you sent them."

"I did not send them."

Glenn considered that, didn't reply.

Only two possibilities: either this guy was lying or the man in the chamber had been.

Glenn had the sense that a man whose life was being threatened would be a bit more likely to tell the truth than someone who'd hired an assassin to kill an old man.

"I want some answers here," Glenn said. "This whole thing is—"

"The way it is." A tense, hard tone. "I tell you what you need to know. Don't get demanding with me. You wouldn't want me to start considering you a liability."

Glenn felt his grip on the phone tightening. "I'm not the only one in this conversation who's at risk of becoming a liability."

For a moment neither man spoke. Both held their ground, both retained their status, until Glenn decided he was ready to move past his threat and get on with business. "I'm set to take care of Tanbyrn at three."

"I'll have your money waiting."

"What about the couple from the research facility?"

"Forget 'em. I didn't send them. Just take care of your job, the one you were hired to do."

He didn't send them? Did someone else from RixoTray? Another firm?

Glenn was surprised that his contact didn't seem concerned that a competitor may have sent the couple. Was he faking it? Or maybe the guy didn't have anything to hide after all. Maybe the whole blackmail idea had been a mistake.

"I'm going to take care of them."

"No you're not. You're—"

"They might've seen my face."

"I don't care about that. I just want you to do the job you were hired to do and then get out of there without leaving any evidence behind."

Glenn responded by hanging up.

Abruptly.

He shut off his phone.

Pissed off now.

Not happy.

No.

No, he was not.

He placed his hands palms-down on the table. Took a breath.

Alright. He would do what he'd been hired to do. The transaction with the doctor was a done deal. That was professional. That was business. The matter of the couple from the chamber was personal. A loose end he could not risk leaving unattended.

He thought about how to kill Dr. Tanbyrn.

Though he'd obviously deliberated on it earlier, he preferred not rushing into a decision as important as how to murder someone without thinking through all the options. It was better to make your decision closer to the actual event and adapt as necessary.

For the most part, Glenn avoided guns. Because of that, he'd used wire in the past, plastic bags (twice), and once—on a unique and rather memorable assignment—a blowtorch. But all in all, he preferred his knives, and they'd served him well the six times he'd used them for their intended purpose.

When you use a knife, almost always, even if someone knows what he's doing when he's fighting you, he will get cut. A Kevlar vest will stop a bullet, but because of the amount of force generated at the tip of a blade when you thrust it forward, even a vest won't stop a knife.

Yeah, well, what about the guy last night? He didn't get cut. He did pretty—

Irritation.

Anger at himself.

Save the knife for the couple.

Wound for wound.

Something else for the old man; what you were thinking of before.

So after a short internal debate, Glenn decided to go ahead with his original idea.

Fire.

Tanbyrn's office was located at the end of the hallway on the lower level. There was a reception area just outside his office that would serve Glenn's purposes well. More accurately, it was a waiting room. There was no receptionist there. No secretary. All of which made it ideal.

The building was constructed of logs, and with its central air system, it would circulate the smoke even as the wooden structure burned. The smoke and the alarms would clear the building of other people.

But Glenn would seal Tanbyrn in the office so he couldn't escape—easily enough done.

Elevator—no problem.

Stairwells and exit doors—chain them shut.

Glenn would light the fire just outside Tanbyrn's door. The campus was isolated enough so that the county's volunteer fire department would never be able to arrive in time to save the building, and the center had only rudimentary fire suppression resources on-site.

Either the flames would get Tanbyrn or the smoke billowing up the vent just outside his door would do the trick.

Glenn could use the furniture in the waiting area along with a petroleum-based accelerant to create the thick smoke he was looking for. Yes. And since fire destroys most, if not all, forensic evidence, and fire investigations usually take weeks to complete, Glenn would have plenty of time to disappear.

Admittedly, he wasn't an expert at arson, but he had torched two buildings: a warehouse and a duplex. Both assignments had gone well, both resulted in the intended insurance payouts—although he did have one small regret. He hadn't meant to kill that little girl in the apartment. He'd been told it was empty.

Well, you know what? Live and learn.

In this case, fire would be a good choice.

But it'll destroy the computer files you were looking for.

Screw it.

Let that be.

Just get this done, get the money. Find the couple from last night. Take care of them. Close this thing up.

And then move on.

He reviewed his plan for the next couple hours: check out of the motel, grab a copy of *USA Today*, stop by the hardware store in Pine Lake and pick up the items he would be needing, then get back to the center by two to make sure he had enough time to get everything ready for the big show at three o'clock.

Flocking

12:43 p.m.
2 hours 17 minutes until the fire

Dr. Tanbyrn, Charlene, and I walk down the hallway of the research center. Philip trails behind us as if Tanbyrn is royalty and he's giving him the wide berth he deserves.

Charlene has changed shirts, and the sleeve puffs over the fresh bandage on her arm.

No one comments on it.

I notice that the drops of blood that were on the floor in here last night have been washed off.

Again, I think of how Tanbyrn studied Charlene when he saw the blood on her arm earlier. I can't imagine that he'd helped mop the floor or clean up the blood, but regardless of who did—or even whether or not Tanbyrn knew about it—somebody had seen the blood, so someone was aware that there'd been at least one wounded, bleeding person in here last night.

Entering the room where we encountered the assailant is a bit surreal.

I look around, searching for any sign of blood or of a struggle

131

in here—or in the chamber whose door is now wide-open—but I don't see any.

Illuminated by the overhead fluorescents, the room has an entirely different feel than it did when I was directing my flashlight around here last night. A slightly built but stately African American woman stands near the desk, introduces herself as Abina; she's apparently another research assistant. She gives us the same reverent prayer-gesture bow that Serenity offered us when we checked in last night. Charlene and I respond in kind.

"That's a pretty name," Charlene tells her. "Abina. What does it mean?"

"It's Ghanaian. It means 'born on Tuesday.' I was born on a Wednesday, though. Wishful thinking on the part of my mother. She was in labor, actually, longer than she expected."

Charlene smiles. "Ah."

Abina is wearing a flowing, colorful African dress that swirls around her resplendently as she moves through the room. A myriad collection of metal bracelets jangles from her delicate wrists.

A photograph of a shimmering mountain vista sunset glimmers on the screen of the computer that our assailant was using last night. From the view, it looks like the picture might've been taken from one of the LRC's scenic overlooks.

I wish I could get alone with the computer, look up any recently accessed files.

Specifically those opened last evening.

"Well." Dr. Tanbyrn smiles. "It looks like we're all set."

I decide to say goodbye to Charlene before she enters the Faraday cage, and I offer her a hug. "See you in an hour, dear."

She holds me. "Goodbye, honey."

I whisper to her as softly as I can, "If you get a chance, check the computer."

She nods. Kisses me on the cheek.

Though simply for show, the terms of endearment and the show of affection impact me, and I gaze into her eyes a moment longer than I probably should.

As I step back, Abina smiles at us.

Well, at least we were being convincing.

Dr. Tanbyrn still doesn't seem sure of himself with his cane as he leads me and his impressively sideburned graduate research assistant 120 feet down the hall, to the room where I'll be watching for Charlene's face to appear on a video screen.

I don't want him to lose his balance again, so I stay close as we travel down the hall.

We enter the room and I look for transmitting devices, video cameras, anything the researchers might be using to alter or fake their findings. While I do, I make sure that I surreptitiously turn in a full circle so that the button camera gets a 360-degree view of the room.

Obviously, Dr. Tanbyrn could simply have programmed his computer to print out fake results—that was something we would need to check on before we went on air with our show, but for now I wanted to eliminate as many other factors as I could.

I see the window, the reclining chair, a desk, a few office chairs, the same view as the photo in the center's brochure.

Nothing out of the ordinary.

Positioned in front of the reclining chair is a widescreen, hi-def television, blank now, but I anticipate that it's where the video of Charlene sitting in the chamber will appear once we get started.

Dr. Tanbyrn picks up a tablet computer from the desk and finger-scrolls across the face of it. The TV in front of me flickers on and a video starts, but it's not Charlene in the chamber; it's a nature special about how birds fly in flocks, simultaneously changing direction as if they have a collective consciousness.

A collective consciousness.

Well, that made sense, considering the doctor's area of interest.

Philip stands quietly by the door. "We've found that leaving people alone helps them to not be distracted or nervous." He smiles, but for some reason it makes him seem less trustworthy. His teeth are just too straight, too white. A televangelist's grin.

I decide I'd rather keep an eye on the two of them during the test to make sure they don't alter any of the test conditions. "Thank you, Philip. But feel free to stay. You won't be distracting me. I assure you." I indicate toward the two chairs near the window. "There's plenty of room."

His momentary hesitation is a red flag to me, and I begin to not trust the graduate student from Berkeley.

Dr. Tanbyrn gives Philip a glance, then tells me, "Of course, Mr. Berlin. Whatever will help you relax."

"Wonderful."

Somewhat reluctantly, Philip takes a seat, and Dr. Tanbyrn dials the Venetian blinds down so they shut out the meager light that's seeping in from the fog-drenched day outside.

So now, relax.

When you're doing water escapes, especially cold-water escapes, if you don't learn to lower your heart rate at least a little, you end up using your oxygen too quickly, and it dramatically decreases your chances of escaping in time, so all escape artists learn to control their heart rate, at least to some degree.

In the days when I was performing my stage show, I not only had to learn to hold my breath for up to three and a half minutes, but I had to learn to relax enough to lower my heart rate to fewer than thirty beats per minute. Now that I haven't done it in over a year, it seems pretty impressive. Back then it was just me going to work, doing my job.

Right now I figure I'll relax as much as I can, try to stick as closely as possible to the test procedures. After all, we were making our own recordings of Charlene's physiological state, so we would know if their test results were faked or in some way falsified.

I lean back in the reclining chair and lay my hands across my stomach, not just so that I can relax, but so I'll be able to tap the lap timer button on my stopwatch every time Charlene's image appears. This way we'll have an accurate record of the instances when her image was being transmitted onto the screen, and we'll be able to compare it to changes that might appear in the printed record of her physiological states.

Dr. Tanbyrn dims the lights and takes a seat while I watch the birds flock across the screen in unison and wait for the video of Charlene to appear.

The Placebo Effect

It was the middle of the afternoon, and Riah had spent most of the day so far reviewing the journal articles written by Dr. Tanbyrn and his team at the Lawson Research Center in Pine Lake, Oregon.

Some of the material, particularly the unconscious communication between two lovers, she found unbelievable, but yet surprisingly well-supported by the center's detailed documentation.

And she did agree with a few things.

She knew that the mind is a powerful thing, that it's possible to alter your own physiology through your thoughts, a puzzling fact that physicians and scientific researchers have known since the 1780s.

The placebo effect.

Just give people a harmless pill, a sugar pill, an aspirin, whatever, tell them it's the latest pain medication or a drug to treat a severe medical condition they have, and depending on the ailment, 30 to 95 percent of them will be helped, at least to some degree—more than those in a control group that isn't receiving any treatment.

Of course, the effectiveness of the placebo isn't the same with every illness or injury or with every patient, but in some cases the placebo group actually experiences more of a positive effect than the people taking the drug that's being researched.

Yes, at times the brain can heal the body even better than medicine can.

And astonishingly, according to a 2011 study, patients even benefited if they took a placebo *and were told it was a placebo*.

Honestly, no one really had a clue how that worked.

And the placebo effect was far-reaching.

Placebos hadn't been used just to control pain, but people taking them had been healed of cancer, had controlled their schizophrenia, and even, in a few isolated cases, had been cured of Parkinson's disease. Body builders who thought they were taking the newest anabolic steroids gained muscle mass as fast as those who were taking steroids—and even suffered the negative side effects they would've if they were actually taking the steroids.

How is it possible that our thoughts alone can cause us to feel less pain—even allow patients to feel no pain during amputations? How can our thoughts cure us of cancer, or manage the symptoms of schizophrenia or Parkinson's, or help us build muscle mass?

All of that? Just by our thoughts?

It was a medical mystery.

Riah also knew that thoughts can do more than heal, they can have a negative effect as well—sometimes called the *nocebo effect*.

In her research into humanity, she'd read the aptly titled book *Man's Search for Meaning* by Viktor Frankl, a Jewish psychiatrist who was a survivor of the Nazi death camps in World War II.

In the book he tells the story of another prisoner who'd had a dream that the war would end on March 30, 1945. But as the day approached and the men heard reports of the battles, it seemed less and less likely that the fighting would end on that date. On March 29 the man became ill. On March 30, when the war didn't end, he became delirious. On March 31 he died.

In his case, he hadn't died from any diagnosable medical condition, he had died from lack of hope.

His thoughts had ended up being fatal.

Undeniably, thoughts can heal and they can kill.

And as far as affecting another person's physiology, we do that all the time. All you have to do is kiss someone or aim a gun at his head or slap him in the face. He may get aroused or afraid or angry, but in every case his heart rate, breathing, and galvanic skin response will change. In fact, when two people are alone and in close proximity, their heart rate and respiration begin to emulate each other's and they begin to breathe in sync with each other.

But the issue here wasn't the physical effects of thoughts on your own body, or the effect of your presence with or actions toward someone else. The question was: could your loving thoughts affect another person's physiology when you're not present, when you're not communicating with him in any tangible way?

Medical science, of course, said no.

But the quantum physics that Dr. Tanbyrn was researching seemed to say yes.

All of this made Riah increasingly interested in what would be on the video that Cyrus was going to show her at seven o'clock tonight.

With traffic in central Philly, she would need to leave her apartment by six.

That gave her just over two hours.

And there was one thing left that she needed to do.

Someone named Williamson would be at the meeting as well.

Riah was going to find out who that person was.

I see Charlene's picture appear on the screen.

Without letting Philip or Dr. Tanbyrn notice, I gently tap the button to start the lap function of my watch.

"Okay, Mr. Berlin." It's Dr. Tanbyrn from behind me, speaking softly. "I'd like you to concentrate on the image of the woman you love. Imagine what it's like being with her, holding her hand, kissing her, having intimate relations with her."

Admittedly, I'm a bit surprised by the bluntness of his request. Not only would it be a little distracting to take things as far as he's suggesting, but the idea of sexually fantasizing about Charlene while watching her on the screen has a sleazy, voyeuristic feel to it. Doing so would've made me feel more like a Peeping Tom than a co-worker and friend who respects her as a woman. So instead of following his request to the letter, I focus on my affection for her rather than my physical attraction to her.

Think loving thoughts.

Loving thoughts.

Concentrate on the image of the woman you love.

The woman . . .

She looks relaxed and comfortable sitting in that metal chamber, and I can tell she has no idea that I'm watching her.

. . . you love.

Despite my efforts to keep my thoughts on a purely platonic level, I can't help but notice how attractive she is—not runway-model beautiful, but naturally pretty—the kind of woman who doesn't need makeup to turn heads but can really dial up the volume and be striking when she wants to be.

What really is love? At its essence? Action? Emotion? Attraction? All three?

Think about the woman you love . . .

When I first started looking into this research, I'd thought I might end up inadvertently thinking about Rachel during the test, might return to the feelings I had for her while she was still alive. But although those feelings are present to some degree, they're bookended by time—we met, we fell in love, we married, had kids, and she died. I'll never stop caring for her, loving her, but I'll also—

No, Jevin, she didn't just die, she killed herself and she murdered your sons.

Grief marked with a sting of caustic anger grips me, making it harder to be present in this moment, and while I'm trying to focus on Charlene again, her image disappears and the bird documentary comes back on.

I tap the watch's lap function button again to record the end of the video segment of Charlene.

I'm not sure how well I did in sending my positive thoughts through the building to her, but at least I couldn't be accused of not putting forth my best effort. Dr. Tanbyrn encourages me to try to stop thinking about Charlene now and let my attention drift toward other things.

I've already started to do that, but it's not easy to put her out of my mind, or to obviate my thoughts of Rachel and the boys.

The birds flock across the screen, moving together just as fish do, as if guided by an unseen hand, and watching them, I can't help but be struck with a sense of wonder at the natural world.

An admiration, an awe, a sense of marvel I've always had.

Ants build intricate tunnel systems. Bees build hives. But how does each member of the hive know what his job should be? How does each ant know where to dig? Ask a biologist and she'll typically answer "instinct," but that's like explaining how you saw a woman in half by saying it's "magic." It's an explanation that doesn't explain anything; just more smoke and mirrors, misdirection, to keep you from asking the questions that really get to the heart of the matter.

Instinct.

Really?

That's the explanation for every adaptation, trait, and inborn desire of every species? Even of behavior that could not possibly be taught to offspring, or of environmentally cued responses that could not be passed on in the genetic code? There's a gap in logic there that most people simply overlook or aren't willing to acknowledge.

Charlene's picture appears again, and I turn my attention to her, start the timer on my watch.

Over the next half hour or so, her image appears twenty-six times—I keep track as I tap the button on my watch to record the exact timing of the appearances.

140

And although I'll need to analyze it later, the timing of the image generation certainly does seem to be random.

Sometimes the segments come on only a few seconds apart, other times several minutes pass between them, so unless I'm missing something, I can't imagine how Charlene could ever guess when her image is being played for me—and even if she could, there's no believable way she could alter her heart rate and respiration within a handful of seconds in ways that would coincide with each of the video segments.

Every time her image disappears, I do my best to lend my attention to the bird video, but with each passing minute I become more and more curious about what the tests will show, about whether or not Charlene's physiology will have been altered, even in the slightest degree, by my thoughts.

Finally, Dr. Tanbyrn announces that we're done. He graciously thanks me for being part of the study, and then consults the tablet computer again. "Give us just a few minutes, and then we'll go down the hall and see how Jennie is doing."

The DVD

1:38 p.m.
1 hour 22 minutes until the fire

Glenn arrived at the center.

With his fake beard and wig, he knew he would never be positively identified, even after the surveillance video was analyzed later, after the fire.

Rather than hike through the woods on his injured leg, he drove straight to the registration building, pulled into the parking lot, and went inside to get a visitor's pass for the day.

~

RixoTray Corporate Headquarters
Philadelphia, Pennsylvania

Caitlyn Vaughn, Dr. Cyrus Arlington's faithful receptionist, ushered the courier into his office.

An earlier arrival than Cyrus expected.

The courier handed him a package stamped "Official business. Requested material."

Cyrus knew, of course, that it was the DVD containing the video footage of what had happened in Kabul thirty-one hours earlier.

He also knew that he needed to watch the footage privately before allowing the twins, Riah, or Undersecretary of Defense Oriana Williamson to see it. And definitely before passing it on to Akinsanya. He was not someone Cyrus was prepared to disappoint.

He paid the courier, closed the door, and locked it so that even his nicely endowed and seductive young secretary, the one he'd slept with when she was in accounting and then transferred up here before starting his relationship with Riah, wouldn't interrupt him.

It was vital that Williamson was on board with this—the funding depended on it, and it was important that the twins were reassured about the efficacy of the program, since it would affect how things went with the president's policy speech tomorrow morning here in Philly in front of the Liberty Bell.

The Liberty Bell.

How very patriotic of him.

Cyrus carefully opened the package.

According to the administration's press releases, the speech was going to "contain broad and far-reaching initiatives aimed at strengthening the economy and regaining the confidence of the American people in Washington's ability to make a positive and lasting impact in their lives and throughout the free world."

The speech would include policy proposals for reinvigorating the economy, decreasing unemployment, broadening health care coverage, enhancing the development of alternative energy to reduce dependence on foreign oil, and making "judicious" cuts to the military—pretty much the same topics the president had tried to tackle during his last three years in office but had made almost no headway on.

But if Cyrus's sources were right, this time the announcement he was going to make regarding health care was going to change everything in the pharmaceutical industry for years to come.

Cyrus flipped open his laptop, inserted the DVD.

Waited for the password prompt to come up.

Really, the footage was the fulcrum upon which everything balanced. That, and the work of—

What about Riah? What will she think when she sees it?

Well, yes, what about Riah?

Truthfully, she'd become more of a distraction lately than she was probably worth. It might be necessary to get her out of his hair in a way that she would not bother him again. If the video showed what he thought it would, she wouldn't be needed anymore.

Maybe when this was over, that thug Glenn Banner would be interested in making another twenty-five thousand dollars.

A possibility.

Either that or Atabei.

Yes, the woman from Haiti, the one he'd met on one of his trips down there to help out after the earthquake. She might actually be a better choice.

In either case, Cyrus decided he could deal with Riah later, when everything was completed; for now the main issue was the video. He couldn't take any chances that the footage would be unconvincing to Williamson and the twins.

The prompt came up, he typed in the password to unlock the video and pressed Play.

Loving Thoughts

1:43 p.m. Pacific Daylight Time
1 hour 17 minutes until the fire

I return to the room that contains the Faraday cage.

Dr. Tanbyrn and Philip walk quietly beside me.

We find Charlene standing in the corner near the computer workstation, chatting lightheartedly with Abina. I'm struck again by the contrast between how innocuous things in here seem now compared to how menacing they'd become last night. Charlene smiles at me. "So, how do you think it went?"

Although I'm glad to see her, I'm a little upset at myself for not discovering anything so far about how—or if—the staff here might be faking the tests. "I'm sure it went as well as it could," I tell her vaguely.

She turns to Dr. Tanbyrn. "When will you have the results?"

"In about an hour. There are some numbers I still need to run, and I have to check in with another couple. If you could kindly meet me in my office at, say, a quarter to three?"

I would've expected that he could use his tablet computer to analyze the data within seconds, but when I think about it, actually,

145

this would give Charlene and me a chance to see if our tests, the ones taken from the heart rate monitor that Xavier had given her, showed anything close to the findings that the doctor and his crew typically found. Charlene and I might even have enough time to look over the footage I took with the button camera I'd worn during the test.

"Alright," I tell him. "We'll see you at 2:45."

We leave the building and find that the day is still foggy, still devoid of wind. The smokelike tendrils of mountain mist seem to drain sound from the air, creating an almost eerie stillness that not even birdsongs are able to taper into. Even the squish of our steps on the soggy trail seems dampened by the heavy air.

"Seriously, Jevin, how did it go?" Charlene asks. "Did you do your best to think of me in a positive light?"

"I did."

"And to think loving thoughts?"

"And to think loving thoughts. Yes."

I wait for her to ask a follow-up question or crack a joke about how difficult that must've been—sending loving thoughts to her—but she's quiet, and I'm not sure if that's an invitation for me to speak or a way of letting the conversation drift in another direction entirely.

"Hopefully, it'll be enough," I add.

"Yes." She takes a few steps. "Considering."

"Considering?"

"That we're not in love."

"Of course. Exactly . . . So what were you thinking about while you were in the cage that whole time?"

Her answer comes without any hesitation. "I was thinking about you."

"About me."

"Yes."

Her words both surprise and do not surprise me, assure me and unsettle me. "Well . . ." I'm really not sure how to proceed here. "It'll be interesting to download the data. Print it out."

"Yes, it will."

And we wouldn't have long to wait.

The outline of our cabin lies fifty yards ahead of us in the fog.

~

Dr. Cyrus Arlington ejected the DVD from his computer.

The video was convincing.

Very convincing.

After watching it, he didn't foresee any problem in assuring Williamson and Akinsanya of what was possible. And the twins would certainly be heartened by the footage.

He looked at the clock.

4:51 p.m.

So, 1:51 in Oregon.

In just over an hour the doctor would be dead and there wouldn't be any chance of him going public with his findings regarding Project Alpha. With what he knew, there was just too much of a possibility that he could piece things together, and now that things were this close, it wasn't the time to take any chances that Tanbyrn would be able to do that.

Cyrus's eyes landed on the two aquariums in the corner of his office.

Last week Riah had asked him about them, but he'd never explained why he kept the *Ampulex compressa* wasps or the *Periplaneta americana* roaches. So now, perhaps the best way to explain would be through a little demonstration.

And besides, letting one of the wasps do her work would lend a certain irony to the occasion of the four people watching the DVD in the next room. Considering what the footage contained.

Predator.

Prey.

Submission and helplessness.

Two hours might be cutting it a little close for the wasp to finish her burrow, but at least it would be enough time for her to get started with the roach.

Cyrus walked toward the aquariums.

It was time to let his little parasitoid play.

Parasitoids

Back at the cabin, Charlene and I connect her heart rate monitor to the small printer we'd brought along and print out the results of her EKG. Then I compare the results with the times recorded on the lap timer of my watch, which denoted specifically when her image appeared on the screen.

Strangely, even though it would be evidence of something I didn't believe in, I find myself hoping that the test results will match, as if that would be some sort of sign that Charlene and I were meant to be together.

But you don't believe in signs.

You don't believe—

I stare at the two sets of data.

And the results are bewildering.

In almost every case, the fluctuations of her heart rate correspond directly to the times when I was focusing my thoughts and emotions on her.

I literally scratch my head. "Honestly, I have no idea how to explain

149

this, Charlene. You put the RF jammer beneath the cushion on the chair like we talked about last night?"

"Yes."

Everyone's heart rate, respiration rate, blood pressure, and other physiological processes are constantly changing as we move, as we respond to our surroundings and other people, as we feel apprehension or guilt or fear or pleasure or excitement. Still, there's a baseline that our bodies will return to when we're in a relaxed state, as Charlene was in while she was in the chamber.

However, what I'm looking at here are not random fluctuations; rather, they match, with startling uniformity, the instances when I was focusing my thoughts on Charlene.

But when, of course, she had no idea I was doing so.

These are our results, not the center's. This was with our equipment, not theirs. There was no way they could be faking this. And I could think of no explanation as to why her physiological signs should have fluctuated as they did, when they did.

I try to keep an open mind, but it's hard to know what to think.

This morning I started out trying to debunk this research, not confirm it, so despite my reservations, I have to rule out the variable of confirmation bias, however unlikely that would be.

Keep an open mind.

Charlene stands beside me, studies the printouts I'm holding. "So, Jevin, it looks like you and I are entangled."

"So it would seem."

"I wonder how long this has been going on."

"Our entanglement?"

"Yes."

"I, um . . . I couldn't say."

I feel like a junior high–age boy standing next to the girl who's just given him a note with the question, "Wanna be more than friends?" And two boxes, "Yes" and "No." And then the words, "Check one." And I know which one I would check, I know how entangled my heart

150

is, but I'm afraid to tell her. Something holds me back. Maybe it's the fact that I haven't been with a woman since my wife died. And how to act now, in this moment with Charlene—the right thing to say eludes me.

We look into each other's eyes and she doesn't look away, and I almost get drawn beyond myself, almost let the shock of seeing the data we were just reviewing drift away. Almost, but not quite. Because the impact is still there—the results have snagged my thoughts and I just can't shake them, can't ignore the implications.

I think she can tell I'm distracted because a flicker of disappointment crosses her face and she looks away, toward the window. Toward the fog. "It's almost two. I know Xavier will be anxious to hear about the test. Let's see if we can find a way to reach him or Fionna, tell them what we found. We might be able to reach them if we drove a little ways down the road."

Go on, Jevin, say something.

Wanna be more than friends? Yes or no?

Yes.

Now she looks at me. "What do you think?"

I start to reply, to answer her previous question about how long this entanglement has been going on, but all that comes out is, "Sure. We can head straight to Tanbyrn's office from the parking lot. Save some time. That should be fine."

A pause. "Yes."

"Okay."

"Okay."

Tell her how you feel. Tell her!

My hands feel awkward and unsure of themselves as I fold the printouts, put them in my pocket.

Yes or no?

I just can't find the right words to say.

Then Charlene steps out of the cabin and I follow her, thinking back through the conversation, replaying it, rehashing what I should have said but didn't.

I wonder how long this has been going on.

I have evidence that there really is something to Dr. Tanbyrn's tests. That there really is something tangible to my feelings for Charlene.

What measurements could you ever come up with to test the depths of true love?

Maybe I had them on that sheet of paper in my pocket.

～

For a few moments Cyrus admired the beautiful, sleek jewel wasps. Perfectly evolved predators. Beautiful *Ampulex compressa* specimens.

A parasitoid is an animal or organism that takes control of another organism, killing it so that it can implant its offspring inside the host.

But in this case, Cyrus's female jewel wasp wasn't actually going to kill the cockroach herself—her offspring would do that when it hatched and then consumed the cockroach from the inside out while it was still alive.

He leaned over the aquarium that contained the inch-and-a-half-long, squirming *Periplaneta americana*. There were twenty roaches in there, but he would just be needing one today.

He eased the cover to one side.

Fast little creatures. Able to move up to four feet per second, which was comparable to a human running over two hundred miles per hour. It took him a few tries, but in the confines of the aquarium, it wasn't too difficult for him to corner one. He picked it up, pinching it firmly to keep it from twisting free from his grasp.

With his other hand he closed the aquarium, carefully edged the cover to the wasps' aquarium slightly to the side and dropped the cockroach in, then quickly closed the opening again before any of the fifteen wasps could escape.

The roach immediately skittered across the dirt floor, instinctively looking for a place to escape its wide-open, exposed position, especially with so many predators buzzing around it.

The roach hit the aquarium's glass wall, began scurrying along the edge of it, desperate to find cover in the small leaves scattered across the floor. Millions of years of evolution willing it to run, to hide, to survive.

The cockroach was five times the size of a wasp, but that made no difference to the wasps.

One of them took the lead and flew in a tight, circling pattern, undoubtably working out the best way to approach the future host for her child.

~

Glenn pinned the visitor tag to his shirt, left the registration lobby, and returned to his car to retrieve the pack of supplies for the job at hand.

With the wound in his leg, he couldn't help but limp, and that bothered him, made him irritable, but he would spend time recovering when all this was over. After he'd been paid.

In the distance, near the registration building, he noticed two people—a man and a woman—round the corner and head toward the parking lot.

~

2:07 p.m. Pacific Daylight Time
53 minutes until the fire

We're not yet to the car, but I pause, try my cell.

Nothing.

"Let's drive down the road toward the valley," Charlene suggests. "The gorge might be wide-open enough for you to get a bar or two."

As we walk toward the car, she hands me her cell. "You know how much I like talking on these things. I'll drive; you try to reach Fionna. We have different carriers. Who knows? It's worth a shot."

"You're the only woman I know who can't stand talking on the phone."

"Careful now, dear."

"I'm just saying."

I hand her the keys and we cross the parking lot.

~

Glenn could hardly believe it.

The two people angling toward him were the ones who'd been in the chamber last night.

Don't let them see you!

He slipped into his car and tilted the rearview mirror. Watched them climb into a sedan not fifty feet away.

No indication they'd noticed him.

Good.

He didn't know if they'd gotten a glimpse of him last night in the Lawson building. He'd kept his light in their eyes nearly the whole time, so it was unlikely they could identify him, but still, it was a possibility. So now as he observed them, he was careful to keep his head turned slightly so they wouldn't be able to see him if they looked in his direction.

The woman was behind the wheel. She backed the car out of the parking spot, aimed it toward the road that led from the center to Pine Lake.

Glenn took note of their license plate number.

So.

It looked like he had a decision to make.

Yes, he wanted to follow them, of course he did. See where they were going, then corner them, do some work on them. But that would put the time frame with the doctor in jeopardy.

They'll be back. They weren't carrying their luggage, the bags they had on the video when they were checking in.

Yes.

True.

You know their plate number now, what kind of car they have. You'll be able to find them again. Just get to the Lawson Center, check out the reception area, make sure the chairs will work. Take care of the doctor, then deal with them. You'll have plenty of time.

Okay.

Glenn waited for the sedan to disappear, then left his car. Carrying his backpack with the supplies in it and walking as quickly as his injured leg would allow him, he headed toward the Lawson research building.

First things first.

Visit the maintenance closet on the first floor and disable the building's sprinkler system.

~

Two miles from the center, I'm able to reach Fionna.

"Jevin, I've been trying to get ahold of you since yesterday. What happened?"

"No cell reception up here in the mountains."

"So you didn't get the files I sent you?" She sounds exasperated.

"No. What did you find?"

Her tone changes. I can tell she's calling to someone across the room. "Maddie, put down those scissors and let go of your brother's ponytail!"

I hear a faint, disgruntled "Yes, ma'am."

The joys of being a mom.

I motion for Charlene to pull the car to the shoulder so we can make sure we don't lose the connection.

"Here's what I found." Fionna is back on the line with me. "Rixo-Tray isn't just working with the Lawson Research Center. They're working with the Pentagon. DoD."

"Really."

"Yes, it has something to do with the president's speech tomorrow and with Kabul, the suicide bombing attempt earlier this week. The guy who was going to blow up the mosque."

I hadn't heard anything about that. "What happened?"

"There's not much to tell, just that a suicide bombing attempt was unsuccessful. The media isn't saying much. A couple al-Qaeda cell members were killed. There are differing accounts of how many."

I couldn't see how that would have anything to do with what was going on here at the center, but if there was a connection, the timing of the bombing attempt in Kabul and the confrontation with the thug here last night might be more than coincidental.

"You should hear Xavier," she tells me. "He's all over this. Conspiracy stuff, you know him."

"I can only imagine. What else?"

"A few things. That's the big—" Here she stops again, calls away from the phone to her kids: "I'll be there in a minute. Just stick the noodles in the pot and cover it." Then she's back on the line with me. "Late lunch. We had a field trip this morning."

She's in Chicago, where it really would be a late lunch. I would've called it an early supper. "No problem."

"Anyway, I was about to say, the files might be too large for you to download to your phone. You'll need to use my FTP server." She gives me the info I'll need to log in, but it looks like I'll have to wait to get the files until I can use my laptop after the meeting with Dr. Tanbyrn.

Charlene taps the clock on the front console of the car: *We need to hurry.*

2:18 p.m.

I give Fionna the quick rundown of what happened last night: sneaking into the center, meeting the assailant, Charlene getting injured. Before I can tell Fionna about today's tests, she asks concernedly about Charlene, "Is she alright?"

"Yes. Do you want to talk to her?"

"Yes."

Charlene unequivocally shakes her head no.

I hand her the phone.

She glowers at me, then speaks to Fionna. "Hey . . . Good." I try to fill in the blanks, guess what Fionna might be saying: "How's your arm? Are you sure it's not serious?"

"Yes . . . Fine . . . Okay," then Charlene hands the phone back to me.

Five words. That's it. Less than ten seconds.

This woman really does not like talking on the phone.

I accept the cell, tell Fionna, "It's me again."

"Xavier's done getting the B-roll for you. He offered to slip up there, meet with you two tonight, catch up."

"I'll call him. Set something up."

Now it really is time to go.

"So you mentioned the guy looking through the computer files . . ." Fionna seems to be anticipating what I'm about to ask her. "Let me guess, you want me to dig around, find out what he might've been searching for." It was more of a conclusion than a question.

"Searching for or deleting, yes."

"I had a look at their files before you went there, Jev. You know that. I didn't see anything suspicious."

"Take another look. Go deeper. Explore the military connection."

A pause. "Alright. Lonnie's looking for a little extra credit. I'll get him on it." Lonnie is her seventeen-year-old son. Not even out of high school yet, and already he's presented twice at DEFCON.

We end the call, and only after I'm lowering the phone do I realize that I didn't get a chance to tell Fionna about the test results, about my entanglement with Charlene. It doesn't look like there's enough time to call Xavier right now, but I text him, tell him I'll call him later this afternoon after our meeting with Tanbyrn. I leave out the news about the watch for the time being. Later I'll drive down here again, download the files from Fionna, and fill Xavier in.

Charlene pulls onto the road, does a U-turn, and takes us back toward the center for our appointment with Dr. Tanbyrn.

～

5:27 p.m. Eastern Daylight Time
33 minutes until the fire

Riah locked her apartment and left for her meeting with Cyrus, the twins, and the person named Williamson, whom she had not yet been able to identify. Yes, it was a little early, but if she got there before the twins did, she could spend a little time talking with Cyrus, find out more about the connection with the Lawson Research Center.

As she climbed into the car, she was thinking about all she'd learned over the course of the day concerning Dr. Tanbyrn's research in Oregon, and she was becoming more and more curious about exactly what the video Cyrus was going to show them would contain.

～

Cyrus watched as the beautiful *Ampulex compressa* made her move.

She flew toward the cockroach and they seemed to battle for a moment, curling and twisting and tussling with each other, the cockroach trying to escape, the wasp trying to make her first sting.

And then she did—with a quick flick she inserted her stinger into the roach's spine, into its central nervous system. In only seconds the cockroach lost control of its front legs and collapsed.

That was the first sting, the one that paralyzed the roach just enough to set it up for the second sting.

The one into its brain.

The venom of this second sting was a dopamine inhibitor. It wouldn't stop the roach from moving, but it would stop it from moving under its own volition. Once this venom was injected, even after the venom from the first sting wore off and the roach had control of its legs again, it would not try to run away. It would be completely under the wasp's control.

Now she wrapped herself carefully and tightly around her prey's head so that she would be able to slide her stinger into the precise spot she was looking for. Just a millimeter to either side and she would kill the roach. She had to get it right the first time, but evolution had taught her what to do.

Truly remarkable.

Of course Cyrus was aware that this was an act, not a genetic trait; neither was it a behavior that she was able to pass on to her offspring. Inexplicable, yes.

So be it.

She knew how to do it, so instinct must have taught her.

But now, as he watched her position that stinger, he thought again of the astonishing precision of this act. How could any wasp ever develop these two separate venoms, know to look for this type of a roach in the first place, then know exactly where to make each of the stings? She wouldn't be able to reproduce unless she could do all of this, so how could this knowledge ever be passed on genetically? It was almost enough to make a person believe that there was a designer behind the process of natural selection.

But would the benevolent deity that religious people believe in really design something like this? A wasp that could create, for lack of a better term, a zombified cockroach to use as a living host for her offspring?

A god with a streak of sadism, sure, but a loving one? That seemed incomprehensible.

The wasp pressed her stinger against the roach's head.

Inserted the stinger into its brain.

Injected the venom.

And waited for it to take effect.

Charlene guides the car into a parking space.

It only takes us a few minutes to walk across campus to the Lawson Center.

We enter through the front door and decide to take the elevator instead of the stairs down to Dr. Tanbyrn's office on the lower level.

And as we wait for the doors to open, she asks me about my father.

Old Wounds

"So now that we know you can get cell reception," Charlene begins, "maybe later—after we meet with Tanbyrn—you can get in touch with your dad."

"I'm not sure that'd be the best thing to do."

The elevator doors slide open and we step inside.

"What happened between you two, anyway? You never told me."

I press the "L" button. "We didn't do so well together after my mom left. He changed, he . . ." Is there a good way to say this? Not really. Just the simple way, the blunt truth: "He became angry."

There's so much more to explain, but it would be opening up a can of worms that I didn't think this was the right time or place for.

The doors close and we descend.

On the lower level, Charlene is quiet as the doors whisk open again. She remains quiet as we exit and head down the hallway toward Tanbyrn's office. Any blood that she or the assailant might've left behind last night on this level has been cleaned up, just as it was on the third floor.

"So, you're saying he wasn't just angry at her for leaving?" We're halfway down the hall. "Not just at her?"

"I suppose that's a good way to put it."

As we approach the small reception area in front of Dr. Tanbyrn's office, I see a man sitting on one of the chairs reading a magazine. A daypack rests on the floor beside him.

He looks up as we join him.

"Do you know if Dr. Tanbyrn is in?" I ask him.

He shifts his gaze from me to Charlene before answering, and when he does he clears his throat slightly. "No. Not yet."

～

A sweet feeling came over Glenn. A secret rush of quiet power.

He could tell that they didn't recognize his voice. Last night he'd tried to mask it, and apparently, it had worked. However, when he went on, he was somewhat tentative, testing the waters: "Do you know where he is?"

"I know he had a few things to take care of. We're scheduled to meet with him at 2:45."

"2:45?" Yes. This was working. It really was. Still no glimmer of recognition on their faces.

"Yes."

"Well"—Glenn nodded knowingly—"I'm in no hurry. I can wait until you're done."

～

Charlene and I give him some space and sit on the other side of the room, a small footstool between us. I expect that now that we're no longer alone, she'll drop the subject of my father.

But she does not.

Instead she lowers her voice. "It's not your fault that your mother left."

"I know."

"It's . . ." She hesitates. "It would be good if you could try to fix things between the two of you. Between you and your dad."

"I'm with you on that."

Although the man across the room is still staring at his magazine, I can only imagine that he's also doing what anyone would be doing in his situation if they heard two people nearby talking in hushed tones—eavesdropping.

Just in case he is, I go with Charlene's assumed name. "Jennie, we've never been close." I'm doing my best to not let the stranger hear me. "I don't want to call him because it would be uncomfortable for both of us, it wouldn't solve anything, it would just open up old wounds, and I think in the end one of us would probably say something he would regret."

"How do you know it wouldn't solve anything?"

"Experience."

A moment passes.

Where is Tanbyrn?

"You know my dad died, right?" Her voice is low but has an intensity to it. "When I was twenty-five, I told you about that? Right after my divorce?"

Charlene had been married for only a short time before her husband decided he preferred the eighteen-year-old girls taking his high school lit class to her. She rarely spoke about it, and now I'm a bit surprised she's even mentioned it.

"The car accident."

She nods and it takes her awhile to respond. "I never had the chance to say goodbye to him. There were things between us that, well . . . should have been said. Things . . ." Her sentence trails off, and it's clear that she's deeply moved by the thoughts of the father she lost and the things she never told him. "Well, I think you understand what I mean."

I'm not sure what to say. I do understand, and for her sake, as a way of showing that I empathize with her, I want to tell her that yes, I'll call my dad and talk with him about all those things that accumulate over the years, but I already know he won't want to see me or talk to me.

"Let me think about it. I'm not brushing you off. I need to figure out what I might say."

She accepts that and agrees that it's a good idea.

Then we're both quiet.

I check my watch.

Ten minutes to three. Dr. Tanbyrn is running late.

Charlene picks up a magazine that she is almost certainly not interested in.

I do the same.

Honestly, Glenn could not believe his luck.

Here they were, delivered straight to him, and if they were going to meet with the good doctor in his office, that meant that he could deal with all three of them at once.

But what about what you had in mind for the woman? About making the guy watch?

As tempting as all of that was, Glenn had to admit that it would be smarter to let them burn alive with the physicist. Simpler. Easier.

Wound for wound for wound.

A tidy, happy ending after all.

Then move on.

He kept his eyes trained on the magazine he was holding.

Despite himself, he felt his heart beginning to hammer.

Don't give anything away. Don't let them guess who you are.

He turned the page of the magazine he was not reading.

Eavesdropping is nice, listening in on people's secrets, peeking into their lives, but as Glenn had learned over the last couple years, there's an even deeper thrill you get from eavesdropping on the people you're about to kill.

There's something special when they have no clue, when they think that life is just going to keep going on the way it always has. Status quo. Time in a bottle; nothing to worry about.

But when you know that's not the case, when you know that the person's death is imminent, only minutes away, the secret knowledge is like a drug. The feeling is rich and sweet and intoxicating, and there's nothing else like it. That's probably what drives serial killers to act out their urges so often. The sense of ultimate, godlike power over your helpless little prey.

Even though he wasn't able to concentrate at all on the words, Glenn dutifully kept pretending to read the magazine.

As soon as the doctor showed up.

As soon as all three of them were in the office.

Then he would act.

He realized that deep in his heart, he really did feel an obligation to something greater than just a paycheck—a calling to do this sort of thing. A duty, so to speak, to death.

His heart raced, his anticipation sharpened.

Yes, there really were moments of pleasure and satisfaction in this job.

Most days it wasn't like this, but today he had to admit that he could lose himself in this work if he wasn't careful, could become more than just a guy doing a job, could start to view himself as something he'd never before been able to admit to himself that he was.

An assassin.

～

The venom took effect.

The roach made no further effort to squirm or get away.

And it would make no further effort to escape. Not ever. Even when it was being burrowed into or eaten from the inside out by the wasp's young larva.

Sometimes the wasp that has stung the roach will break off one of the roach's antennae and drink some of its blood, which was what the wasp in Cyrus's office now chose to do.

Afterward, she waited until the roach had the use of its front legs again, then led it into the corner of the aquarium. She guided it by grabbing its one remaining antenna and directed it to the place where she was about to entomb it with bits of leaves and mud.

The process could take hours, but she would seal the helpless roach in her tomb and then lay her egg on its abdomen.

The roach would remain there, still alive but without trying to escape. After three days, the wasp larva would hatch and, a few days later, burrow into the roach and devour some of its internal organs to make enough room to form a cocoon.

Still it wouldn't try to crawl away, even as this was happening.

Six weeks after that, the young jewel wasp would emerge from the hollowed-out cockroach carcass, make her way out of the nest, and fly away.

Dr. Cyrus Arlington considered all of this and its symbolic connection with all that he was trying to accomplish with the twins, with how the predator controls the prey. More than simply a matter of national security, as Williamson believed, this project would help usher in the next step in human evolution.

A string of facts, of connections, only he was aware of.

As long as the twins did their job.

Adaptation.

Survival.

Adding twenty healthy years to the average life span of *Homo sapiens*.

Twenty years or more.

And he would be at the forefront, leading his species' foray into a bold and uncharted future.

～

Dr. Tanbyrn arrives, greets Charlene and me, as well as the man who was waiting for him when we came in. "May I help you?" Dr. Tanbyrn asks him.

He stands, shakes Tanbyrn's hand. "Dr. John Draw. I contacted the center and they told me I'd be able to meet with you at three. I'm doing some research in superstring theory and its connection to the emerging research in M-theory. I've been a fan of your work for a long time. I was in the Northwest and hoped that perhaps we could sit down and chat for a few minutes."

A question mark crosses the doctor's face. "With whom did you speak? To set up the appointment?"

"Honestly, my office manager made the arrangements. I can come back another time—if that's better?"

"No, no." Dr. Tanbyrn taps the screen of his tablet computer, checks the time. "I'll be glad to meet with you. Can you give us half an hour?"

"That would be perfect."

Then Tanbyrn addresses me and Charlene and gestures toward his office door. "Let's take a look at these results."

Yes, Glenn had been somewhat arrogant, talking so freely in front of them, trusting implicitly that they would not recognize his voice. But it was just another part of the thrill he was tapping into.

He waited until the three of them entered the office before limping to the far end of the hallway to take care of the exit door.

Entombed

Dr. Tanbyrn's office is a small, paneled cubicle. Overstuffed bookshelves line the walls, and a computer monitor that must be at least ten years old sits on his desk next to a dusty ink-jet printer, all a stark contrast to the cutting-edge technology of the research room.

The office isn't as small as the Faraday cage, but it's certainly not one I would want to spend much time in. Windowless, cramped, dominated mostly by the behemoth gray industrial desk. A calendar and a variety of papers with dozens of scribbled equations lie pressed beneath the thick sheet of glass covering the desk.

An overwhelmed inbox sits beside the computer.

Tanbyrn ambles around the desk to have a seat in the chair on the other side. "Forgive the clutter. I'm afraid my cleaning lady is off this week." I'm not sure if he meant that as a joke or not, but I smile. Two folding chairs are propped against the bookcase, and I set them out for Charlene and myself.

Despite the fact that I want to talk to the doctor, the tiny office distracts me, reminds me of a time when I performed a show in Rome three years ago. A Vatican official who'd attended the performance and had been impressed by my escapes took me and Charlene on a tour—albeit an abbreviated one—of the tunnels and crypts that lie beneath the Vatican.

The guide told us that in medieval times, some monks would use bricks and mortar to seal themselves into small alcoves, leaving out only one brick just a small opening through which the other monks would deliver food and water, and out of which the entombed monk would pass his waste.

For years that cell would serve as the monk's home as he prayed and reflected on God in solitude—until he died, and the other monks would slide the final brick into place, making the cell their brother monk's tomb.

Our tour guide praised the monks for their "sacrifice of holiness," but I wondered how anyone who purposely cut himself off from the opportunity of ever serving someone else could be considered holy. Charlene, calling on her university classes in religion, had asked our guide how the actions of these monks squared with Basil's words in his *Rule*, the guidebook for monks since the fourth century: "Whose feet therefore will you wash if you live alone?" Our guide had simply told us somewhat cryptically that there were different kinds of service and different levels of sacrifice.

It'd struck me then, and in the doctor's office now, it strikes me again that in medieval times the holiest men chose to live in solitary confinement, but today we consider that to be one of the worst punishments imaginable and reserve it for only the most heinous of our criminals. We sentence our greatest sinners to the life the Church's saints used to freely choose.

Dr. Tanbyrn spreads a sheaf of papers across his already cluttered desk and looks up at us. "Let's just be honest with each other, now. You're not here for the program, are you?"

I feel a stone sink into my gut. "Excuse me?"

His gaze shifts from me to Charlene, then back to me. "Kindly tell me what you're really here at the center for."

～

Glenn finished chaining the far exit door shut.

Strode toward the door to the stairwell to take care of that as well.

～

I stare at Tanbyrn, taken aback, unsure how to respond.

Option one: try to keep up the charade that Charlene and I are lovers and simply entered this project to be a part of the study in the emerging field of consciousness research and the entanglement of love.

Option two: be honest with him, lay my cards on the table, and see where that might lead.

Obviously he knows you're here under false pretenses. He knows or he wouldn't have said anything.

I wonder if it's possible that the test results he ran have something to do with his conclusion about why we're here. Could they have given something away? As extraordinary as that seems, it's possible.

Tell him the truth.

Get some answers.

"Truthfully, Dr. Tanbyrn, you're right. When we applied for the program, we did have a different agenda in mind than simply participating in your research."

Charlene gives me a look of surprise.

"And that was?"

"Debunking it."

A pause. "I see."

"But how did you know? How did you—"

"Philip told me about the blood he cleaned up from the floor. When I accidentally grabbed Jennie's arm—is that even your real name? Jennie Reynolds?"

"Charlene Antioch," she tells him.

"And I'm Jevin Banks," I add.

"I see." He takes a long breath. Intertwines his fingers. "Yes, well, after I grabbed your arm, Charlene—and I am quite sorry about that—I noted the amount of bleeding, and since no one had checked in with our staff nurse last night or this morning, it got me to thinking. I looked up the address you provided on your application forms and found that it doesn't exist. It did not require a great deal of deduction to conclude that you were likely the one in the Faraday cage last night, the one bleeding on the floor."

This is it. This is where he asks us to leave, tells us that we shouldn't be here. I'm about to speak, to try to finesse whatever information I can from him, but he leans forward. "However, two questions remain: why were you bleeding on the way out of the building and not on the way in, and who left the blood going in the other direction?"

"We weren't the only ones here," Charlene tells him. "A man attacked us with a knife; Jevin was able to wound him before he left."

The doctor looks more than a little concerned. "Attacked you with a knife?"

She nods.

I cut in, "We think he was trying to find something on the computer in the room with the Faraday cage. Is there anything in your files or on that particular computer that's sensitive? Something an intruder might be interested in?" I think back to last night, add one more question. "Perhaps someone from a pharmaceutical company?"

"RixoTray?"

"Or a competitor. Yes."

Tanbyrn is quiet.

Charlene gestures toward her injured arm. "The man might have hurt me much worse if my arm hadn't been in the way when he swiped that blade at my abdomen. Thankfully, Jevin knew what he was doing and stopped him. The man threatened to kill us both if we didn't tell him who'd sent us."

"And who did send you?"

"EFN," I tell him. "Entertainment Film Network."

"Entertainment Film Network."

"I have a television show."

"Oh. I see."

Guessing that the information Fionna found out for us earlier is the key here, I go on quickly: "The computer files the man in the room last night was looking for, I think they have something to do with the military, a suicide bombing attempt earlier this week in Kabul."

He stares at me. "Who did you say you are again?"

I decide to go with the truth and launch into telling him everything he needs to know.

Interruption

Glenn chained the stairwell door shut, snapped the lock closed.

Walked to the elevator.

Disabling one is remarkably easy.

You simply insert something into the base while the doors are open in order to keep them from closing. As long as they don't close, the elevator won't leave that floor.

Glenn reached into his pack and pulled out a hammer, pressed the up button, and waited for the doors to open.

When they did, he jammed the handle of the hammer into the opening between the floor and the shaft, then pounded it down with his heel, making sure it was so tightly forced in that it wouldn't come out without something like a crowbar to pry it loose.

He took care of the remaining stairwell but left the exterior exit door closest to the doctor's office alone for the time being so that after he'd started the fire he would have a way out of the building.

The other rooms on this level were small meeting rooms. No other offices. No other people.

The floor was sealed off.

Glenn returned to the reception area, removed the magazines from the end table, then carefully and quietly tilted it beneath the doorknob to the doctor's office. He wedged it securely in place so that there would be no opening that door from the inside.

When you're lighting a fire in a building that you're trying to bring down, you need to direct the flames to where they'll spread the quickest. Typically, that means starting the fire on the building's lowest level in a corner where there's plenty of combustible material, where the walls and ceiling reflect both the heat and the movement of the combustible gases even while channeling the flames upward.

Which was precisely what he was about to do.

There were six chairs in the lobby outside the doctor's office. The plastic coating along with the latex foam and the gasoline would form a fast-growing fire with plenty of smoke. By using two piles of chairs, Glenn was confident the reception area would be fully involved within minutes.

He began to stack the chairs, making sure that one pile was directly beneath the vent that fed air into the doctor's office.

<hr/>

The more I tell Dr. Tanbyrn about my history of researching psychic claims, the less pleased he looks that Charlene and I are here. I finish by admitting that our test results matched the ones he'd been finding, the ones he'd published in the literature. "I'm no longer trying to debunk anything you're doing. I'm just trying to get to the bottom of what's going on here."

As he evaluates what I've said, he slowly and gently rubs two fingers together.

Charlene leans forward. "Dr. Tanbyrn, do you have any idea who that man last night might have been?"

He takes a small breath. "Your life was in danger last night, Miss Antioch, Mr. Banks—both of you. That troubles me deeply. I think there are a few things you should know." He nods toward Charlene, then gestures toward a manila folder on the bookshelf near her. "My dear, do you mind getting that folder?"

She rises.

Retrieves the folder.

Dr. Tanbyrn lays it out on the desk in front of him and begins flipping through it, carefully scrutinizing each page of equations as he does.

～

Glenn finished with the chairs and was reaching into his bag to get out one of the two-liter bottles of gasoline he'd brought with him when the nearest exit door opened and a slim black lady wearing a gaudy African dress walked in.

She looked at him, then at the stacks of chairs. "What are you doing?"

He set down the bag. Folded it shut. "Oh, I'm sorry, didn't they tell you?"

"Tell me what?"

"We're cleaning the floors."

She lowered her head slightly, one eyebrow raised. "Cleaning the floors?"

"I'm from the agency." Glenn smiled innocently.

"What agency?"

He smiled. "Here, let me show you my ID." As he approached her, he made like he was reaching for his wallet, but instead, with his side turned to hide his hand, he was sliding it along the back of his belt toward his knife's sheath.

Her gaze went past him to the end table he'd propped against the door to trap the doctor and his two visitors in the office.

"Why is that table leaning against the door?" Caution bordering on suspicion. She took a small step backward toward the exit.

He found the sheath, snapped it open. "I just needed to slide it out of the way."

She was about ten feet away, but he knew he could be quick when he needed to be, even with his wounded leg.

The woman leaned to the side and called, "Doctor Tan—" but that was as far as she got. It was all she could say, all she would ever say, because then he was on her. He clamped one hand over her mouth and whipped out his knife with the other. She tried to call for help and was certainly a squirmy one, but he managed to hold on to her long enough to tuck the blade up into her tight little belly.

Even though he still had his hand over her mouth, he could hear her gasp.

"Shh, now. Don't fight it."

She was still trying to pull free, but the strength was beginning to seep out of her, allowing him to firm up his grip.

He slid the blade out, raised it to her throat. Drew it to the side in one swift, firm motion and let go of her body.

She fell clumsily to the floor. The only sounds she made now were the wet, sputtering ones from the base of her throat, and she didn't make those for long. Her body twitched a little before lying still at last, a dark gaping wound across her neck, a spreading stain of blood across her belly.

Quiet now.

No more trouble.

That's a good girl.

Glenn wiped off the blade on his jeans.

Alright.

It was time to finish this up.

He dragged her toward the chairs.

Pulled out the gasoline bottles.

And set to work.

~

"There it is." Dr. Tanbyrn points to a page, spins the papers around so we can see what he's pointing at. "Project Alpha. I work with two men. They fly in, do some tests, fly out. I don't even know their real names. We call them 'L' and 'N.' It's funded through the Department of Defense."

The Pentagon. Yes. The same thing Fionna had uncovered about the research at RixoTray.

The page is covered with detailed algebraic and scientific equations that I have no idea how to decipher. "What kind of tests?"

Dr. Tanbyrn has been surprisingly open with us, but now seems to second-guess himself. "I'm not sure how much more I should . . ." His eyes come to rest on Charlene's arm and he hesitates.

The chapters I've read of his books flash through my mind: quantum entanglement, nonlocal communication, the interconnection of life on the subatomic level, relationships—

That's it. That has to be it.

"They're twins, aren't they? 'L' and 'N'?"

He looks at me long and hard. "Yes, Mr. Banks. They are twins. Quite special twins indeed."

~

Glenn soaked the chairs with gasoline, then splashed some on the dead woman, just because he thought it might be interesting to watch that dress stick to her skin, and then take her with it as it went up in flames.

~

"How are they special?" I ask him.

For a moment I think I smell gasoline.

Gasoline? But that's—

"Well, you see—" Dr. Tanbyrn begins.

Charlene grabs my arm to stop me. "That's gas, Jevin."

"Yes."

I stand. Start for the door.

~

Glenn backed up.

Lit a match.

Tossed it onto the stack of chairs beneath the air vent and watched the flames lick up the fabric. They were hungry and immediately fell in love with the wood.

No, this fire would not take long at all to devour the building.

～

I smell smoke and tell myself it's from outside the building, just like when I smelled wood smoke last night when Charlene and I first entered our cabin.

But I know that's not the case.

I try the doorknob. It turns, but the door won't open.

Oh, not good.

Not good at all.

"What's going on?" Dr. Tanbyrn asks.

"Grab your things. We're getting out of here."

～

Glenn lit the other stack of chairs.

Lit the dead black woman.

Then he splashed the rest of the gasoline on the floor as he backed toward the exit door.

～

I slam my shoulder against the door, but it stays firmly in place. Smoke is beginning to curl beneath the door and billow down through the vent above my head. It's acrid and black and it's coming in fast.

"It's the project." Dr. Tanbyrn coughs. "'L' and 'N.'"

"What's it about?" Charlene urges him. "What makes the twins so special?"

I go at the door again, harder, hoping to jar loose whatever is jammed up against it.

～

Glenn lit the pool of gasoline on the floor. Stepped out the exit door. Pulled out his remaining chain, lock, and key, threaded the chain through the door handle, wound it through the metal post of the fence beside the walkway, and snapped the lock shut.

There was no way out of the building's lower level.

~

Nothing.

The fire alarm goes off, the sprinklers on the ceiling do not.

I search for something to smash against the door.

The desk is too large to move, or at least too large for me to push with enough momentum to take out the door.

"Communication. Physiology—" Dr. Tanbyrn's explanation is chopped up by hoarse coughing. "Identical twins are much more effective than individuals. I was providing feedback to help them direct and focus their alpha waves, studying the negative . . . the effects . . . if they were . . ."

Charlene has snatched up Tanbyrn's desk phone, but the line must be dead because she drops the receiver again. Pulls out her cell.

Smoke is quickly filling the room. "Get the papers," I tell them. "On the desk. Project Alpha. And the iPad."

"Eleven o'clock." His voice is harsh. "When the eagle falls at the park . . . The twins said—I don't know what it . . ."

I back up and try a front kick against the door, directly beside the doorknob.

A tremor runs up the door, but that's all.

No reception. Charlene pockets her phone.

Tanbyrn is coughing. He's stopped trying to explain the research and is just trying to breathe.

Go. You have to get out now!

With the thick smoke filling the cramped quarters, it isn't going to take long at all for the air to become too toxic to sustain life. I pull my shirt up over my mouth, shout for Charlene and Tanbyrn to do the same.

The vent above us is far too small to climb through.

Back to the door. I try a side kick, but whatever's holding the door shut doesn't budge.

Flames snake down through the vent on the ceiling.

Charlene is supporting the doctor. "Hurry, Jev!"

No windows. No other doors. This is it.

You need to get this door open.

Now.

I try to think of what might be holding it shut.

If this fire was started by a professional, it might be an angled door jammer, a rod with suction cups on its two ends, one that attaches to the door, the other to the floor, so the harder you press on the door, the more firmly the other end suctions to the floor. I did an escape from a room sealed shut with one in a show in Denver a decade ago—

A chair? The end table, a doorstop of some kind?

Impossible to know.

Whatever was there, I can think of only two ways to get out: pop the hinges off the door or slide something through the space beneath the door and push it hard enough to break the seal and knock the jammer—or chair legs, or whatever—out of the way.

The door's hinges are on the other side, so that's not an option. Instead I'd need something thin enough, long enough, strong enough to push under the door and shove whatever was there out of the way.

And I know exactly what that is.

I turn away from the door.

Toward the thick sheet of glass covering Dr. Tanbyrn's desk.

The Glass

I sweep my arm across the desk, knocking everything to the floor.

Glass is fragile when dropped on end or when pressure is applied to the middle of it, but lengthwise, a sheet as thick as this might just do the trick.

As long as it's not too wide to fit under the door.

Dr. Tanbyrn is coughing harshly and leaning awkwardly against the bookshelf.

"Help me get this glass," I shout to Charlene. "We need it over by the door!"

～

As Glenn limped away from the building, he could see a dozen or so people stream down the front steps. None of the three people he'd sealed in the office were among them.

He ducked out of sight behind a tree to watch the place go up in flames.

And fingered the folded-up copy of the front page of the current issue of *USA Today* he had stuffed in his jacket pocket.

～

Charlene and I have to slide the desk aside to make enough room to get the glass onto the floor.

We position it in front of the doorway, I push it forward, and—thank God—it fits beneath the door. It's at least five feet long, surely long enough to reach the bottom of whatever is lodged against the doorknob. I guide the glass forward a few feet until it meets with resistance.

Dr. Tanbyrn slumps to the floor. Charlene hurries to his side.

Okay, this is where things either went right or very, very wrong. There's nothing else in this room we could use to get out of here.

If the glass cracks or shatters, you're going to die in here.

You're going—

Stop it.

I pull the glass toward me, then press it forward again, nudging the far edge firmly against whatever's holding the door in place. I don't have a great grip, but it seems like it should be sufficient enough to give me the force I need. I push harder, but the glass goes nowhere, the object it's touching doesn't move.

I try again. Nothing.

"Slam it," Charlene calls urgently. "Jar it loose!"

No choice. I have to try.

Praying the glass won't crack, I grip the end firmly, draw it toward me, and then as swiftly and solidly as I can, I shove it forward.

This time I feel a brief bump of resistance, then the glass keeps moving. Whatever was propped up on the other side of the door clatters to the floor.

Yes!

By now the doorknob will undoubtedly be too hot to touch. I leap to my feet and bunch up the front of my shirt around my hand, but as I'm about to open the door, Charlene yells to me, her voice coming from the floor beside the desk. "Jevin, get over here! It's Tanbyrn! He passed out!"

Oxygen

I kneel beside the doctor.

He's lying still. Breathing but unconscious. Charlene tries to shake him awake, but he doesn't respond.

I shake him myself, call his name. Nothing.

The room is nearly filled with smoke.

You need to carry him, get him out of here.

Yes, but how would we—

The glass will be too hot to hold.

Maybe not, maybe you can get past the fire.

Quickly, I tug off my leather jacket.

"What are you doing?" Charlene is gasping for air herself.

I hand her the jacket, then hurriedly guide the glass back into the room and prop it upright against the desk.

"Jevin, what's the jacket for?"

"Hold the glass in front of you." I can barely see her through the smoke. Both of us have to yell now to be heard. "I'll carry Tanbyrn, follow you out the door. Tilt it, slide it across the floor, use it like a shield to protect you from the flames." I help her pull the jacket sleeves over her hands to protect them from getting burned. "Keep your head low and move fast!"

I lift Dr. Tanbyrn, drape him over the back of my shoulders, fireman's carry. Charlene holds the edges of the glass, her hands protected by the leather sleeves of my jacket. The glass plate is heavy, but she should be able to lean into it, move it in front of her along the floorboards, even with her injured arm. At least I hope she can.

With my shirt bunched up around my right hand, I reach for the doorknob.

"Will the flames rush in?" Sharp concern in her voice.

All fires are hungry for oxygen and it's possible the flames would pour in, but we don't have a choice. I needed to open this door.

They might, yes—

"I don't know."

I grasp the knob.

Turn it.

And open the door.

Flames

A rush of smoke swirls around us, but thankfully, only a few flames lick into the room. The door gets hung up for a moment on what'd been holding it shut—which I now see is the end table from the lobby—but with enough pressure I'm able to slide it aside and open the door all the way.

Heat rages everywhere.

Flames are already consuming the walls. Much of the floor is also on fire, but there are enough spots that look free of the blaze that we should be able to get to the nearest exit door.

"Go on!" I holler to Charlene, and she leads the way, holding the glass in front of her. I follow closely behind. I'm not sure how effective the glass shield is, but it does seem to be keeping some of the flames away from her face.

Even though in my shows I've been set on fire, escaped from burning buildings, and been blown up innumerable times by Xavier, those were all controlled situations. None of that compared to the heat singeing my face and arms, burning my throat with every breath right now.

After only a few steps, I notice a body lying nearby. It's scalded, and I can't identify who it is until I see the metal bracelets encircling one of the charred wrists.

Abina.

A thick knot of anger forms inside me.

Whoever did this can't be far. Find him. Stop him.

Charlene doesn't pause, and I take that to mean she hasn't seen the research assistant's body. It's a small thing, but at least it's one thing to be thankful for.

We shuffle forward.

The air is rigid and fiery in my lungs.

We're about ten feet from the exit door, but by now I can tell that the glass idea doesn't seem to be working as well as I'd hoped. It's awkward for Charlene to maneuver and seems to be slowing us down. In front of us, blocking the way to the exit door, is a pool of flames.

"Tip it forward!" I yell. She does so immediately, and the glass hits the floor and shatters across the floorboards, sending a whoosh of smoke and displaced flames to every side. But the place where the glass fell is momentarily clear of the blaze, so we rush across the glass shards, make it to the exit door.

"You okay?"

"Yes!" Her reply is muffled by the popping, crackling fire.

I lean my hip against the push bar and the door pops open, but only about six inches, then catches on a stout chain.

No!

A rush of desperation.

I shift Dr. Tanbyrn's weight to keep him balanced on my shoulders, then smash my side against the door, but it's useless. I study the chain and see that it has a keyed lock, not a combination lock, holding the two ends together.

Oh yes.

"Charlene, my belt!"

She's worked with me on hundreds of escapes and knows about the belt buckle, the narrower-than-normal prong. I have no idea how many locks I've picked with it while sealed in trunks, coffins, airtight tubes—

She tugs the jacket off her arms, unbuckles the belt, snakes it out of my belt loops, and hands it to me, buckle first.

Holding it carefully, I slide my hand outside.

A one-handed pick, not easy, and it's been months since I've picked this brand of lock . . .

But I haven't lost my touch. It takes less than ten seconds, the lock clicks open, the ends of the chain dangle free. I grab one of them and yank the chain loose even as I throw my hip against the door.

It bangs open.

Charlene and I emerge from the building and run toward the clearing to escape the smoke and the raging flames.

You're okay. You made it!

Hopefully, Dr. Tanbyrn did as well.

Assault

As gently as I can, I lower him to the ground.

Charlene leans close. "Let me." She's more experienced at first aid than I am. I clear out of the way.

She tilts Dr. Tanbyrn's head to open his airway. Checks to see if he's still breathing.

I stand, look around.

The day is still damp, still gray, smudged darker now by the heavy black smoke from the blaze.

The guy who set that fire is probably still on the campus, probably—

I see someone standing just off the trail that leads along the edge of the forest behind the building and recognize him as the man who was waiting in the reception area when Charlene and I arrived.

"He's still alive." Relief in her voice.

The man is half-hidden by a tree, and he must have seen me watching him because he turns and heads into the woods, limping.

From last night's knife wound.

That's it.

You're mine.

"Take care of Tanbyrn," I shout to Charlene. I'm already sprinting toward the woods, wrapping my belt around my left hand. "I'll be right back."

188

~

Glenn glanced behind him.

The guy was pursuing him.

Alright. Let him follow.

The fog would help.

Find a spot out of sight from the rest of the campus.

Take care of this guy for good.

Then get to the parking lot and clear out before the fire trucks and the cops show up.

~

I throw a branch aside, jump over a root, and race toward Abina's killer, eighty yards ahead of me, barely visible on the edge of the fog.

You're a runner. He's injured.

You can catch him.

Catch him, yes. But then what?

Stop him. Do whatever it takes to stop him.

Whatever it takes.

Seventy yards, maybe sixty-five.

He killed Abina. Tanbyrn might die. He tried to kill Charlene.

Yeah, I would stop him.

With my lungs still feeling like they're filled with smoke, I'm short of breath and I can sense that it's slowing me down, and despite the wound in this man's leg, he's amazingly fast. Last night he had a knife sticking out of his thigh, now he's racing through the forest like he was never hurt at all. It was quite possible the knife hadn't gone in as deeply as I thought it had.

But still, I'm gaining.

Sixty yards.

He reaches a ravine and disappears into a patch of thick fog that has settled into the valley. Logs covered with moss. Dense ferns on the ground. The trees here are ancient. Primeval. Fog lurks between them like threads of living smoke.

The mist brushes against my face and arms and it feels good, cooling the reddened skin. I can only hear the sound of my choked breathing, my muted footsteps on the forest floor. Other than that, all is still and quiet in the fog.

I'm jacked on adrenaline from the fire, the chase, the thought of fighting this guy, and my heart is slamming against the inside of my chest. I arrive at the edge of the ravine and then descend into it, trying to find the path through the underbrush where he might've gone. At last I come to a small clearing in the trees.

Fog all around.

No sign of him.

I slow to a jog.

Stop.

No sound of him running. The ground has leveled off and the fog is thicker here. I can only see fifteen or twenty feet in any direction. Towering trees surround me. He could be anywhere.

Puffs of breath circle from my mouth in the cool air as if they were bursts of steam evaporating before me. I listen but hear nothing apart from my ragged breathing.

I was in a fire only minutes ago, now I'm in the chilled forest and a shiver runs through me.

Backtrack? Did he backtrack?

No, he's here.

Fists raised, I crouch. Ready stance.

If he were still running, I would hear him, at least be able to tell what direction he was heading in.

But I hear nothing.

He's close.

He's here. Behind one of the trees.

I inch toward a large tree to my left, one wide enough to conceal a person.

"They're following me," I shout, I lie. "You won't get away. I've seen your face. I can identify you."

That much was true.

I move closer to the looming tree and hear a crunch of leaves ten feet to my right. Instinctively I whip around toward the sound, but no one is there.

A trick.

Misdirection.

Tossing something away from yourself—it's what you would have done!

I snap my head in the other direction and see a branch as thick as a baseball bat swinging toward me. I try to duck, drop to the side, but I'm too slow.

The branch collides with the left side of my head and sends me reeling to the side. I fall hard, face-first onto the forest floor. A rock that's jutting up between the roots smacks into my right side, and I hear a muffled crack.

A burst of pain shoots through me.

My rib.

My head throbs, feels like it's filled with its own heavy, thunderous heartbeat. The world becomes a splinter of dots, stars splintering apart in my vision. I try to push myself to my feet, but the world is turning in a wide, dizzy circle and I can't seem to make my limbs obey me. My side screams at me, and I don't make it past my hands and knees.

Focus. Focus!

Out of the corner of my eye, I see the man approaching me.

I don't make it to my feet. He kicks me hard in my injured side and the ground rushes up at me again. I barely hold back a gasp of pain when I land. If the rib wasn't fractured before, it's almost certainly broken now.

Everything around me seems to be edging outside of time, but in my blurred vision I see him raise the branch, step closer. I roll away from him and feel the whoosh of air beside me as he brings the branch thwacking down right where my head had been only a moment earlier. A spray of mud splatters across my face.

My injured side squeezes out a jet of pain that courses through my chest every time I take a breath.

Get up, you have to get up to fight this guy.

Forcing myself to stand, I feel another swoop of dizziness, but I hide it from him. Face him.

He discards the branch, flips out a knife.

So he has a weapon.

But so do I.

Carefully, I wrap one end of the belt around each hand. It's one of the simplest ways to defend yourself when someone comes at you with a knife. If you know what you're doing, you can trap the wrist of your opponent's knife hand, control the arm, and take him down.

And I know what I'm doing.

As long as you can stay on your feet.

The pain coursing up my side and pounding through my head makes it hard to focus.

He's stationary, less than ten feet away, studying me, no doubt planning how best to attack me.

He holds the blade straight out to slice at me like he did last night when he went after Charlene.

No ice-pick grip this time. He's learned his lesson.

As I breathe, breathe, breathe, try to relax, somehow, even though I'm distracted by the pain, my senses seem to become sharper, more focused. I catch the sound of a stream nearby that I hadn't noticed. I smell the pine needles and the moist decay of the soil, feel the droplets of sweat trailing down my forehead and the warm blood oozing from the side of my head where he hit me with the branch.

He watches me.

Don't black out. Do not black out.

But I'm unsteady and feel like I might.

I blink, rub the back of my fist across my eyes, and my vision clears enough for me to see the streak of blood splayed across his sleeve. I can only guess what he did to Abina before setting her on fire.

A shot of anger tightens my focus again.

"Her name was Abina," I tell him.

"What?"

"The woman you killed in there. Before you started the fire."

"Ah." He taps the edge of his lip with his tongue. "Stuck her in the belly like a squirmy little pig. She would have squealed and squealed. Died quick, though. When I did her throat." He demonstrates how he killed her, miming the action with the knife. "Burned kinda nice in that outfit too. Almost like she was dressed for the occasion."

Rage, white and hot and like nothing I've ever experienced, overwhelms me and I like it. Feel fueled by it. I snap the belt taut between my hands and realize I'm no longer thinking in terms of stopping this man. That's not exactly the right word.

Everything becomes clear: only one of us is going to walk out of this forest alive.

"How's your leg? How about we do the other one too?"

His grin flattens. He flips the knife into his other hand. "Wound for wound."

Stall, Jevin. Stall long enough and help will arrive.

But no, I don't want to stall.

I want to take care of this right now.

Besides, I know help isn't on its way. We're hidden in the fog more than a quarter mile off the trail and down a ravine. Even if I called for help, the dense forest and the drizzling rain would devour the sound. No one knows where we are, no one is looking for us. Besides, there aren't any cops around, so even if someone from the center did come, that would only mean one more unarmed person for this guy to attack.

~

Glenn eyed the man who'd bested him last night in the chamber.

A line from a movie came to mind: "You are the pus in a boil I am about to pop." Glenn thought that, thought it, but did not say it.

But yes, popping a boil was a good way to describe what he was about to do to this man.

~

I move toward him.

He's passing the knife back and forth from hand to hand, trying to intimidate me. Not wise—it leaves you unprotected for a fraction of a second each time you do it.

"I like it better this way." His voice is all acid and filled with disdain. "I can make it last longer than the fire would have."

"So can I."

He feints left, lunges right, sweeping the knife toward me. I stop the attack with an inside block and let my momentum carry me through and land a left leg round kick to his side, then I twist away, sweeping my leg backward to take him down, but he's quick and plants himself, blocks with his left shin.

Kick his leg. His thigh. It's injured.

I go for it as he maneuvers toward me, but he evades the kick. He jabs right, then slashes the blade toward my stomach, catching my shirt, grazing my skin. He quickly goes for me again, but I block his hand, get in close, and smash his jaw with the back of my fist. It's a solid punch and it hurts my hand, but I know it must have hurt his face even worse.

He has the knife in his right hand, and I go for that wrist with the belt, try to wrap it so I can disarm him, but he savagely slashes the blade against the belt, severing it. I drop the two ends as he punches me hard in my injured side, and I can't help but crumple backward in pain.

My head is pounding fiercely and my balance is still off. I'm queasy, dizzy. It feels like everything around me is slipping off the rim of reality into a widening gray blur.

I straighten up. Face him. Give him no indication of how weak I feel. "Why set the fire? To kill Tanbyrn or destroy his files?"

Spittle hangs from his lip and he sneers, blood covering his teeth from where I punched him. He doesn't speak, but there's a stony hardness in his eyes, a look that seems to say, "I'm willing to do anything it takes to see this through. Are you willing to do as much to stop me?"

That's the look in his eyes.

And I know it's the look in mine.

The fog swirls aside as he rushes at me. His blade flashes toward my cheek and I deflect his arm, land another punch to his jaw. He spins, but I step to the side, heel-kick his injured leg, then his knee, buckling it, and as I do I strike the back of his neck as hard as I can with the straightened edge of my right hand.

He goes down quick, with a heavy, wet thud. I expect him to be on his feet in a second, and I wait, ready, my heart jackhammering in my chest.

The man does not rise.

Two thoughts flash through my mind—*he's hurt and he can't get up; he's faking it and he's going to stab you as soon as you move closer.*

There's no way my knife-hand strike disabled him. I'm strong, but I'm not that strong.

He's faking it.

Only then do I see that his right arm is buckled beneath him. That was the hand that held the knife.

Still he does not stand.

I call to him. He doesn't answer.

Check, you have to see.

Sparring didn't prepare me for this, didn't teach me what to do next. When you're in the gym, you help your partner up when he goes down. But not here, not in a real fight. There's no way I'm going to flee, but I'm not sure I want to get closer to him either.

He doesn't move.

I edge toward him.

If I go in any closer and he rolls toward me with the knife, I'm not sure I'd be able to jump out of the way in time. He might manage to stab my leg, even my stomach.

I take a breath, try to calm myself, but it's not exactly happening.

Something I'm going to have to work on.

If there was a way to roll him over without getting close enough for him to cut me, then I would—

The branch he hit me with.

Yes.

I retrieve it and approach him.

His back is rising and falling slightly with each breath, and that makes me think he really is hurt. Someone who was faking it would probably hold his breath to make it look like he was dead.

Only a couple feet away now.

I call to him again, but still he doesn't reply.

Using the end of the branch, I press against his shoulder to roll him onto his back. He's a big man and it takes some effort, but then he does roll over and I see the blood soaking his shirt and the handle of the knife protruding from his abdomen.

The blade is buried almost to the hilt, angled up just beneath his sternum. I can only guess that the knife tip either punctured his heart or is close to it. Either way, it went through his lung, and the frothy blood he's spitting out tells me how serious the wound is.

His eyes are open. He's still breathing, but his teeth are clenched and he's obviously in a lot of pain. He coughs up a mouthful of blood and it splatters across his chin. If I turned him onto his side, it would keep the blood from pooling in his throat, help clear his airway, and keep him from aspirating on his own blood, and if he hadn't killed Abina, I might have done that right away. But because of what he did to her, I'm not sure I want to help him at all.

But then I have another thought.

You need to find out what he was looking for before it's too late.

Alright.

I kneel beside him.

Last night I saw him yank a knife out of his leg without flinching. To make sure he won't pull out the blade now and kill me with it, I remove the knife. Toss it to the side.

He winces, then sneers.

I turn his head to the side to help clear his mouth of blood, and it does seem to help him breathe.

"What were you looking for in the center last night?"

He spits, coughs a little, doesn't respond.

"Who are you? Who sent you here?"

"Akinsanya will find you." His voice is sputtering and wet with blood.

"Akinsanya? Who's Akinsanya?"

No response. Just a smug grin.

"Who's Akinsanya?"

Nothing.

A compassionate person might've reassured him, told him that he was going to be okay, that help was coming. But that would have been a lie, and besides, right here, right now, more than compassion was at stake. There's justice too, and after what he did to Abina, what he tried to do to Charlene, what he might've succeeded in doing to Dr. Tanbyrn, I don't try to comfort him. Instead I lean close. "You're dying. But it might take some time. I'll help it along if you tell me what you were looking for."

Something in his eyes changes.

"Go on," I tell him. "I'm listening."

"Screw"—his word is stained with hatred and a pathetic kind of defiance—"you."

Alright then.

I stand up.

Watch him.

I don't hurry things along, but let him die at his own speed.

It takes awhile.

And I'm not at all sorry that it does.

The last thought Glenn Banner had was not regret for what he had done, not remorse, not sorrow, just anger that he hadn't killed this man, that he hadn't gotten to spend some time with that woman from last night.

Well, at least you got to watch that skinny little whore burn.

Then the darkness descended.

And the silent, writhing journey toward forever began.

The Photos

I wait a minute or two after his breathing stops just to make sure that he's gone, then I check his pockets.

A set of car keys, a cell phone, a lighter, a crumpled-up copy of the front page of today's issue of *USA Today*. A wallet.

Opening up his wallet, I find out that his name was Glenn Banner. He lived in Seattle. A felon. I'm surprised to see that noted on his license, but it's there, probably some helpful little law that I wasn't even aware of.

I figure I have a right to know as much as I can about the man who tried to kill me, so I don't feel any guilt searching him like this. I'm not going to take anything with me, I'll leave everything here for the cops; I just want some information.

There's twenty-nine dollars cash in his wallet, four credit cards, no family photographs. But there are photos—eleven of them.

A dark chill slides through me when I realize what they're pictures of.

Corpses.

Eight men, two women, plus one body that's mangled so badly I can't tell the gender of the victim. Some corpses had been stabbed, two have plastic bags over their heads, others were strangled with wire. The first page of a *USA Today* newspaper lies beside each body.

To prove they died on that day.

Eleven horrible crimes that will finally be solved when the police follow up on this. Eleven families who'll find out the truth. Terrible, brutal, yes, but at least they would get some sense of closure to their pain, and surely there's some degree of justice to that, to knowing the truth?

Hard to say.

I've never been able to find the reason lurking behind why Rachel killed herself and our sons. I tell myself that knowing the truth would make a difference, would help me move on. But there's no way to tell if it would really help anything at all.

I put the photos back in the wallet, slide it into his pocket.

On his phone, I check the last ten numbers called and received. Since I have nothing to write with, I record them on my own phone, typing them into the notepad. When I'm done, I return Banner's phone to his pocket as well.

The last thing I find is a crumpled sheet of paper with a seemingly random series of sixteen numbers, upper- and lowercase letters, and punctuation marks: G8&p{40X9!qx5%8Y

All I can think of is that it's a password or some kind of access code. I record it in my phone's notepad as well, then stuff the scrap of paper back into his jeans pocket again.

The rain is picking up now, and I'm anxious to see if Dr. Tanbyrn has awakened—and to find out if anyone else might've been trapped in that fire.

All around me the forest looks the same, so as I navigate through the mist, I snap off twigs at regular intervals to mark the way so I'll be able to lead the police back to Banner's body.

I know I was acting in self-defense when he died; in fact, when he fell on the knife, I was just trying to keep him from killing me. I hadn't planned that, it was an accident, but still, I hope there won't be any kind of trouble with the police when I show them his corpse.

After I find the trail, it's not far to the research building, which, despite the rain, I can see is already mostly consumed by the blaze.

Rain and smoke smudge the day.

Charlene isn't in the place where I left her and Tanbyrn, and I'm not sure if that's a good sign or a bad one.

I study the area, searching for her.

Emergency vehicle sirens scream at me from the access road to the center, but it's too late for the firefighters to save much of the structure, and unless Banner had a partner we don't know about, there is no arsonist for the cops to track down. All I can think of is that hopefully no one else in addition to Dr. Tanbyrn and Abina was hurt or killed in the fire.

A group of about twenty people has gathered beneath the roof of a deck built along the back of a nearby cabin, presumably to escape the rain. A few people are silently watching the blaze, others have formed a semicircle and are staring down at a body.

Tanbyrn.

I quicken my pace.

Two people lean over him, Charlene and a woman I don't recognize. Two of the women in the semicircle are holding their hands over their mouths, and I can't imagine that's a good sign.

The attention of the crowd turns to me as I approach, and the people part to let me through. Someone asks if I'm alright, perhaps noticing the blood smeared across the side of my head or the hitch in my step from the pain in my side.

"I'm fine. Thanks."

I make it to Tanbyrn's side and Charlene looks up at me. "He still hasn't woken up."

But at least he's alive.

At least—

"Did you . . . ?" she begins, then seems to catch herself and stands. The woman who's kneeling beside Tanbyrn apparently knows what she's doing—perhaps she's a doctor or a nurse—and Charlene must feel comfortable leaving him alone with her because she leads me away from the group of bystanders to the corner of the porch, where we can talk privately.

"What happened? Did you catch him?" Then she sees the wound on the side of my head. "Jevin!" Out of concern she reaches for it, but instead of touching it, just ends up pointing at it instead. "Are you okay?"

"Yes. Was anyone else hurt?"

"No. It doesn't look like it."

"Good." I lower my voice. "The arsonist, he's dead."

"What?" She stares at me. "You killed him?"

The first fire truck appears, lumbers toward the flaming building with one set of wheels on the trail, the other on the wet, uneven ground beside it.

"It was an accident. He came at me with the knife. I blocked his arm, kicked out his leg, and when I hit him again, he went down. He landed on the blade."

She lets that sink in.

I gesture toward Tanbyrn. "How is he?"

"Hard to say. He needs to get to a hospital. You killed the guy? Honestly?"

I'm not quite comfortable phrasing it like that, but technically I have to admit that it's correct. "Yeah, I guess I did."

Her eyes have returned to the gash on my head. "Are you sure you're okay?"

A few police cars and an ambulance emerge from the fog, following the fire truck. One of the men who was on the porch leaves and signals to the ambulance to come this way. The driver veers away from the path and aims the vehicle toward us.

Gingerly, I touch the wound. It's already swollen pretty badly and is quite tender. I'd been so distracted thinking about Tanbyrn that I hadn't been as aware of the pain pumping through my side, but now that I pause and breathe and think about where I am, what happened, it seems to become more pervasive again. The knuckles of my right hand are sore from when I punched Banner's jaw. The skin on my hands is still red and tender from the fire.

"A little beat-up," I admit. "But yeah. I'm okay."

She's quiet, and I imagine she's mentally running through the fight, trying to picture me—or maybe trying not to picture me—killing a man.

"He was the guy from last night," I tell her. "The same guy who was outside Tanbyrn's office when we arrived."

"Did he . . . Did you find out anything?"

"His name was Glenn Banner. From Seattle." The ambulance pulls to a stop. Two paramedics leap out, and the crowd parts to give them access to Tanbyrn. "I found a note with a code on it, and I've got some cell numbers for Fionna to follow up on." I'm not sure how to tell her the rest, so in the end I decide to just go ahead and say it. "Charlene, he killed Abina."

"What? Abina?"

I nod.

"How?" Shock and disbelief in her voice.

"Charlene, it's not really—"

"What did he do to her!"

I hesitate, realize she will settle for nothing less than the truth, and give her the whole story. "He stabbed her, then he slit her throat. He burned her body in the fire."

Charlene's face hardens into a mixture of revulsion and rage.

For a moment I debate whether or not to tell her about the photographs in his wallet, but it's pretty clear this isn't the time for that. Unsure what to say, I finally just mumble an honest but inadequate acknowledgment that I understand how devastating this news is. "I'm sorry."

The paramedics are giving Dr. Tanbyrn oxygen and transferring him onto a gurney that they've lowered beside him.

"Did he suffer?" Charlene's words are soft, but there's fire beneath them. "Did he suffer before he died?"

"Yes. He did. It wasn't quick."

"Good."

She stares past me for a moment, then notices the slice in my shirt where Banner's blade made its mark when he came at me. She reaches out and tenderly slides her finger along the edge of the frayed fabric, the light cut underneath it. The pain and anger on her face fade, and a look of deep concern takes its place. "Thank God you're alright."

"Yes."

"But that poor woman." Her voice breaks. "I can't believe she's dead."

I see a tear form in the corner of Charlene's eye, and I draw her close. She wraps her arms around me and leans against me, and despite the pain that crunches up my side as she does, I don't flinch. I just let her try to draw strength from me, even though at the moment I don't really feel like I have a whole lot of extra strength to offer anyone.

The words from a few moments ago echo through my head:

"Did he suffer before he died?"

"Yes. He did. It wasn't quick."

"Good."

Yeah, maybe there is a degree of justice to that after all.

Bloody Soil

The sheriff's department deputies question me about the assailant, and I walk three of them to the place where Glenn Banner's body lies sprawled on a bed of soggy, bloody pine needles. They ask me to explain what happened, talk them through the fight, and I do. Blow by blow.

Two of them jot notes while the third, a man with a snarled brown mustache whose name tag reads Jacobs, slowly circles the body, taking photographs with his mobile phone. I figure I don't need to tell them about the pictures in Banner's wallet. They'll find them soon enough.

I'm finishing recounting what happened when Deputy Jacobs begins to go through Banner's pockets.

He locates the phone, the note, the keys, the newspaper page, the wallet. He flips it open and after a moment pulls out the photographs.

Pauses.

He quietly calls the other men over, and the three of them go through the photographs of the dead and mutilated bodies one at a time. A dark, uncertain storm of shock and fury seems to settle all around us in the small clearing.

I wait for them to finish.

Honestly, I'm unsure how much they'll want to question me, or even if they might take me to the station or arrest me. After all, a man is dead, and I was the one fighting him when he died. I have no idea what the legal ramifications might be, but the longer I stand here, the more I begin to wonder.

Finally, one of the officers, a looming, sloping-shouldered man with a stern face, turns to me. "Looks like you're lucky to be alive."

"Yes."

I wait to see what will happen next. He folds his notebook shut, turns to Jacobs. "Walk Mr. Banks back to the center. He needs to have those EMTs take a look at that contusion on his head." Then he addresses me again. "And Mr. Banks . . ."

Okay. Here we go.

"Yes?"

"Looks like you saved us some trouble here, saved the taxpayers a lot of money. I'm sure as questions arise, we'll be in touch." Without another word, he puts away the notepad, turns back to the body, and Deputy Jacobs motions for me to return with him up the hill.

It takes a moment for the facts of the situation to settle in, but then it strikes me that although there'll undoubtedly be more questions to answer and probably sheaves of paperwork to fill out, for now it looks like the officers aren't going to give me a hard time about Banner's death.

Instead the tall officer had essentially thanked me for getting Banner off their hands.

I'm a bit surprised by my initial thought, but in the end I agree with it: *Actually, you know what, Deputy? It was my pleasure.*

Jacobs trudges beside me as we ascend the muddy hill. "They'll probably want to take you to the hospital. Check you over."

Actually, that wouldn't be bad. It would give me a chance to see how Tanbyrn is doing.

And get your ribs X-rayed. A fractured one could puncture your lung.

Yeah, that would ruin my day.

You can't do the kind of stunts I've done over the years and not come away with your share of broken bones, and I've cracked ribs before but never seriously broken one. Either way, deep breathing or coughing was not going to be fun for the next couple weeks, but it would be good to find out the severity of the damage.

"Also," I tell him, "there's a woman who needs to come along. That guy cut her last night. Sliced her arm. She's back at the center."

"Alright." He pulls out his walkie-talkie. "Let's get you two an ambulance."

Riah presented herself at Cyrus's office, and the receptionist, Caitlyn Vaughn, led her grudgingly through the door.

She entered and found Cyrus alone, studying the aquariums containing the wasps. Without even mentioning their meeting with the twins last night, he invited her to join him. "Come here, Riah. There's something I want you to see. She's building her nest around the roach. I think you'll like this part."

Riah presented herself at Cyrus's office, and the receptionist, Caitlyn Vaughn, led her grudgingly through the door.

On the way to the hospital, I call Xavier and tell him to meet us there, then I contact Fionna and give her the phone numbers I'd pulled from Banner's cell and the alphanumeric code I'd gotten from the sheet of paper in his pocket. I also mention Project Alpha, the name of the research program Dr. Tanbyrn had started to tell us about just before the fire. "Look into it. See what you can find out. And see if you can find any reference to someone named Akinsanya."

When we were in his office, right after we smelled the gasoline, Charlene had taken Tanbyrn's folder of notes and his iPad and stuffed them into her shirt to save them from the fire. Now, in the ambulance, she has the iPad on her lap, but we find that it's password protected and we can't access the files. The algorithms on the sheets of paper are still as unintelligible to me as they were earlier when I was sitting at Tanbyrn's desk.

I ask Charlene how she's holding up.

"I don't know . . . I mean, what happened to Abina . . ." A deep sadness pervades her words. "It's so senseless. She seemed really nice and I can't believe that guy just . . ." She shudders. "I'm worried about Tanbyrn too. And about you—about your head." I'm a little glad I hadn't told her about my ribs.

The paramedic had given me an ice pack and I'm holding it tenderly against my swollen temple. I take a shot at trying to lighten the mood: "You didn't see that branch. It got the worse end of the deal."

She smiles faintly at that.

I reach over and take her hand.

For a moment she's quiet, then speaks softly: "The test is over, Jevin. We don't need to pretend anymore."

I don't always know the right thing to say to her, but this time I do. "I'm not pretending."

And instead of pulling away, she repositions her hand to hold more tightly onto mine.

Savants

Things at the hospital proceed quickly.

Xavier is waiting for us and, despite the objections of the nurses, hovers while they fret over the contusion on my head and while a doctor takes a careful look at Charlene's arm. I overhear the doc tell her that she's still in the window to get stitches, but that it was good she came in now.

Tanbyrn is still unconscious, and because of the amount of smoke inhalation, his age, and his apparently frail health, he's listed in critical condition. The doctors say it's possible he may slip into a coma.

I take some Advil for my mild concussion, the nurses leave me alone while they order an X-ray for my ribs, Charlene heads down the hall to get her stitches, and I start bringing Xavier up to speed, but I'm distracted by the furry-looking bologna and cheese sandwich he's eating. "Where did you get that thing, anyway?"

"A vending machine."

"A vending machine."

"Yup."

"Looks like it's been there a month."

"Tastes like it too." But that doesn't stop him from taking another bite. "But I've had worse."

"I'm not sure I needed to know that."

He listens carefully as I go on with my summary of what happened at the center, and in between bites of his sandwich, he interrupts to make observations about the heat flux of the fire, the likelihood of full-room involvement—flashover—in the doctor's office. "The paneled walls lined with books—man, you wouldn't have had much time."

"Let's just hope we got out soon enough for Tanbyrn."

"Yeah." A pause. "You did good back there, bro."

"Thanks."

"I bet it felt good too." Talking with his mouth full.

"You mean helping Tanbyrn?"

He polishes off the sandwich, licks the grease off his fingers. "Yeah, that and escaping—getting out of the office, through the fire, picking that lock to get out of the building. I bet it felt good to be back in the zone again."

"The zone?"

"Who you are, Jev. What you do. You're an escape artist."

"I'm a filmmaker."

"No. You're an escape artist."

No, you're not. Not anymore.

I leave the topic alone. "Hopefully, Tanbyrn will pull through."

"Yeah." A moment passes. "So you got the footage with the button camera?"

"It's at the cabin back at the center."

"And the test didn't appear to be faked?"

"Not that I could tell, no."

"So that means if the entanglement stuff is for real—that means you and Charlene are—"

"Friends."

"Friends."

"Right."

He winks at me knowingly. "Gotcha."

"No, no. Don't do that, Xav."

"What?"

"That whole innocent 'gotcha' routine. We're just friends."

"Who are entangled."

I open my mouth to respond, change my mind. "Never mind."

He produces a pen from his pocket and flips open his leather-bound journal. Actual paper. Very old-school. "You mentioned that Tanbyrn told you about something called Project Alpha."

"He said it involved two men, twins. He just called them 'L' and 'N.' Said they'd fly in . . ." Something else the doctor mentioned comes to mind, distracts me.

Right before you smelled the gasoline, what did he say?

Negative?

Negative what?

Xavier waits. "You alright?"

"Yeah, I'm just . . ." My thoughts scurry off in a hundred directions.

"So they'd fly the twins in . . . and . . . ?"

"Sorry. Right. He mentioned that the studies involved communication and physiology, alpha brain waves, that identical twins are more capable of . . . well, he didn't clarify. I assume that he was studying the negative effects of something concerning the mind-to-mind communication. He never had the chance to explain."

Xavier writes in his journal while I verbally try to sort through what we know: "RixoTray is funding research on mind-to-mind communication. According to Fionna's research—wait . . ." This was high-stakes conspiracy stuff, right up his alley. "Dr. Tanbyrn was studying the phenomenon of one person's loving thoughts nonlocally affecting the physiology of the person he or she loved."

"Uh-huh. And your results with Charlene bore that out."

Not this again. "I told you we're—"

"Friends."

"Right."

"Gotcha."

"Stop that. And don't say 'gotcha.'"

"See, you really can read minds." He crumples up the wrapper from his sandwich. Sets it aside.

"Xav, my point is, it's two people who genuinely care about each other. I'm not certain they would need to be lovers exactly."

He sees where I'm going with this. "So, you're thinking family members in this case? These two twins?"

I stand. Pace. Weave the 1895 Morgan Dollar through my fingers to help clear my head. "Right. Tanbyrn mentioned they were special. Well, what if they have a really close emotional connection like my boys did? Drew and Tony. You remember that. At times they seemed to almost read each other's minds."

Even though Xavier wasn't related to the boys, he'd fulfilled the role of the cool uncle every kid wishes to have, and I know he misses them acutely.

"Yeah, I do remember. There were times when they would finish each other's sentences. Like they were connected in a way no one else is."

For a moment I'm quiet. "I don't think I ever told you about what happened one day with Drew. When his side started hurting."

"What was it?"

"I was playing with him outside. T-ball. I was behind him holding his arms, helping him with his swing, when suddenly he dropped the bat and turned and clung to me, hugged me. 'What's wrong?' I asked him. And he started crying. I knelt and held him. 'What is it?' And he said, 'It hurts, Daddy!' He was holding his right side. That's when I heard Rachel calling for us from inside the house. It was Tony. His appendix had burst."

"You're kidding."

"No. Drew's pain went away while we were driving to the hospital, but still, I wracked my brain trying to figure out how it had happened. It couldn't have been a coincidence—but if it wasn't, then what was it? What caused Drew to feel Tony's pain?"

Xavier taps his pen against the page. "You hear stories like that sometimes. People waking up in the middle of the night with chest pains and finding out later that their mom or dad had a heart attack at that very moment, or having a gut feeling not to walk down a certain street and then finding out there was a mugger who was caught down there. Once when my sister and I were in high school, she had the sense one night that she was being watched, and when she turned off the light to her bedroom, she saw a face of one of the boys from her class outside her window."

"That's disturbing."

"You should have seen what I did to him when I caught up with him the next day. Anyway, all this stuff, these gut feelings, déjà vu, premonitions, UFO sightings, stigmata appearing on people—I know you don't like to hear this, but there's a lot that happens out there that just can't be easily explained."

Discounting his reference to UFO sightings, he's right that there are a lot of things out there that can't be explained, at least not in the typical ways, and since I've spent the last year trying to prove that those things can be explained, the fact that he's right annoys me.

He goes on, "Do you think there might be senses that some people have that others don't?"

"You mean a sixth sense?" I don't even try to hide my skepticism at that. "No. I don't buy that."

"Step away from the idea of psychic powers for a minute."

"And aliens."

"Okay, and aliens. Think about it, what if there are senses that we're supposed to have, that aren't breaking any physical laws or depending on any divine or malevolent forces—only gifts, skills, talents that aren't any more supernatural than twins sharing behavioral traits that genetics can't explain. Nobody calls autistic savants who can perform complex quadratic equations in seconds 'psychics.'"

"You mean even though they haven't studied math."

"Yes. Or Down syndrome children who can hear a tune once on the piano and can perform it flawlessly—"

"Okay, I see what you're saying."

"In the past those people, or maybe child prodigies, might've been considered psychic or witches or demon-possessed, but modern science—although it can't always explain the behavior—has, for some reason, grown to accept them as unusual, outside of the realm of normal experience, but not paranormal."

He pauses, then out of nowhere he waves his hand through the air as if to erase our conversation, and I'm not sure why; he seemed to make a good point. "Anyway, I don't want to lose my train of thought. You were telling me that these twins, 'L' and 'N,' they flew in, Tanbyrn did some sort of tests, they'd fly out. We don't know what the tests are about, but we do know that RixoTray has been funding them."

I'm more than happy to leave the topics of psychics and UFOs behind as well. "Last night Charlene was reading over the notes that Fionna drew up on RixoTray, and she came across the name of a doctor in Philadelphia. Riah something."

Negative.

The doctor said he was studying the negative effects—

Oh.

Flipping the coin faster. "Xav, what if it's not just loving thoughts that affect people?"

"You mean negative thoughts? That's what Tanbyrn was looking into with these two guys?"

"I don't know, but—"

Negative.

Why would the Pentagon be involved with this?

Xavier waits. "But?"

"But what about this." I stop finger-flipping the coin. Stare at him. "If one person can affect the heart rate of another person—even slightly—just by his thoughts, could he learn to do more than that?"

He straightens up. "Are you saying what I think you're saying?"

"Yes, affect his heart rate to a greater degree—possibly give it an uneven rhythm, cause it to beat faster, or—"

"Stop it."

"Yes, exactly. Or stop it."

Project Alpha

For a long time neither of us speaks. It all seems unbelievable to me that the research might have gone in this direction, but whether this was all conjecture or not, the facts we have so far do seem to fit this line of reasoning. "Project Alpha is a cooperative program with the Department of Defense."

"The government." Xavier nods as if that explains everything. "Just like Star Gate."

"What, you mean the TV show?"

He waves his hand dismissively. "No. It has nothing to do with that or the movie. Star Gate was a CIA program back in the nineties. They were studying psychics to try and use remote viewing—basically, observing something without being physically present."

"Clairvoyance."

"Right. They were hoping it would help with intelligence gathering."

"Which, obviously, it would have." Normally I'm doubtful about Xavier's government conspiracy theories, but in this case, considering everything that's happened over the last twenty-four hours, I'm a lot more willing to listen. "Go on."

"They also tried to use psychics to manipulate objects—telekinesis—so you could conceivably cause a Russian nuclear reactor to overheat, or a torpedo to explode while it was still in the firing tube of a sub. That sort of thing."

Telekinesis is one of the most common tricks of television "psychics," and one of the easiest ones to replicate—bending spoons, making objects float or vanish, affecting the performance of machines—I'd been doing this stuff since I was a teenager. But those were all illusions, and what Xavier was talking about here was on a whole different level. "So did the CIA have any success?"

"The short answer is no." He seems to balance that mentally, re-evaluate it. "There were mixed results in the remote viewing arena, but that's about it. Anyway, they dropped the program. The Air Force and DoD dabbled in similar research over the years, but nothing really came of it."

Knowing Xavier and his predilection for conspiracy theories, if there was anything at all to this research, he would've been all over it.

I reflect on what he said. "Okay, but that was a couple decades ago. Now, with Tanbyrn's research, with recent discoveries in neurophysiology and neurobiology, the nature of consciousness, this deeper understanding of quantum entanglement—"

"The Pentagon has picked it up again—that's what you're thinking?"

"That's what I'm wondering."

Everything I've done exposing fake psychics seems to argue against what we're talking about here. Telekinesis, clairvoyance, altering someone's heart rate by your thoughts. The idea of directing negative energy toward someone to harm him in some way, or even kill him—it was just too much. Reminded me of River Tam in *Firefly*: "I can kill you with my brain." This couldn't possibly be the right track.

"No, Xav. To kill someone by your thoughts? That's crazy."

If it were possible, why not just do that with Tanbyrn? Why hire an assassin to take him out?

"But," Xavier replies, "there are stories of shamans, witch doctors, voodoo priestesses doing that—cursing people—stories that've been around for centuries."

"That's just folklore. Like the legends about the fakirs in India levitating or being buried alive for years on end, and so on. You know as well as I do that every trick in the book can be replicated without any supernatural explanation. You helped design half the effects in my last stage show."

Xavier taps his lip, deep in thought. "'But to emulate is not to disprove.' A wise person once told me that."

"I appreciate the compliment but—"

"He also told me that replication is not refutation, that just because you can find the counterfeit of something doesn't mean there isn't the real thing. Just because there's counterfeit currency doesn't mean there isn't actual currency out there somewhere."

"Xavier, I—"

"It could be that science is just now discovering what people of faith have always known—that our thoughts and expectations about reality affect its outcome in real, tangible ways. That's what quantum physics is all about, right? The role of consciousness in collapsing quantum wave functions, that without an observer, reality never manifests itself?"

"You read Tanbyrn's books too?"

"Skimmed a few chapters while you were at the center. Think about it: nearly every religion believes in the power of thoughts and prayers, curses and blessings. They're a huge deal in the Judeo-Christian tradition, especially the Old Testament. And then of course you have the New Testament where Jesus was clairvoyant, telepathic, and telekinetic."

I stare at him. "What are you talking about?"

Xavier ticks the reasons off on his fingers as he lists them: "Clairvoyance—he saw Nathanael under a fig tree when he wasn't present. Telepathy—he read the thoughts of the Pharisees. Telekinesis—turning water into wine, having Peter catch a fish to pay the temple tax and the fish has a coin in its mouth . . ."

"Oh, so you're saying that Jesus either made the coin appear there or somehow made the fish swallow it and then swim into Peter's net."

"Right." Next finger. "And as far as prayers and curses—his prayers drove demons out of people, healed them, even raised people from the dead."

"He didn't curse anybody."

"He cursed a fig tree and made it wither."

I'm not sure if Xavier just made that up or not.

He looks triumphant at his list, however, it's easy enough to rebut what he said. "Okay, suppose for a moment that those stories are true, not just folklore. If Jesus was who he claimed to be, if he was God, then those were just miracles."

"Just miracles? What do you mean *just* miracles?"

"I mean, he was God. He could do anything."

"No, he couldn't."

I look at him skeptically. "Jesus couldn't do anything."

"The Bible says he couldn't do any great miracles in his hometown because of the people's lack of faith. It doesn't say he wouldn't do them, it says he couldn't."

I shake my head. "No. I can't imagine that's in the Bible."

"Look it up. The power of God himself was strangled by the lack of belief."

"That's a little extreme, I'd say."

"Besides, he told his followers that nothing is impossible if you have enough faith, that they would do even greater things than he did if they believed: that if they had enough faith, they could tell a mountain to stand up and move across the street."

"How—how do you know all this, anyway?"

"Sunday school. I was a very attentive child. And I've done a little research over the years. Some people think Jesus was from another planet. Or another dimension. Could have been a time traveler. It's not really clear."

"Aha." Now that sounds more like Xavier.

I'm not exactly sure where all of this leaves us. The inexplicable test results from the study earlier today come to mind—my thoughts actually causing Charlene's heart rate to change. Maybe there is something to this idea that thoughts alter reality, but I still feel really uncomfortable going there. "Xav, regardless of the power of curses or blessings or prayers or faith or miracles or focused thoughts or chi or any of those things to alter reality, there's one tangible step we can take to verify if any of this relates to Project Alpha."

"What's that?"

"Find out what Dr. Tanbyrn's diagrams and algorithms mean. And figure out a way to access his iPad." I stand, open the door. "Come on. Let's find Charlene. Last I heard she was down the hall getting stitches."

Stitches

Riah was watching the wasp build a nest around the helpless cockroach when the twins entered the office.

"Oriana called us," Daniel told her and Cyrus. "She's running a little late but should be here in the next twenty minutes or so."

So, Williamson's first name is Oriana. But who is she?

"We'll wait for her before starting the video," Daniel said to Cyrus, then: "But more importantly, did you hear about Dr. Tanbyrn?"

Riah immediately recognized the name; after all, she'd spent the day studying his research findings.

"No. What happened?"

"There was a fire at the center. He's in the hospital."

Cyrus looked puzzled. "In the hospital?"

"He was almost killed in the fire. Apparently, the arsonist who started the fire is dead."

"Really?"

Darren answered for his brother, "The news report wasn't really clear if he died in the fire or if he died when he was fleeing and the authorities tried to apprehend him."

Cyrus was quiet for a long moment. "Well, let's hope Dr. Tanbyrn pulls through."

Darren set a tablet computer on the edge of the desk. Scrolled to an online news feed. "I'll keep an eye on the story. Dr. Tanbyrn's condition will no doubt be of concern to Oriana."

"No doubt." Cyrus reached for the intercom button on his desk phone next to his open laptop. "I'll have Caitlyn bring us some coffee. While we wait."

~

It takes a few minutes, but finally Xavier and I find Charlene in an exam room two doors down an adjacent hallway. There's a fresh bandage on her arm.

"How many stitches did you need?" I ask her.

"Sixteen."

"Sixteen." Xavier nods. "Nice. We're talking some quality scar material there."

"I don't want a scar, Xav."

"Hey, they make great conversation starters. I've got one here on my knee from—"

"How's it feeling?" I cut in, directing my question at Charlene. It's really not a good idea to get Xavier started on scar stories.

"Local anesthetic. I can't really feel it at all."

"Glad to hear that."

We move on to the reason we came, and she listens reflectively as I tell her what Xavier and I have been debating. When I finish, she gets right to the point: "If your thoughts could be fatal to someone else, it would be almost like having the ability to spread a thought-borne virus. How on earth could anyone fight against that?"

"Magneto," Xavier mutters. "His helmet blocks Professor X's telepathy from working. We could use a couple of those."

The irony that Xavier's first name is Professor X's last name isn't lost on me.

"Too bad they're not real," Charlene responds.

"You never know."

Actually, knowing Xavier's friends, I wouldn't have been surprised if some of them were working on something like that as we speak.

A thought-borne virus.

An apt way to describe what we're talking about. Frightening. I tell Charlene, "We came in here so we could take another look at the pages from Tanbyrn's files. See if we can find a way into that iPad."

As she's pulling out Tanbyrn's notes and iPad, the door beside me opens and a severe-looking nurse emerges, straddling the door frame. "There you are." She levels her gaze at me as if she's sighting down the barrel of a gun. "They're waiting for you in the X-ray room."

Charlene looks at me concernedly. "X-ray?"

"Just to check on something." I'd kept the rib injury to myself, but now I gently tap my side. "Might be a cracked rib."

"You broke a rib?" she gasps.

"Cracked it, maybe. Just a little. I'm not sure if it's—"

"Jevin, why didn't you say anything!"

A guy's gotta at least try to be heroic.

"Um, no reason. Exactly."

She looks at me reprovingly. "That rib better not be broken or I'm going to have to hurt you."

"I'm not sure that's really going to—"

The nurse clears her throat.

I signal to her that I'll be with her in a moment, but say to Charlene, "I'll be back as soon as I can. See if Fionna can help you get into that iPad. And Xavier, this guy Banner killed at least one person today. I want to find out what's at the bottom of all this. Call your friends and have them pull up everything they can on Star Gate and Project Alpha. Any other telepathic research the military might be doing. I want the best conspiracy theorist minds out there on this thing."

He smiles. "Groovy."

As I leave, I notice I have six text messages from my producer at Entertainment Film Network telling me to call her.

Well, I guess someone's been watching the news.

But this doesn't feel like the right time to talk with her. I need to sort through some things first, decide exactly where we are on this project. Pocketing the phone, I follow the rather stout nurse to the X-ray room.

~

Cyrus Arlington knew that if that idiot Banner had been careless, there was the possibility that the police would be able to tie him to the fire. To the attempt on Tanbyrn's life.

He'd never given Banner his name, had used only a prepaid cell phone that no one would be able to trace, had paid him the down payment of $12,500 in unmarked, nonsequential bills. But still . . .

As he waited for Oriana to arrive and drank the coffee that Caitlyn had brought in, Cyrus thought of what he would tell the police if they ever came knocking at his door.

While his jewel wasp finished encasing her roach.

Oriana

I'm lying on my side on the X-ray table finishing the second of four X-rays of my ribs when my phone rings. The technicians had asked me to leave it on a counter inside the protected area where they were working, but even from here I recognize the ringtone.

Fionna.

Well, that was quick.

I excuse myself, and the frizzy-haired woman working the X-ray machine declares in no uncertain terms that she needs two more slides before I can go anywhere.

"No problem." I slip past her into the hall and answer my phone. A bit chilly without my shirt on.

"Nothing yet on Akinsanya or Tanbyrn's iPad," Fionna tells me. "It would be a lot easier if I had it in hand. But I do have something for you. Guess who your arsonist has been calling?"

"Who?"

"The CEO of RixoTray Pharmaceuticals."

"What?"

"It was with an unregistered prepaid cell, but I was able to backtrace the call and follow the GPS location to—"

"Wait a minute. If it was unregistered, how did you backtrace it?"

"Through AT&T's tech center."

"You hacked into their—"

"Not exactly. They hired me to do that last quarter. I kept my notes. Anyway, the GPS location for a previous call matches his residential address, and the most recent call just happens to line up with his office at RixoTray's corporate headquarters."

"Nice work."

"That's why you pay me the big bucks."

Actually, it was.

"Also, that passcode, the one you found in Banner's pocket, well, it's not just a password to the Lawson Center's RixoTray files, it's the one to a certain person's computer."

"You're not saying it's the same guy? The CEO?"

"Yup. Dr. Cyrus Arlington."

Okay, now that's interesting.

How would Banner have gotten Arlington's personal password?

"So, Fionna, this is all illegal, of course? Everything you just did?"

"Well, RixoTray did hire me to try getting past their firewalls and hacking into their system. I guess I'm just good at my job."

That works for me.

"Anyway, I pulled up Arlington's computer screen. There's an image, the beginning of a video. It's paused. It has something to do with—"

"Let me guess." I think of our earlier conversation, anticipate what she's going to say: "Kabul. The bombing that was averted."

"Right." Fionna sounds disappointed. "Of course, I can't be positive, but it looks like it, yes. How did you guess that, by the way?"

"What you told me earlier; I'm starting to think like you. Listen, can you send me a copy of that image?"

"Better than that. I'm going to send you a link to the screen. If he starts the video, you'll be able to watch it right along with him."

"You deserve a raise, Fionna."

"I could use one. Donnie needs braces."

We hang up, and against the firm objections of the X-ray technician, I grab my shirt and leave to find Xavier and Charlene.

The X-rays can wait. Right now it's movie time.

～

Riah heard the door open.

A woman entered, brisk and businesslike. Hair short, an Ellen DeGeneres boy cut. She was slightly built, just over five feet tall, but carried a commanding presence that drew the immediate attention of everyone in the room.

She nodded toward the twins, greeted Cyrus, then directed her gaze at Riah. "You must be Colette."

Riah was a keen enough observer of human behavior to realize that there were certain societal protocols on how to address people, how to treat them. It didn't mean that she necessarily understood why those conventions were in place, but it was immediately obvious that this woman did not follow them.

"Dr. Riah Colette, yes," she told her. "I'm the head researcher on this project." She decided to try something. "You don't have to call me Dr. Colette, though. I'm fine with Riah."

A small fire appeared in the woman's eyes, and Riah could tell she was not used to being spoken to so directly. The response intrigued her. Oriana might be an interesting person to observe. To test.

"I am Undersecretary of Defense Oriana Williamson. And that's what you will call me."

Undersecretary of Defense? Riah wasn't sure how high exactly that went up in the Pentagon's command chain, but she knew it had to be close to the top.

Fascinating.

Undersecretary Williamson, who was currently dressed in civilian clothes, looked away from Riah toward Cyrus. "I don't care if she's been vetted. I told you it was too late to bring anyone else in on this. I do not like—"

"I'm not just being brought in on this," Riah corrected her. "I mentioned a moment ago that I'm the head of the project at the R&D facility. I'm the one developing the neural decoding—"

"Synthetic telepathy."

Riah had never liked that term. It made what she was doing sound somehow paranormal when it was simply the development of a brain-computer interface. "What's your connection with it? Again?" She purposely posed the question in a challenging way to gauge how Oriana would respond. Riah was struck by the fact that Cyrus had at some point vetted her, gotten her military clearance to be here tonight.

Or did the twins do it?

The undersecretary scoffed at her. "You have no idea what this project is about."

"Ma'am." Daniel stepped forward, interrupting them. "Dr. Colette knows more about deep-brain stimulation of the Wernicke's area than anyone. If we're ever going to make this work with individuals, rather than just twins, she'll be the one to figure out how."

Darren nodded. "My brother and I need her in on this project if we're going to be able to move forward with it on the time frame we've discussed."

Williamson let out a small sigh of resignation. "Dr. Colette—"

"Riah really is fine."

A set jaw. "Dr. Colette, you realize that the material on this video is absolutely confidential and you may not share what you see with anyone. It concerns matters of national security."

National security?

She really had been vetted.

"Well?"

Riah had no idea who she might even be tempted to share the contents of the video with. "Of course."

The Undersecretary of Defense pulled out a sheaf of papers. "Before we move forward, I need you to sign these release forms."

"She's been cleared," Cyrus reiterated. "She wouldn't be part of the project if she weren't."

"It's alright," Riah told him, then quickly scanned the papers and signed them.

The undersecretary collected the papers, filed them in her briefcase. "Alright. Let's watch this video."

Cyrus gestured toward the hall and picked up his laptop. "It'll be easier for everyone to see if we use the screen in the conference room."

The Footage

Charlene, Xavier, and I find an empty exam room. Slip inside. Xavier closes the door behind us. "I made some calls. I have some of the best people out there working on Project Alpha and Star Gate."

"Good."

As he's locking the door, my phone vibrates.

A text.

The link from Fionna.

I click it.

An image comes up: a room with plaster-covered walls, a ceiling fan, and a window overlooking a Middle Eastern city.

~

The twins sat across the table from Riah and Undersecretary of Defense Williamson. Even though Riah knew that all the other people in the room were previously acquainted, she didn't feel out of place. A lack of social anxiety was actually one of the perks for people with her condition.

The sprawling oval conference table lay centered in the room. Cyrus tapped a button on a console on the table, and the lights dimmed to a preset for watching videos. Then he depressed another button, and a large screen lowered from the ceiling and covered the front wall.

Williamson steepled her hands, leaned forward, asked Cyrus, "So have you seen it yet?"

"Not yet. No." He connected his laptop to the projector system.

She faced the twins. "And you?"

"No."

Riah didn't wait for the question. "I haven't seen it yet either. But I'm looking forward to it."

"Well. So am I."

The image from the laptop appeared on the projector screen. A room in Kabul.

Cyrus tapped the space bar and the video began.

The video begins.

We watch as the camera pans across the room, revealing two bearded men in Middle Eastern clothes standing beside a table. They're speaking rapidly in a language I don't immediately recognize.

"It's Arabic," Xavier announces.

"How do you—" Charlene begins.

"Shh."

One of the men steps aside, and I can see a table littered with wires, cell phones, detonators, a pile of nails, and several boxes of ball bearings. The audio on the recording is remarkably good, and I can hear the rush of traffic and the intermittent blaring of horns outside the window.

The taller of the two men walks toward the window and tugs at the threadbare curtains. They don't close all the way, however, and leave a gap nearly a foot wide, allowing for a narrow view of the building across the street.

"The guy who's filming this . . ." Xavier points to my phone's screen. "He's gotta be wearing a button camera like the one I gave you. Doesn't look like his buddies know they're being recorded." He studies the video carefully, mumbles something about the grade of the C-4 on the table. "Oh yeah. That's gonna leave a mark."

There are three suicide vests beside the explosives.

A few more words in Arabic.

I'm pretty sure I know how this is going to end, and I can feel a palpable rush of apprehension.

You're about to watch these people die.

The man beside the table faces the person filming the scene and speaks to him. I have no idea what he's saying, but I do make out the words "Allahu Akbar." The person with the camera repeats the words, and the tenor of his voice confirms that he's male. Then all three men echo the phrase again.

The man closest to the table takes off his long-sleeved shirt and picks up the suicide vest.

I think again of what Fionna told me earlier: there was a thwarted attack on a Kabul mosque, an unconfirmed number of terrorists were killed.

The research Dr. Tanbyrn was working on before the fire was a joint project between the Pentagon and RixoTray Pharmaceuticals.

RixoTray's CEO, Dr. Cyrus Arlington, was in communication with Glenn Banner hours before the fire.

Mind-to-mind research . . .

Telepathy . . .

The twins . . .

If you can affect someone's physiology, can you consciously change it?

If you can alter someone's heart rate, could you stop it?

All the facts circle elusively around each other, and I try to find a way to fit them together.

"Oh," I whisper. "They're going to kill him."

"What?" Charlene breathes.

"Watch. The guy with the vest, they're going to kill him."

The man slips the vest on, tightens some straps to secure it in place, then puts his loose-fitting long-sleeved shirt back on over the vest. It's not noticeable beneath his shirt, and if I didn't know he was wearing it, I never would have guessed that he was an armed suicide bomber.

I can feel my chest tensing up.

The taller man, the one nearest the window, peers past the ratty curtains for a moment, then joins his two cohorts in the middle of the room.

I hear the words "Allahu Akbar" repeated again by the three men in the group.

The man wearing the vest turns toward the window.

And then.

Explodes.

For a fraction of a second you can see the blast, a blur of color and fabric flaring toward the camera lens overwhelmed by a deafening roar.

And then there's nothing but a blank, silent screen.

Neither Charlene nor Xavier speaks.

So I was wrong.

They didn't stop the guy's heart.

Manipulating matter? Telekinesis? They made the bomb explode?

That seemed even more implausible.

At last Charlene speaks: "Wow."

Xavier shakes his head. "How did they get this footage? The camera was destroyed, so this footage was obviously being transmitted to someone—and then that person sends it to the CEO of one of the world's largest pharmaceutical firms? Are you kidding me?"

"I don't think he intended to do that," I tell them.

"Who?"

"The suicide bomber. It's hard to tell, but it didn't look like he reached for the vest. Neither of the other guys touched the cell phones to detonate it. Also, he put his shirt back on right after putting on the vest. Why would he do that if he was just going to blow up his buddies right there in the room?"

"You think it malfunctioned?"

"No. And I don't think he detonated it. I think somehow the twins did it for him."

~∾~

Cyrus shut off the video and Riah waited for him to comment, for any of the four people she was with to speak.

Finally, Williamson did. "So it works."

"Yes," Daniel said quietly. "Apparently it does."

~∾~

I expect Xavier to be on the same page with what I just said, to agree with me about the evil schemes of the federal government's secret psychic research and black-ops assassination programs, but both he and Charlene seem skeptical. "Tanbyrn's study concerned mind-to-mind communication," he reminds me, "not telekinesis."

"As far as we know. But it could have something to do with quantum entanglement. Manipulating matter nonlocally. Remember? Like the nuclear reactor or the torpedo?" But even as I try to convince them, I begin to doubt it myself, and the more implausible the whole telekinesis angle seems. I sigh. "You're right. I don't know. We'd need more information to tell."

The link on my phone expires, and when I try to refresh it, I'm unsuccessful.

I doubt Fionna would have severed the connection. Maybe someone at RixoTray did.

Just in case the video comes back on, I leave the browser open, set down my phone, and ask to borrow Charlene's. She's more than happy to give it to me.

I really have no idea how deep all this goes or who we can trust, but Abina is dead, Dr. Tanbyrn might die, the three people in the video are dead. RixoTray's CEO is involved with this and has ties to the Pentagon as well as to the guy who carried those eleven photographs of corpses in his wallet. There's no way all of this was simply a local law enforcement matter, and with the DoD's involvement I don't trust going to the federal government with what we know either.

For a moment I consider contacting the media, but then the obvious fact hits me in the face—*You film documentaries, Jevin. You are the media.*

I'm not about to just sit on the sidelines until more people start showing up dead.

"Charlene, last night you told me about a researcher at RixoTray who was in charge of this program. What was her name again?"

"Dr. Riah Colette."

I navigate to the internet browser on her phone.

"Are you going to call her?"

"No, I think we need to talk to her face-to-face."

I find what I'm looking for. Dial the number.

"Then who are you calling?" Xavier asks.

"I'm getting us a plane. We're going to Philadelphia."

Family Ties

Charlene looks at me curiously. "Philadelphia?"

"Arlington is there. He's connected with Banner, with the attempt on Tanbyrn's—and our—lives. Colette is there. RixoTray's headquarters is there. If we're going to crack this open, we need to be there too."

"What about the police?" she asks me. "Or the FBI? Shouldn't we just go to them?"

Xavier shakes his head. He must've been thinking the same thing I was a minute ago. "And when they ask why we suspect that the CEO of one of the largest pharmaceutical firms in the world is involved in conspiracy to commit murder, I suppose we'll just tell them that we hacked into his computer and phone records after getting the information off the body of the man Jevin killed."

That was an interesting way to put it.

I'm still on hold, waiting for someone from the charter plane company to speak to me. "Right now we have ties between all these things but no proof. Until we know more, we'd be accused of making unfounded accusations."

"Which would be true," Xavier points out.

She considers that.

"We do exposés, right?" I think of Abina again, of justice, of un-covering the truth. "Well, let's expose something that really matters."

The charter service's rep picks up, apologizes for the wait, and asks how she may be of assistance to me.

So far no one had offered Riah an explanation.

At last Cyrus typed on his keyboard and a photo appeared on the projector screen.

Three people: a Middle Eastern woman in her late thirties standing beside a dark-skinned, attractive girl in her teens, and the bearded man who'd strapped on the suicide vest in the video. Riah was surprised that a fundamentalist Muslim suicide bomber would allow his wife and daughter to be photographed without their burkas' veils cover-ing their faces.

Is it a fake?

"Malik was married," Cyrus explained. "He had a wife and a fourteen-year-old daughter. If he'd backed out, not gone through with it, they would have been punished."

Riah had heard enough about the culture and beliefs of Islamic fundamentalist society to know that "punished" in this case probably meant publicly shamed, or quite possibly raped or even killed.

"What do you mean if he'd backed out?"

"This way," Undersecretary of Defense Williamson said, not an-swering her question, "by all accounts it looks to the other members of his group that it was an accident."

"What does that mean: this way it looks like it was an accident?"

"We let him do it."

Still no direct answers. "You let him do what? Detonate the vest?"

Cyrus said, "Riah, your research, your work with the twins, helped save innocent lives, protected Malik's wife and daughter from retribu-tion had he failed to go through with his mission, and it helped eliminate a terrorist threat and take care of three members of an al-Qaeda cell."

"I research ways to decipher neural activity related to linguistic patterns. How did my research do any of that?"

"Dr. Colette," Daniel offered, "this man was planning to kill himself and possibly hundreds of innocent people at a mosque. People who had assembled to worship God."

"But you're saying this wasn't an accident? That somehow you let him do it. Does that mean you influenced him to do it?"

"He was planning to do it already."

Riah wasn't rattled by the fact that no one was giving her a straight answer, but she was becoming more and more curious about why that was the case. "You're telling me that you somehow convinced this man to kill himself?" She looked at the twins. "But how?"

It took Darren a long time to answer.

"The circumstances concerning his death are one of the reasons we wanted you here. We need you to help us put them into context."

Okay, so that was finally an answer, but it was certainly not the one she'd expected.

"How can I do that?"

The twins rose almost in unison. Daniel said, "We'll meet you tomorrow morning at 9:15 in the R&D facility, room 27B. We'll explain everything then."

Based on the concern Cyrus and the twins had shown earlier for Dr. Tanbyrn's condition, Riah had expected that the topic of the fire at the center in Oregon would come up again, but now it appeared that everyone was ready to leave. All of this was fascinating and intriguing to her. She agreed to meet with the twins in the morning, if only to find out what they were using her research for: "I'll be there. I'll see you at 9:15."

And that was that.

They headed toward the door, Oriana mentioned to Cyrus that she would tell her oversight committee to extend the funding, and then she excused herself as well.

The meeting had ended in the same shroud of questions that had pervaded it.

Cyrus escorted Riah past Caitlyn Vaughn at the reception desk and down the elevator. "About last night, coming over to your apartment . . . the sleepover. Does the offer still stand?"

Riah understood that his question was a test, a way of feeling out how needy she was, how dependent on him, and she decided to show him that she was not the dependent one in their relationship. "I'll have to think about that."

She paused, then turned to him, looked deep into his eyes, and trailed her finger across his cheek. "Say hi to Helen tonight for me, will you? Tell that thoughtful wife of yours that coffee tomorrow afternoon sounds like a wonderful idea."

"She invited you out for coffee?"

"Good night, Cyrus."

Then Riah left for her car.

Let him chew on that for a while.

If she'd been a person capable of feeling pleasure, she would have smiled. As it was, she tried one on to see how it felt, but it didn't make her feel anything at all.

I'm not really a fan of commercial airlines, and thankfully, my stage shows over the last decade have done well enough to give me the freedom to be able to bypass those long security lines and groping TSA employees.

It didn't take me long to book the charter plane.

Both Xavier and Charlene know that money isn't really an issue for me, so neither of them bats an eye when I tell them the price tag— just under six thousand dollars per hour. Plus landing fees, fuel, and overnight expenses. "It's really not that bad, actually."

"What does that work out to per peanut?" Xavier asks.

"Hors d'oeuvres," I correct him. "And lobster bisque. Only the best for my friends."

Excusing myself from them for a minute, I find the restroom, then on my way back down the hall, I call Fionna to see if she recorded the video. "I did. I'll get you a copy. Sorry I lost the connection to the laptop after it was finished. Someone on their cybersecurity team must have stumbled onto the breach. But don't worry, I got out before anyone would've been able to find out who was there."

I tell her about our plans to go to Philadelphia.

"How can you be sure that Dr. Colette will even be there?"

Good point. "Um . . ."

"Hang on a second."

Momentarily she gets back into their system and confirms that Dr. Colette's schedule includes some meetings in the morning there in Philly.

"So," Fionna says, "have the charter plane swing by and pick me up."

"What do you mean?"

"Pick me up. Here in Chicago."

"Are you serious?"

"Sure. I'm already up to my neck in this with you, Jevin, and it'll be easier if I can work things from the inside."

"From the inside of what?"

"With Rixo Tray. It looks like I have some rather troubling news to give them—their cybersecurity isn't nearly as good as it needs to be. In fact, the CEO's personal computer is at high risk of a security breach."

There was no arguing with that.

She goes on, "That's something I should discuss with him in person. If I'm with you, I can guarantee you a meeting with Arlington. Besides, you're flying from Oregon to Pennsylvania. You'll practically go right over my house. I'm not sure, but I'd guess a charter plane will need to refuel on a flight across the country."

"Actually, these planes are equipped to—"

"You know as well as I do"—she refuses to give up—"that you'll make more progress if I'm there. I can do a few things from here to try and access that iPad, but from what I've seen, the security on it is reasonably good. It might take me awhile remotely, but I guarantee that if I had it in front of me, I could hash that password in two minutes or less."

Even though I have complete confidence in her ability to work something like this from an off-site location, I have to admit that it would be good to have her there with us in Philadelphia, especially when it came to getting us an audience with Dr. Arlington.

Stopping by Chicago won't really add that much time to the trip. You could still make it to Philadelphia by morning.

"Okay, you've convinced me. I'll set it up and let you know the details about when and where to meet us."

"And my kids come too."

"What? No, that's not—"

"This might take a couple days. I can't leave them alone that long, and it's too late to find someone who'd be able to take in four children."

Lonnie is seventeen and very responsible, but I couldn't help but agree with Fionna that it wouldn't be a good idea to leave him alone to watch his three younger siblings. Fionna doesn't have family in the area, and while she could farm the kids out to their friends' houses, that might be awkward. She was also right that this would likely involve a couple days of work. Still, even taking all that into account, I'm hesitant to say yes.

"I don't know, I'm—"

"They'll be safe in the hotel rooms you're going to get us, if that's what you're worried about. They'll have plenty of security. After all, we're staying at a nice hotel, right? Because it'll really be a lot easier if there's room service."

"This isn't exactly—"

"My kids like to swim, so let's make sure there's an indoor pool."

I wish I could tell her that there wouldn't be enough room on the plane for her and her kids, but the Gulfstream 550 that's on its way to Portland would actually have just enough seats.

I rub my head. "Really? You want me to fly your kids to Philly?"

"You're already paying for the flight, why not get your money's worth? Besides, they're due for a field trip, and they've never been to the City of Brotherly Love."

"You told me earlier today that you took them on a field trip this morning?"

"That doesn't really count. It was in the same state."

Oh. Is that how it works.

"I see."

"You won't regret having them along. Trust me. They can help me out, and from what I've seen, you could use it. I mean, this project is about as confusing as when you have two dozen gerbils running around a pet store and you're trying to catch the one with the little white tuft on his left ear, and you can't seem to find him because all the other ones are just too dang frisky."

I knew a simile would sneak in here eventually. Or an analogy. Or metaphor. I'm not really sure what that one was.

"Where do you get these from, Fionna?"

"Sometimes they just come to me. So?"

I hold back a sigh. "Okay, they can come. But I'm not guaranteeing you a pool."

"Hot tubs in the suites will be fine." She turns from the phone and I hear her calling to her family, "Kids, pack up your things. We're going to Pennsylvania!"

Part II

MEANS of DISPOSAL

Critical Condition

Cyrus slipped into his Jag and took a deep breath.

Had Helen really invited Riah out for coffee? Or was that a lie? If Helen had asked her to meet, did she know about the affair?

He felt his temperature rising.

Who was the wasp here and who was the cockroach? Who was the helpless one? Riah was not the one calling the shots in this, he was. And he was not about to have her try to control him, try to seal him in a corner.

Her mention of Helen annoyed him, really annoyed him. And then, of course, there was this whole botched job with Tanbyrn.

The assassin was dead and the doctor was not.

Cyrus pounded the steering wheel.

How could you have been so stupid to hire an inept goon like him!

Frustrated, he drove toward the drop-off point at First Central Bank, the place Akinsanya had told him to leave the DVD of the footage in Kabul.

Earlier, while they were waiting for Oriana to show up, Cyrus had decided that if the police came knocking, he would tell them the truth: yes, he had been in touch with Banner, had spoken with him on several occasions.

And he would also tell them a lie—Banner had been blackmailing him from the beginning, threatening to expose his affair with Riah.

The conversation played out in his head:

"How did he find out about you and Dr. Colette?" the cops would ask him.

A lie: "He told me he had a tip. That's all he said. He had photographs. Compromising ones."

"What did you pay him?"

The truth: "So far, $12,500. He wanted more. Another twelve five."

"Then why would he burn down the building where they were doing research related to Rixo Tray?"

A lie: "I have no idea. Dr. Colette is in charge of the research project. She might be able to help you with that."

The blackmail angle worked. It explained the money, the fact that Banner had been in touch with him, and the reason Cyrus had kept it all a secret. Admitting to the affair might not help his marriage, but he could work through all that, play the repentant husband, reconcile, move on. Or maybe go back to Caitlyn. She really was a fine little office helper.

But for now there was still the issue of Tanbyrn.

Put quite simply, he knew too much.

You never know—he might already be dead.

Cyrus put the DVD in the mail slot of First Central Bank. The bank was, of course, closed. He had no idea who Akinsanya was, had never met him, only spoken with him on the phone.

He didn't know why Akinsanya had chosen this location, but he was not going to question him, not after the photos Akinsanya had sent him of what he'd done to the people who'd betrayed him or failed him in the past. All using a needle and thick, black thread.

Back in the car, before starting the engine, Cyrus considered his course of action.

He had a meeting tomorrow morning at nine with the vice

president at the White House. Papers to verify, a myriad of details to arrange.

Cyrus took out his cell phone, surfed to a dozen news sites, one after another, to see what details had emerged about the fire at the Lawson Research Center.

He found out that the famous Nobel laureate Dr. Tanbyrn wasn't dead yet. Some guy had gotten him out of the building just in time. But the doctor was in critical condition with carbon monoxide poisoning and had slipped into a coma within the last twenty minutes or so.

Well, that was a bit of good news.

The circumstances surrounding Banner's death were still sketchy, but apparently he was killed while fighting one of the people at the center.

Some professional he turned out to be.

Tanbyrn's in a coma. Nonresponsive. If he ever does recover, he'll probably have brain damage. Just get through until tomorrow night. There'll be time to deal with Tanbyrn later, once things have settled down.

After thinking things through, Cyrus decided to go home, get everything ready for tomorrow, and keep an eye on the situation with Tanbyrn. Yesterday he'd briefly considered contacting Atabei. Maybe, with Tanbyrn in a weakened condition like this, that would be the best route to take after all.

Yes, keep tabs on his condition and make a decision in the next couple hours regarding Tanbyrn.

~

After contacting the charter flight service again and making arrangements for us to stop by to pick up Fionna and her children in Chicago, I put in a call to make our hotel reservations. With people streaming to central Philly to hear the president's speech in the morning, there aren't many vacancies, so it takes a little time to find some rooms, but finally I do.

Because of our early morning arrival, I book the rooms for both tonight and tomorrow so we'll be able to check in immediately when we get there and not have to wait for the normal check-in time later in the day. It's only a couple thousand dollars more for an extra night for the four rooms, and it would save us the hassle of stowing our luggage until the afternoon. I figure it's worth it.

I return to Charlene and Xavier and ask him if he can give us a ride back to the Lawson Center so we can get our car and our things from the cabin.

"What about your X-rays?" he asks.

"Only if they can get me in quickly. Our flight leaves from Portland in less than four hours, and with the drive back to the center, it's going to be cutting it close." I watch Xavier carefully to see how he responds to the next bit of information. "We'll be meeting up with Fionna and her kids in Chicago on the way. They're coming with us."

"Fionna?"

"That's right."

"And her kids?"

"Uh-huh."

He's quiet for a moment. Despite his unwavering support for people living off the grid and his suspicion of the federal government's role in just about every evil of modern society, he's surprisingly never been a big fan of homeschooling and has made the mistake of mentioning to Fionna that he thought she should've sent her kids to a charter school or a private academy of some type.

Families who homeschool usually have pretty strong convictions for why they do it, and Fionna was no exception. I'd seen her and Xavier really get into it a few times.

All good-naturedly, of course.

I think.

I pat him on the shoulder. "Just don't bring up the homeschooling thing and you guys will do fine."

"Uh-huh," he mutters. "As long as she doesn't try out any of her similes on me, we'll do even better."

I'm tempted to tell him about the gerbils-on-the-floor analogy but hold back. "Let me get those X-rays, and then I want to check on Dr. Tanbyrn again before we leave."

Malik's Daughter

Two cracked ribs. Neither serious.

The ER doctor and the radiologist both interpret the X-rays the same way. It's a welcome piece of good news in the sea of an otherwise dark and turbulent day.

Rest and time would help me heal. And that sounded a lot better to me than dealing with a pierced lung.

We proceed quickly to Tanbyrn's room.

Even though Pine Lake is a small town, with the news of a Nobel laureate nearly dying in a purposely set fire, it's no surprise that the national media is already camped outside the hospital doing live feeds. Thankfully, the sheriff's department has kept them from getting through the doors.

At the room, Deputy Jacobs, the mustached cop who'd gone through Banner's pockets when I led him and two of his fellow officers to Banner's body, is standing sentry outside the door.

At first I'm a little surprised to see him stationed here, but considering the fact that this crime spree involved arson, at least one homicide, and possibly eleven others by the same person or team of people, the extra security made perfect sense.

Deputy Jacobs gives us a nod as we approach and anticipates what we came for. "He slipped into a coma."

What? Charlene mouths.

A silent nod.

"Is it possible we could see him?" she asks.

"I'm afraid not. They don't want him disturbed."

"How would we disturb him if he's in a coma?"

Jacobs has no answer for that.

"It's possible that he's aware of what's going on, that he needs to have someone reassure him—"

"I'm sorry, that's—"

Charlene folds her arms. "Can you imagine what it would be like if you were lying there and part of your brain was aware of how alone you were, how hopeless your situation was, and no one was there to comfort you? How do we know for sure that's not the case?"

Deputy Jacobs isn't up for a fight tonight. "I suppose it can't hurt. I'll go in with you. But just for a couple minutes; I don't want the docs walking in on us."

"I'll stay here in the hall," Xavier offers, "and knock if I see any doctors coming."

Inside the room, we find Tanbyrn lying motionless on the bed, the blankets tucked neatly around him, leaving the outline of his slight frame sketched beneath the covers. Only his head and arms are visible. He's on a ventilator and has tubes running into his arms, and all of this makes him look vulnerable, frail, and smaller than he really is. The subtle hum of hospital machinery and the lemony scent of antiseptic fill the air.

The room has only dimmed lights and the generic, nondescript feel of hospital rooms everywhere.

I think of how many people die in these generic rooms and how tragic that is. A whole life of uniqueness and individuality funneled down into a room that's interchangeable with a hundred thousand others just like it all around the country.

Feel-good movies will tell you, "Pursue your dreams," or "Follow your heart and everything will work out in the end," or "Love conquers all," or some other cliché that sounds good at first but doesn't stand up to reality, to the way things really are.

Because dreams don't always come true.

And following your heart sometimes only leads you deeper into despair.

And love doesn't conquer all. Death does. Like it did with Rachel and the boys. Death won. Death always wins in the end.

We approach the bed.

I have no idea if Dr. Tanbyrn can hear me or not, but I tell him, "We got the man who started the fire." I doubt that talking about anyone dying is the best thing to do at the moment, so I leave out the news about Banner's death and Abina's murder.

Charlene sits beside the bed and takes Dr. Tanbyrn's hand. "You're going to be okay."

Considering his condition, I'm not sure she should be telling him that, but truthfully, when she does the words sound so heartfelt and confident that I almost believe they'll come true.

Positive thoughts. Remember, they make a difference.

And prayers.

Thoughts and prayers.

Even though I wish we could ask him about Project Alpha, I'm at least reassured that we have a plan, that we're on our way to—

A series of knuckle raps on the door from Xavier tells us that there's a doctor on his way to the room.

"We should go," Deputy Jacobs tells us quietly.

I assure Tanbyrn that we're going to find out who was behind everything. Charlene gives him a light kiss on the forehead and tells him she'll be praying for him, then we slip out of the room, meet up with Xavier, and leave to retrieve our things from the center so we can make it to Portland by the time our plane lands to pick us up.

~

Riah did not find herself sad that the three men in the video had been killed in the explosion, but she did find their deaths to be unfortunate and untimely in the sense that the men probably had more things they would've liked to accomplish before they died.

Possibly, but they were planning a suicide attack, after all.

In either case, other than acknowledging that a premature death might not have been on their agenda for the day, Riah felt no sorrow or pity or grief.

It was her condition, her curse.

Her reality.

However, she couldn't help but remain curious about Malik's wife, the woman who would now be forced to fend for herself in a male-dominated, patriarchal society, and Malik's daughter, the fourteen-year-old girl who would now have to grow up without her father. Riah guessed that the girl had loved him and wondered what she was going through.

What would that be like? To grieve the death of a loved one?

Would the Afghan girl see her father as a hero who'd died for his beliefs, or as a coward who chose to escape a harsh life and slip into paradise, leaving his wife and daughter living on the hellish outskirts of a war zone?

Riah thought back to when she was that girl's age, to the days when her father first started tying her to the bed and having his way with her. What if she'd loved him and then he had died? How would that've felt? Or what if she'd hated him instead? Would she have celebrated?

But he had not died.

Instead he was living in a decrepit farmhouse in the middle of Louisiana. Riah's little sister, Katie, was still alive too, was on her third marriage, rented a squalid little apartment in San Diego, had three kids, and hadn't spoken with her since their mother's funeral.

Their mother had fallen down the basement stairs six months ago and broken her neck when her head hit the concrete floor.

The coroner labeled her death "accidental." Riah's father had been home at the time, and Riah thought that it was at least as likely that after decades of physically abusing his wife, he'd pushed her down the stairs or smashed her head in and then shoved her body down the steps to make it look like an accident, but there was no way to prove his involvement one way or the other.

But regardless of the circumstances regarding her mother's death, Riah knew that her father was a guilty man, guilty for what he had done to his daughter.

Or daughters.

She had her suspicions, but never could get Katie to tell her if their father had done the same things to her.

Riah knew that someday she would visit him and discuss the fact that he had not treated his children in an honorable manner, discuss it in a way that he would understand.

She was confident she could come up with something unforgettable.

But now, tonight, she went to bed thinking about Malik's daughter, about watching that fourteen-year-old girl's father explode.

Tomorrow morning she would be meeting with the twins to find out what role her research had played in that man's death, in that fourteen-year-old girl's loss.

And, presumably, based on what Darren had said to her in the conference room, what her role might be in killing even more fathers just like him.

Heading East

The drive to Portland goes surprisingly quickly, and Xavier, Charlene, and I find the Gulfstream 550 waiting for us on the tarmac.

The pilot, a fortyish woman with golden retriever eyes and an enigmatic pair of pigtails, introduces herself as Captain Amy Fontaine. The copilot is a quiet, slightly overweight man named Jason Sherill.

Our flight attendant, a young Indian gentleman who speaks with only a faint Indian accent, tells us he is Amil and is at our service.

We shake hands, give them our names, and take our seats in the jet's cabin.

Though the price tag for this flight isn't cheap, I've used this company before, and as I look around the jet, I'm reminded that I'm getting my money's worth. The cabin is ultra high-end, elegant—swiveling, reclining captain's chair seats, four flat-screen televisions, not to mention the individual monitors for each seat. A couch sits at the back of the plane near the galley and restroom.

Xavier stows a duffle bag full of his toys. He winks at me. "You never know what tricks you're going to need up your sleeve."

"No, you don't."

"I have a few things here I've been working on."

"What are those?"

"Oh, well, you see, that's a surprise, Petunia."

I stare at him.

"Charlene filled me in."

"Great."

As Captain Fontaine pulls the plane onto the runway, Amil informally gives us the required preflight information—apart from the senseless instructions about powering down your phones and electronic devices. "If it were even remotely possible that your electronic devices could affect the navigation of an airplane during takeoff or landing, do you really think the FAA would allow you to bring the items on board?" He almost slips into a stand-up routine. "Can you imagine a jet crashing and they find out that the cause was someone forgetting to turn off his noise-canceling headphones? My friends, you could run a cell phone kiosk next to the cockpit and have an MRI machine stationed in the back of this cabin, and it wouldn't affect the navigation of a plane one bit."

I liked Amil already.

We take off, and as we break through the clouds, I see the final glimpse of sunlight fading along the edge of the sky. I can't help but think of all that has happened since the sun went down yesterday evening: the fight in the chamber, the test this morning, escaping the fire, seeing Abina's body, watching Glenn Banner die at my feet.

It feels like a lifetime has passed since the last sunset.

Like a dream.

But it's real.

The pain and death and questions, all real.

My thoughts float back to my nightmare last night about seeing my wife and sons drown. How I felt. How helpless. How terrified.

Needless to say, I'm not too excited about going to sleep now, on the plane.

In the waking world, when you're haunted by the past or troubled by the present or nervous about the future, you can distract yourself—go for a run, watch a movie, check your email—but when you're asleep and you're facing something terrifying, you can't turn away, can't even close your eyes and pretend it's not happening.

In a sense, I guess, we're powerless to escape our dreams. We're forced to live them out, forced to watch whatever our haunted past wants to throw in front of us. Even though we may know it's not real.

～

Cyrus made his decision.

He slipped quietly to the garage, careful not to wake his faithful, innocent, and rather oblivious wife.

The more he'd thought about it, the more he'd realized it would be best not to wait until morning to deal with the situation with Tanbyrn.

He backed the Jag out of the driveway, pulled onto the silent, deserted street.

Over the last nine months, Cyrus had explored every avenue available to him for clearing the way for his research concerning the release of the new telomere cap. During that time he'd considered the broad-reaching implications of Dr. Tanbyrn's research on quantum entanglement and its connection to human relationships, its connection both in positive ways and in negative ones.

Cyrus was a man of science, but if there was one thing quantum physics was teaching us, it was this: there is not always a scientific explanation for what happens in the world. Logic evaporates when you reach the subatomic level. Reality is much more malleable than it seems.

He wasn't sure he believed in Mambo Atabei's practices, but he had seen some things in her ceremonies that he couldn't reasonably explain. Based on Tanbyrn's research, there were scientific reasons, matters of quantum entanglement, that might have been able to explain some of the effects, but that seemed to Cyrus to be a bit of a stretch.

Admittedly, he was somewhat embarrassed by his forays into this field, but when tens of billions of dollars were at stake, it was worth a little unorthodox dabbling.

He had a relatively good relationship with the Haitian woman, and he speculated that she might just be able to help if he gave her a big enough donation.

Guiding the Jag down the street, he aimed it toward South Philly. Toward the high priestess's house.

~

After we level off, Amil offers us caviar hors d'oeuvres and wine in tall, fluted glasses.

Xavier takes out his button camera and puts it on. When he sees me looking at him curiously, he explains, "We were supposed to be filming a documentary. You never know what kind of footage we're going to need. We may end up with a film yet. Don't worry, I'll be unobtrusive." Then he asks Amil if he has any cheese, crescenza if possible, and Amil looks at him blankly.

"We have some cheddar in the back, sir."

"That'll do."

Amil passes us to get to the refrigerator in the back of the cabin.

I suggest to Xavier and Charlene that we review what we know, make a game plan for the rest of the night, and they swivel their chairs toward me.

Charlene flips open her computer, positions it on her tray table. I ready my iPad. Xavier produces his pen and journal.

"So," I begin, "here's what we know. Fact: RixoTray Pharmaceuticals funded a research program that focused on the quantum entanglement of people's consciousness and its effect on the physiology of partners who have a deep emotional relationship."

Xavier summarizes the research of Tanbyrn in one simple, succinct phrase: "The entanglement of love." He looks at me slyly. Then at Charlene.

Uh-uh. We are not even going to go there.

"Fact," I go on, "a pair of men, twins known only to us as 'L' and 'N' who are special in some way, would fly in, meet with Tanbyrn, and fly out. We still don't know what the tests consisted of, only that they had to do with the negative effects of something."

"And with alpha waves," Xavier adds, then graciously accepts an elegant platter of sliced cheddar from Amil. "Directing them. Focusing them."

"Yes."

"Fact"—he takes a bite of his cheese—"Glenn Banner killed the young woman at the center and started the place on fire. Motive still unclear."

Charlene is typing as she tracks along.

"Fact," he continues, "Banner's cell phone was used to contact Cyrus Arlington, the CEO of RixoTray Pharmaceuticals. Also, Banner had a passcode with him that led Fionna to get past the firewall and into Arlington's personal computer."

At that, Charlene pauses, lets her fingers hover over the keyboard. "Which brings us to the video. One of the people from a terrorist cell was recording and transmitting footage of another cell member putting on a suicide vest. The vest—by the way, Xavier, you knew what language they were speaking. Do you know Arabic?"

"I can identify it, can't speak it. I once worked for a Middle Eastern singer in Las Vegas."

"Well, the vest detonates . . . where does that leave us?"

I sigh. "Square one."

She glances at me. "Square one?"

"We have a collection of facts and interrelationships but no *why* behind them. No motive. Why was RixoTray funding Tanbyrn's research? Why have Banner burn down the Lawson research building? Why was one of the terrorists filming and transmitting the video? Why was Banner in touch with Arlington? Why was Arlington watching the video? Why is the Pentagon interested in any of this?"

Xavier adds, "And how does Dr. Riah Colette fit into the mix?"

"And who is Akinsanya?" Charlene chimes in.

"Right. A pile of whys, one big how, and one big who."

A moment passes. Xavier takes another bite of cheese. Chews. Swallows. "By the way," he asks me, "did you ever review the footage you got when you were taking the test at the center?"

"No. Do you think that still matters?"

"Probably wouldn't hurt to have a look at it. Stick it on a jump drive and I'll glance it over."

I'm reminded of Banner's watch and I retrieve it from my carry-on bag, explain to Xavier how I got it.

"I don't think we need prints anymore. Looks like you got yourself a new watch, bro."

"Looks like I do." I slip it on. It looks good.

"So . . ." I type in a few notes myself. "I know we all need some sleep, but let's see if we can make a little progress before we reach Chicago. Xavier, could you follow up with your friends about Project Alpha and Star Gate?"

"Sure."

"Banner warned me about someone named Akinsanya, that he would find me. Let's see if anything about Akinsanya or this video has been leaked to the internet or to any of the conspiracy theorist circles."

"Gotcha."

I glance at Charlene. "You still have the notes that Fionna dug up earlier, right?"

"Sure."

"Why don't you go through them and see if you can find out more about the telomerase research or the EEG research. If you have time, go online and pull up what you can on Drs. Riah Colette and Cyrus Arlington."

"Check."

"I'm going to study Tanbyrn's books and look for anything related to the negative effects of mind-to-mind communication."

Then we turn our chairs from each other and get started with our work as we head east, toward a new day.

The Needs of the Many

Dr. Cyrus Arlington had never killed anyone.

Per se.

Yes, people had died because of his actions, or, more accurately, because of his lack of action, but that's the way the system was set up, the only real means of scientific advancement when you're doing medical research on human subjects.

After all, you need a control group, a baseline. So if you're testing a new drug, you give your experimental medication to one set of patients, a placebo to another, and you need a third group, a control group, that receives no treatment at all. It's the only way to measure the true efficacy of a drug.

Of course, as the test progresses, even if the drug appears to be working, you don't stop the trials in the middle to administer it to the dying people in your control group. It's not just a matter of protocol, it's a matter of science. Even with a double-blind study, there are too many factors that can affect the research, so you need a large enough sample to really verify your findings. If you assume too much too early, it could be detrimental to the lives of millions of people in the long term.

So, yes, some people will inevitably die during the process, but it's the only way to collect the data that you need to determine whether or not a drug is effective.

The needs of the many outweigh the needs of the few.

And of course, the more people you have in your control group, and the more time they go without getting their potentially life-saving drugs, the more of them that will die.

But they would, of course, die anyway. Eventually.

Ultimately, health care is a numbers game, and there are only two rules, two guiding principles that are taught at every school of medicine in the country:

Rule #1: Everyone dies.

Rule #2: There's nothing you can do to change Rule #1.

"We prolong life; we do not save it," one of Cyrus's professors at Harvard Medical School had told him. "Don't try to be the savior of the world. Just do your best to help ease the greatest number of people's pain as much as you can, for as long as you can. At its heart, that's what medicine is all about."

The Hippocratic Oath: *Primum non nocere.*

First, do no harm.

Not quite as in vogue today as it used to be, not with physician-assisted suicide and third-trimester abortions, but the point was well-taken.

And so, during his twenty years of overseeing research before taking over as RixoTray's CEO, Cyrus had been part of hundreds of studies and seen thousands of people die. It wasn't his fault that cancer or AIDS or congestive heart failure took those people from the world. But paradoxically, even though he had not killed them, if you wanted to be technical about it, he could have stopped the tests. It was, in one sense, his fault that the people didn't live.

They might've been saved if compassion for them trumped the scientific advancement that their deaths advanced.

But it had not.

It could not.

The needs of the many outweigh the needs of the few.

For a while, watching others die, even though he knew he could stop the process, had been like a thorn in his thoughts, an uncomfortable irritation that made his daily work less enjoyable, but you have to move on, have to come to terms with your role in life. And Dr. Cyrus Arlington had done just that.

He'd begun to look at the big picture and had initiated the most expensive research program in the history of his company to find the cure for aging, which would, in many ways, be the cure for everything.

Telomeres, protective caps on the ends of chromosomes, erode as cells reproduce, and so the cells eventually degrade and enter a state referred to as "senescence" when they no longer reproduce. This causes the effects we associate with aging—dementia, increased risk of stroke, muscle atrophy, and decreased organ function, sight, hearing, and so on. Put simply, the enzyme telomerase protects the telomeres from degrading and thus slows aging.

If it were possible to use telomerase on humans to stop telomeres from shortening when cells reproduce, there would be no reason for those cells to begin breaking down. Would it add years to your life? Yes. And undoubtably, it would also dramatically increase your quality of life during the decades up until then.

Stopping senescence halts the negative effects of aging and, at least in the 2010 Harvard studies on rats, *reverses* those effects by increasing neural function, regenerating nerves, and rebuilding muscle tissue.

But there was a problem. Cancer cells initiate telomerase, which is one reason cancer cells don't degrade with time, so increasing telomerase in the body of a person who has no cancer would cause him to become more immune to it, but someone with cancer would become more riddled with it.

All of this means that if you could create a drug that releases telomerase, you would either need to administer the drug to people who don't have any cancer cells growing in them, or give the enzyme to people in short doses so that it decreases the risk that the cancer cells they already have would spread.

Unless the drug increased the level of telomerase only in cells that were not cancerous.

And that's exactly what RixoTray was on the verge of producing.

It would be the one drug that everyone on the planet would want to take, and it would make thousands of other drugs obsolete.

The pharmaceutical company that could create the first-generation telomeres protector would be positioned to become one of the most financially lucrative firms on the planet. Perhaps one of the most profitable companies of all time.

And that company was going to be RixoTray Pharmaceuticals.

They needed a little more funding, yes, and a little more time. The funding would come from the Pentagon, and the time would come from—well, it certainly wouldn't come from the added restrictions the president was going to propose in his speech tomorrow at eleven at Independence Park just outside of the Liberty Bell building.

Cyrus threaded his Jaguar down the narrow streets of South Philly. Groups of gangbangers huddled on the street corners; abandoned buildings littered the block. The row houses in this primarily African American neighborhood were all in disrepair. And it was not the kind of place someone of Cyrus's stature would normally venture.

He was heading to the house with the dumpster in the cramped alley behind it. The dumpster that accepted the remains of what happened in the basement of that building during the night.

Despite the low-income demographic of the neighborhood, Cyrus wasn't afraid to leave the Jag on the street. He was known as a friend of Mambo Atabei, and no one around here would dare cause any trouble for one of her friends.

He parked in one of the four spots in front of her house left vacant for her visitors. Walked to the porch, knocked on the door.

Waited for her to answer.

There were generations of African Santería practitioners in Philadelphia who have been around since colonial times. And although Mambo Atabei was not from Africa, the ceremonies she performed had been originally exported from there to Haiti, adapted, and then imported from Haiti to North America.

The cloth doll in Cyrus's office was, of course, a gimmick. No one who was a serious voodoo worshiper would use a doll like that. It was for the tourists in places like New Orleans and some of the neighborhoods in Miami. Real voodoo has much deeper roots and much different methods.

When the door opened, Cyrus could smell incense. It was meant to mask the other smells that emanated from the house, or peristyle, as it was known in Mambo Atabei's religion.

She stood in front of him, fiftyish, slim, black—she hated being called African American because, as she said proudly, she was Haitian, not from Africa, not from America. "You don't hear Caucasians preface their identity by naming their ancestors' continent of birth: 'European-American' or 'North American–American.' All of this political correctness is only thinly veiled bigotry used to create divisions between people groups that need to be drawn closer together, not separated by hyphenating their identities."

"Dr. Arlington." Her voice was soft and congenial but had a raspy edge to it. The result of a throat injury sometime in her past.

"Mambo Atabei."

"It's been, what? Two months? Three?"

"Something like that."

Without another word she invited him into the living room.

The brown and white doves that she would use in the basement were caged in the corner of the room, out of reach of the gray cat that stalked across the footstool in front of her couch. The doves squabbled with each other, oblivious to what awaited them. The cat eyed them with calculated interest.

Cyrus wondered about the cat. He hadn't known Mambo Atabei

to use cats, but he wasn't really sure what all went on in her basement. He'd only witnessed her using doves and chickens—although he did know that larger animals were part of some of the ceremonies she performed.

A wide variety of liqueurs and rums were collected on an end table in the corner of the room. An HDTV, two chairs, a lamp, a crucifix on the wall, a shelf of DVDs, and knickknacks rounded out the room. A typical living room.

At the far end of the room, a curtain was drawn across an open doorway. He knew that the curtain concealed the steps that led to the basement.

A basement that was not quite so typical.

He'd been down there on numerous occasions, just as an observer. But he'd seen what went on around the pole, the *poteau-mitan*, in the middle of the main room, had seen what caused the dark stains on the dirt floor beneath it.

There is, of course, a dark side to voodoo, a strand that's not about dancing and drinking or trying to find out some insights about life from a Loa. There's a side that has nothing to do with blessings or celebration.

It was the side Mambo Atabei counted herself a part of, the highly secretive Bizango Society.

Cyrus was not easily rattled, but Atabei had a certain unnerving quality about her and studied him with a quiet intensity that made him slightly nervous. "And what exactly can I offer you tonight, Dr. Arlington?"

"I'd like to put something into play."

"Regarding?"

"A man who is in a coma."

"A coma."

"Yes."

He knew that in Atabei's tradition, a donation for services was expected. The nature of the request determined the size of the donation.

"I'm willing to make a donation to the peristyle." For now he held back from telling Mambo Atabei exactly what he wanted from her. "A sizable one."

She tapped the thumb of her right hand against her forefinger, evaluated what he'd said.

He heard bleating from the stairwell to the basement. A goat.

He pretended not to notice it.

"What is it exactly that you want me to do?" she asked.

And Dr. Cyrus Arlington told her, in depth, the nature of his request.

Production Value

The jet's engines purr, but other than that the plane is quiet as Xavier and Charlene do their research beside me.

It's been half an hour and I've been scanning Dr. Tanbyrn's book. He actually does make reference to potential negative effects of quantum entanglement when it comes to thoughts, mentioning some of the same examples as Xavier used with me earlier today—shamans and witch doctors. Curses.

After all, if placebos can be used to help people heal themselves merely by their thoughts, could their thoughts also be used, conversely, to destroy them? Certainly, the debilitating effects of psychosomatic illnesses and depression were just two examples. And if a person really can affect another person's physiology by his thoughts, as Tanbyrn had demonstrated, there was no reason to believe that the effects would necessarily always have to be positive.

His conclusion: if either blessings or curses affected reality, the other would imperatively do so as well.

As Dr. Tanbyrn wrote:

Most religions believe in the power of blessings and curses. In medicine we have placebos that eliminate pain or, in some cases, treat diseases. In psychology we find that the power of positive thinking affects behavior, and there is ample evidence that those thoughts can actually rebuild neural pathways that have been damaged by severe depression. From quantum physics we know that an observer's thoughts and intentions determine the outcome of reality. So we have religion, medicine, psychology, and physics all saying essentially the same thing—our thoughts and intentions have the ability to affect reality in inexplicable, but very real, ways. To shape the outcome of the universe.

The last statement seemed like hyperbole to me, but it was a similar point to the one Xavier had made when we were talking earlier in the hospital.

A couple of observations that I find significant: according to Dr. Tanbyrn, it's more effective if the person who is cursed knows it and believes in the power of the curse. Research on curses that were spoken over people who were unaware of it or didn't believe in them had mixed results. The deeper the personal connection, the more pronounced the effect, just like in his love entanglement studies at the Lawson Research Center.

Tanbyrn didn't mention Jesus cursing the fig tree, but he did mention Balaam being hired to curse the Israelites in the Old Testament.

After a lifetime of studying the secrets behind illusions and mentalism, I can't help but be skeptical about all of these claims. However, the test results from when Charlene was in the Faraday cage showed that my thoughts had somehow affected her physiology, and the dozens of research studies mentioned by Dr. Tanbyrn in his books add validity to the theories. Needless to say, the findings at least piqued my curiosity.

Whatever the actual relevance of all this, one thing is clear: Xav was right; for thousands of years people of faith have believed in the power of words, thoughts, and intentions to both heal and to harm. And recent breakthroughs in the study of quantum entanglement and human consciousness support those claims.

My phone vibrates, and I see another text message from my producer at Entertainment Film Network.

Oops. Forgot all about that.

Now that I'm on my way to Philly, it's definitely time to give her a call.

I speed-dial Michelle Boyd's number and she picks up almost immediately. "Jevin! What happened? I've been texting you all night."

"It's been a crazy day. I assume you heard about—"

"Of course I heard. Are you kidding me?" She's excited, sounds almost exuberant. "Fill me in. I need to hear it. Your take on everything."

It takes me a few minutes to relay the story of the fire at the center and Abina's death and the fight with Banner and Dr. Tanbyrn's hospitalization. For now I leave out the detail that I'm in the air on my way to Philadelphia.

"What about the study? Were you able to debunk it?"

"No, but at this point I don't think that's really the primary issue."

"Of course it's not the issue. This Tanbyrn deal, this fire, that's the story. This whole thing with the doctor is great."

I feel myself bristle at her words. "Great? How is it great that a man is in a coma?"

"No, no, no, not that. That he survived! I'm talking production value. What a great story—human tragedy, heroism, a life-and-death struggle. Viewers will love it. If we can just pull some footage together before tomorrow's—"

"Production value? That's what this is to you? Viewers will love the fact that a man—"

"You're missing the point here, Jev. This is a Nobel laureate who was the target of an arsonist's flames. Viewers will love that you saved him, that he's valiantly fighting for his life. Don't you see? It's the perfect way to take your series in a new direction. We were aiming for more of an investigative approach this time around anyway. And I mean, let's be frank, debunking psychics and sideshow acts? Come on, Jev, even you have to admit that that gets old after a while. Viewers want something unique, something fresh, something different."

"So, a dying man is fresh and different."

"Listen to me, Jev, every news station in the country is following this story, but you have the inside scoop. You were there. You saved a man's life, for God's sake. This isn't just Tanbyrn's story, it's yours."

On one level, I know that what she's saying is true—other networks will cover this, and I had been there; I'd experienced it all firsthand. It was certainly a tragic and gripping story that viewers probably would love, and it made sense that Charlene and I would be the ones to tell it. I can't put my finger on precisely why I'm not excited about pulling what we have together into an episode, apart from the fact that it seems to be leveraging a man's suffering to promote ratings.

Which, of course, it is.

"Dr. Tanbyrn might die," I tell Michelle. An obvious fact, yes, but I feel like it needs to be said.

A pause. "Yes, well, that would be tragic, but viewers would be forced to think about their own mortality in light of his death and would be inspired to live better lives themselves. They'd be moved to tears, would remember him and his work in a positive light. If he makes it through, he's a fighter; if he succumbs, he's a martyr in the name of scientific advancement. Either way, we come out ahead."

That's it.

No one comes out ahead when an innocent man suffers. And no one comes out ahead when an innocent person dies.

"I'm out."

"What do you mean, you're out?"

"I mean I'm out. I'm not going to be involved with this."

"You have to be. You drop this and I'll drop your show, I swear to God—"

"Do it. You just said that debunking psychics and sideshow acts gets old after a while. And yeah, you're probably right. I don't need the money and you don't want the show. Find something you're excited about and we both win. There's plenty of extra footage left over from previous shows. I'll give it all to you. It should be enough for you to round out the season."

"I don't want that, I want *this*. I want Tanbyrn."

"Get used to disappointment."

I hang up and notice Charlene eyeing me. "Breaking out lines from *The Princess Bride* now, are we?"

"In this case it seemed appropriate."

"So, I couldn't help but overhear that—your side of the conversation, at least. We're officially freelancers now, I take it."

"Yes. I suppose we are."

"It actually might be better this way."

"Yes." I feel an unexpected spark of excitement at the thought. "It just might."

Daymares

I find myself dozing on and off as we fly east. Eventually I wake to Amil's voice telling us that we're approaching Chicago's Midway International Airport. The lights in the cabin, which have been low for the last few hours, are still dimmed, but he turns them up slightly.

Xavier is in the back of the plane snoring contentedly, but Charlene is across the aisle from me resting, her eyes closed. I'm not sure if she's asleep.

She has a blanket pulled up to her chin, and I watch her for a moment, thinking about when I observed her in the Faraday cage earlier today. She's as unaware now that I'm watching her as she was when I was viewing her on the video screen.

I feel like I'm intruding on her somewhat, admiring her like this, and just as I'm looking away she opens her eyes. "Hey."

"Hey."

She yawns. "So we're almost to Chicago?"

"It looks like it, yes."

She rubs her eyes and repositions herself in her seat so it's easier for her to talk with me. "I guess we didn't get a chance to connect with your father."

The comment takes me back a bit. I hadn't even thought of my dad since my conversation with her earlier in the day.

"When this is over, I'll be in touch with him. I promise."

"It might not be over for a while."

I wasn't exactly sure why it was so important to her that I talk with my dad, especially since she'd never brought it up before this week, but I figure she has her reasons, and right now I decide I'm not going to probe. "Give me a couple days. I'll call him on Friday afternoon, okay? Even if we're still caught up in the middle of all this."

Another small yawn. "Fair enough."

She closes her eyes again, snuggles up in the seat, and I wonder how awake she really was, if she'll even remember our brief conversation later.

Far below us, the steady flow of cars accelerating, decelerating, pumping through the city streets looks like glowing blood cells passing through dark veins. The cars look so small, but obviously, their size and speed are distorted by distance and by the plane's velocity.

It's all about perspective.

Only by taking into consideration our current elevation and airspeed could a person calculate the actual size and speed of the cars. As my mentor in magic, Grayson DeVos, used to tell me, "Only perspective brings truth into focus. Where you stand when you look at the facts will determine how they appear. Never forget that when you design your show. The audience's perspective is even more important than how well you execute the effect."

Maybe that's what we needed here.

Perspective.

Maybe you're looking at all of this from the wrong angle entirely.

When you study illusions, you have to study the limits of memory to better understand short-term and long-term memory and how to use them to your advantage in a performance. Long ago I read about memories people have in which they see events not through their own eyes but as if they were hovering in a corner of the room watching the events take place.

Most people have them, often from traumatic incidents. In fact, they're so common that neurological researchers have a name for them: observer memories.

I have one of them myself, from when I was nine and a group of half a dozen junior high–aged boys surrounded me. They began to drag me toward an old quarry that people had turned into a junkyard before it was filled with water to create a small lake for fishing and ice-skating on that otherwise neglected side of town.

No one dared swim in the lake because the bottom was still strewn with junk—bedsprings and broken glass and rusted car parts that were visible beneath the surface on the rare days when the lake was clear enough for you to see down more than a few inches.

It was a lake we all feared. But they dragged me toward it, and when I recall it now, it's not from the point of view of a boy being pulled toward the water by the other boys, but from a distance, as if I'm watching it unfold from a perch in a nearby tree.

I can see the older boys laughing and I can see myself struggling to be free, crying out for them to let me go. Finally, at the water's edge they shoved me to the side, into a stand of tall grass. Then they smiled at each other and patted me on the shoulder: *It was just a joke. We were never gonna hurt you; we were just kidding around.*

I ran home but never told my parents for fear that they would think I'd overreacted or, worse yet, been a coward.

And since then, when I remember that day, I don't see the events through my own eyes, but as if I were watching it all happen from somewhere beyond myself.

Observer memories.

But how could they even be called memories when my mind was filling in the blanks, making up the details, viewing things from another, imaginary person's point of view?

Observer memories are fictions that our minds tell us are true.

The same as optical illusions.

In magic we play people's expectations against them. The observer's mind fills in what he or she would *expect to see* rather than what's *actually being seen.*

I notice that Charlene has her eyes open again. She's watching me quietly. "You look deep in thought."

"Just thinking about how our minds can do strange things, can convince us of things that aren't real. Sometimes we see things that aren't really there, sometimes we don't see things that are. We're all experts at fictionalizing the truth."

For a moment she's quiet. "There's a legend that when Columbus was sailing toward the New World, none of the natives saw the boats, that the idea of the giant boats approaching was so foreign to their way of thinking that even though their eyes sent the signal to their brains, it didn't register."

"Not until they landed onshore, you mean?"

"Well, actually, while they were still out in the water, a shaman saw the ripples and was curious what was forming them. He stared at them, studied them, until eventually he saw the boats. When he told the villagers, they were shocked and at first didn't see anything. But they all believed in him and eventually came to see for themselves that the ships were there. So the story goes."

"So, it was their belief in him that helped them see the boats."

"Yes."

We begin our initial descent to the airport.

"Jevin, you've told me you have nightmares. About your boys. About Rachel in the van."

"Yes."

"Have you ever had one when you were awake?"

"You mean a hallucination?"

"A nightmare, but only you have it during the day."

"No." But there's something in her tone, something beneath the words. Then I catch on. "But you have? Is that what you're saying?"

"When I was a girl, a man killed three people in my neighborhood. Stabbed them. His wife, his daughter, then the woman who lived next door."

I'd never heard this before. "That's terrible."

"I was eight at the time and I heard the sirens outside—you know, from the police. Someone from the neighborhood had called them. I was standing at our front window; I saw the man walking toward our house, right down the middle of the street, holding that knife in his left hand. It was still dripping blood."

The plane banks and we slope down into the final descent.

"My parents had gone over to a neighbor's house just down the block when it happened. I don't remember exactly what they were doing or why they'd left me alone, but they didn't make it home until it was over. The first police car came racing around the corner, but the man, Mr. Dailey, didn't stop. He just kept walking directly up the driveway to my house. He must have seen me inside the window because he smiled and tipped the knife in my direction. I should have run, I suppose, or hidden in the closet or something, but I didn't. I was just too terrified to move."

I hear a palpable chill in her words from the dark memories that haunt her.

The ground draws closer. My ears pop from the pressure, refuse to equalize.

"Right as he was walking up our steps, they shot him. The police did. He wouldn't put down the knife. I was watching through the window, just a few feet away. He died right there on our porch, his blood splattered across the glass right in front of me. That's when I ran to hide. I've never told anyone I saw him die. Not even my parents or the police knew I was there when he was shot. They thought I was downstairs watching TV."

When she pauses, I sense that it's just to regroup, not to give me a chance to respond, so I wait and at last she goes on, "Since that day, I sometimes see Mr. Dailey. I'll look up from reading and he'll come around the corner in my bedroom and hold that knife up and smile and just stare at me. I've seen him in restaurants and at bus stops. Sometimes I'll be sitting talking with my friends and he'll walk into the room, just like you or me, and I can't tell if he's real or not. And then he pulls out a knife. Sometimes he'll walk up to me and swipe it toward me, toward my stomach."

I'm reminded of what happened in the chamber last night when Banner tried to kill her by swiping the blade toward her abdomen.

Apparently she's thinking the same thing because I notice her gazing at the arm where she got her stitches. "I guess it's a hallucination, but I've always thought of it as a nightmare that I have while I'm awake. A daymare. I know it's not real, but everything inside of me tells me that it is. That's how powerful our thoughts can be. They really do change things, Jev, our thoughts do."

There's not a whole lot of difference between her daymares and my observer memories. In both cases our minds were filling in details, forcing us to see what wasn't real.

Why don't we just call observer memories what they are: retrograde hallucinations?

The saying about our eyes playing tricks on us comes to mind. But the saying isn't true, I've known that since my early days of magic. Our eyes don't play tricks on us, our minds do. Our eyes only gather information; our minds interpret it. We perceive the world not so much by what we actually see but by how our minds expect it to look, by what construct we use to make sense of the data.

Observer memories.

Fictionalized truth.

Hallucinations.

Perspective.

Our wheels touch down. The landing is a little rocky, as if the plane is unsure of itself as it settles onto the runway.

Clearly, Charlene is deeply moved and upset from sharing the story about Mr. Dailey. I reach across the aisle, put my hand gently on her shoulder. "You okay?"

"Yeah."

It's not true what they say about things being "only in your head." If it's in your head, it's in you, and you can't escape your thoughts, can't flee their effect on you. Call it psychosomatic if you want, but when thoughts affect your physiology, the problem is never just in your head.

Misdirection.

Seeing what you expect to see.

Why did the suicide bomber put the shirt on over his vest? If the video was simply of a malfunction in the vest, what did it have to do with RixoTray? With Dr. Cyrus Arlington?

I consider that for a moment. The implications for what we're trying to do here.

Eyes playing tricks on you.

A different perspective.

Captain Fontaine stops our taxiing beside the charter jet terminal.

Charlene folds up the blanket. "I hope Dr. Tanbyrn will be alright."

"So do I." But my thoughts are still on the video, on the behavior of the suicide bomber, the ways perspective and expectations affect what our minds tell us is real.

I'm not sure what any of it means and I make a decision to look into it later, but it'll have to wait. For now Fionna McClury and her four children are already waiting for us just outside the nearest hangar.

Socialization

I put a call through to the hospital in Oregon and find that there's been no change in Dr. Tanbyrn's condition, and by the time I'm done the door is open and Fionna and her kids are lining up to board the plane.

Fionna has a shock of red hair that she always seems to have a hard time taming and endearing green eyes that beg you to look deeply into them, but it's not easy to. One of her eyes wanders, and when we first met, I found it difficult to guess which of her eyes to look into when I spoke to her. For a while I kept switching my focus from one eye to the other until she abruptly told me to just choose one because going back and forth like that was making her dizzy.

She has two girls and two boys, all four years apart, almost like clockwork. Mandie is five, Maddie nine, Donnie thirteen, and Lonnie is seventeen. I'm not sure why she gave her boys and girls names that sounded so much alike, and I have no idea how she keeps the names apart, but from the first time I'd met her, I've never heard her call any of the children by the wrong name.

After two marriages that didn't work out, she's sworn off men, but she's also mentioned to me how important it is for her kids to have a good male role model, and I could tell she was conflicted about the whole issue.

STEVEN JAMES

Amil stows the McClurys' luggage in the back of the plane, and Fionna lets the kids troop aboard first, their eyes wide, mouths gaping.

"Sweet." It's Donnie, the ponytailed thirteen-year-old who has looked up from his cell phone just long enough to take a quick glance around before texting someone again. Last year he'd somehow convinced his mom that he needed an earring, and in his tattered jeans and long hair, he looks more like an aspiring rock star than your typical Midwestern homeschooled kid.

Lonnie strolls aboard, confident, perceptive, lean, and already handsome at seventeen. Mandie, the youngest, has both arms wrapped around a stuffed dog that's nearly as big as she is. Nine-year-old Maddie wears stylish glasses and is toting a well-worn copy of *The Count of Monte Cristo*.

Fionna ascends the plane's steps just behind them. She's wearing two buttons on her jacket: "Moms against Guns" and "NRA Member."

She is not an easy woman to figure out.

She offers me a nod and a smile. "Jevin."

"Hey, Fionna."

Because of how often we use videoconferencing, it's been a few months since we've all been together face-to-face. She leans in for a peck-on-the-cheek greeting.

As the kids pass by Xavier, they all greet him as "Uncle Xav." Then they settle into their seats.

"It's great to see you, Fionna," Charlene tells her.

"You too."

Xavier shakes her hand. "Hello, Ms. McClury." He lends a degree of respect to her name.

She regards him lightly. "Hello, Mr. Wray."

"And how is the homeschooling going these days?"

"Quite well, thank you. How's the search for the Loch Ness Monster?"

"It's coming along."

It doesn't take long before we're in the air again. Fionna asks for

281

an update and I quickly brief her on what's going on, what we've found out.

When she hears about the documented negative effects of mind-to-mind communication and the idea of using a thought-borne virus to stop someone's heart, she shakes her head. "That's about as unnerving as a warm toilet seat at a highway rest stop."

"Ooh . . ." Charlene cringes. "That one's just troubling."

"And memorable," Xav mutters. "I don't think I'll ever look at rest areas the same way again."

Fionna smiles. "Thanks." Then she turns to me. "So, you have Tanbyrn's iPad?"

Charlene retrieves it and hands it to her.

Earlier, Fionna had said that she could hash the password in two minutes or less. I decide to time her. A password prompt appears on the tablet's screen. She begins to tap at the virtual keyboard. I start my watch.

From behind us I hear Xavier talking with Maddie, the nine-year-old, who's staring out the window at the receding lights of Chicago.

"So, a field trip, huh?" he remarks offhandedly.

"Yes."

"Should be fun."

"Yes."

"A chance to get out of the house."

Oh, don't do this, Xavier. You're going to regret it if you—

"Uh-huh."

My watch tells me Fionna has one minute fifty seconds left. Without looking up, she calls back, "What makes the biggest difference in a child's education, Mr. Wray? According to the latest research, what's more important than the teacher's educational background, the school district, technology available in the classroom, socioeconomic and racial demographics, even parental involvement?"

She's still working on the iPad.

One minute thirty-five seconds left.

"Let's see . . . the culture of the school? At some inner-city schools, no one even takes books home because of peer pressure. Because it's not considered cool."

"Yes, that's a factor," Fionna admits—her fingers are flying across the virtual keys—"but I'm talking about the most important factor: class size. The smaller the class, the better kids learn. Until you get down to twelve students, where it levels off. And what educational alternative offers that the most readily?"

"But what about socialization?" he counters.

Oh, bad move, Xav.

This was going to be brutal.

I look his way and notice Maddie staring at him questioningly. "Socialization?"

One minute left.

"Yes," he tells her. "It's how you make friends." He directs the next part of his answer toward Fionna. "Some people call it preparing for the real world." It's not sarcasm, not even criticism in his voice, but there's definitely a challenge there.

Fionna stops typing. Gazes at him.

Forty-five seconds left.

Here we go.

"Yes, that's right," she agrees, "socialization. It means preparing for life beyond school and learning to get along with people of all ages in a healthy manner. Maddie, why don't you go ahead and answer Uncle Xavier. Does homeschooling do that?"

Back to the iPad's keyboard.

Thirty seconds.

The socialization objection is such a typical one leveled against homeschooling that I wonder if Fionna has coached her children on how to respond to it. But Maddie doesn't look like she's trying to recall what her mother might've told her, she looks like she's really thinking about it.

Xavier waits.

We all watch Maddie to see what she'll say.

After a bit she replies, "So do you think the best way to prepare kids for the real world is to bus them to a government institution where they're forced to spend all day isolated with children of their own age and adults who are paid to be with them, placed in classes that are too big to allow for more than a few minutes of personal interaction with the teacher—"

Twelve seconds left.

"—then spend probably an hour or more every day waiting in lunch lines, car lines, bathroom lines, recess lines, classroom lines, and are forced to progress at the speed of the slowest child in class?"

Two seco—

Fionna punches one final key. "Done," she announces, looking up from the iPad.

Man, she really was worth her pay.

It's quiet in the back of the jet for a moment, and Charlene whispers to me, "Not too many times you find Xavier speechless."

"I heard that," he calls to her, then clears his throat slightly, addresses Maddie. "Your mom taught you to say all that, didn't she?"

"No." She pauses, thinks about that. "But if she had, wouldn't it show that she prepared me for the real world?"

Silence. Then Xavier's voice. "Amil, do you have any more of that cheese?"

Fionna smiles faintly: *Gotcha.*

The password prompt clears away, revealing the desktop screen. "Now, let's see what Project Alpha is all about."

Fionna is fast, but most of the files require her to type in another unique password. I have no idea how Tanbyrn could have kept them all straight, but it's taking Fionna awhile to work through them.

Finally she gets discouraged and sighs. "I think I need a break from this."

"You probably need some sleep," Charlene tells her. "Rest. Get back at it when we reach Philadelphia."

The truth is, we probably all need some sleep.

So that's what we do until the sun begins to glow on the eastern horizon and the City of Brotherly Love lies beneath us, its bridges straddling the Delaware and Schuylkill rivers, its skyscrapers rising into the cobalt-blue, unfolding day. Strands of high and lonely clouds stretch across the lower part of the sky.

And we land at the Philadelphia International Airport.

Philly

Wednesday, October 28
7:21 a.m.

I've been to Philadelphia at this time of year before, and the temperature is usually in the midfifties. Today the temps are lower, the day is clear, and the wind bites fiercely at my face as I step onto the tarmac.

Everyone is quiet as we head to the terminal; no doubt they, like me, are still half-asleep, still transitioning back to the waking world.

Memories of the path that led us here, the events of the last thirty-six hours, pass through my mind, bringing with them a hailstorm of harsh emotions.

Fury.

Grief.

Curiosity.

Confusion.

Abruptly, my thoughts are interrupted by Fionna. "Did you get the hotel rooms all figured out?"

"Should be all set. Sorry, no pool, but the suites do have whirlpools."

"How many rooms did you get?"

"Four. I figured I could share with Xavier and you and Charlene could stay in the same room, as could your boys and your girls—don't worry, the girls' room adjoins yours so you can leave the door between them open."

"Actually, I'm more concerned about my boys. It might be best if you could room with Lonnie and Xavier could room with Donnie. Keep an eye on them."

"Um . . ."

She smiles. "Just kidding. I appreciate everything."

"No problem. Anyway, their room is beside ours. We'll make sure they don't party too late."

"Much appreciated."

We're almost to the terminal. Amil has his cell phone out and asks me how many taxis we'll be needing.

I'm about to tell him two when Xavier leans close to me and whispers, "Get a limo for Fionna's kids. They'll love it."

Nice.

Good thought, Uncle Xav.

"One taxi," I tell Amil. "And one limousine."

On the helipad on top of RixoTray's corporate headquarters, Dr. Cyrus Arlington boarded one of his company's three Sikorsky S76A executive helicopters.

The drive to DC would have taken nearly three hours—more if traffic was bad—and he didn't have that kind of time today. Too much to do before this afternoon.

As the pilot completed the last-minute safety checks, Cyrus wondered what Mambo Atabei had accomplished for him last night and how it might affect his agenda for the day. Already he found himself thinking of her as a loose end. One that might need to be tied off permanently, just like Tanbyrn.

As the largest individual shareholder in the company, Cyrus stood to lose tens of millions of dollars if the legislation went through. He knew that name-brand drugs are safer and more effective than their generic counterparts. But also, yes, of course, more expensive.

For good reason.

If you were a novelist and spent a decade writing a book, and then someone came along and copied 95 percent of your words, packaged the book similarly to yours, and sold it at a fifth of the price, that person would be guilty of copyright infringement. It's the same as the Chinese and Russians producing designer handbags or watch knockoffs that sell for a fraction of the price of the original products.

Yet generic pharmaceuticals are enthusiastically welcomed by the general public.

Because they're cheap, not because they're ethical.

But still, incomprehensibly, they are legal.

There were two factors at play in the pharmaceutical industry regarding protection from generic drug infringement: data protection and patents.

According to the 1984 Hatch-Waxman Act, generic drug companies can release drugs to the marketplace without clinical trials as long as the companies can prove that their drug is equivalent to the name-brand drug. This allows them to earn income off the millions or billions of dollars of research and development that they don't have to pay for. There's only a five-year span of time after the release of data related to the drug's research before the equivalent generic drug can be released to the public.

Thankfully, however, for RixoTray and other pharmaceutical firms, their biopharmaceutical products also have patents that run not for five years but for twenty. However, considering that the only way to protect intellectual property on a research-based project like this is to file for the patents early, and research and development of the drug might take eight or ten years, the twenty-year protection shrinks to ten or perhaps twelve at the most.

Since the five-year data protection and twenty-year patent protection time frames run concurrently and generic drug companies will often sue to have patents overturned, the actual length of time between the release of the name-brand drug and its generic equivalent can drop to five or six years. Not a lot of time at all to recoup your R&D investment.

And that was about to change.

Cyrus's man had told him that if the president got his way, the time frames were going to be cut in half.

The helicopter took off.

He sent a text to the vice president's people that he was on his way, then reviewed what he was going to say to Vice President Pinder about the legislation initiative that the leader of the free world was going to propose in just under four hours.

~

We step into the Franklin Grand Hotel down the street from Independence Park.

Xavier was right. The kids went crazy over the limo ride.

I figure that neither Dr. Colette nor Dr. Arlington will be at work yet and we have some things to get together before meeting with either of them anyway, so after stopping by the front desk to check in, I suggest that we get settled and then the grown-ups meet in Xavier's and my suite to figure out our plan for the morning.

In the elevator, Mandie gets the honor of pressing the button to the twenty-second floor.

One wall is glass, and as we ascend we see the Comcast building nearby. Fionna mentions that it was built to look like a giant flash drive, and everyone agrees that it really does. For a homeschooling mom, school is always in session, and she explains to the kids that Philadelphia is sometimes known as the "City of the Nation's Birth" and that it has the largest number per capita of Victorian-style homes in the US. "The city hall is also the largest city hall building in the world. No steel reinforcement; it's all concrete, brick, and marble. It was built in 1901 and has more than two hundred statues surrounding it. The statue of William Penn on the top of the tower is thirty-seven feet high, and the circumference of his hat is more than twenty feet."

The elevator pauses at our floor and the doors open.

"Who can give me a definition of circumference?" she asks her kids.

As Maddie does so, we all troop off to our respective rooms, and Xavier mentions quietly to me, "She's quite a woman, isn't she?"

"She sure is."

The Question Behind
All Questions

7:55 a.m.
3 hours left

After dropping off my bags in the room, I decide that before our meeting begins I'll grab some coffee and bagels for our crew from the coffee shop across the street.

As I pass through the crosswalk, a young mother pushing a stroller ferrying a warmly bundled-up baby boy joins me. She greets me and I wish her good morning back. "That's a cute baby you have," I tell her honestly.

She beams. "Thank you. His name is Frankie."

A moment later she and Frankie walk out of my life, but they send my thoughts cycling back to the days when my sons were that age.

And I think of Rachel too—the young mother who loved them and then took their lives.

In the months following their deaths, lots of people gave me advice, and almost none of it helped. Especially not the line about the ones who've passed away "living on in our hearts."

My family lives on in my heart as much as the memory of the night I got drunk in college and totaled my car, as much as the recollections of food poisoning sending me to the hospital for a whole weekend last year.

A memory is a memory is a memory. And that's all it is, so if that's all we can claim for our loved ones when they die—that they live on in our hearts—then that's a pretty puerile and insulting thing to say to a grieving person.

Memories. The fictions we tell ourselves are true.

But perhaps wishful thinking is less painful than the brutal truth: "Don't worry, you'll remember Rachel and the boys for a while, then life will go on and they'll slowly get crowded out of your heart by other, more trivial things. And then, of course, before too long you'll die too, and eventually all of you will be forgotten in the sands of time."

Unless eternity is real, unless heaven is more than a fairy tale, death always wins in the end.

The air inside the coffee shop is interlaced with the sweet smell of freshly baked cinnamon rolls and aromatic coffee. I load up on half a dozen giant cinnamon rolls drenched in icing, some bagels and breakfast sandwiches, as well as coffee and lattes for the adults, and head back to my room.

One piece of advice that did seem to help, though, at least a little bit, was something one of my ultramarathoner friends told me: "Hang in there. It'll never always get worse." It's a saying ultra-runners have to remind themselves at eighty or ninety miles into their hundred-mile races that eventually the trail will get easier. At least for a little while.

Obviously, life for everyone has its ups and downs, and I've had lots of good times over the last year, but a pervasive heaviness has settled into my heart, as if the default setting of my life has changed from joy to disappointment. Grief might actually be a better term.

Life might get worse, but it'll never always get worse.

According to my friend.

But maybe it should. Maybe if you're the guy who fails to notice the warning signs in the actions of the woman who would eventually become your sons' murderer, maybe then it should get worse for you until you die and are forgotten in those sands of time too, along with them.

All these thoughts are stirred up simply from seeing that ebullient young mother's joy over her child. Charlene's words from last month come back to me, when she told me that joy is evidence of God.

Well then, if that's true, what is grief evidence of?

On my way through the lobby, I contact the hospital again and find out that Dr. Tanbyrn is still in a coma. I ask the nurse in charge to text me or call me if his condition changes. Since I'm not family, it takes me awhile to convince her, but in the end she agrees.

As I approach my room, Charlene meets up with me in the hallway. "So how are your ribs this morning?"

"Still tender. Your arm?"

"The stitches are tugging a little, but not too bad. Your head?"

"Manageable. Burns from the fire?"

She shrugs. "Nothing serious. You?"

"I'm good."

"Good."

Remarkably, I do feel better. Not 100 percent recovered, but at least on the way, and that's one thing to be thankful for. I'm glad she's doing alright too.

Inside the room, we find Xavier has showered and changed. His eyes widen when he sees the food, especially the box of cinnamon rolls. "I'll take some of those to the kids."

I hand him the bag and he leaves to deliver breakfast to the Mc-Clury children.

"He really likes those kids," Charlene observes.

"I'm thinking it might be more than just the kids."

"I'm thinking you might be right."

We pull out our notes and for a few moments we're quiet, and I realize I'm slipping back into my retrospection about the loss of my family.

At last when Charlene speaks, I hear gentle caution in her words. "Jevin, you need to be careful."

"About?"

"The times you disappear."

"The times I disappear?"

"Into the past." A pause. "Into your pain."

Her words hit me hard and ring as true as Xavier's did on Monday, when he talked about my past being a part of my story but not what defines it. "Stop feeding your pain and it'll dissipate," he'd told me. "Be where you are; let where you've been alone. Do that and the universe will lean in your direction."

But how? How do you get to that place?

I take a long time before responding. "What are we supposed to do when life makes no sense, Charlene? And don't just say we need to make the best of it. There's no best to make of it when your sons are murdered by your spouse."

"I know."

"So?"

A moment passes. "I don't know, Jev."

I let my thoughts crawl over everything again. "I guess it all comes back to the question behind all questions."

"I don't know what you mean."

"The question 'Why?' Why do bad things happen? There are never enough 'becauses' to answer that final 'why.'"

"I have to believe that there is, that there's a reason why God would—"

"Would what?" The words come out before I can stop them, taut and cutting and fueled by my brokenness: "Would allow two little boys who're strapped in their car seats to drown? Would allow their mother to sit by and let it happen?"

"It makes no sense to me either. I don't know why we hurt so badly and hope so much for something better. But I do believe that somewhere there's a reason behind it all."

"God works in mysterious ways? Is that it?" Even as I'm saying the words, I feel bad about the tone I'm using with her, but it's as if these feelings have been churning around inside of me and now they're geysering out all on their own.

Charlene seems to be at a loss for words. Finally she stands and walks to the window. Gazes at the day. "Jevin, when Jesus was dying he cried out to God, asked him why he'd abandoned him."

"And what did God say?"

Her eyes are on the skyline. "Nothing."

I'm quiet. So not even Jesus could unriddle the mystery of suffering, the feeling of being abandoned by God. I'm not sure if that's supposed to reassure me or not. Honestly, it only serves to make the answers I'm seeking seem more elusive than ever.

Charlene faces me, says softly, "There's a teaching in the Bible that all things work together for the good of those who love God."

"And how did being tortured to death work out for Jesus's good?"

Oh, that was just great, Jev. Just great. Keep attacking what she's saying when she's just trying to help.

"Charlene, I'm sorry. I shouldn't have—"

"It wasn't the end when he died."

"He rose."

"That's what Christians believe. Yes, St. Paul said death has been swallowed up in victory."

The idea that death could be conquered, that life would win in the end, strikes me as too good to be true, but also as the most necessary truth of all.

"Do you believe that?" I ask her.

"If I didn't, I'm not sure how I'd find enough hope to make it through the day."

I have no idea how to respond to that. I haven't felt hopeful in a very long time. And I haven't felt very prepared to make it through my days either.

She approaches me. Her voice is tender. "Jevin, who are you angry at, yourself or God?"

"I'm not angry."

"No, don't do that. Not with me."

"Do what?"

"Brush me off. Hide. I know it's there. I can see it. How you've changed."

I find I can't look her in the eye, but then she puts her hand gently on my chin, turns my head so I'm facing her again. "Rachel had problems, Jevin. She was ill—"

"Okay, let's just—"

"Something broke inside of her and she didn't have the chance to get it fixed."

"Charlene, stop."

"There's no way you could have known, no way you could have—"

I pull away. "That's enough!" I've never spoken to her like this before, and I'm sorry, so sorry, for snapping at her. "Charlene, I'm—"

"It's okay." She pauses and I can tell there's more she wants to say. "I loved her too, Jevin. We all did. But her choice wasn't your fault. She's the one who did that terrible thing, not you."

"Ever since it happened, ever since that day, I've been trying to hate her for what she did to my boys."

"I know."

"I can't seem to."

"I know."

All the questions and anger and desperation that has been piling up for the last thirteen months overwhelms me. It's like a weight too heavy to bear, one that's smothering me and isn't ever going to let me go. "I don't forgive her, Charlene. I'll never forgive her. And don't tell me I need to forgive myself, because I don't even know what that means."

"No, I wasn't going to, Jev. You don't need to forgive yourself. You need to stop hating yourself."

I'm standing there, reeling from the impact of her words, when the hallway door opens and Xavier and Fionna step into the room for our meeting.

Dilemma

8:10 a.m.

2 hours 45 minutes left

"Hey, kids," Xavier calls. "You two behaving yourselves?" He's halfway through one of the mammoth cinnamon rolls. Fionna has Dr. Tanbyrn's iPad in hand.

I turn to the side so no one can see my face. I'm afraid a tear will escape, but I make sure it doesn't.

The question behind all questions.

The one not even Jesus knew the answer to: *Why?*

And Charlene's words: *"You don't need to forgive yourself. You need to stop hating yourself."*

Yes, yes, I do.

But how?

She assures Xavier that, yes, we were behaving. It takes me a few seconds to collect myself, then we all gather around the suite's executive conference table beside the window that overlooks Independence Park.

I try to refocus my thoughts, dial us back to the task at hand. It's not easy. Shutting away your pain never is. "Okay, I know we were all working on different things on the plane. Let's take a sec, summarize

298

what we have, then move forward, see if we can figure out what Arlington's connection with Glenn Banner might be." From the looks on Xavier's and Fionna's faces, it doesn't appear that they can tell I was so close to losing it.

Charlene offers to go first. "I found Colette's and Arlington's vitas online, as well as some references to the research and patents they've been involved in, mainly in the area of recording brain waves and electrically stimulating parts of the temporal lobe. Also, the further you delve into Arlington's background, the more you find the telomerase studies coming up again and again. There's proposed legislation that could affect its release date. RixoTray has started clinical trials. I'll email everyone what I have."

"I think we should contact Dr. Colette first," Fionna suggests, "before we do anything else, see if she can help us."

It seems reasonable. Fionna goes online, locates Colette's home phone number, and I try it. No answer. I'm about to leave a message when Xavier stops me. Taps my phone's screen to end the call for me.

"What?"

"Really, what are you going to tell her, Jev? That you're a magician who thinks her boss might be connected to a homicide and arson in Oregon, a top-secret military thought-borne virus psychic research program, and a conspiracy to stop suicide bombers in the Middle East?"

"Hmm. Yeah. Maybe better to talk in person."

"And what if she's involved? Did you think about that?"

I set down the phone. "Okay. Let's table that for the time being."

My emotions are still wrenched from my conversation with Charlene. They feel raw and exposed. Concentrating on this meeting isn't going to be easy.

How do you stop hating yourself? Where do you even begin?

I have no idea.

Xavier takes a final bite of his cinnamon roll and out of habit begins his explanation with his mouth full. "I didn't find out—"

But the mom in Fionna immediately kicks in: "Let's not talk with food in our mouth, Mr. Wray."

"Oh. Right." Some people might have taken offense, but the way she said it was friendly enough, and Xavier swallows, apologizes. "Sorry. I was saying I heard from one of my buddies who's . . . well . . . connected. He said he did a little checking, and Project Alpha was started just over a year ago."

Fionna is typing on her virtual keyboard. "Which would correspond to when Dr. Tanbyrn's studies were first published."

"Exactly. It was named Project Alpha after the first published article detailing a researcher's ability to translate brain waves of linguistic information. Back in 1967."

"1967? This line of research has been around that long?"

"Yup. That was the year Edmond M. Dewan taught himself to turn on and off the alpha rhythms in his brain—they're brain waves that are associated with mental states and relaxation. So, by relaxing himself at conscious intervals while recording those alpha wave changes with EEG, he was able to communicate Morse code messages. Through his thoughts."

Charlene leans back. "Whoa."

"Of course, scientists have come a long way since then in recording brain waves through functional magnetic resonance imaging, diffusion tensor imaging, and magnetoencephalography. Lots of people think the government is already monitoring their thoughts." He pauses and looks at us ominously. "I know people who know people who've already had it happen to them, and pretty soon it's going to be as widespread as—"

"And the military connection?" I direct him back to the topic at hand before he can launch into a tirade on how the government is controlling and policing our thoughts.

"Yeah. Project Alpha goes high up in the Pentagon; in fact, the second in command in the DoD, Undersecretary of Defense Oriana Williamson, is on the oversight committee. There's no sign of the

Kabul video on YouTube or WikiLeaks, so whoever received it has kept it under tight wraps. Nothing on Akinsanya either, except that the name is Nigerian. It means 'the hero avenges.'"

He takes a breath. "Jev, I watched the footage you managed to get while you were taking Tanbyrn's test and didn't see anything unusual. As far as I can tell, you and Charlene really are entangled."

"Really?" Fionna raises an eyebrow. "Entangled?"

A clarification is in order here. "I'm not sure that's really the best word. Charlene and I have been working together for a long time. It's natural that we would have a close interpersonal relationship."

"A close interpersonal relationship." Xavier nods. "That's a good way to put it."

"Yes," Fionna agrees. "That sounds accurate."

Charlene is watching me expectantly.

After a fumbling silence I say, "Um . . . let's figure out the right terms to use later." I indicate to Fionna. "So? Anything?"

She holds up Tanbyrn's iPad. "Well, I wish I had some good news, but so far I haven't been able to find anything more specific about Project Alpha on this thing. If there was some secret data floating around out there somewhere, it must have been on another computer."

"The one Banner was checking just before he attacked us in the chamber?" Charlene muses.

"Possibly. And it looks like Tanbyrn had some doubts about the future of the program. Funding. President Hoult apparently wants to nix it. Oh, and Lonnie isn't bad at math, so I left the sheets from Tanbyrn's folder for him to look over, see if he can decipher them." Most seventeen-year-old guys wouldn't exactly be excited about deciphering a Nobel laureate's scientific quantum mechanics equations, but Lonnie was not your typical teenage guy. "What about you, Jev? Dig up anything?"

"Tanbyrn touched on studies about both prayers and curses. It seems there's more than just anecdotal evidence supporting the effectiveness of both of them—the one to heal, the other to harm. A . . . well . . . close interpersonal relationship seems to be vital to both."

We all take a minute to process what everyone has said.

I draw things to a close: "I think the first order of business is setting up that meeting with Arlington."

Fionna types on the iPad, then announces that he'll be out of the office this morning. She consults the screen. "According to his personal calendar, he'll be back at noon. He has a meeting in DC this morning." She sounds disappointed, and for good reason. We'd all been hoping that by announcing that she'd hacked into his personal laptop, she could get us an audience with him this morning.

"What about the people from RixoTray's cybersecurity department?" I suggest. "Certainly there'll be someone there interested in speaking with you before you report your findings to the company's CEO?"

"That makes sense. But that doesn't help you get to Arlington. And what exactly would you want me to find out from them?"

"When we first watched the video of the suicide bombers yesterday, it was after office hours here in Philly. See if you can get a look at the footage of the surveillance cameras in the lobby or, ideally, the reception area in Arlington's office suite. Find out if anyone else entered. It'd be helpful to know if Arlington watched the video alone or had company with him."

"Nice." Xavier holds his fist out toward me until I bump it with my own, then he offers to go with Fionna. "It might be good to have two of us there to deal with anything that might come up."

"What might come up?" she asks.

"Stuff." He looks around awkwardly. "You know. That might need handling."

"Handling."

"Hey, you never know what you might run into."

"Well . . . I suppose I could use a minion."

"Let's go with 'assistant.'"

"I can work with that."

I collect some of my notes. "Good, and Charlene and I can try to set up a meeting with Dr. Colette. Fionna, see if you can find out where she'll be."

It takes a few minutes, but finally she finds what she's looking for. "According to her calendar, Dr. Colette will be at RixoTray's R&D facility up near Bridgeport this morning. I'm guessing it's about half an hour drive from here."

It strikes me that somewhere along the line I forgot to get us all cars. It's less than a mile to RixoTray's headquarters, but I figure Fionna and Xavier should at least have a car at their disposal. I make a quick call, get two executive cars and drivers for the day, and we get back to business.

"But how'll we get through security?" There's skepticism in Charlene's voice. "Surely they won't let us just walk into their R&D facility, not without an appointment."

I find myself palming my 1895 Morgan Dollar, finger-flipping it. "True. Security is sure to be hypertight."

"Go in as custodians?" Fionna suggests. "Or service workers?"

Xavier shakes his head. "Not enough time to put something like that into play. Besides, those people would almost certainly be vetted. Possibly even fingerprint ID'd."

"New employees?" Charlene suggests. "We just got a job? We show up for the first day of work?"

"Too easy to check."

"How about we're there for a business meeting? Or what about the truth: we're working on a documentary and have some questions we need to talk with Dr. Colette about concerning her research?"

That's actually a tempting thought, but I doubt it would work. "It'd be too easy for them to just deny us access; we need something they can't say no to."

Fionna has been typing and now sighs. "There are three security checkpoints to go through. And Xavier's right. They have fingerprint identification at the front gate."

"Okay . . ." Xavier is thinking aloud. "So we need a way of getting two people who've never been there before, who the guards aren't expecting and won't be able to verify the identity of, into an ultra-high-level security pharmaceutical R&D complex in a way that won't arouse suspicion."

And that's when it hits me. Misdirection. The thing I do best. "Well put, Xav. And I think I know just how we can pull it off."

Complaint Procedures

They all eye me curiously.

"Government inspectors from the Food and Drug Administration following up on a complaint about the treatment of human subjects in their telomerase research."

Everyone mulls that over for a moment.

Xavier gives a slow nod. "Government agencies are always reshuffling staff, renaming divisions, reworking their logos. Bureaucracy at its best. Shouldn't be that hard to fake the paperwork, and it would make sense that they wouldn't know you. But what if they decide to follow up? Call the FDA?"

"We'll put your phone number on our cards."

"We'd need IDs." Charlene taps her chin thoughtfully. "Official ones."

"There's a FedEx Office store down the street. I saw it when I was getting the coffee. It's amazing what you can pull off with a color printer, some card stock, and a laminator."

Oh yeah. I was liking this. I could get used to being a freelancer.

"Fionna, we'll need official-looking documents. Can you come up with those in an hour?"

She screws up her face. "No. Not ones that could fool the guards. But . . . maybe my kids can help me—do a little research on FDA complaint procedures. Extra credit." After a moment of reflection, she nods. "I'd say we should be able to come up with something."

"I'll give you a hand," Charlene offers.

"Great." I stand. "I'll help Xavier with the IDs and business cards. Charlene, you and Fionna tackle the paperwork; there's a business center on the second floor. You can print what you need down there, or join us at the FedEx Office."

We use my phone to take Charlene's and my pictures for the IDs, then the two women head out to convene with the kids and Xavier grabs his computer. "Come on," he tells me. "Let's go do something illegal."

Dr. Cyrus Arlington landed in DC.

Strode off the helicopter pad.

There was already a car there waiting to take him to the White House.

Mambo Atabei carried the goat's headless carcass into the alley behind her home and tipped it into the dumpster.

She'd been ridden by her Loa for more than six hours last night, so long that the other members of her peristyle who were involved in the ceremony had begun to worry about her.

But she was thankful. Being possessed for long stretches of time was the most rewarding part of what she did, the reason she'd gotten into all of this in the first place.

Some people claimed that Loa possession was a hallucination brought about by cultural expectations, wishful thinking, and a little too much rum. That was an easy way to explain away what happens. Let them think what they wanted.

After turning from the dumpster, she brushed some of the goat's hair off her shirt. The blood was still there. That wasn't going to come out nearly as easily.

Then she went to check the news to see how everything had panned out concerning the doctor in Oregon.

~

Darren took a deep breath, said to his brother, "Ready?"

"Ready. Lancerton, Maine, huh?"

"Let's see how well this works."

Then the twins closed their eyes, relaxed, and focused their thoughts on the same thing. Just as they'd been training for so long to do.

Oil and Blood

Adrian Goss had slept in a little and was still a bit groggy as he walked toward the woodshed.

Behind him, smoke curled from the cabin's chimney, wisped into the crisp Maine day, and wandered toward the steel-blue sky like a slowly uncurling snake.

He trudged through the mud and thought of the wood stacked by the side of the shed, of splitting it, and he thought of his wife, who would be home anytime from working the graveyard shift at the hospital.

And he thought of his son.

It would be his birthday next week, turning eleven, and Adrian had decided to buy him a football—real pigskin. Official NFL size and weight.

Eleven next week.

A fifty-year-old guy with an eleven-year-old kid to raise. Not ideal in some regards, but not that unusual. Besides, love can overcome something as trivial as the age span between a father and his boy.

308

Adrian passed the 1972 Chevy Impala chassis in his yard and the thick stump he used to balance the wood on when he chopped it, pressed open the shed door, heard the harsh squeal of the hinge.

Oil it.

He'd been meaning to.

Yes.

Later.

He stepped into the woodshed. Light filtered through the cracks between the boards that made up the walls. The shafts of light seemed like giant slivers that he should avoid but would never be able to if he was really going to cross over to the other side of the shed.

Yes. Oil the hinge.

His thoughts seemed to blur together. Strangely, as if they were sliding over each other. Layers of ideas. A mesh that was impossible to sort through.

Shadow and light. Just like the shed.

A birthday present for his son. Eleven.

For a moment Adrian stared at the dust filtering through the slanting light and tried to remember why he'd come into the shed in the first place. He blinked and looked around.

It was something to do with his wife. Something to do with her and the argument they'd had last night.

His eyes landed on the shelf. A chain saw, tools, grease for the lawn mower. Spark plugs. A small metal oil can.

Adrian felt light-headed, like he had in high school after that tackle against Woodland in the state semifinals, when he'd had to sit out the rest of the game because he was seeing two of everything. That running back—what was his name? Terry something. Or Tommy. Something like that. Number eleven.

No, wait. His son was Terry. Yes. His son.

Adrian walked toward the shelf, braving the slivers of light, but they passed across him like they didn't care, like they weren't interested in eviscerating him, in slicing through his flesh and meat and bone.

At the shelf with the chain saw. Paused—

No, the game wasn't in the semifinals. They didn't make it that year.
Reached for the oil can.

No.

He came in here to get something for his son.

No, it was somehow about that argument with his wife.

Yes. About the house. The wood, the stove, and outside there wasn't
enough wood around, so why couldn't he have split more of it, because
when she got home from work in the morning, what was she supposed
to do, chop their wood too?

No, he'd told her, of course not. He would do that. He would
take care of it.

He passed the oil, the chain saw, went to the southwest corner of
the shed, toward the axe.

Southwest corner? Why would he even think of it like that? He'd
never called it the southwest corner before.

The shed's angled sunlight brushed against his face in between
the flutters of velvety black shadows. It didn't hurt at all. Not one
little bit.

He blinked and tried to collect his thoughts again. Something wasn't
right. Something wasn't clicking. There was the high school football
game and his son's birthday and the wood to be chopped and the
number eleven, the number of the player.

No, that's what Terry was turning on his birthday, and Adrian still
didn't have a gift for him.

Light and shadow and light.

Toward the axe.

His son's birthday, yes.

He lifted the axe, swung it gently. He was a man used to hard work,
and the axe felt comfortable in his hand. At ease, as if it were an extension of himself. Another limb with a sturdy-bladed end.

Something for his son.

Adrian was aware of the sunlight becoming alive, crawling against his skin. Every particle of dust, friction, friction, flowing sandpaper coursing through the air! Rubbing. Troubling!

Split the wood.

Split.

Adrian left the shed, shut the door behind him. Heard it creak.

Fix that. Oil it.

After Terry's birthday.

The azure sky above him seemed to stretch forever. Beyond forever.

He went to the woodpile, axe in hand, sunlight falling all around him.

Azure? Where did that word come from?

After he turned eleven.

Trish had argued with him last night and accused him of being lazy. Lazy.

He wasn't lazy.

He positioned the wood upright on the stump. He would show her. Prove it.

She was always doing this. Always nagging him, getting on his—

He would show her.

He raised the axe; yes, yes, he would prove it to her.

Adrian felt the muscles in his shoulders and back flex, his forearms tighten as he gripped the axe handle with a stranglehold, raised the blade above his head, and then, slicing through the sunlight, shredding it and leaving it hanging in tatters around him, he swung the blade down. It struck the log but did not cleave it in two.

Swing through the log. Don't aim at the top of it, aim at the stump. Swing through it.

Through it.

Focus not on connecting with the top of the log, but rather the stump on which—

On which.

The log rests.

He tugged the blade free, repositioned the wood, heaved the axe

311

backward over his head, then brought it forward again, harder than before.

Vaguely, he heard the axe connect with the stump. The two split logs dropped to the sides, but for some reason they did not bleed. For some strange reason he thought of this, of how nice it would be to see them bleed.

In the sunlight.

But they did not.

Blood could be used to oil that hinge on the shed.

He tossed the split logs aside and grabbed another log off the pile.

His wife accused him of being lazy.

He would need blood to fix the woodshed.

Behind him, from the end of the long driveway that wound along the edge of the woods, he heard the sound of a car's engine and the crunch of gravel. Trish. Coming home from work.

The graveyard shift.

She mocked you last night. Accused you of being lazy. But you're not lazy. You're a hard worker. You're—

Anger fueled the force of his next swing.

The two split logs flew to each side of the axe head as it hewed the log and sank into the stump beneath it.

But once again the split logs did not bleed.

The car stopped beside the house.

He wrenched the blade free.

Your son doesn't turn eleven until next week. You can pick him up at school today when you're done here. Pick him up early. Bring him back home.

He would need that blood to fix the woodshed door.

A car door slammed.

Eleven years old. Next week.

"Hey," Trish called. "How's it coming?"

Adrian turned toward her and realized that she was mocking him even now. It was her tone of voice. It was all there in her tone of voice.

312

You need to oil that hinge.

"It's coming," he heard himself say, but it wasn't really like he was saying it, instead it was more like he was somewhere else nearby hearing another person talk to his wife.

The axe felt comfortable in his hand.

An extension of himself. Another limb. With a bladed end.

Blood in the sunlight.

He walked toward her.

Oil and blood.

And then the door to that troubling woodshed would never bother him again.

"Hello, honey," he said. "Welcome home."

Preemptive Justice

8:51 a.m.

2 hours 4 minutes left

"Well?" Daniel asked his brother. "Do you think it worked?"

They were both easing from their trancelike states in the dimly lit research room at the RixoTray R&D facility. No one else was there with them. This was one experiment they'd been careful to conduct on their own.

After what happened in Kabul, they'd decided they needed one more test. After all, it was essential that they see this through, finish their mission successfully, and neither of them felt quite ready to do that yet. What they were attempting was unprecedented in their field and would change the landscape of espionage and covert warfare forever. It wasn't something they could fail at, not when so much was at stake.

"We should check the news," Darren said. They both rose, he went to the computer on the desk. Daniel made a few phone calls, including one to their contact, the one who'd salvaged things in Kabul. The one who'd told them about the man in Lancerton.

Riah was the kind of person they were confident could help them. Not only because of her expertise in deep-brain stimulation but because of who she was inside—how much like them she was. Even though she might not've been aware of what she was really capable of, they could tell. It'd become more and more clear to them over the last few months.

She would be here soon and they wanted to tell her everything.

True, they would have to kill her when this was over, just to be safe. But she could be of use to them in the meantime in completing their assignment.

The two brothers hadn't yet decided which of them would eliminate Dr. Colette. That little detail was still up in the air.

~

At the FedEx Office, I buy two clipboards, one for me, one for Charlene. No government inspector impersonation kit would be complete without them.

"You do know," Xavier tells me, "we'll probably get in big trouble with this."

"I'd say almost certainly."

"Too bad there isn't any fine print somewhere, a way to skirt around possible prosecution."

I kick that around for a minute. "You know what, let me get in touch with my lawyers. They might be able to come up with something that Fionna can add to the forms, noting that we're there for entertainment or educational purposes only, or that by allowing us to access the facility, the guards release all liability. Something like that."

Xavier looks at me skeptically. "You really think your lawyers can come up with something that'll cover our butts?"

"Hard to say, but that's what lawyers do best. And my lawyers are very, very good at what they do."

"Well, you pay them enough."

"True. And it's not like the guards would take the time to try to translate the legalese double-talk."

"No one reads fine print on forms like that anyway."

"That's true too. They don't even read iTunes updates."

"I do."

I pause. "I know. But honestly, regarding a waiver, when you know what you're doing, you can create a disclaimer big enough to cover your butt even if you were to steal the moon."

"Steal the moon?"

"I don't know. I was trying to think of something big."

"You keep using analogies like that and you're going to start giving Fionna a run for her money."

Now he was just being mean.

I gesture toward the cards he's holding. "The lamination machine's over there in the corner." Then I fish out my phone and make the call to the law firm.

Riah arrived at the R&D facility and passed through security.

She was still uncertain what all this was about, but she sensed that helping the twins was a good thing, the right thing, to do.

If that was indeed the case, it looked like she would get a chance to help the government stop terrorist threats by working with Daniel and Darren to do whatever it was they actually did when they thwarted that potential suicide attack in Kabul.

"We let him do it," they'd told her last night.

How did they "let" the suicide bomber do it?

She wasn't sure, but obviously it had something to do with her research and Dr. Tanbyrn's findings.

Hundreds of people might've been killed at that mosque, and if she could assist in stopping things like that, help to remove terrorist threats, that was probably an honorable, perhaps even, in one sense, a noble thing to do.

Preemptive justice?

One way to look at it.

She was obviously no expert on morality, but even she could anticipate that if the man in the video had been shot or arrested, insurgents would've claimed that he was an innocent civilian who'd been unjustly killed or imprisoned by imperialist Americans. After all, news is all about spin, almost never about truth. Scratch away at the surface of what people say and you'll always find an agenda lurking beneath the words.

That was one thing she'd learned about human nature. One thing she knew for sure: you can't take what people say at face value.

And spin like that would put more American soldiers at risk.

Yes, if there really was a way for her to help the twins eliminate threats without endangering the military's intelligence assets or personnel, it would certainly help the war efforts, probably save lives, and—

It would be the right thing to do. A way to serve the greater good.

So, yes, the greater good.

As she walked down the R&D facility's east corridor toward research room 27B for her meeting with the twins, she became more and more curious about what exactly she could do to help them kill.

Or eliminate targets.

Whichever term you preferred to use.

The Recruit

9:13 a.m.
1 hour 42 minutes left

Dr. Tanbyrn died.

We receive the news while we're gathered in Xavier's and my room getting ready to head out.

It shakes us, all four of us.

Personally, I hadn't been seriously considering the possibility that he would pass away but rather had settled on the expectation that he would recover.

The tragic announcement lends a renewed sense of focus and intensity to what we're doing. Now Dr. Cyrus Arlington is not only somehow connected to the death of Abina but also to that of Dr. Tanbyrn, the researcher he and his company had spent millions of dollars funding.

And Arlington was somehow connected to the video of the three men in Kabul, although how he might be tied to their deaths was still unclear.

We quietly take the elevator to the lobby, step outside, and find our two executive cars waiting for us out front.

Charlene and I climb into one of them, Fionna and Xavier disappear into the other, and the four of us leave the hotel to find out how RixoTray Pharmaceuticals was entangled in arson, terrorism, conspiracy, and murder.

~⌒~

Cyrus was waiting outside the vice president's office when he saw on his phone's news feed that Dr. Tanbyrn had died.

So.

Atabei had come through for him.

Or the fire did, that coma did. Tanbyrn could've simply died from complications brought about by smoke inhalation.

Possibly, but—

"Dr. Arlington?" It was the receptionist, jarring him out of his thoughts. She wore a telephone headset and was tapping the receiver by her ear to end a call.

"Yes?"

"The vice president has been held up talking with Congresswoman Greene. He told me he'll be here within the hour. He apologizes for any inconvenience."

"Not a problem." Buoyed by the news of Tanbyrn's death, Cyrus didn't mind waiting another hour for the vice president of the United States. "Not a problem at all."

~⌒~

"Please, Riah, have a seat," Daniel told her.

She positioned herself across the table from the two brothers. The mammoth MEG machine took up the far end of the room. Countertops covered with medical instruments lined the walls. A sink, two computer desks, and a small conference area rounded out the room. All familiar to her. All part of her everyday world.

"Last night," she began, "you told me that you would explain

319

how I could help you do . . . well, whatever it was that happened in Kabul."

"What do you think happened?" Darren asked.

"Somehow you made that man detonate his vest. I don't understand how—except that it must involve my neurophysiology research and Dr. Tanbyrn's psi studies."

"Yes, of course." Daniel stood. "Riah, if we could identify a threat, a terrorist, and without putting any soldiers in harm's way—"

"Get him to blow himself up."

"That's one option, yes. Or kill him quietly, in a way that was untraceable. Think about it. If it were possible."

She did think about it.

Identify a terrorist and somehow convince the person to blow himself up—like the man in the video. Let the terrorists take themselves out.

Or kill him quietly?

In an untraceable manner?

What did that even mean?

Tanbyrn's research: altering galvanic skin response, respiration rate—

Heart rate.

She took a shot at it: "Cardiac arrhythmia."

Daniel nodded. "Or a cerebrovascular accident."

In other words, a stroke.

But how?

She didn't know, but she did realize that what they were saying didn't quite fit with what she'd seen on the video of the suicide bombers. "Is that what you're telling me happened in Kabul?"

"At this point we're not quite ready to cover all that happened," Daniel said apologetically. "I wish we could, but we're awaiting word on an incident in Maine, then we can explain everything. But for now, we promised to tell you how you can help us."

Darren continued for him, "My brother and I were engaged in a

study with Dr. Tanbyrn regarding the effects of mind-to-mind entanglement. Ways to nonlocally affect another person's physiology.
Daniel and I share a certain connection with each other, you know
that. Even more so than most identical twins."

"Yes."

"In the studies, by working cooperatively, we were able to cause a
person a great deal of—"

"Discomfort," Daniel cut in.

"Discomfort?"

"Pain," Darren specified. "Fluctuations in cardiac activity and syn-
apses in neural activity in the centers of the brain that register pain."

"And you're saying you did this nonlocally?"

They nodded.

She reflected on what she knew of Tanbyrn's research. Did it really
involve the possibility of negatively influencing another person? If it
were possible, as he claimed, that your thoughts could affect another
person's physiology, then—

Especially if you know which areas of the brain to alter. Especially
if you had an identical twin with whom you shared the ability to
communicate in unexplainable ways . . .

Especially if—

Ah.

So that's where she came into the picture.

Stimulating the Wernicke's area.

Exciting that specific area of the temporal lobe.

"You're actually talking about—"

But before she could finish, Darren got a text message, looked at
his phone, then interrupted her: "Goss's wife and son were found dead
at the house. The sheriff has Adrian in custody."

"His son and his wife?" Daniel said.

"Yes."

Riah had no idea who Adrian was or who the Goss family was, but
she was intrigued that more people connected with the twins had died.

Discomfort.

Pain.

Death.

She waited; Darren took a breath. "Well, it looks like we can tell you exactly how you can help us after all."

No Wind

Charlene and I sit quietly in the back of the executive car as our driver maneuvers through traffic, taking us to Bridgeport.

The silence accentuates how affected we both are by the news of Dr. Tanbyrn's death.

I think of what Michelle Boyd, my producer at EFN, told me last night about viewers being forced to think about their own mortality if Tanbyrn died, and then being inspired to live better lives themselves.

But that's not exactly how I feel.

Not inspired to live a better life for myself—inspired to bring down the people who took his life from him. That was more like it.

In a way, I feel like I did yesterday afternoon when I was facing down Abina's murderer in the forest in Oregon—a sharpening of my senses, a dialing in of my attention.

And it felt good.

It's like the higher the stakes are being raised, the clearer my focus is becoming. It reminds me of the times when I was performing my stage show and I would do stunts other people referred to as death-defying.

323

I always liked those.

Kinda miss them.

Knowing that I'm all in, that there's no turning back and no backing down, it's what I'm made to do. And it's good to have that feeling back. I just wish it wasn't coming today on the heels of someone's death.

I couldn't shake the thought that the footage of the suicide bomber and his two associates blowing up was one of the keys to unlocking what was going on here.

On the plane, I'd made a mental note to take a closer look at the footage, and I figure now's probably a good time to do so.

To give Charlene and me privacy, I close the sliding glass shield between the front and back seats. Then, on my laptop, I pull up the video Fionna had sent me. We watch it several times, study it carefully, looking for anything we might have missed earlier.

But find nothing.

Just when I'm about to abandon the idea, Charlene motions to me. "Hang on." She reaches over, taps the space bar, pauses the video. "I think I saw something. Back it up a little bit."

I finger-scroll backward, to the moments immediately preceding the explosion.

She points to the screen. "There. Outside the window, across the street. You can see it between the gap in the shades. A glint."

I enlarge that part of the video, study it closely. "On the third-floor window of that building."

"Yes."

I zoom in on the image even more, but the footage isn't the highest resolution and the image becomes blurry. I back it up a bit, and Charlene reads my mind: "Could that be a scope? From a sniper's rifle?"

The picture isn't clear enough for me to tell for sure. "I don't know. It's possible."

"Play it again. From the start."

We cue the video at the beginning: the men in the room, the table with the vest and explosives, the man tugging the curtains partway closed, the glint, the explosion—

"Why doesn't it billow outward?" I whisper.

"What?"

In the sharp sunlight I really can't tell for sure. "Let me play it through again."

I start at the beginning again, pause the video just before the explosion, then play the footage forward as slowly as the computer will let me.

"The curtain. It looks like it billows into the room as the explosion happens."

Once more we study that crucial moment in the video, and it certainly does appear that a fraction of a second before the explosion occurs, the curtain on the left side swirls inward.

"The wind?" she suggests. "Or a breeze from the ceiling fan?"

"There wasn't any wind, there weren't any ripples in the curtain earlier, and the ceiling fan wasn't on. So that leaves us with . . ."

It's all about sight lines, misdirection, and—

"A bullet passing through it." She leans back in her seat. "It's a fake. A sniper shot the vest, blew it up."

Expectation. The audience sees what they expect to see.

I think through what we know, balance it against what we don't. "Let me ask Xav if that type of C-4 would detonate from the impact of a sniper's bullet."

I speed-dial him while Charlene slides the computer onto her lap to watch the footage again. Xavier picks up, speaking quietly; apparently they'd just been escorted into RixoTray's corporate headquarters and I've caught him in the hallway leading to the cybersecurity office. After quickly recounting what Charlene and I noticed, I ask him about the possibility of detonating C-4 by firing a round into it.

There's a pause as he considers my question.

"No. C-4 is a secondary explosive, needs a primer . . . but if the sniper aimed for the primer or the electronic control, it might. Depends on the configuration and design of the vest, where the bullet struck. The point of impact might also explain the brief delay, why there was actually time to see the curtains flutter. But a sniper wouldn't aim for the vest. He'd aim for the head."

"Unless the whole intention was to make the video look like something other than a sniper attack."

"So you're thinking a sniper was stationed in that other building, knew what room these men would be in, sighted through the window, waited until one of them put on the vest, then shot it in the exact place to detonate it?"

"When you put it that way, it doesn't sound quite so plausible," I admit.

"I'm not saying it isn't plausible, just thinking aloud. Let's suppose it actually went down like that. It would mean that all of our postulating about the entanglement research—"

"Was completely off base."

"Yeah."

Perspective.

You only find the truth when you look at the facts from the right perspective.

I try to evaluate things. "The sight line would've allowed the sniper to hit each of the men. Maybe the vest just played into the narrative better."

"Like one of your tricks."

"Like one of my tricks."

"Is it definitive? Can you tell for sure if there's a sniper over there?"

"No. But the curtains, the glint across the street, the fact that the guy didn't reach up to detonate the vest himself—they all make it a legitimate possibility."

"I'll have a look at it as soon as I can with Fionna. She might be able to do something about the resolution. But it might be a little while. We're almost to the cybersecurity office."

"Good. As soon as you can."

We end the call.

Reviewing the footage had only brought more questions—if there was a sniper, did that mean someone was faking the effects of this research? Could everything we'd been hypothesizing be on the wrong track entirely?

Hopefully, meeting with Dr. Colette would bring us some answers.

Because for the moment it felt like, as Fionna might say, someone had just knocked over another cage and there were even more gerbils than before underfoot.

The Need to Kill

The twins asked Riah to help them kill someone.

It was that simple. That's why they'd called her in.

Given all that she knew, all that'd happened in the last couple days, the request wasn't by any means out of the blue, but hearing Darren actually say the words, actually ask her to help eliminate a threat to national security, was instructive.

And inviting?

Yes, admittedly, it was.

Before letting them go on with their explanation, she returned to the topic of Goss and his family. "So you did that?"

"Yes," Darren said.

"But how?"

"Something went wrong. We were trying to influence him to take his own life, but he did not. He slaughtered his family instead. With an axe. We weren't able to—"

"Who did he kill first? The mother or the son?"

They stared at her. "I don't know," Daniel said.

I wonder what their wounds look like. How much blood there was.

"Why him? Why Adrian Goss?"

"He was the man who raped our mother." Darren's words were matter-of-fact. "The man who impregnated her."

"Adrian Goss was your father."

"Yes."

A close personal connection.

The prerequisite for Tanbyrn's research.

"Did you love him?"

Another quizzical look, but then both twins avowed that no, they had not loved him. Had not even known his identity until recently.

"We failed," Daniel began. "We need you to—"

"Use the electrodes to stimulate the Wernicke's area of your brains."

"Yes."

"To enhance your ability to cause discomfort in others."

"Yes."

Pain.

Death.

Exactly how all of this was possible was still unclear to her, but if Dr. Tanbyrn was right, the answer lay somewhere in the realm of quantum entanglement, an answer she would have to investigate more in-depth later when she had time.

"How did it feel?" she asked them. "To find out that a boy and a woman whom you had not targeted died in such a violent manner?"

"Disappointing," Darren admitted. "It meant that on our own we weren't as effective as we'd hoped."

There was no remorse in his voice, not even a hint of sorrow over the loss of the two innocent lives.

She trusted the twins implicitly, knew that they were patriots, knew that they had only the best intentions in mind. And she trusted that they truly did need her help, that the next target truly was, as they said, a well-funded terrorist, an enemy of the state.

But could she help them kill?

She thought again of the fourteen-year-old girl in Afghanistan whose father had blown up, she thought of the son and wife of Adrian Goss, and she remembered being a teenager herself, holding that fragile-boned bird in her hands. Most of all, she remembered snapping its neck simply to see what it would be like to kill it. She knew that just like everyone, she had the capacity to kill. And to do so for no other reason than curiosity.

But could she kill a human being?

Yes.

Yes.

She absolutely could.

In an illuminating rush of insight, she realized that in a certain sense it was something she'd always wanted to do. Just like with the bird—to find out what it would be like. To find out if it would make her feel anything at all.

But there was one thing she needed to know before she would agree to help the twins. "People say that love lies at the core of human nature. To love and be loved. Do you believe that?"

"No," Daniel told her.

"Then what do you think people want?"

"People don't want to *be* loved; they want to *feel* loved."

"To feel loved."

"Yes. Would you rather be secretly despised by a partner, a lover, a spouse, but live your whole life believing that he deeply loves you, or would you rather be deeply loved by someone and yet never find out about it? Would you prefer a lifetime of feeling loved or a lifetime never finding out that you were?"

Riah wasn't sure how most people would answer that question. She'd been told she was loved many times but had never known what it was like to feel it. Not for one minute of her life.

She took a moment before responding. "Don't people want more than to simply believe they're loved? Don't they want the real thing—without any deception, without any betrayal? Don't people fundamentally want both love and truth?"

"It's very rare to have both," Daniel said, not quite answering her question. "Wouldn't you agree?"

"Yes. I would imagine that it is."

Rare. Too rare in this world of so many people who were so soon going to die.

She realized that the feeling really must be what mattered most, and that given her nature, it was not something she would ever experience.

Not ever.

Given her nature.

She made her decision.

"I'll help you," she told them.

Darren looked satisfied at her response. "We'll call you within the hour to tell you where to meet us. Bring the equipment."

With the nanowire electrodes already in place in the twins' brains, the instruments she would need to send the electrical impulses to their Wernicke's areas were minimal. She could carry them in a small day pack.

Darren pulled out three cell phones. "There's a time frame here. We need to move on it this morning. There are two numbers pre-programmed into each phone, one for each of the other two. After each number has been connected to, the phone's chip will erase itself, so if anything goes wrong, just hit number one and number two to speed-dial the other phones. It will erase the chip in yours."

Everyone took a phone.

The twins left.

And Riah went to her computer to verify what they'd told her regarding the man who lived in Maine slaughtering his family with an axe earlier that morning. She hoped she could find some photos.

After all, she really was curious about the details, about what fatal axe wounds in the body of a woman and a young boy would look like, if they would bear any semblance to the wounds in the snake her father had beheaded when she was just a girl, the one whose body she held until the wriggling stopped.

Killed but not yet dead.

Then finally, after a few minutes, both.

GPS

"It's as hot as a monkey's armpit in here."

The three computer technicians from RixoTray's cybersecurity team stared at Fionna.

"Um . . ." The youngest of the three techs nodded toward the only woman on the team. "Can you take care of that?" She headed off to fiddle with the thermostat.

A few minutes ago Fionna had introduced Xavier to the RixoTray cybersecurity team as her associate, promoting him from minion and assistant to associate. It seemed like the right thing to do. Now he stood by her side.

"So, you were able to get into Dr. Arlington's laptop?" The guy asking her the question looked like someone you'd picture appearing on Wikipedia's "computer geek" entry. Young. Skinny. Black-framed glasses. Messed-up hair. Holding a Dr Pepper in one hand and a bag of Doritos that Xavier was eyeing in the other. He seemed to be the one in charge, but from what Fionna had seen so far, her son Lonnie would've been more than a match for this guy at a keyboard.

"Yes," she said. "I was able to get in."

"We identified the attempt. Blocked it." Nacho Chip Boy was defending himself, but Fionna wasn't impressed.

"Only after I was in for five minutes and forty-two seconds. I could have erased data, altered research findings, transferred funds, anything I wanted to, long before you identified the breach." She didn't tell him about getting in again earlier that morning to access Dr. Colette's and Arlington's personal calendars.

The young man opened his mouth as if he were going to respond, then closed it. Said nothing.

She gestured toward the computer desk. "May I?"

He stepped aside and she sat down.

Xavier moved next to her, asked the guy if he was planning on finishing his Doritos.

"Yes."

"Right."

Fionna tapped at the keyboard.

First she went to the company's mail server to show the tech team how she got in. She fudged on that just a little, didn't give away all her tricks, but it offered her a chance to note any emails to Dr. Arlington's account. The latest was encrypted. She typed. Not encrypted anymore. "Oops." She acted like that'd been a mistake.

The message was from someone named Brennan Sacco concerning the president's speech. Interesting. She flew past it. "Video surveillance? Last night? In Arlington's suite?"

A pause. "Why do you need that?"

"When I was in the system yesterday, I found evidence that someone else had been there, had compromised his computer from inside his office." Yes, it was a lie, and since telling lies was not something she would ever want her children to do, she felt a little bad about it. But in this case it seemed necessary, and sometimes grown-ups have to make grown-up decisions.

After a small hesitation, he showed her which directory to use to access the footage.

Fionna pulled up the cameras and the screen split into four sections, one for each of the security cameras in the lobby and in Arlington's executive suite. She cued them to thirty minutes before the video had started and pressed play, then fast-forward.

"The system is set up so that when people check in at the security station," the guy with the Doritos said proudly, "one camera is directed at their face. Then, after the guard types in their driver's license number or RixoTray security code clearance number, their name appears on the screen."

Xavier grunted. "Is that the best you can come up with for a multi-billion-dollar international pharmaceutical company? A security code number? You never heard of facial recognition? Unbelievable."

My sentiments exactly, Fionna thought.

On the screen, a woman entered. Her name appeared: Dr. Riah Colette.

Fionna took note of it, then fast-forwarded the footage again.

Soon two men came in. Twins. No identification came up on the screen, but yet they were allowed to pass through both the main entrance and Arlington's office suite, just like Colette had done.

"There aren't any names for them," Xavier said. "That a glitch?"

"They've been here before," one of the techs answered. "They have clearance."

"Of course they do," Xavier replied somewhat rebukingly. "They're walking right through your checkpoint."

And then, as the footage rolled, one more person came through the door and one more name appeared on the screen.

Undersecretary of Defense Oriana Williamson.

While Fionna continued working on the keyboard and schooling the pharmaceutical firm's cybersecurity team, Xavier slipped into the hallway to call Jevin and Charlene to share the information about the Sacco email, the names of Dr. Colette and Undersecretary of Defense Williamson, and the fact that a pair of identical twins had entered Arlington's office just minutes before the video began.

~

So now there were gerbils everywhere.

I end the call with Xavier so he can get back to Fionna and the cybersecurity team.

Mentally, I review what I know about the research, the video, the Pentagon connection, the thwarted terrorist attack.

The twins, Undersecretary of Defense Williamson, Arlington, and Colette all saw the video.

A thought-borne virus.

What had Fionna said yesterday when she first mentioned the bombing attempt earlier this week? A reference to the president's speech . . .

Now this email from Brennan Sacco about the speech.

"Charlene, see if you can find out who Brennan Sacco is."

She thumb-types on her phone. Goes online. Surfing she doesn't mind—just talking on the phone.

I close my eyes, try to process everything.

Tanbyrn was worried about funding.

The president wants to end Project Alpha.

"He's the president's speechwriter," she explains.

All the facts merge, pass each other, then lock into place again.

We had the connection between Cyrus Arlington and Glenn Banner . . . brain imaging . . . Charlene's mention of the legislation that could affect the telomerase drug release date . . . the clinical trials—

I have no idea if the sniper was real or not or how the video related to any of this, but it obviously concerned killing those—

Affecting someone nonlocally. A top-secret research program on the negative effects of nonlocal psi activity . . .

Oh.

Eleven o'clock at the park.

"Charlene. The president's speech. That's it."

"What?"

"Track with me here. Tanbyrn told us 'when the eagle falls at the park'—something he overheard the twins say. The timing isn't a coincidence—remember what you told me Monday night? Banner and now the Kabul video. The legislation, the speech. Everything is converging."

When the eagle falls at the park—she's mouthing the words. "Independence Park?"

I tap at the phone to bring up the image I'm thinking of, the one she needs to see. "Yes." I spin the phone toward her, showing her the image of the Great Seal of the United States. "And the eagle is—"

"You're not thinking that the twins are going after the president!"

"That's what I'm thinking."

"No, that's crazy." But it doesn't sound like she's convinced of her words. "I mean . . ."

We had threads weaving everything together, but for the moment they were still tenuous, more like strands of a spiderweb—the design was only visible when you moved back and looked at the whole thing at once.

Perspective.

But did we have all the strands yet? I backpedal a little. "No, it's not enough. Not with what we have."

"It doesn't matter if it's not enough to prove it, Jev, there's enough there to make it feasible. We need to warn the Secret Service."

But with each passing moment, I'm feeling less confident of my conclusion. "What would we tell them? That a pair of identical twin telepathic assassins might try to send a thought-borne virus to the president? We don't have proof, a time frame, an established motive, anything. We don't even know who the twins are." I sigh as I realize the truth. "Really, all we have is a collection of circumstantial evidence. If that."

But she doesn't budge. "Jev, if there's even a slim chance that his life might be in danger, we have to report it. We at least have to tell them what we know."

"They'll probably take us in for questioning."

"Yeah. Probably."

That's the last thing I want right now, but I do sense that she's right about contacting the authorities. However, I'm not exactly thrilled at the prospect of convincing them to take a threat like this seriously.

If you call the Secret Service, they'll be able to track the phone's GPS.

Staring out the window, I assess our situation. How to give the Secret Service everything they need without being brought in as accessories or suspects?

"Charlene, let me use your phone."

She hands it over. "Why my phone?"

"You'll see."

It takes me a few minutes to get through to someone who'll actually talk to me. I thought there'd be some sort of hotline to report threats against the president, but I have to go through almost as many prompts as you do when you call for computer tech support. Finally a real woman's voice comes on. Boredom and annoyance in her first two words: "Name, please."

Using an alias right now would probably not be a good idea.

But neither would giving her your real name.

"I have information about a possible threat against the president's life."

"What is your name?"

"I just said I have information about a threat against—"

"Name."

"You're not listening to—"

"Who am I talking with?" She's losing what little patience she might have had.

"Jevin, and this is important."

With an audible sigh, she decides not to push me for a last name: "What information?"

"It involves a pair of twins. Who, well . . . they might attack President Hoult at any time."

"Who are they?"

"I don't know. But they go by the initials 'L' and 'N.'"

"'L' and 'N.'"

"That's right."

"And how are they going to attack the president?"

I'm aware that the answer to her question is going to sound ridiculous. I could spend time trying to explain the quantum physics of it all, but I didn't even understand most of that myself. I just go ahead and say it: "By their thoughts."

A stretch of silence.

"Sir, you do know that it is a federal offense to threaten the life of the president of the United States. Even to joke about it."

"No, I'm not threatening his life, and I'm not joking. I'm telling you that I think there's a plot against him. It has to do with a top-secret Pentagon program called Project Alpha. The twins work for the Pentagon. Sort of." With every word, I can tell I'm losing more and more ground.

"So this assassination plot was hatched at the Pentagon."

"Well, that or a pharmaceutical company."

"I see."

I rub my forehead.

"And how did you come about this information?"

It would take way too long to explain everything. "That doesn't matter, this is—"

"Sir, how exactly are these twins going to kill the president by their thoughts?"

"Maybe stop his heart. I'm not sure."

"With the use of their psychic powers?"

"You have to believe me—"

"Excuse me for just one moment." When she puts me on hold, I know it's over. This is never going to work. I imagine she's calling for a car to pick us up right now, or possibly checking to make sure she has a lock on our GPS.

I hang up.

"Well," Charlene acknowledges, "maybe that wasn't the best idea after all."

"Maybe you should have made the call."

"Are they going to follow up on anything you said?"

"I doubt it. We need to find the twins ourselves. Lead the Secret Service to them."

"Then we can't let them find us first."

We come to a bottleneck in traffic. "That's why I chose your phone. I thought I'd give you the honors." I hand her cell to her.

She catches on. "Are you saying . . . ?"

"Yup. Something we both know you've wanted to do for a long time."

With a gleam in her eye, she rolls down her window and pelts her cell phone onto the road. It shatters in a lovely little explosion of technology.

"That felt really good."

"I'll bet it did."

Of course, it was certainly possible that NSA or the Secret Service had already tracked our location, even traced the phone number back to Charlene. In fact, they might've already dispatched agents to find us, but I was counting on the fact that in the congested traffic they wouldn't be able to figure out which car the phone had been thrown from and, as we drove on, wouldn't be able to find us.

Yet.

The plan: find Dr. Colette.

Then the twins.

And then let the Secret Service find us.

The First Baby

Riah found no photos of the axe murder victims.

Which was a bit disappointing.

But the search for the pictures of the dead family made her think of her own family once again. Her dead mother. Her father. Her sister. And the question of what people really want: feeling loved or being loved.

She loved you when you were a child.

Yes. She did.

But you never loved her.

Riah drew out her phone, tapped in a number that she hadn't called in six months but had committed to memory long before that.

A woman answered. "Hello?"

"Katie Burleson?"

Immediate suspicion. "Who is this?"

"This is Riah."

Silence.

"Your sister."

"How many Riahs do you think I know?" Katie's words scorched the air.

"It's been a long time since we spoke and—"

"If I wanted to talk to you, I would have called you. It's not like you're hard to find. I'm hanging up now and I don't want you to call this number again."

"Katie—"

"Goodbye—"

"He did things to me."

Riah waited for the line to go dead but it didn't.

"Our father," she went on, "he did things to me. Things a father should never do to his children."

"Of course he did."

A pause. "You knew?"

"Is that why you called? To try and make me feel sorry for you? What do you think happened when you went off to college? Do you think he just got interested in Mom again? Really? Are you kidding me?"

Riah found her sister's words informative and sensed that she should feel a deep sense of rage against their father for violating Katie too.

In the background, Riah could hear Katie's youngest child crying, and a thought struck her: Katie had her first pregnancy, her first abortion, shortly after moving out of the house. She'd always said her boyfriend Jose was the father.

"It wasn't Jose's baby," Riah said softly.

"Don't call this number again." And then, without saying goodbye, Katie hung up.

This bitter woman, this hurting woman, had known innocence, known love as a child, but both had died over the years because of their father.

Or perhaps because Riah had never done anything to stop him.

She was left wondering what to do.

She could never help her sister feel loved, it wasn't in her nature, but could she do something else, not out of love exactly, but in the service of justice? An act on her sister's behalf?

Yes.

A very specific act.

Yes.

To right a tragic wrong.

The greater good.

Riah made a firm and certain decision to pay a visit to their father as soon as her duties with the twins were completed.

Credentials

9:48 a.m.
1 hour 7 minutes left

RixoTray's R&D facility lies on the outskirts of Bridgeport, surrounded by a dense wooded area that I suspect also belongs to the firm to create a buffer between their facility and any corporate or residential encroachment.

Our driver slows, gets in line behind the four cars in front of us. They all pass through the checkpoint without a hitch, and only moments later we pull to a stop beside the guard station.

The driver and I roll down our windows. The guard looks at me with a practiced air of suspicion but ignores our driver as if he doesn't even exist. Apparently, Charlene and I are the ones he's most interested in.

"Driver's licenses, please."

We produce them, as does our driver. We all hand them over. Charlene and I also give him our fake FDA credentials. "J. Franklin Banks," I tell him, avoiding drawing attention to my real name, my stage name, the one I used on TV. "Food and Drug Administration." I briefly hold up my clipboard and its attached documents to show him that I mean business.

He gazes at the driver's licenses, then studies the creds carefully. Fionna had told us they would check our fingerprints, but that didn't concern me much, since, unless you've been printed by law enforcement or as part of a corporate security program, your prints won't show up on any kind of watch list.

As expected, the guard holds out a small electronic pad about the size of a smartphone. "Fingerprints, please."

All three of us, in turn, place our forefingers on the pad and no red flags come up. He goes on, "What is the purpose of your visit?"

"We're here because of complaints involving a research project," I tell him. "We need to speak directly to Dr. Riah Colette."

He hands the creds to his partner to study as well. Then looks over a clipboard of his own.

"I don't see your name on our appointment list."

"No, of course not."

He looks at me questioningly.

Charlene scootches toward me, leans toward the window, addresses him. "The FDA no longer announces spot inspections or visits of this nature before they occur. In the past, people have shredded documents and destroyed evidence when they've received prior knowledge of our visits. Arriving unannounced is the only way to assure that none of that happens."

Before he can reply, she goes on, "This complaint involves ethical violations involving the use of human test subjects in experimental drug trials. It is a highly sensitive matter and these are serious allegations. I'm afraid that's all we're authorized to tell you."

Oh, she was good.

I've saved the clipboards and their paperwork as the pièce de résistance. Now I hand them to him.

The line of cars behind us is growing longer.

The guard flips through the official-looking documents that Fionna and Charlene drew up based on the information Fionna's children had gathered on actual FDA complaint report forms.

I can tell he isn't reading any of the fine print.

They never read the fine print.

Except Xavier on iTunes updates.

At last the guard looks at his partner, who shrugs and passes the IDs back to him. He returns the clipboard, driver's licenses, and FDA credentials to us and waves us through.

Charlene whispers to me, "One down, two to go."

～⌒～

Air Force One touched down at the Philadelphia International Airport.

Originally, before delivering his eleven o'clock speech, the president had been scheduled to visit a charter high school to encourage the students to be good citizens and strive toward academic excellence, but he'd changed his plans earlier in the morning to give himself more time to review what he was going to say.

The Secret Service, of course, mentioned nothing about the reported psychic assassination plot as they escorted him from the plane.

Not only was this latest threat ludicrous, but the Secret Service has a policy: never notify the president of any threats against his life unless there is immediate and imminent danger. Considering the fact that he receives more than twelve thousand death threats a year, keeping him up to speed would mean updating him hourly about all the people who wanted to kill him.

And the Secret Service never cancels presidential events just because of uncorroborated death threats.

The speech at the Liberty Bell would go on.

Still, as absurd as this threat was, they had to follow up on it, just as they have to follow up on every threat to his life—all twelve thousand. Two agents had been sent to bring in the person who'd called it in, and whose GPS location had been pinpointed and verified by NSA.

～⌒～

In the lobby of the research facility, Charlene and I again produce our credentials and paperwork.

We place our things on the conveyor belt, step through the full-body scanner, and the security guard working the X-ray machine tells us we'll need to leave our cell phones with him. "I'm sorry. There are no pictures allowed, no recording devices of any kind inside the building." He sounds tired. Looks tired. I wonder how long he's been working already today. Or last night.

I hadn't thought through this part of the plan. I'm not sure if government inspectors would need to keep their phones with them. While I'm debating what to say, Charlene speaks up. "Only one of us carries a phone and it's illegal for us to leave it behind. Look at page fourteen of the complaint form."

"I'm sorry, it's our policy to—"

"I'll give you a phone number. Call it and explain your policy to the federal agents who will—"

He cuts her off by holding up a hand in surrender.

Yeah, she really was good.

He exhaustedly motions for us to move along. At the final checkpoint we're handed visitors' passes, and one of the sentries, a mountain of a man who must weigh at least three hundred pounds, tells us he will escort us to Dr. Colette's office.

I jot something on the clipboard. A shopping list, actually, but taking notes is a way to mess with him, to show that Charlene and I will be the ones calling the shots and not him. "Yes. Please"—I gesture toward the hallway, indicating for him to lead us—"take us to Dr. Colette."

Brandy

9:57 a.m.

58 minutes left

"Thank you for seeing me, Mr. Vice President."

"Of course."

Cyrus had been at the White House to meet with other high-level administration employees a dozen times, the vice president half a dozen. He wasn't a lobbyist, but he'd been consulted about the ongoing health care legislation debate and the issue of counterfeit pharmaceuticals—a growing problem, especially the ones being smuggled in from southeast Asia.

And of course, anyone who'd donated as much to a presidential campaign as Cyrus had personally done, and as RixoTray had corporately done, was welcome at the White House. It was the way the system was set up, the way institutes of power have always operated. Money speaks. And the more of it there is, the more loudly it's heard.

"Have a seat, Cyrus," the vice president invited. "Would you like a drink?"

Of course, it was too early to begin drinking socially, but the vice president was not a coffee kind of guy. Not many people knew how early he typically got started on his brandy each day, but he had not kept it from Cyrus.

"Cognac. Thank you."

"Good choice."

Over the last couple years, they'd occasionally discussed the fact that the vice president hadn't gotten his party's nomination last time around, but it wasn't a topic he liked to address, so Cyrus typically refrained from bringing it up. But with the election next year, and considering the nature of his visit here today, he decided to address it, at least tangentially.

As the vice president produced an elegant bottle of cognac from his desk and poured each of them a drink, Cyrus said, "So, Hoult is already in election mode?"

Vice President Pinder brought Cyrus his drink. "You know how these things go," he said evasively. "Now, before we get down to business, how is Helen?"

"She's good. Luci Ann?"

"As beautiful, supportive, and as much of a shopaholic as ever."

Cyrus raised his glass. "To our wives."

"To our wives."

They clinked glasses. Drank.

The cognac was extraordinary, and Cyrus complimented the vice president on it.

"Camus Cognac Cuvee 3.128, rated by many connoisseurs as the best cognac in the world. We have only so many heartbeats, my friend. It'd be a shame to waste any of them on cheap brandy."

They both drank for a moment. Cyrus knew they didn't have a lot of time to talk, especially since this meeting had gotten started late, but he also knew that etiquette required that he not jump immediately into discussing business.

"So"—Pinder was the one to break the silence—"how is the telomerase research going? Have you come up with a cure for aging yet? A way to offer me a few more of those heartbeats?"

"Working on it. We've started clinical trials. Another year or so and we're hoping to have FDA approval."

"Well, I'd ask to be one of your human guinea pigs, but I think I'll wait until you get the kinks out."

"Probably a good idea."

A small smile. "Hopefully, I'll still be around to benefit from it."

"Hopefully, we both will."

They sipped their drinks, then the vice president moved things forward: "I'm guessing you're here about the speech."

Cyrus set down his glass. "You know the president's new initiatives will not serve the American people: the proposals regarding the expedited release of generic pharmaceuticals."

The vice president scratched at the back of his neck, then stood. "Let me play devil's advocate here for a moment, Cyrus. Pharmaceutical companies are some of the most profitable companies in the world. Every year they post billions of dollars of profits while millions of working-class Americans struggle under the exorbitant price of prescription drugs. Making generics more readily available could save thousands of lives each year."

Prolong, not save.

Rule #1: Everyone dies.

Rule #2: There's nothing you can do to change Rule #1.

Cyrus had heard all this before. "Actually, pharmaceutical firms aren't as profitable as most people think. Oil companies, tech firms, insurance companies, banks all have higher profit margins. Big business has always been an easy target for liberals to take potshots at. You know that."

The vice president rolled his shot glass back and forth in his fingers reflectively.

Cyrus continued, "Also, the Food and Drug Administration has made it harder than ever to get new, life-saving drugs onto the market. Out of a thousand compounds studied in prediscovery and then put through a decade of preclinical and clinical trials, only one will ever become an FDA-approved drug. The R&D costs are—"

"Yes, yes, I know. Astronomical."

"The FDA allows generics to be up to twenty times less effective in crossing the blood-brain barrier than trade-name pharmaceuticals. So when you're talking about anticonvulsants, mood stabilizers, and antidepressants, the public ends up suffering the consequences. Not to mention that 10 percent of generics are inert."

Vice President Pinder sighed. "Cyrus, I am on your side on all this, always have been. But the president isn't going to change his mind. At this point there's really nothing I can do."

"But if you could?"

"If I could?"

"If you could make it easier for us to get our pharmaceutical products to the public without the added restrictions the president wants to put on the industry, would you? If you could keep producers of generic pharmaceuticals from taking advantage of our research and then undercutting us on the price, would you do it?"

"I've always done all I can to support scientific innovation and the advancement of pharmaceuticals for the betterment of the American people."

"Yes."

"So are you asking that I speak with the president about this? Because I assure you that he's not going to back down. He is quite firm on what he intends to do."

Cyrus knew the president wouldn't back down. That wasn't what he'd come here to talk about. "We could really use someone at the top who sees things more clearly than Hoult does. Who realizes that without our R&D, the life-saving drugs would never exist in the first place, that we need time to recoup our investment before we're undercut by generics."

"Once again we are on the same page."

The vice president laid his hand on the desk and gently massaged the elegant wood as if it were the skin of his lover, who Cyrus knew was not Luci Ann, his beautiful, supportive, shopaholic wife.

Varied love interests.

Something else the two of them had in common.

"If I were able to effect change," the vice president said, "if I were ever to become president, I would never unfairly target pharmaceutical firms or the important work they do in improving the life and health of the American people."

So.

Yes.

Cyrus had what he'd come here for. The reassurance that the VP would promote legislation that was in line with RixoTray's goals.

"If you were ever to become president."

Vice President Pinder looked at him knowingly, said in his eyes much more than he said with his words: "If that were ever to happen. Yes."

Cyrus rose, warmly thanked the vice president for his time and his cognac.

"Have a safe flight back to Philadelphia," Vice President Pinder said as they were walking toward the door. "I hope we'll be able to speak again soon."

"I'm confident that we will."

Riah got the call from Daniel sooner than she thought she would. He asked her to meet him and his brother at 10:45 just off the I-76 Belmont Avenue/Green Lane exit. "Darren will call you with the exact location as soon as possible. Bring everything you'll need."

"I will."

And then she began to gather her things.

Departure

10:04 a.m.

51 minutes left

Our hulking escort leads us to Dr. Riah Colette's office and announces that we're from the FDA and would like to speak to her. She appraises us, notices the official-looking documents attached to our clipboards, invites us into her office, and closes the door.

Gotta love those clipboards.

Her purse is on the desk. Her car keys and folded-up laptop beside it. Either she's just arriving or she's on her way out. But if she was following the schedule Fionna had pulled up earlier, I knew that Dr. Colette was not just coming in to work.

"My name is Jevin Banks." Time for the truth all the way around. "This is Charlene Antioch."

"Dr. Riah Colette." She's an attractive woman, dressed respectively but not pretentiously. She doesn't look the least bit intimidated to see us or to have heard from the guard that we're inspectors from the FDA. I have the sense that most people in her position would, at least to some degree, be nervous or defensive. Not her. She doesn't ask why we're here or how she might help us.

How to do this.

Don't jump into talking about an assassination conspiracy. Find out what you can first. Find out if she's involved.

"We have a few questions," I tell her, "and we think you're the right person to answer them."

"I'm afraid I'm in a bit of a hurry. I have an appointment I need to be preparing for. Perhaps you could talk with one of my assistants?"

Charlene speaks up. "It really needs to be you, I'm afraid."

"What is it concerning? Exactly?"

I take a breath. "The twins."

She gazes at Charlene, then at me.

"You're not from the FDA." It's a statement, not a question.

"No, we're not. Yesterday at the Lawson Research Center in Oregon, we were investigating Dr. Tanbyrn's research for a television documentary. A man named Glenn Banner started the building on fire. We barely escaped. Dr. Tanbyrn got out with us, but died this morning from complications caused by smoke inhalation."

She takes a seat on the edge of her desk.

"I had not heard that."

I don't detect any sense of loss in her words, but there's no coldness either. It's as if the news is informative to her, that she's acknowledging how tragic it is but isn't in the place right now where she's ready to mourn for the dead doctor.

Charlene lowers her voice. "A woman was also killed in the fire. One of Tanbyrn's research assistants."

Dr. Colette is quiet. "I'm not exactly sure how I can help you."

From doing cold readings while emulating the tricks of professed psychics, I'd gotten good at reading people and I catch no sign that Dr. Colette isn't being straight with us.

She isn't involved. Trust her.

I go with my gut. "The man who started the fire, Glenn Banner, had been in touch with Dr. Arlington."

"And how do you know this?"

"Banner's cell phone. We know you're in charge of the division that has a connection to Dr. Tanbyrn's research. The Pentagon is involved as well."

She studies me carefully. "You're doing a documentary?"

"Right now we're just concerned with stopping more people from being killed."

A moment passes. "Is there anything else?"

Get to the assassination plot.

The twins.

"There's a connection to the video that you, Dr. Arlington, Undersecretary of Defense Oriana Williamson, and the twins watched last night."

"Well." She seems more impressed than taken aback. "You have done your homework."

Charlene steps forward. "Dr. Tanbyrn told us he was studying the negative aspects of the twins' special abilities. His research points to using avenues of quantum entanglement to affect another person's physiology in a negative manner."

Dr. Colette doesn't seem surprised by that. "Nonlocally."

Man, she's not hiding anything.

I nod. "Yes."

"Anything else?"

The plot. Tell her what you suspect.

"The suicide bomber didn't kill himself. He was shot by a sniper." I take a stab at this, go for it: "We think the president of the United States might be the next target."

"The president?"

"That's right."

"And why do you think that?"

I tell her about our line of reasoning about the telomerase research, Tanbyrn's murder, the press release, the proposed legislation, the phrase the twins used about the eagle falling at the park, the Brennan Sacco email. The more I explained it, the more everything seems to fit together in a pattern of gossamer threads.

When I finish, rather than sticking to the topic of the potential assassination plot, surprisingly, Dr. Colette focuses instead on the footage in Kabul. "How do you know it was a sniper?"

I pull out my laptop. "I'll show you."

Dr. Cyrus Arlington was in the helicopter on his way to Philadelphia when he got the text from Caitlyn telling him that the police were waiting for him at the landing pad. "It has something to do with a man named Glenn Banner."

Not a surprise.

He texted her back a word of thanks.

Then rehearsed what he would tell the officers about his relationship with the dead arsonist.

Riah carefully evaluated what the two people who'd been imitating FDA inspectors told her. They had all their facts straight, that much was true, but how could the enemy of the state mentioned by the twins be the president of the United States?

It wasn't possible to tell for certain whether or not a sniper had been involved in detonating the suicide bomber's vest in Kabul, but after reviewing the footage she had to admit that it was certainly possible.

The sniper might explain why the twins were so adamant that you help them.

But sniper or not, they had affected Adrian Goss's neural processing abilities on their own, so the president could still be in danger. After all, what if they were able to do the same thing to one of the Secret Service agents guarding the president?

But some things just didn't compute. Did the twins know that they'd been unsuccessful in Kabul? If there was a sniper, who hired him? The twins? Oriana? Cyrus?

What if they all did? What if they've just been playing you ever since the beginning?

Less than forty-five minutes ago, she'd agreed to help the twins eliminate a national security threat, but there was a lot more going on here than met the eye, a lot of currents flowing beneath the surface, and she wasn't sure she was in the right position at the moment to trace where they all came from or in which direction they were flowing.

The man who'd introduced himself as Jevin Banks was watching her closely, waiting for her response.

Honestly, she had no reason to doubt anything he or Ms. Antioch had said, especially considering the risk they'd taken getting this information to her, the effort of creating fake IDs and documentation, of working their way past three security check—

"Who are the twins, Dr. Colette?" I ask her.

She hesitates only slightly before answering. "Darren and Daniel are military-trained assassins."

Oh.

Well, that made sense.

Darren, ending with an N; Daniel, ending with an L. Is that it? The reason for the initials?

I couldn't be sure, and right now it didn't matter.

But why would they target the commander-in-chief? Why, if they worked for the military? What possible motive could they have?

I realize that at the moment that doesn't matter either. Their plan, whatever it consisted of, did.

"We need to stop them," I tell her. "Do you know where they are?"

"No. But I'm supposed to meet them at 10:45. They told me we needed to move on it this morning."

"Before the president's speech," Charlene notes.

"It would seem so. It won't take long to send the electrical impulses to the electrodes once I get there. I'm not sure how long it would take for them to focus their thoughts, but I'm guessing not too long. Are you certain that it's the president they're trying to kill?"

"No," I admit, "but—"

Her desk phone rings, startling all of us.

"Excuse me." She picks up the receiver, listens to someone on the other end, acknowledges that she understands, then hangs up.

"There are two Secret Service agents at the front gate. They're asking about you."

Oh, not good.

Somehow they'd tracked us after all.

And now they were here, and undoubtedly, they were going to bring us in for questioning.

For a moment Dr. Colette stares out her office window at the trees surrounding the property, then picks up the phone again, taps in a number, and speaks into the mouthpiece. "Yes. Those two agents? Send them in."

She hangs up.

So.

That's how it's going to go.

"If the Secret Service goes after the twins," she explains, "there are going to be a lot of dead Secret Service agents out there. Daniel and Darren are that good. But they'll listen to me, and they're going to wait for me. I think I can stop them, stall them at least. And you know more about this than I do. I want you to come along." She snatches up her purse and a small daypack. "We'll take my car. By the time those agents get here to my office, we'll be off the property. Let's go stop the twins."

Oh yeah.

That's what I'm talking about.

"I could really grow to like this woman," Charlene whispers to me as we hurry out the door behind her.

"Me too."

The Embalming Room

10:27 a.m.
28 minutes left

Darren snapped the man's neck as his brother took care of the woman just a few feet away.

Both of the targets died quickly and with very little struggle.

Darren let go and the man's body thudded to the carpet. Daniel was more considerate, lowering the woman's corpse gently to the floor.

Both the male funeral home director and his female embalmer lay staring unblinkingly at the ceiling.

They had, appropriately enough, died in the building where they'd prepared and then displayed so many other bodies. Dying in this place dedicated to the dead.

Darren closed the shades of the funeral home's west-facing window.

The Schuylkill River flowed swiftly past the edge of the property, providing a panoramic view of the late autumn trees lining the other bank. A prayer garden and flower bed lay in the funeral home's yard, but the lawn stretched fifty feet beyond them to the six-foot drop-off to the river.

The Faulkner-Kernel Funeral Home was located on River Road, less than twenty minutes from central Philly. The tranquil setting provided "a picturesque, restful setting that no other funeral homes in the city can offer," according to the brochure the twins had picked up earlier while they were scouting out sites they might use.

A picturesque, restful setting for families to come and view the embalmed corpses of their loved ones.

A place far enough from the city center to allow for on-site cremation.

The brothers had wanted that option available to them for disposing of Dr. Colette's corpse.

Out front, the hearse sat in the curving driveway leading to the front doors. Parking was limited, so Darren imagined that during an actual funeral, the people attending would have to park on the side of the narrow road winding along the riverbank. He'd parked their sedan behind the hearse.

He and his brother had needed a place where they would be isolated and would have equipment that Dr. Colette could use for any medical procedures she might have to do if things didn't go as planned. So, a place that would have at least a rudimentary operating room.

The embalming room would work.

After all, that wasn't the kind of place someone would be tempted to suddenly walk into, even if for some reason a visitor were to show up at the home. The room offered them everything they needed. Seclusion. Isolation. A private setting where they would be able to relax and focus their thoughts enough to kill the leader of the free world.

For a moment Darren studied the two bodies on the carpet. Then, for the time being at least, he and his brother laid them to rest in two of the caskets in the funeral home's small but well-stocked showroom.

A pair of unfortunate but necessary civilian casualties.

He checked his watch.

10:29.

Twenty-six minutes before they were scheduled to begin with Riah.

"She'll be at the exit at 10:45," he told his brother. "I'll call her a few minutes beforehand with the address. That should give us just enough time."

Last-Minute Revisions

"Read me what we have."

"Mr. President, I would rather—"

"I want to hear it while there's still time to change it."

Brennan Sacco had only been brought in as one of the president's speechwriters six months ago, but he'd discovered right away that it was always this way with President Jeremiah Hoult—last-minute changes. Some of which never even made it to the teleprompter.

Now the presidential limousine caravan turned onto Market Street and passed Declaration House. Five limos so that no one would know which one actually carried the president. Today Brennan was in the fourth, along with the president and two Secret Service agents.

Yes, it was unusual for a speechwriter to work this closely with the president, but Hoult had always insisted that the most important part of his job was sharing his vision for the future with the American people, and the way to do that was through communication.

Obviously, he didn't know that Brennan was being bribed by Dr. Cyrus Arlington to share his own communication with him, leaking the contents of the speeches concerning health care issues.

President Hoult had a copy of this morning's speech on his lap, but rather than read along, he studied his reflection in his ornate handheld mirror. Tweaked his hair a bit. "Go on. Read it to me."

"Yes, sir," Brennan said reluctantly. "We'll pick it up in the middle. 'The American people are tired of the status quo, tired of politics as usual, tired of Washington insiders and Wall Street millionaires controlling their lives and finances when they're barely able to make ends meet. And they're tired of oil conglomerates and giant pharmaceutical firms making record profits while they can barely make their monthly mortgage payments.'"

"'That's nice. I like the contrast between profits and payments. Nice alliteration there, and also with 'make, monthly, and mortgage.'"

"Thank you, sir."

President Hoult noticed a few hairs out of place, took a small spot of hair putty, rubbed it between his fingers to warm it, and worked it into his hair. "Plays off class envy too. That works well with my constituents."

"Yes, sir, Mr. President."

"Go on."

Brennan cleared his throat. "'They want change, and one of the ways we're going to give that to them is through health care reform. Today I'm pledging to sign an executive order to cut the waiting period in half between the time when drugs are released to the public and when the generic equivalents of those drugs can be made available. That's the kind of change Americans want. That's the kind of change they deserve.'"

Normally it would be Congress's job to pass new legislation, but a president can bypass all sorts of laws by issuing an executive order, as both Bush and Obama had made eminently clear.

The limos entered the cordoned-off underground parking garage below the Independence National Historical Park's visitor center.

No other cars had been allowed inside it today.

With the Secret Service's presence, for the time being at least, this was the most secure parking garage on the planet.

"Go on. What's next?"

"This is the part I'm still not quite happy with. It has a little too much spin, seems to make those who disagree with you sound heartless and cruel."

"Let's hear it."

"Yes, sir. 'This isn't just a matter of politics, it's a matter of deep humanitarian concern to all Americans. It's a matter of the basic human right of every individual to have affordable health care. It's unconscionable for millionaires and billionaires to keep lining their pockets while letting millions of hardworking middle-class Americans suffer or even die when the drugs that could save them are already available but are prohibitively expensive. This profiteering at the expense of the welfare of fellow Americans in need cannot go on any longer.'"

"Perfect." President Hoult folded his hands in his lap, looked reflectively out the window at the concrete walls passing by. "Yes. Very nice. Now, the rest. The part about cutting frivolous military spending on dead-end programs to reinvest in our country's treasured public school system: construction paper for kindergartners instead of ESP programs that'll never produce results—but don't put it quite like that."

"Of course not, sir."

Their driver parked the limo.

"Come on. I want you to help me make sure we have that last section nailed down."

"Yes, sir, Mr. President."

Then Brennan Sacco, the president, and his entourage went to the preparation room in the Independence Visitor Center to finalize the speech.

A Distraction

Lonnie deciphered Dr. Tanbyrn's equations.

Fionna and Xavier were back at the Franklin Grand Hotel in Xavier's room, reviewing the footage of the suicide bombers, when he knocked on the door. Fionna had been able to enhance the image enough for Xavier to verify that it really was a rifle's scope in the window across the street. They were about to contact Jevin when Lonnie appeared.

"What did you find?" Fionna asked him.

Lonnie explained that the notations had to do with differences in quantum entanglement related to the amount of alpha wave activity in the brain during various mental states. "Apparently, a relaxed state of mind is necessary for both the sender and receiver during mind-to-mind communication."

"Both?" Xavier said. "Both the sender and the receiver?"

"Yes. Mom, I was wondering, these algorithms, are they for real or was it just an assignment?"

Both.

363

"It was an assignment."

The truth, but not quite the whole truth.

Grown-ups making grown-up decisions.

"Nice work, Lonnie. It's possible that Mr. Wray and I will have to step out for a bit, so I may need you to watch your siblings again."

"We'll be fine. The girls are reading, Donnie's playing video games."

As soon as he'd exited the room, Fionna speed-dialed Jevin, put the call on speakerphone, but before she could tell her friend anything about what they'd found, Jevin detailed his and Charlene's deductions regarding the possible attempt on President Hoult's life. "Dr. Colette told us that the twins are military assassins."

"Of course." Xavier nodded soberly. "I knew black ops would fit in here somewhere. It all makes perfect sense."

Fionna relayed to Jevin what Lonnie had found regarding the necessity of both the sender and receiver being relaxed at the time of the connection.

"I don't know for certain the kind of time frame we're looking at here," Jevin said. "The reference to the eagle at the park, the eleven o'clock time mentioned by Tanbyrn—"

Xavier cut in, "Means it's going down this morning."

"Yes. I think we need to assume that. Dr. Colette thinks the twins will wait for her, but they'll want to move on it as soon as we get there. We're on our way to find them now."

"What can we do to help?" Xavier asked. "Do you want us to meet you there?"

"No. If Lonnie is right and the relaxed state of mind is vital for both the sender and the receiver, we need to make sure the president isn't going to be able to relax until the twins are stopped."

"You're thinking a distraction."

"Yeah. A big one."

He looked at his duffle bag and Fionna saw his eyes light up. "I have just the thing."

They ended the call.

Fionna asked him, "You're not thinking of blowing something up, are you?"

"Oh, something even better than that."

"Hmm . . . would it be safe for the kids to see?"

"Oh yeah. This'll be a great educational experience. In fact, I think I'm gonna need their help."

~

Dr. Cyrus Arlington met Detective Rothstein and Sergeant Adams as he departed the helicopter at the landing pad on top of RixoTray's corporate headquarters.

He told the two Philadelphia Police Department officers the story about Banner blackmailing him, and he was surprised at how readily they seemed to believe him. They informed him they would be contacting him later to follow up on a few things, then left him alone. Just like that.

Problem solved.

Or at least postponed.

It was time to contact the twins. Make sure everything was in place. And then let Akinsanya know things were a go.

~

10:43

12 minutes left

Just as we reach exit 338, Dr. Colette gets the call from Darren with the address—the Faulkner-Kernel Funeral Home on River Road, beside the Schuylkill River.

A funeral home? Why a funeral home?

"It's not far," Riah tells us. "Should be less than ten minutes."

Charlene suggests we try the Secret Service again, but Riah is against the idea. "Believe me, if law enforcement shows up, the twins will think nothing of slaughtering everyone there. These two are specialists, but they won't move on the president without me."

But in the end I decide there's too much at stake.

I call the Secret Service and tell them the address on River Road, however, just like before, it doesn't sound like they're taking me seriously. They insist that I not hang up, but I do. They know as much as we do now and it's up to them to take action.

I keep the cell on.

Let them track my GPS. We'll take them right to the twins.

~

· For the president's visit, the Secret Service had stationed agents throughout the greater Philadelphia area and had two on the north side of the city near the Schuylkill River.

· Policy dictated that they follow up on every threat, no matter how preposterous, so the district command center immediately dispatched agents to the funeral home.

~

President Hoult straightened his suit coat, checked his tie, then looked over the final notes and revisions he'd made to the speech.

His press secretary leaned into the room. "They're almost ready for you outside, Mr. President."

"Fine."

"Is there anything you need?"

"No. How does my hair look?"

"It looks perfect, sir."

Then she left and President Hoult took a moment to calm himself, as was his custom, before addressing the nation.

Collateral Damage

Special Agents Wendy McAuley and Tyron Harris approached the funeral home's front door.

It was a routine check, one of dozens they'd been assigned to do in the last two weeks. Yes, you try to take every call seriously, but after a while it's hard. Especially when 99.99 percent of them turn out to be crank calls.

Just like a paramedic who's no longer affected by seeing severe trauma, or a homicide detective who gets numb after viewing corpses day after day, Secret Service agents eventually get so used to investigating death threats against the president that it becomes run-of-the-mill.

Agent McAuley gave the door a knock. "Unbelievable," she muttered. "Psychic assassins."

"What are you going to do?" Agent Harris yawned. "So, remember the last time we were in Philly?"

"Cheesesteaks."

"Get this call over with, go grab some lunch?"

"Geno's or Pat's?" McAuley asked him.

"You know I'm a Pat's fan."

"No, it's gotta be Geno's all the way—with the onions well-done. They're so much—"

A nondescript man in his late twenties opened the door and greeted them cordially. "Yes?" He wore a name badge that told them he was the funeral director. "May I help you?"

They showed him their Secret Service creds. "We have a few questions for you," Harris said. "May we come inside?"

"Of course." The man stepped back, ushered them in. And swung the door shut behind them.

Three Cars

10:51 a.m.
4 minutes left

Dr. Colette draws her car to a stop along the side of the road leading past the Faulkner-Kernel Funeral Home.

A hearse, a sedan, and an SUV with shaded windows and government tags are in the cramped parking area. Charlene gestures toward the SUV. "What do you know, the Secret Service beat us here."

Riah identifies the sedan as that of the twins.

The morning is quiet, just the sound of the river flowing by and a few geese honking as they settle onto a small boat landing just north of us. The sunlight is warm, but the wind funneling down the river valley feels crisp and wintry.

There's no sign of the twins or the agents.

"So?" Charlene asks. "Plan of attack?"

Riah retrieves the bag of medical instruments she'd brought with her from the research facility. I'm not certain why she brought them along, unless it was somehow to convince the twins she was going to help them after all, to buy time. She turns toward the front door. "I need to talk with them."

But something's not right. It's too quiet. "Hang on."

"What?"

"If the agents have the twins in custody, why haven't they brought them back to their car?"

She stops.

The twins got to them already.

"Wait here," I tell the women. "I'll go."

"They'll be expecting me," Dr. Colette reiterates. "Even if they've done something to the agents, they won't harm you if you're with me."

"She has a good point," Charlene agrees.

A quick internal debate. "Alright. But I go first."

I lead the way to the door. When I knock, no one responds. I try the doorknob and find it locked.

"If the twins are expecting you, Riah," I'm thinking aloud, "why don't they open the door, and if the agents are safe, they'd answer the door too, wouldn't they? To see if we might be coconspirators?"

"I'm not sure."

I stare at the keyed lock. It looks manageable. I don't have my lock-pick set with me or the belt buckle prong of the belt Banner severed yesterday, but I can use something else.

"Charlene, can I borrow one of your earrings." She hands it to me and I kneel to work at the lock. "This'll only take a second."

The Empty Holster

"Dr. Arlington."

Cyrus immediately recognized the voice. Akinsanya. His heart almost stopped.

He turned and saw a dark-haired, stocky man close the office door behind him.

"How did you get in here?"

"Your receptionist was kind enough to grant me entrance. I convinced her that I was an old friend. Cyrus, you've been compromised."

"No, I—"

"Those who've been compromised"—Akinsanya approached him—"have become liabilities. And you know what I do with those who've become liabilities."

"No." Cyrus was backing toward the window. "You have to listen to me, there's nothing to—"

But then Akinsanya was on him, a choke hold to knock him out so the young redheaded receptionist in the next room wouldn't hear what was going on.

Then Akinsanya began to do to him what he did best, working quickly and proficiently with the needle and thick thread he had brought along. Today he tried something unique, something he'd never done to anyone else before, but he was a creative man and always ready to expand his horizons. Especially when it came to utilizing the items that his immediate environment provided him.

In this case, the contents of two aquariums.

～

A crowd of more than a thousand people had gathered in Independence Park. At first they were focused on the stage and the much-anticipated arrival of the president, but then a woman and her four children pointed to the top of the Franklin Grand Hotel. "There's a man!" they cried. "He's gonna jump!"

The attention of the crowd immediately shifted to the man standing on the edge of the hotel's roof.

～

I ease the door open. I think about calling out for the agents or the twins but then think better of it.

The lights in the foyer are off, but a shaft of light escapes from the cracked-open chapel doors on our left and from a hallway twenty feet beyond them. Before us, elegant cushioned chairs sit next to a guest book on a lectern. Thick carpet. Heavy shades keep out the sunlight. A quiet, reverent mood.

No movement.

No sounds.

I hand Charlene her earring, and she edges closer to me as she puts it back in. "Jevin, I don't think—"

I hold up my hand: "Wait." I hear footsteps, then a voice somewhere in the hallway or just beyond. It's indistinct and I can't make out the words.

Riah hears it too. "It's the twins." Her voice is low. "I can't tell which one."

So, not the Secret Service agents, and even though I can't discern the muffled words from the other room, there doesn't seem to be any fear in them, no urgency, no intimidation.

I don't take that as a good sign.

They're assassins. This is stupid. Get out of—

"I don't like this, Jevin," Charlene whispers.

Riah hasn't moved. "I should go ahead. Talk to them."

"Just a sec." If the twins had done something to the Secret Service agents, I doubted they were going to take kindly to Riah's arrival. They would surmise that someone had leaked their location, and I doubted they would have shared it with too many other people besides her.

I don't like the idea of putting either of the women in danger, but I don't like the idea of backing away either, not when we're this close. Even without Riah's help, the twins still pose a threat to the president.

Glancing around, I look for a weapon. A hall tree for hats and jackets and a small coat area with empty hangers sit to my right. A decorative bin holding half a dozen umbrellas rests beside it.

No, not an umbrella. That won't do anything. Not if a couple Secret Service agents had been overpowered by these assassins.

All in. Remember? No turning back, no backing down. Just like your escapes. It's what you were made to do.

I indicate for the women to stay where they are. "I'll be right back." I sense that they're about to protest but move forward before they can.

Edging closer to the chapel, I press the door open a little more.

Two rows of wooden pews, ten in each row. A closed coffin sits in the gentle light at the front of the room. Paintings of serene meadows on the walls. Other than that the room is empty.

I take a few more steps to get a better view of what lies down the hallway—

That's when I see the legs of someone on the floor in a room partway down the hall. Trousers. Men's loafers. The person isn't moving.

From where Charlene and Riah are waiting by the front door, I can't imagine they can see the body and I don't want them to.

He might still be alive.

Quietly returning to Riah and Charlene, I hush my voice. "Get to the car. Drive away. And call 911. I think someone's hurt. I have to check; don't argue with me. Go. Call 911. Get out of here." I eye Riah. "Both of you." I make it clear by my tone that there's no room for debate. I'm not sure how she's going to respond, but after a small moment she nods. I hand them my phone.

A voice inside of me tells me that I really should go with them.

No, Jevin.

That person might be alive.

Stop the twins.

All in.

No, I wasn't about to leave the building and wait for who knows how long for cops or more agents to show up, only to find out later that I'd left someone dying on the floor when I could've saved him.

Besides, I really doubted that the Secret Service would've sent only one agent here. That meant there might be another victim.

Or someone else to help you. Someone's who's armed.

Finally, the women step silently toward the door.

I decide that an umbrella's better than nothing and go for one after all. The end is tipped with metal, and I figure I can use it like a bayonet if I need to. It might not be lethal, but it would sure slow someone down.

Cautiously, I creep past the chapel again and make my way toward the hallway. As I get closer, I see more of the man's legs. For the moment, no other sounds.

I tighten my grip on the shaft of the umbrella and realize I haven't heard the front door opening. I glance back, see the women still in the foyer. Charlene is talking softly, urgently, on the phone. Dr. Colette is standing stoically beside her, watching me. I gesture again for them to go, and Charlene holds up a finger to indicate that they will in just a moment.

At last they ease out the door.

Good.

Okay.

Heart hammering, I round the corner.

The man on the floor has an earpiece attached to a white coiling cord that disappears into his suit coat. His head is twisted gruesomely to the side at an angle a head was never meant to turn. Eyes open. Staring.

Quickly, I scan the room. More elegant furniture. A prayer stool in the corner. A cross hanging from the wall. Heavy floor-length drapes pulled across unseen windows. No one else is present.

No sounds.

Two other doors are propped open. One leads to the crematorium. Through the other doorway, I can see a tiled floor. Old metal gurneys and countertops of chemicals and medical instruments.

The embalming room.

I make a decision: *See if this guy is alive, then go. Get out of here.*

Silently, I crouch and press two fingers against the agent's neck. No pulse. Nothing.

But then I hear movement in the embalming room, someone walking across the tiled floor.

See if he has a gun. Move!

I'm no marksman, but I am a practiced shot. Mostly I've fired guns at Charlene while I'm blindfolded. That was for part of our show.

This was for real.

I feel for a shoulder holster on the dead man, find his gun, and as I'm removing it, I hear indistinct voices in the embalming room, and a man in jeans and a black sweater crosses the doorway, walking backward, dragging a woman across the floor. She's not moving.

The other agent.

Then the person dragging her speaks. This time I hear him clearly: "Go get the man."

I scurry to the wall, duck behind one of the chairs.

Stillness. Perception. Expectation. There's no reason for him to suspect that anyone else is in the room.

He'll focus on the task, why would he look your way?

Still, I hold the gun ready, umbrella tucked behind the curtain beside me.

The man enters the room. He's athletic, walks with poise, confidence. Doesn't look my way. Identical to the other man except he wears a green sweater.

This twin grabs the wrists of the dead Secret Service agent, tugs him toward the door to the embalming room, but as he turns the corner, the flap of the dead man's jacket flips open, revealing the empty shoulder holster.

Countdown

In a beat while I still have the advantage, I respond.

Ditching the umbrella and swinging the handgun in front of me, I dash across the room, through the doorway, and shout, "Do not move!"

But only one man is here now, and it's not the one who pulled the male agent's corpse into the room. A wicked scar scribbles down this twin's left cheek. He looks at me calmly, holds out his hands, palms up, to show that he's unarmed. The dead woman whom I saw him dragging a moment ago lies at his feet.

"Who are you?" he asks.

There's one other door leading out of this room. His brother must have fled the second he realized the agent's gun was missing.

"Don't move." Then I call out the door, "I have the gun! I'm aiming it at your brother. Step out with your hands up."

No response. No sound. The man in front of me appears unfazed. "Who told you to come here? Dr. Colette?"

I'm trying to keep an eye on both him and the doorway. "I said I have your brother!"

No reply.

How to do this?

How to do this?

Make sure this guy's not a threat.

"Get on your knees."

He doesn't move.

"Now."

But that's when I hear the front door bang open and Charlene cry out, "Jevin, he's got—ouch!"

"Don't!" Anger flares up inside me. "Touch her!"

He got outside, got to the women!

"Give my brother the gun," the man down the hallway demands. He's still out of sight, as are Charlene and Riah.

The twin I'm aiming the pistol at speaks to me calmly. "My brother will kill her, I assure you. He has the other agent's gun. Now set down your weapon. Kick it to me."

From the foyer: "I'll give you five seconds."

No!

"Five—"

Thoughts whip through my head: *If you shoot this guy, his brother will kill Charlene, Riah too—*

"Four—"

But if you stall long enough—

"Three—"

The police or more Secret Service agents can get—

Charlene: "Jevin, he—!"

"Two—"

"Okay!" I lower the gun. "I am. Let her be!"

The man with the scar indicates toward the floor. "Slowly."

I bend down and place the gun on the floor, then slide it toward him. While he retrieves it, I stand, brushing my hand across my pocket. He doesn't notice but gestures toward the wall to my left. "Stand over there."

I cross the room.

"Okay, Daniel," he calls to the foyer. "Bring her in."

I survey my surroundings. The surgical tools on the counter across the room could serve as weapons. There's a scalpel, a small saw, and a trocar—a hollow, spear-like probe about a foot and a half long. One end is attached to a rubber tube that leads to a pressure pump and plastic tub of yellowish liquid, the other end is sharpened, with a hole it. It doesn't take a genius to figure out that the trocar is used for filling body cavities with embalming fluid.

The plastic tub has a warning on it: FORMALDEHYDE.

Yes. If I could get to that—

Riah and Charlene enter through the doorway, followed by Daniel, who holds a gun identical to the one I'd found.

⌐∾

The crowd gasped as the man stepped off the roof of the Franklin Grand Hotel.

Then exploded.

And disappeared in midair.

⌐∾

I berate myself for leaving the women alone, for not getting them out of here. "Are you two okay?"

They both nod.

"Riah." Darren's voice is flat. "Who are these people?"

She doesn't respond to his question but asks one of her own: "Why the president, Darren? How is he a threat to national security? Why are you doing this?"

He motions for her and Charlene to stand beside me and they do. All of us have our hands up. Daniel joins his brother, who replies to Dr. Colette, "He wants to shut down Project Alpha, but what we're doing here, Riah, this will save the lives of thousands of American soldiers."

Daniel goes on, continuing as if he's thinking the exact same thoughts as his brother: "It'll give us the upper hand around the globe in fighting terrorism. You must know that too. We can't just abandon it."

"More people like Malik?"

"Yes"—it's Darren now—"his death saved hundreds of lives. That's just one example. We can save tens of thousands more." He looks at Daniel, who says, "The cuffs."

"Yes."

Daniel stows his gun on the counter next to the trocar and embalming fluid. He leans over the dead woman's body and removes the pair of steel handcuffs she was carrying, slips them into the back pocket of his jeans, then visits the man's corpse and retrieves the cuffs from him as well.

I'd given Charlene back her earring a few minutes ago. If I were cuffed right now, I wasn't sure how I would pick the lock.

I opt for stalling and think back to what Glenn Banner said when he was dying—the threat, the man who would find me, the hero who avenges. "It was Akinsanya, right? He was the sniper in Kabul, wasn't he?"

The men look at me with interest but say nothing.

"Okay, Riah," Darren begins. "It looks like we're going to have to move to a new location. We'll take care of things from there. You're still going to help us, aren't you—or have you changed your mind?"

She points to Charlene and me. "I'll help you if you let these two live." I'm not sure if she's bluffing. I sense no deception in her words. She brought the medical instruments, and I wasn't sure if maybe she'd been planning to help them all along

It was definitely possible.

The brothers exchange glances, then Darren nods. "Come over here, Riah. Daniel, cuff them."

Riah obeys while Daniel strides toward us. Charlene lifts her hands so that they're behind her head.

I want to keep them talking. "You had the sniper shoot the guy's vest because you can't do it, can you? That's why you need Riah. You can't do it without her. But Arlington thinks you can, so—"

Darren cocks his head. "Who are you?"

"Jevin Banks, the magician."

"Magician?"

My thoughts are racing. "What about Williamson? Is she involved, or were you just using her to help secure funding for Project Alpha?" Honestly, I'm not certain about any of these conclusions, but I'm not really trying to get them to admit anything. It's all misdirection.

What I do best.

Daniel tells Charlene to turn around, put her hands behind her back. She does. When she lowers her hands from behind her head, I see that one of her earrings is missing.

I hold up my hands to show him that they're empty.

But the right one is not.

When I stood up a few moments ago, I palmed something from my pocket.

The 1895 Morgan Dollar.

Sight lines. Darren hadn't seen me do it.

It's the only advantage I have.

And I'm going to use it.

The Trocar

Daniel handcuffs Charlene's wrists behind her, then she turns her back to the wall and I know what she's doing: using the earring she just palmed. I'd give her just under thirty seconds to get free. She's not quite as fast as I am, but she definitely has skills.

He approaches me, and I turn and feel him click the cuff around my left wrist, but that's when I make my move. I whip around and, in one motion, swipe the Morgan Dollar violently toward his right eye.

Based on how deeply it gouges in, I'm guessing there'll be no using that eye again. I don't care how tough you are, that was going to hurt.

He cries out and throws his hand to his face, and while he's disoriented I grab his shoulders and tug him toward Charlene, positioning him in front of her to use as a human shield, but Darren is leveling the gun at us, and even with Daniel in the way, I have a feeling he might be able to pick off me or Charlene. He eyes down the barrel, but Riah throws herself against his arm, and when he fires, the bullet ricochets off the floor.

The other gun is on the counter.

Get it. Go!

I shove Daniel to the floor and rush at Darren, who tugs free from Riah. I have enough speed and connect with a front jump kick to his brachial plexus on the inside of his upper arm, whip my hand out, and manage to knock the gun away—sleight of hand, instinct—but he's so quick he snags my leg in midair before I can retract it and whips me around, sending me crashing against one of the metal gurneys.

As I leap to my feet, I hear Charlene cry out from behind me, and I glance back only to see Daniel grab her arm and hustle her out of the room toward the hallway that leads to the funeral home's entrance.

No! Stop him, he—

But Darren comes at me. He's better than I am, and every move I make he's one step ahead of me. He deftly blocks my uppercut, does a spinning side kick that connects with my fractured ribs. I gasp and stumble backward, almost toppling over the dead female Secret Service agent.

A crippling throb of pain overwhelms me when I try to draw in a breath, and as I struggle to regain my balance, Riah valiantly tries to help and goes for Darren's arm again, but he backhands her brutally in the face, sending her reeling into the wall. She smacks it hard with her forehead and sinks limply to the floor.

As he's bending down to retrieve the gun, I grab him with both hands and drive him backward. He crashes into one of the metal gurneys, the momentum sends it spinning toward the counter, and that's when I see that Riah has risen and flipped on the switch to the motor attached to the trocar. Embalming fluid immediately floods the tube.

On his feet again, Darren reaches for my head.

He broke the necks of the Secret Service agents. He's going to—

I spin, rotating him toward Riah.

And she plunges the trocar into his side. And depresses the trigger.

He draws in a strangled, horrid-sounding breath and looks down, stunned, at the hollow metal rod that's augered in between his ribs, that's filling his lungs with embalming fluid. He grips it with both hands to pull it out, but Riah rams it in farther and he gasps, then crumples to the floor, making sounds I never want to hear again.

Charlene.

Go!

As Riah watches Darren die, I bolt across the room, down the hallway, through the foyer, and out the front door.

Daniel is sliding into the driver's seat of the Secret Service agents' SUV. Charlene lies on the driveway next to the hearse, her hands still cuffed behind her. She isn't moving.

No!

I rush to her.

No, no, no!

When I turn her head toward me, she groans.

Oh, thank God you're alive. Thank—

"Stop him." She coughs slightly. "He's still going to kill . . ."

"Are you—"

"Yeah." She still seems dazed, and I don't know why Daniel didn't kill her, but I'm thankful—

"I'm fine. He's going after Hoult." There's no hesitation in her voice. "Stop him!"

"Alright." I jump to my feet. "I will."

And how exactly are you going to do that?

Improvise.

Daniel is backing up to pull around the sedan. The SUV rides high, has runner boards beneath the passenger's and driver's side doors.

That'll work.

I sprint alongside the vehicle and reach for the passenger-side door handle but can't quite catch it. Daniel aims the SUV toward the road and I try for it again.

Can't hold on.

Do this!

Now!

He accelerates.

On the third try I snag the door handle, yank the door open, and, striding off the runner board beneath it, leap inside. Either it surprises him or he's trying to throw me from the vehicle because he swerves wildly, but I'm already in with him. The door bangs shut and I reach for the wheel to crank it to the right. Toward the yard. Toward the Schuylkill River.

Where I'll have the advantage.

Yeah, improvise.

He elbows me savagely in the face, but I hold on, wrench the wheel again, and we bounce across the lawn toward the drop-off to the water.

And as we launch off the edge, I hit the button to roll my window down.

Cuffed

The impact is even more jarring than I expect.

The air bag smacks me in the chest and knocks the wind out of me, causing a whole new flood of pain to rupture up my side from my cracked ribs. The current grabs the vehicle, tilting it forward and redirecting us downstream. We're low enough for water to pour in through the open window, and the SUV tips in my direction.

After all the cold-water escapes I've done, I'd figured I'd be more able to withstand the shock of the river water than Daniel would, but I'm out of practice, and with the fractured ribs I'm having a hard time breathing at all.

Both of the air bags are deflating, giving us more room to move. Daniel, who's handling the chilly water better than I thought he would, wrestles to get his door open, but I clutch his arm and hold him back.

"Your brother's dead," I tell him. "It's over." Pain wracks my side with every breath. With the open window, the SUV is sinking fast and the water is almost to my chest.

"I know. His left side."

But how? He left before—

Oh, just like your boys. He feels the pain his brother felt.

He punches my jaw, stunning me, then wraps his hands around

my throat and shoves my head down. I struggle to get free, but his grip is fierce and he manages to get my face beneath the water that's cascading into the SUV.

I wish I could smack the handcuff dangling from my wrist into his face, but the angle's not right for that arm.

But it is right for the other arm. I'm still wearing the watch from Banner, the one built to withstand a bullet, so I use that instead. I swing my wrist backward, smash it into Daniel's face. His grip weakens just enough for me to fight free, sit up, grab a breath.

Water is rising fast. He goes for his door again, then sees the handcuff still hanging from my wrist, seizes my arm, and drags it toward the steering wheel.

Oh—

No.

I try to pull free, but he hits me hard in the jaw again, causing me to see stars.

"I'll kill her," he says evenly. Looks at me with eyes fierce and cold. "The woman back there. Her life for his."

Don't let him get out. Do not let—

He angles my wrist to snap the cuff to the steering wheel—

Now.

You've done it before in your stage shows. It's not that hard of a move.

In an instant, I twist my hand around, slap the open side of the handcuffs to his wrist, and smack the lock mechanism against his chest to ratchet it shut, cuffing his wrist to mine.

Descent

For a moment it's as if he doesn't realize what just happened, then he yanks powerfully at his arm, but there's no getting free. The water is almost up to our necks. I don't know how deep the river is—we haven't hit bottom yet, and it looks like water's going to fill the vehicle before we do.

Water splashes into my mouth. We won't have air for more than a few more seconds.

Daniel wrenches at the cuffs again but it does no good.

"Never threaten a guy's girl, Daniel. It's not a good idea."

The force of the current swirls the SUV and takes us farther down, and the water roils higher. I snatch one final, deep and painful breath, then the water is over my head.

As his mouth goes under, I hear a fierce, enraged scream that uses up a lot of air, and that's bad for him. It's seriously going to shorten his life.

I used to be able to hold my breath for three and a half minutes, but not in water this cold, and that was back when I was practicing every day. I figure the temperature will cut into that time; I might have a minute, maybe less.

You can still get out of this.

Pick the lock. You need to pick the lock.

How?

Beside me, Daniel is struggling to get away, but that's a mistake because he's using up the precious oxygen in his blood. You want to stop moving. That's the secret.

Hang on, Jev.

His hand goes for my throat. I try to pull it away, but he's stronger than I am.

Not like this, Jev.

Don't let it end like this.

Again I try to pry off his hand but can't.

The water is too cloudy for me to see him anymore, but I can feel him squeezing harder. He jerks again at the cuffs, but then his grip on my throat begins to weaken. A moment later his arm goes slack and he begins to shake uncontrollably. I know what's happening, what he's going through. I've been there myself. It'll go on for a few more seconds.

And then it will stop.

Which it does.

They died like this. Your boys did. And Rachel did too. Drowning in that minivan.

How much time?

Thirty seconds.

Maybe.

Maybe not.

Cuffed to him like this, I can't think of a way to get out. My first thought is to try to get his body out of the vehicle and swim it to the surface, but I have very little air left in my lungs, the current is strong, and I'm exhausted. I'd never make it.

This is your punishment for not stopping Rachel. Dying like your family did.

Drowning.

All is dark and cold as the SUV comes to rest on the river bottom. My strength is fading.

I'm sorry, Rachel. I'm sorry, Tony. Drew. I loved you.

I do love you—

Relax.

Maybe I deserve to die.

I hear Charlene's words: *Stop hating yourself . . . Rachel had problems . . . She was ill . . . Something broke inside of her and she didn't have the chance to get it fixed.*

Death always wins in the end.

It was her choice, Jevin, not yours.

Death always wins.

Yes.

In the end.

I did love you, Rachel. I do. I can't help it.

But I couldn't save her.

No one could.

I think of the two women. Rachel, Charlene. One gone. The other waiting for me. Three lives wound around each other. Destinies intermingled.

Entangled.

I think of how much the death of those I loved affected me, wonder how much my death will affect Charlene.

You can postpone death, but you cannot conquer it. Only one person, the one who rose, ever has.

One day death will have its way with me.

But that doesn't need to be today.

You're an escape artist, Jevin Banks. So escape.

Yeah, I think I will.

Pick the lock. You have to pick the lock.

I don't have anything with me to—

Well—

Except for one thing.

The car key.

But not the key exactly.

What it's attached to.

Convergence

With my free hand I feel for the key, find the looped wire ring that connects it to the keyless entry fob. I try to twist it from the ignition, but the car is still in drive. I pop it into neutral, remove the key.

My air is giving out fast. I don't have long.

Stay calm, Jevin.

Lower your heart rate.

Just like you used to. In your show.

But a torrent of air bursts up from my mouth.

No! Come on, focus!

The wire resists at first, but when I jam my fingernail in and twist, it uncurls a little bit. I don't need to unloop it all the way, just enough to get it into the handcuff's lock.

It takes a few seconds, a few precious seconds, but I manage, and once it's in the lock mechanism, my fingers know what to do. Instinct.

The cuff snaps open, I pull my hand free from the assassin's corpse and snake my way out the open window, then push off the side of the SUV with my feet to propel myself toward the surface. I stroke as best I can with my broken ribs, and as soon as my head breaks through, I sputter and gasp for breath.

The current has pulled me toward the middle of the river, and the bank is more than fifty feet away.

With the water moving this fast and as weak as I am, it won't be easy to make it that far.

I hear my name and see Charlene, cuffs gone, sprinting along the shoreline. I'm too out of breath to reply, but pivot in the current and start to swim toward her.

Fighting the current is tough. I wish I'd done laps with her this last year, kept in shape for swimming. I manage a few strokes but that's it. I'm too weak, it hurts too much, strains the muscles around my fractured ribs.

I begin to sink again, and the last thing I see before the dark water swallows me is Charlene throwing off her jacket and rushing toward the water.

Riah stared at Darren's body, the trocar still embedded in his side, still pumping embalming fluid into his corpse.

She'd always wondered what it would be like to kill a human being. And now she knew.

It felt like nothing. No more impactful or moving than tying her shoes or putting on makeup.

Watching him while it happened had only made her wonder how long he would twitch before he stopped quivering for good, just like that snake's body that she held when she was a girl.

Killed but not yet dead.

But now Darren was both.

Finally, she turned off the pump.

Leaving the funeral home, she saw that the SUV was gone. Tire tracks led to the river, but none of the three people—Daniel, Mr. Banks, or Ms. Antioch—were anywhere to be seen. Perhaps they all drowned. That would be unfortunate if they had other things they were hoping to accomplish today.

She had killed one person and could kill again. She could kill her father. Yes, she could do it and feel no remorse whatsoever.

Now you know. Do it for Katie.

At her apartment she already had the items she would need to restrain him while she did her work—the things she'd acquired for her sleepover with Cyrus.

He raped Katie, the incestuous pedophile sexually abused and raped both of his daughters.

Both of them. So many times. He impregnated his youngest daughter and caused her to stop believing in love.

Perhaps killing him was the closest Riah would come, could ever come, to loving her sister and even her dead mother.

It wasn't much, but it was something. Yes, human beings do want to love and be loved. To experience the real thing. Riah had wanted that for herself but had been unable to ever attain it or express it. But even if she couldn't, she could at least act on behalf of justice, on behalf of those she wished she could have cared about.

Planning how she would take care of her father, Riah Colette, the psychopath, left the funeral home to get the items she would be needing from her apartment.

The president's speech was postponed. The police disbanded the crowd and thoroughly searched the rooftop as well as the pavement below, but they found no sign of the man who'd leaned off the edge of the Franklin Grand Hotel, exploded, and apparently disintegrated in midair.

The dark-haired man who'd introduced himself as Cyrus's friend had left a few minutes before, and when her boss didn't answer his phone, Caitlyn Vaughn decided to check on him.

She found him tied to his office chair, slowly regaining consciousness.

His lips were stitched shut with thick black thread. His shirt was off; the skin of his stomach had been sliced open and then sewn back up. Beneath the skin something squirmed, then something else, until the whole surface of his belly began to quiver and bulge unevenly, and when she glanced at the aquariums in the corner, she saw that the one containing the roaches was empty.

There were only a few wasps remaining in the other.

Looking back at Cyrus, she saw a wasp squeeze out from between his lips, tug itself free, crawl across his cheek, and then lift into the air.

Caitlyn had never seen anything so disturbing and she felt repulsed. Turned away.

But then hesitated.

This was the man who'd slept with her and promised to leave his wife to be with her, but had not. This was the man who'd flaunted his affair with Riah Colette right in front of her, and then had sex with her right here in his office while she was just outside the door, forced to listen to everything.

This was the man.

He'd lied to her. Used her. Only. For. Sex. Betrayed her.

And so, as Caitlyn Vaughn went to the desk phone to call 911, just perhaps she did not dial the number as quickly as she might have if Cyrus had treated her more like a woman deserves.

I hear sounds wrestling for my attention. The river. A roar in my head. Sirens. A voice: "Jevin." It's Rachel, coming from somewhere beyond space and time, calling to me. "I love you, Jevin."

Rachel—

No.

She's gone, Jevin.

She's dead.

She's—

"Jevin—"

My head begins to clear.

No, it's Charlene. Not Rachel.

Rachel drowned when she killed your boys.

It's hard to open my eyes, and when I manage to at last, it makes me dizzy, but I see Charlene leaning over me. "Jevin! Thank God you're okay!"

I cough harshly and my side roars with pain. I turn my head, spit out a mouthful of water.

Charlene eases her hand beneath my neck to support me.

Yes, those are sirens in the background. Around me light is swimming with sound. I close my eyes and cough, draw in as deep a breath as I can, try to lean up on my elbow, but my side screams at me again and I end up dropping to my back. Gazing at Charlene, I see that she's soaking wet. "You pulled me out."

"Yes."

"Mouth to mouth?"

"Yes."

Okay.

"That's the seventh time I've drowned and you've saved me."

"Who's counting."

"I'm glad you got out of those cuffs."

"I'm glad I was wearing those earrings."

I gesture toward the water. "Did he come up?"

She shakes her head.

A moment passes. I don't know how to say this. "Charlene, did you, a moment ago . . . I thought I heard someone say 'I love you.' I thought it was Rachel."

"Yes."

"Was it . . . ?"

"Yes."

I can't tell if she means that it was my imagination or if she means that it was her. For some reason it doesn't feel right to ask her to clarify.

There are so many things I want to say to her. So many things I need to say. Her hand is still under my neck. "In the hotel," I tell her, "you said that without hope you wouldn't be able to make it through the day."

Our thoughts can heal us or destroy us. Placebos. Curses.

"I remember."

Blessings. A love that conquers death . . .

The idea that death could be conquered, that life would win in the end . . . an idea too good to be true, but also the most necessary truth of all.

"Prana." The word barely comes out. I'm feeling weaker than I thought.

She leans close. "What?"

"The life-sustaining force. I finally know what it is. It's hope."

The placebo for grief, for hating yourself. The only way to move on.

"Yes." Her eyes smile at me. And I can't remember ever seeing her look so beautiful before. The longer we look into each other's eyes, the more right it feels, and finally she says softly, "We're entangled, aren't we?"

I draw her close, and by the way I kiss her, I doubt she'll need to read my mind to know the answer.

Another Goat

52 hours later
Friday, October 30
3:04 p.m.

"That's really nice," I tell Xavier. We're watching CNN. They're re-airing the footage that a woman at Independence Park took on her cell phone of the guy stepping off the Franklin Grand Hotel on Wednesday. "You can't even see the cables retract, not even on film."

"And the explosion covers everything."

"Misdirection."

"Yup." He dips a cracker into his cheese spread, swipes out a sizable dollop. "People see what they expect to see. Not what's really there."

I shake my head. "And you just rode down the elevator afterward?"

He shrugs. "I had a couple minutes to myself before anyone got up there." He glances at the bag in the corner. "I always wanted to do that stunt. Something I came up with for your next stage show."

"I don't have a next stage show, Xavier."

"Not yet, dude. But I know you, and you won't be able to stay away from it forever."

"Well, you made that look better than I ever could."

He looks pleased.

The women and kids should be here any minute. He goes for another cracker full of cheese spread.

"I gotta ask you, Xav. What's the deal with you and cheese anyway?"

"You want some?"

"No, actually, I have a policy: I never eat anything that smells like my feet."

"I wouldn't eat anything that smells like your feet either."

"What I'm saying is, why are you eating cheese all the time?"

"You've heard of quirks, of course."

"Sure."

"Well, I felt like I needed one to be a more well-rounded individual."

"You needed a quirk? What, are you serious?"

"Sure. It took me awhile to come up with something a little different. Subtle, a little idiosyncratic, but understated. I like cheese; it was a good fit. I'm much more interesting now. Don't you think?"

"Um. Yeah." The news program switches to early polling numbers for next year's election. I flick it off. "Are you still planning to go to that tectonic weapons conference this weekend? You never told me."

"I fly out early tomorrow. Donnie's coming with me. He seems to have an interest in alternative news. Fionna gave him permission. She's really keen on field trips."

"I've noticed."

As if on cue, there's a knock at the door. "Are you guys ready?" It's Charlene.

We join the women and four kids in the hallway and head for the elevators.

We'd decided to stay in Philadelphia for a few more days.

Some of our time had been spent, of course, in interviews with the police, the Secret Service, and the media, but surprisingly, the law enforcement officers hadn't hassled us as much as I'd thought they would. Perhaps because of what we'd been through, or what we'd stopped from happening—the events the government was denying ever occurred.

Which didn't surprise Xavier one bit.

We'd tried to find Dr. Colette to corroborate our story, but she hasn't been seen since the funeral home incident. At first I wondered if she had perhaps been planning on helping the twins after all, but then I remembered that she'd killed Darren and I decided that was unlikely. I figured she would show up soon enough.

And so.

The president was fine. Undersecretary of Defense Williamson was facing a congressional hearing, and Dr. Arlington was in the hospital with some sort of serious infection, although details concerning what'd happened to him hadn't been released to the public. Still no idea on who Akinsanya was.

Earlier today I'd tried calling my dad as I'd promised Charlene I would do, but as I suspected, he hadn't answered or returned my call. For now, the things we all put off saying would have to wait.

As a result of the news coverage, Michelle Boyd begged me to come back to Entertainment Film Network. In addition, I received offers from four other networks to launch a new series, but I declined all the invitations.

Freelancing seemed like a good idea for the time being.

Fionna has offered to act as our tour guide, and as we emerge from the elevator she announces that we're going to visit the Pennsylvania Hospital this afternoon. "It was cofounded by Benjamin Franklin in 1751 and was the first hospital in the western hemisphere. At first they had a difficult time paying for costs, so they charged spectators an admission fee to watch operations."

Five-year-old Mandie wrinkles up her nose. "That's gross."

"Cool." Donnie smiles. "That'd be awesome."

Maddie gives him a sigh and a head shake. "You are such a boy."

"And you're such a girl."

"Thank you."

We leave the hotel. No limos or executive cars today. My side still aches, but walking doesn't hurt too badly. It feels good to get some fresh air, and the Pennsylvania autumn trees are stunning.

Fionna goes on with her explanation. "There was no anesthesia, of course, so people got to choose between opium, whiskey, or getting smacked on the head with a mallet wrapped in leather to be knocked unconscious for the operation."

"What's opium, Mommy?" Mandie asks.

"Something that's very bad for you, dear." Fionna pauses, looks reflectively at the horizon. "Here's one: when the man thought about getting smacked on the head with a mallet wrapped in leather to be knocked unconscious for his operation, he looked about as excited as the second-place kid in the Scripps National Spelling Bee after misspelling the word *idiot*."

"Hmm," Xavier acknowledges. "That one I actually like."

"Thank you, Mr. Wray. I think I'm finally getting the hang of this."

Yesterday Fionna took us to the Eastern State Penitentiary, which is now a tourist site. When I saw the thirty-foot-high walls that were also ten feet thick, I started thinking of ways I could walk through them.

Occupational hazard.

I'd come up with two ideas at the time. Now, on the way to the Pennsylvania Hospital, I think of one more, a good one that'll work even with live audiences watching from both sides of the wall. And the top of it.

Might be a good publicity stunt to launch a new live stage show.

Charlene is by my side and says quietly, "Penny for your thoughts."

"I think I'm going to walk through a wall."

"Sounds fun. Will you be needing a lovely assistant?"

"I could probably come up with a way to work someone in."

"Glad to hear that." She takes my arm in hers. "As long as it's me."

"There's no one else even in the running, Petunia."

"I'm glad to hear that, Wolverine."

The man who had shot the vest of the suicide bomber, the man who went by the name Akinsanya, had, of course, lied to Darren and Daniel about Adrian Goss. Adrian was not their father; he had known their mother, yes, but he was just a person Akinsanya had come up with to serve as another test.

He boarded the plane for Dubai, a place to hide out until he could regroup. Figure out his next step.

In the last two days, RixoTray stock had plummeted and he'd lost over four million dollars. Yes, his investment portfolio had taken a major hit, but in Akinsanya's business, money was easy to make. More significantly, because of Arlington's reckless and illegal actions, the whole telomerase research project was being brought into question.

And that really was the problem.

He took his seat in the first-class cabin.

Yes, lay low until the dust settled, then pursue the second option—the singularity. If he couldn't use the experimental telomerase drug to extend his life indefinitely, downloading his consciousness onto a computer would.

Akinsanya looked out the window.

He was going by an alias today, of course.

After all, he'd served in the US military for thirty years, had just recently left. He was the man who had first found Darren at Fort Bragg and Daniel at Fort Benning. Akinsanya was Colonel Derek Byrne. And he was not at all done with his mission.

Cyrus opened his eyes and saw Mambo Atabei sitting beside his hospital bed.

He would have cried out for help, but the damage to his throat from the wasps was too severe. It wasn't clear if he'd ever be able to speak again. In fact, the doctors were saying it was a miracle that the swelling hadn't completely closed off his airway.

A miracle?

Well, Cyrus didn't exactly believe in miracles, or, conversely, in curses, or in any of the spiritual forces of good or evil that religious and superstitious people acknowledged.

But honestly, he didn't like considering the possibility that there was something to Atabei's practices—or the role they might've played in Tanbyrn's death. And right now, seeing her here, he realized he most certainly did not want to find out.

Atabei assessed him. "The kind officer at the door let me through when I told him I was your spiritual advisor. I wish I could apprise you that my Loa ordered me not to perform a ceremony regarding your well-being tonight, but that would be untrue. She informed me that you had intended to kill me."

Cyrus's eyes grew large. He tried to speak, made only unintelligible sounds. His wrists were strapped to the sides of the bed, so he couldn't press the call button beside him for help.

How?

You never told anyone!

"I just came by to tell you that so you'd know what's coming. Expectation always helps in the equation, belief plays a very important role in shaping the future." Atabei patted his arm and stood. "Well . . . I should probably be going. It looks like I need to be buying a goat on the way home."

Fire and Ice

Two months later

My publicity guys are truly geniuses.

The timing of walking through the Eastern State Penitentiary wall in Philly had been really brilliant. We'd finished the documentary on the events in Oregon and Philadelphia, and it aired the same night as the penitentiary special, coinciding with the week my new stage show opened in Las Vegas. We sold out the first month of the run in the first twenty-two minutes after tickets went on sale online.

We dedicated the documentary to Dr. Tanbyrn and Abina, donated the proceeds from the television special and the run of the show to the Lawson Research Center. All Charlene's idea.

I hear a knock on the greenroom door three minutes before I need to be on stage.

"Yes?"

Xavier leans in. "Jev, there's someone here to see you." I'm about to tell him that I don't have time to see anyone right now, that he should know that, but he goes on before I can say anything. "It's your dad."

"What?"

"He's waiting just down the hall."

My father and I still hadn't spoken. I could hardly believe he was here. Regardless, this was not the time to talk.

At least see him, at least make plans to meet up after the show.

"Okay, tell him I'll be there in a sec."

Two minutes.

As I leave the dressing room, I can hear music pounding through the auditorium and my blood begins to rush. This is it. What I was made to do. What I truly enjoy. Joy as evidence of God, of victory over the pain of this broken world? A place so touched with despair? Charlene believes that. I'm not quite there yet, but maybe I—

I see my father waiting for me. Slim. Salt-and-pepper hair. My features. What I'll look like in twenty-five years.

"Dad."

"Jevin."

He clasps my hand. Our handshake is stiff and unfamiliar.

Charlene stands near the edge of the stage. She looks at me urgently, points to the lift that will take me to the platform hidden high above the audience. I hold up one finger: *I'll be right there.*

"Dad, I'm glad to see you, but could we talk later? I need to go." My eyes are on the lift.

"I'll ride with you."

"Um . . . okay."

We step onto the platform. Begin to ascend. Neither of us speaks. Smoke from the smoke machine hovers in the air and curls past us in ghostlike wisps as we ride through it. Finally I break the silence. "So you got the ticket."

"Yes. Thank you." We ride in silence again. "So you gonna do any escapes tonight?"

"Yeah. It's a good one. I call it 'Fire and Ice.' I'll explode above the audience"—that idea came from Xavier, but I keep that to myself— "then appear in a block of ice onstage."

"Kinda like Blaine, when he was sealed in the ice for sixty-three hours? Or Dayan for sixty-six?"

"Well, I figured instead of standing around in there for three days, I'd just escape from it."

I check my watch.

One minute.

We reach the platform.

"No more claustrophobia, then?"

"You heard about that."

"Charlene might've mentioned it."

"Oh." I didn't know they'd been talking. "Well, I'm not sure I'll ever be over it completely," I tell him honestly. "But you find a way to—"

"Move on."

"Yes. To move on. Listen, after the show we can—"

"Yeah." He puts his hand on my shoulder, looks at me. "Hey, listen. I'm proud of you, okay? You know that, don't you?"

He'd never told me that before. Not once.

"Yeah, Dad," I tell him, because it's what he needs to hear. "Of course I do."

Things'll never always get worse.

He smiles. "So, go do your escape. I'll be watching."

"Okay."

My watch tells me thirty seconds.

My father takes the lift back down as I walk onto the girder. We don't wave to each other, but he offers me a small nod. I nod back.

So, Charlene's been talking with him.

And now it's going to be your turn.

A doorway between us was opening. One worth stepping through.

Below me, the spotlights cut through the vast auditorium, swishing above the crowd, bright sabers welcoming me back home.

I clip into the system Xavier designed. The wire is invisible, as are so many of the things that support us when we fall.

The lights change and the music rolls forward, deep and ominous.

My cue.
I take a breath.
And close my eyes.
And tip into the empty air.
To make an entrance these people will never forget.

WATCH FOR THE NEXT
JEVIN BANKS NOVEL

SINGULARITY

Available Fall 2013

Acknowledgments

A special thanks to David Lehman, Pam Johnson, Dr. Todd Huhn, Trinity Huhn, Jennifer Leep, Jessica English, Heather Knudtsen, Shawn Scullin, Ariel Huhn, and Tom Vick, who all offered me invaluable editorial insights.

Thanks also to Howie and Tom for handing me the trocar, to Noah Tysick for leading me to the peristyle, to Steve Glaze for helping me take flight, to Eric Wilson for showing me the waterfalls, to Kate Connors for your research on pharmaceuticals and patent protection, and to the Mind Science Foundation for expanding my horizons.

Steven James is the author of many books, including the bestselling Patrick Bowers thrillers. He is a contributing editor to *Writer's Digest*, has a master's degree in storytelling, and has taught writing and creative communication on three continents. Currently he lives, writes, drinks coffee, and plays disc golf near the Blue Ridge Mountains of Tennessee.

Come Meet

STEVEN JAMES at

www.stevenjames.net

Learn fun facts,
sign up to receive
updates, and more.

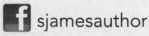 sjamesauthor
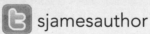 sjamesauthor

SEE WHERE IT ALL BEGAN . . .
THE FIRST
PATRICK BOWERS THRILLER

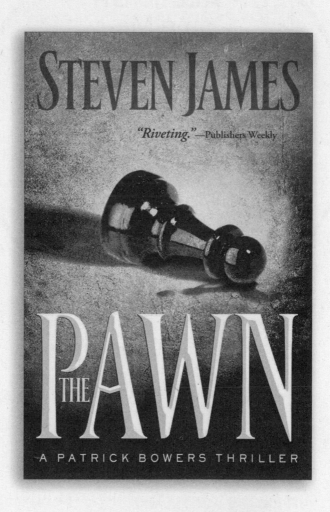

STEVEN JAMES

"Riveting." —Publishers Weekly

THE PAWN

A PATRICK BOWERS THRILLER

"A must-read."
— *TCM Reviews*

Revell
a division of Baker Publishing Group
www.RevellBooks.com

Available Wherever Books Are Sold
Also Available in Ebook Format

MORE ADRENALINE-LACED SUSPENSE TO KEEP YOU UP ALL NIGHT!

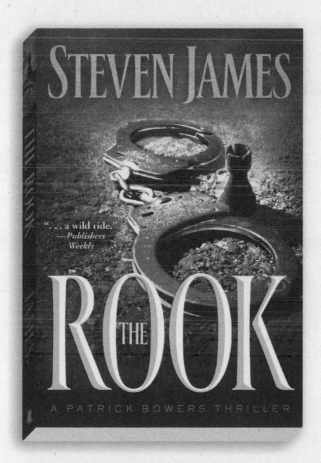

"Best story of the year—perfectly executed."
—*The Suspense Zone*

a division of Baker Publishing Group
www.RevellBooks.com

Available Wherever Books Are Sold
Also Available in Ebook Format

FROM CRITICALLY ACCLAIMED BESTSELLING AUTHOR

STEVEN JAMES

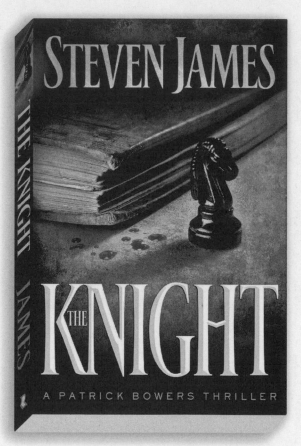

"Top-notch suspense!"
—RT Book Reviews,
★★★★½

a division of Baker Publishing Group
www.RevellBooks.com

Available Wherever Books Are Sold
Also Available in Ebook Format

MORE PULSE-STOPPING NOVELS FEATURING FBI CRIMINOLOGIST PATRICK BOWERS

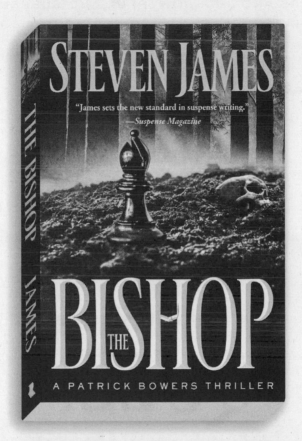

"James writes smart, taut, high-octane thrillers. The endings blow me away every time."
—Mitch Galin, producer of Stephen King's *The Stand*

a division of Baker Publishing Group
www.RevellBooks.com

Available Wherever Books Are Sold
Also Available in Ebook Format

STEVEN JAMES

DELIVERS ANOTHER POWERFUL AND SUSPENSEFUL
BOOK THAT WILL KEEP YOU GUESSING UNTIL THE END

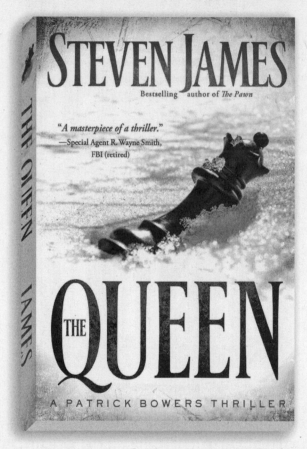

"Steven James continues to raise the bar in suspense writing.
The Queen takes readers to a new level of suspense and is the
best book in the Patrick Bowers series hands down!"

—*Suspense Magazine*

Revell
a division of Baker Publishing Group
www.RevellBooks.com

Available Wherever Books Are Sold
Also Available in Ebook Format